Ms. Never

Other Works by Colin Dodds

Novels
WINDFALL
WATERSHED
Another Broken Wizard
The Last Bad Job
What Smiled at Him
Fun's Monsters
Vice Nimrod, Communications

Poetry
Heaven Unbuilt
Spokes of an Uneven Wheel
Last Man on the Moon
The Blue Blueprint
That Happy Captive
Maybe That's Okay Too

Screenplays
Refreshment
The Sixth Finger of Charlie the Goose
But Let's Not Talk About Work

Ms. Never

a novel

Colin Dodds

Copyright 2017 by Colin Dodds. All rights reserved.

This is a work of fiction. Names, characters, places and incidents either are products of the author's imagination or are used fictitiously. Any resemblance to actual events or locales or persons, living or dead, is entirely coincidental.

http//thecolindodds.com

Published in the United States of America

ISBN: 2 4 6 8 9 7 5 3 1

First printing, 2019

ISBN: 978-1-6907881-4-0

Cover art by Adam Lewin

Farya

It's a nice fall day in Camden, New York. Sunny and cool, and my sweater feels good. The traffic is light; half the city is staying home to watch the game. The stadium is on the other side of town. I can see the blimp above it on the way to Goalposts. Dumb name, but whatever, I say, pulling into the parking lot. I've started to notice that I say "but whatever" a lot when it comes to Romeo.

MS. NEVER

The bar is a half-hour drive usually, but I do it in twenty minutes, so I'm not as late as I'd planned to be. I don't love football, but the sports bar is where Romeo said he'd be, a little too offhandedly. He's a big Camden Railsplitters fan. So, there I go.

He's there with his friends. They've already ordered a five-foot-tall plastic tower of pale-yellow beer. The place is crowded, with new flat-screen TVs mounted flush to the walls or angled down from the corners. Each screen shows a different game. He kisses me hello on the lips, in front of everyone, like it's no big deal. One more thing I'll misinterpret, I think. But then he kisses me again and pours me a plastic cup of beer from the tower.

We're all talking and drinking and watching the game. Time speeds up a bit. The Camden Railsplitters are playing the New York Jets. It's some kind of rivalry, I overhear. The game is close, and the bar is divided. Fans of each team exchange jibes. Romeo is as loud and lewd as any of them. I cheer along, slap high fives with his friends.

And for a moment, things are going swimmingly, and I say, "Oh, I see why people do this." I look past the bar at a big screen with the game projected on it, and before the snap, I start to wonder, even worry, what will happen next. It's a strange flicker of anxiety.

That's when it begins, with one coincidence. The movement, form, and color on one of the smaller televisions—showing a different game—synchronizes with the action on the big screen. Then fans at one end of the bar erupt in unison for different games, but for similar and simultaneous reasons.

Then the different games on the TVs ringing the room coincide. It's eerie at first. A dozen NFL teams making the same third-down conversion on the same play in far-flung cities across the United States.

Then the next play and its outcome match on every screen in the bar. The pauses between plays synchronize, along with the chatter and commercials that fill those pauses. The injuries, timeouts, the cadence of close-up and wide-angle shots uniform themselves. The team logos take on shared attributes and colors. Faces repeat.

Above the beer, chicken wings, and idle jokes about the athletes on the television, I begin to hear a familiar, deafening hum. I know it isn't from the future or the past but from a central point out of which every moment emerges and returns to, like a solar flare ribboning out from the surface of the sun.

In that moment, I know what happens next, but it's gone too far by that point. The images on the screens match, superimpose. So do the faces around me, and the words they say. Then the sensations of the sounds synchronize. Soon there is no room for anything left over from this twinning and folding-in. The process ends with one last numb certainty: The day is all leftover, all the time is time to kill.

Sick with fear and disappointment, I scramble through what little I've learned from having seen this so many times before, and I have some idea of how to stop it: I can yell a racial slur; I can stab myself in the neck with my car keys; I can throw my beer into the face of a girl nearby; I can kick Romeo in the balls—while he's still Romeo. That could throw the moment out of whack just enough so it can continue to be itself. But I don't do any of those things. Maybe I fell out of practice. Maybe I stopped believing I was the kind of girl upon whom these things depended. I trusted normalcy and relinquished such a strange responsibility.

Below the TVs, all the bar's conversations circle the same subject, but not like they're all talking about the game, or the election, or the newest phone or the latest disgraced celebrity. This is more complete. The conversations take on the same emotional tenor, then the same mix of new and old information, the same mix of humor and desperation, the same pauses for refreshment, and finally the same words.

The people in the bar are wearing one of four casual outfits, which they wear in exact sequence, almost like playing cards. It's the visual symmetry—the twinning like the folding up of paper dolls that comes last—just before a collapse. The annihilation of differentiation only escalates. It is too late.

Suddenly, the sports bar with the dumb name isn't exactly that anymore. Unglued from its specifics, from its place on the map and on the calendar, it's a room of busy windows where dozens of alternate possibilities intersect. The beer isn't even beer anymore, but a ritual or mechanical object. I tell myself to wake up, to lash out and interrupt the process. But attention is the best bargain I can make. Seeing and remembering is the closest I can get to controlling what happens next.

The coincidences accelerate like a chain reaction in a nuclear bomb. I have to push my chin up against its terrible force to pay attention and remember.

The sports bar, Goalposts, approaches its moment of criticality. The games and conversations fold in like a roadmap along common fault lines of words, actions, sensations, and habits. Those fault lines extend outward to the metropolis of Camden, New York, in the twenty-first century. The bar, the parking lot, the city of Camden, its history and everyone in it, all crease without a shudder down to a single precise, yet incomprehensible, phrase. Then the phrase grows simpler. It becomes a single sound, a single color, a single sensation.

The sensation vibrates into a hum that eradicates every pretense of somethingness. It happens to me; it happens with a feeling like swallowing and being swallowed at once, like a seizure. It is over fast.

Then I'm outside a gas station on the edge of a small, mostly forgotten town. The town is Camden, New York, where my mother and stepfather live. It has no sports bar. It doesn't have much. I look around and see bright foliage and electrical wires over a two-lane state highway. But I don't need to look to know what I know—the City of Camden is gone, along with most of its two million residents, its suburbs, and many of its unique contributions to the human experience.

That Camden never existed now—except for what I remember. And I know that I'll start forgetting more every day. I look around again for something to do. It is still a nice warm day. The sun is bright through yellow leaves.

I remember promising myself to remember.

It was the worst seizure—her word for it—that Farya Navurian had endured, and the worst damage she had incurred since she was a sophomore in high school. In some ways, it was worse.

Farya spent the next few days afterward in her old bedroom, in the house in Camden that her mother and stepfather shared. When she returned from Goalposts, it was unrecognizable at first—a two-story yellow clapboard house on a sprawling yard that edged into the woods. But just that morning, it had been a yellow-brick townhouse in a quiet section of a lively city.

She told her mother she didn't feel well, said she didn't want to talk about it. Her mother, worried but calm, left her alone for the first few days, brought food to her room.

Farya was afraid to speak, afraid that any word she said would confirm the reality of what she'd done to Camden, to Romeo, to so many people. The woods behind the house and the deep, silent darkness all around whispered new memories of her redacted and adapted hometown. Her bedroom took shape around a revised childhood. She knew the memories but also knew she'd need them—arriving from Ohio to this nowhere of scrub forest, hills, and farmland in the seventh grade. Memories of her stepfather teaching at a regional high school, where the boys knew how to fix a diesel motor, and they canceled classes for the first day of deer-hunting season. Everyone needs a story.

Alone in her room, Farya was devastated. She'd imagined that she had gained some control over her destructive seizures. For all the savvy and discipline she'd earned, this slipped through. If not an illusion, the years she'd spent with a sense of self-control meant the unthinkable: She was culpable. If so, there was no forgiveness for that. And, Farya knew from experience, there was almost no one she could tell.

The house was old. She could hear her mother and stepfather in the living room, talking in the voices they used while trying not to be heard.

By the third night, Farya had to tell her mother something, so she told her mother that she'd lost her job and needed some time to regroup. Her stepfather had gone to bed, and Farya was alone with her mother, drinking tea in the living room. The room was lively—

all busy patterns in Middle-Eastern bright gold and bronze, bold Ohio-State scarlet and gray, and the bright earth hues of Native American rugs. It made the space feel small, warm.

"That can be hard," her mother said. "Do you know what you might do next?"

"I'm not sure. I thought I might stay here for a while."

"Here? You'll be climbing the walls in a week. What about your life in Syracuse?" her mother asked.

Like that, the thing Farya hadn't wanted to think about—her life—was upon her. In those few days, reality had quietly scabbed over after a horrible wound. But upon hearing her mother say the word *Syracuse*, Farya began to remember her apartment there, her job, her life. The freshly made up memory sealed things for the Camden, New York Metro Area. *Syracuse* was the dying tone of a bell that couldn't be unrung.

"I don't know," Farya said, her voice small and choked. "I'm really tired now."

"You rest up. We like having you home. And everyone has their hiccups. I got lost going to the Top Friendly Market, if you can imagine. I hope I'm not going senile."

"You're not, Mom. You're steady as ever."

Alone in her room, kneeling on her bed, Farya wept into a pillow pressed between her face and the mattress. She wondered if suicide would make matters better or worse. She dangled in utter befuddlement, flanked on all sides by terror and guilt. That's when she put on her headphones and turned up the Thelonious Monk. He helped her will herself to a state of mere sickening remorse. If her frustration and boredom could eradicate a whole city, what would her despair do?

The days became weeks. Farya started to go on walks. Camden, the small town, unfolded according to the common logic of small towns. Every new sensation, every new strange bend and twist in the landscape and in Farya's own biography seemed to encourage her to say, *oh yes, of course* to it. She knew that her survival and sanity—and seemingly much more—depended on her saying so.

More than once, her mother asked if Farya wanted to *talk to someone*. As a teenager, she had come close to being committed to an institution after being far too frank with a therapist. And so no, Farya said she didn't want to talk to anyone. To buy time, she lied to her mother, adding a bad breakup, then, a few days later, hinted at some light domestic abuse and, finally, admitted a miscarriage that never happened. Each quieted the hushed conversations in the rooms below hers and won her a few more days alone in her room, alone on her walks.

The pull to forget her life in Camden was like a tide. It challenged Farya's every thought. It relieved and disgusted her. It was one last act of destruction she was being asked to commit, and she refused. It hurt to remember the place, the people, and her life there. But she persisted, focusing on what exactly had happened that day, explaining it to herself, making the pain of it a monument inside of her.

It's a nice fall day in Camden, New York. Sunny and cool, and my sweater feels good. The traffic is light; half the city is staying home to watch the game.

In the many empty spaces and hours of moving to a new city, finding an apartment, applying for jobs, waiting for interviews, sitting in parks, cafes, and bars, while slowly making new friends, she would recite what had happened that one afternoon in a bar and a city that had never been there. Remembering would never be enough. But it was all she could do. *The stadium is on the other side of town. I can see the blimp above it on the way to Goalposts. Dumb name, but whatever, I say, pulling into the parking lot.*

It was a cold afternoon in Brooklyn. The radiator in her room was sizzling. She opened the window a crack. People out in the street talked loudly, going to brunch or bars. She'd always loved New York City. It was a place that didn't need anyone—least of all her. That made her feel safe.

Farya checked her phone and started reciting again, at the beginning, to keep a costly promise. Besides, she had nothing else to do. The store said the mattress would be delivered sometime between eleven and six.

I've started to notice that I say "but whatever" a lot when it comes to Romeo.

The bar is a half-hour drive usually, but I do it in twenty minutes, so I'm not as late as I'd planned to be. I don't love football, but the sports bar is where Romeo said he'd be, a little too offhandedly. He's a big Camden Railsplitters fan. So, there I go.

✛

On the subway, Farya reread her resume. The night before, she'd had to look up where she'd worked last. After the Greater

Camden Metropolitan Area had vanished to a pinprick of a one-stoplight town, the world remembered Farya differently—as having lived and worked in Syracuse, at a small design company, not unlike the place she'd worked in Camden. And reading over her resume, she seemed to remember it well enough.

To be safe, Farya put down her best friend Ethan as her reference. He'd confirm whatever she said in the interview, as she'd done many times for him, impersonating a host of former managers on his behalf. Too smart for his own good, Ethan had his own problems. Going back to their troubled teenage years in Ohio, they'd learned to help each other cheat around their respective shortcomings.

Farya's new heels reverberated through the bright, cavernous foyer. The place was designed to be intimidating. The conference room was old, dark wood, with a huge wooden slab of table and a wide clean vista of the rectangle-busy thirty-story level of Midtown.

She interviewed with a man in an orange blazer—the Chief Creative Implementation Officer, who said, every chance he got, that he wasn't *an insurance guy*. Farya watched him size her up. She knew she was attractive—a strong chin and nose, with shrewd and active eyes—complex, mature. Strong features. Whether or not she was pretty, her mother explained when she was young, was up to her. "No woman is so pretty that a man wouldn't prefer one who he can't quite figure out." Her boyfriends, the ones who lasted the longest, had seemed as if they couldn't decide if she was gorgeous or repulsive, and couldn't look away until they decided. Usually, they ran out of time. Farya was not a patient person.

Her interviewer looked at her for that extra second. Then, with a little awkward laugh, began to ask her questions.

"Some strategy," she responded. She was careful to sound upbeat. But based on his silence, she realized she'd have to make up more. Easy enough—she'd seen all of reality flow and eddy in before her eyes—a plausible lie was never out of reach. Reality was more outrageous than anything she might make up about spearheading a marketing strategy for a real estate developer in Syracuse.

Farya spoke easily about *coordinating a multi-media, multi-strategy campaign as part of overall planning and outreach* at the small company she hadn't even heard of until the night before. Faking it came to her so easily that she often wondered if there even *was* any other ability a person might have. The man interviewing her, close to fifty, in a T-shirt, orange blazer, and sneakers, gave no indication that there was.

"Good," he said, cutting her off mid-sentence. *Disruption*, after all, was all the rage. She could tell from how he looked at her that he was satisfied with her answer.

The only hiccup came as she left, and her interviewer chased after her to hand her the umbrella she'd forgotten. He said her name once, twice, but she didn't respond. Her thick brown hair hid the earbuds she'd hurriedly jammed in as soon as she felt out of sight.

The dissonance of Thelonious Monk's *Epistrophy* pounded, banishing from her mind the belligerent mundanity she'd summoned for the interview. She didn't feel a seizure coming on. But she wasn't going to take any chances.

When the interviewer had his hand on her shoulder, she turned, startled, and could see it on his face that she looked like some typical, young, self-involved idiot wrapped in a cocoon of digital media. Not a great look, but better that than a woman with a serious problem, barely averting catastrophe.

✝

Thelonious Monk always helped. He saved Ohio—maybe not the Greater Majestic Anointed Commonwealth of Ohio that spread from the great Penn Sea to the Indipole Ocean. But he saved it from shrinking to beyond its current form as the seventeenth state in the union. He might have helped more, but Farya didn't discover Thelonious until she was almost fifteen.

Farya's high school years consisted of long days and few friends. The world was boring, predictable, homogenous—highways and suburban houses and neon shopping bazaars and spaceports, then repeat. During those frosty winters, muddy springs, and uncomfortable summers, the commonwealth shrank. Towns and cities slipped off road signs. The tribes of Jacob and the Algonquian Federation merged without a sound, their temples consolidated, and ancient families agglomerated and hardened new, shallower forms. Pyramids, ziggurats, and snake mounds shed their ornaments and retired to quieter existences as sad little ski hills and landfills. Kingdoms became provinces became counties. Ancient cities became shopping plazas. Famous cities became suburban cul-de-sacs. It all happened in the roll of a teenage girl's eyes.

No one was panicked. No one talked about it. So Farya didn't panic, didn't talk about it. What shrank the continent-spanning empire of Ohio wasn't barbarian conquest, redistricting, low birth rates, plague, late-imperial rot or tectonic shifts, but the nonexistence conferred by an exasperated teenage girl.

At some point, Farya realized she was the one doing it, and had been doing it her whole life. She realized that no one said anything because no one noticed. She alone noticed and remembered. It was all small, gradual abbreviations of reality until she hit twelve. The Greater Majestic Anointed Commonwealth of Ohio still existed, but it fell on hard times. People struggled to articulate how or why it was diminished, and a pervasive, mysterious disappointment descended. Her father, a brave astronaut-officer of royal blood, shrank along with that world. One day, she woke up and he was a high school math teacher, as he'd seemingly been for decades.

New memories wrestled with old, at least in Farya's mind. And once she'd seen the response of her peers, parents, or teachers when she asked about a missing castle, stadium, or a shopping mall named for the hero of some sport that no one had ever heard of, she realized that there really was no one she could talk to about these things.

But it was gradual, and to a child, just another part of a vast world she didn't understand. All that changed when she was twelve. She had her first period and her father died in the span of five weeks. And all hell broke loose.

The world began to vanish at a terrible pace. Farya knew she had something to do with it, and that she couldn't do anything to stop it. She spent more of her time alone, in the library, reading, trying to recall a world that was slipping through her fingers. But it kept slipping. She was numb, mute, sent to psychologists and given test after test—EEGs, MRIs, blood tests, flashcards, word association. She tried to explain what was happening to one of the psychologists, a kind middle-aged man with dirty glasses. But he explained it back to her as a runaway metaphor for her father's death. And when he asked if it would help if she went away somewhere where she could get the special attention she needed, Farya stopped trying to explain that it wasn't a metaphor.

So, Ohio vanished one seizure at a time—its space program, its sovereignty, its mountains, jagged seacoasts, and its four millennia of history. She lost friends and acquaintances. And eventually, she found Thelonious Monk. What saved her—and more than her—were the slightly off-key moments in Monk's music, like someone changing their mind in the middle of a decision. It was a tenderness and a willfulness that allowed for creation and yet kept it from running too far on its own steam into doctrine, oppression, and predictability. He kept the seizures at bay. Other things did too, but they all tended to be the kind of outbursts that got her suspended from school.

As alone as Farya was, she could see that, on some level, people did know. It was in their heavy-lidded eyes, their humped shuffle, and their words—the state was in a *recession*, or they had a cousin going through *withdrawal*, or they were *depressed* about the Browns moving to Baltimore, or they had been *downsized*. But whatever they knew about their vanished homeland and history hovered like a hot weight in the base of their skull—an inarticulable tension, a fear.

But some people did notice. There was Ethan.

✝

"Look at you, you *Associate Campaigns Strategist*! You sound so official—like you're the one who decides to close down the plant where Daddy works," Ethan said, and drained the last of his beer. He was wearing a fluorescent-pink puffy coat with gold-foil shoulders, and a black ski-cap with NO CUNTZ stitched into it in rhinestones.

"If only—"

"Now, don't be mad—but I want to know—am I ever going to see you now that you have your big corporate daddy to take care of you?" Ethan asked, refilling their pints. He'd bought the drinks since she got to the city, and tonight's drinks were on her.

"I think so. It's an insurance company, but from the interview, I don't think the job is really too different from what I did back in Camden," she said, taking a sip, catching his eyes on her. Ethan arched an eyebrow, a grin cracking open on his pink and boyish face—the kind of face people were prone to forgive. Everything about him seemed to elude seriousness.

"Wait—what? What did I say?" she said.

Ethan was one of the only people she'd ever met who remembered. Maybe that's why he had the sense of humor he did. Maybe it's why he drank so much. Maybe only by being completely flippant and often drunk could he bear the knowledge.

Through adolescence, there were times when Ethan was the only one who kept Farya from absolute certainty she was losing her mind. He remembered Ohio's space program, the towering pyramids, the undersea heretic-dome tourist traps, the nine-hundred-year tradition of public religious debates, and the post-office murals of the thousand-year war against the giants. They'd talk about these things, and he'd always make her laugh. They were weirdos with a secret language, him saying things like, "So much for the Cuyahoga Monastic period!" in the halls at school. It was a contraband they shared. She never knew why he was able to remember. Even more puzzling, she thought, was why he was willing to.

His friendship wasn't a gift she wanted to question. He was her first friend, her first everything. And she was the only consistent woman in his turbulent life. Now in their mid-twenties, they were past giddiness, lust, and any sense that they would ever be boyfriend-girlfriend or man-and-wife.

Behind the jokes were the millions or more—living until that moment or resting safely in their graves—who were undone, unborn. It was a sacrilege. But in sacrilege, it seemed, was at least a way to live. Farya thought of those nights near suicide in her faux-childhood bedroom in Camden, watching the sun go down over the grim, bucolic scene of the backyard, the trees shedding their leaves, the fall falling, days shortening, trying to catch up with the immense loss that stranded her there. And she said yes, sacrilege would have to do for now.

"You were saying—your last job where?" Ethan asked.

"Oh."

"I thought that Syracuse sounded wrong when you said it," he said. "But you'd think I'd remember Camden. How many weekends did I go up there when I was still living with Cheryl? I remember the tri-tower skywalk, the rickshaws on river heights. That Moroccan place with the homemade wine that tasted like raisins."

"Yeah. I had a problem, a mistake, an I-don't-know. But it was bad, really bad."

Ethan stared over her head, feeling for a memory of Camden, New York—and feeling his sense of what the world had become.

"It was the worst one," Farya said, "since high school—the first big one since then. I don't know; I'm sorry."

"Don't apologize to me. What happened?"

"I was on this date, and there were a lot of TVs. They were all on at once, and it kind of had a way of summing everything up. And I got a little annoyed and a little drunk. Then it was like all the people had the same name and the same problems and the same parents, all halfheartedly making the same point, kicking against the same childhood … and it had been so long that I forgot what was happening."

"Shit, I thought you had it under control, or you'd outgrown it, or, shit, that was a major city," Ethan said, fishing his cell phone out of his pocket.

"I kept wanting to tell you. But I was so embarrassed, and like, ashamed. I thought I was past it."

Ethan whistled at his phone screen. "Gone."

"Not completely."

"I guess not. Gone to like half a page on Wikipedia. Well, drink up—such is life."

"Is it, though?" she asked.

"Oh, gorgeous, you know I wish you were crazy too—just for simplicity's sake. But no such luck, I'm afraid."

"It doesn't scare you? All those people gone?"

"We're all gone, eventually, one way or the other. When I get stressed about having no career or my sham marriage or how I only have like one friend I can trust, I try to think of my life as a bubble among bubbles, waiting for the *pop*. I find a freedom in that."

"I don't know. That doesn't seem like much of an answer," Farya said.

"It's not something you want to hold up to too much scrutiny. But it gets me through most nights."

"Hear, hear."

"I heard that Misty got out of the hospital last year."

Farya shook her head at the mention of Misty. She was a girl Farya and Ethan had known in high school, who seemed to recall bits and pieces of the vanished Greater Anointed Imperial Ohioan Commonwealth. But she lacked a friend, or the protection of teenage sarcasm. And one summer day after sophomore year, Misty took a spray bottle of lighter fluid, squirted her best friend, and said, "You're not real," and clicked a lighter. Both girls learned just how real the world was. Her friend was disfigured, and Misty was locked away for more than a decade. She was a codeword Farya and Ethan shared—a reminder to measure their words and guard their thoughts, and a reminder that the potential cost of knowing what they did was very real.

They shared a look, and Ethan gulped the last of his beer and tapped the pitcher on the table to indicate that Farya needed to go get a refill.

She felt light from the beer and warm from the sense of safety that came with her new job. The bar was filling up. There were men looking at her. Nothing lecherous. But enough to confirm what she knew—she looked good. She squeezed up to the bar beside two professionals—one was describing a company website as "beautiful." She snickered as she ordered another pitcher.

Setting the pitcher on the table, Farya noticed that Ethan was thickening around the neck and face. His face was red, and the rings under his eyes were dark.

"How's the wife?"

"I'd rather talk about my mistress. She's starting her own business—watering plants in big corporate offices: such an adult, civilized thing, my mistress with a business. The wife is doing better, I guess. She's getting out of bed most days since the new pills. Miracle of modern medicine, you know? But her doing better is me doing worse. Didn't you notice that I'm wearing my work clothes?"

"I noticed the clothes—nice hat. On what planet are those work clothes?"

"Well, you know that big, super-tall apartment building in Midtown? You know—the biggest one. It's on the east side, and it looks like a strip of graph paper reaching up to the sky."

"Oh, yeah, that super-tall rectangle—what's it called?"

"I know, right? You'd think it would have a cool name. But it doesn't—just 4-3-2, like a countdown, Park Avenue."

"Okay."

"It's weird, right? This a huge building in the middle of the city, but it's like it doesn't want to be seen—like rich people hiding in the sky. I guess that they're having a hard time selling the apartments, and the people who own the things only live there a few weeks a year. So, to make it look more like a happening place, they hire young, hip things like myself to parade in and out of the lobby, looking imperious, confident, and successful in these cutting-edge threads."

"I can't believe that's a job," Farya said.

"Believe me; it's work. I have to do eight circuits a day—I exit looking fabulous and confident and, thirty minutes later, make an equally triumphant entrance. While I'm out, someone meets me and gives me these huge shopping bags full of crumpled tissue paper to bring back."

"Sounds easy enough."

"It's a lot of walking and a lot of outfit changes. And even with the sunglasses," Ethan said, producing a massive pair of shades from his coat, "it's acting. And the guy in charge, this Luxembourgian lunatic named Stefan, watches us with binoculars to make sure we exude the *432 Park Brand* while we're within eyeshot of the building. Then he'll critique our gait, our posture, our energy, everything. He's not a nice man—at least once a day, one of the girls will storm out crying."

"I don't know what's crazier—your job, or that you went out and got a job at all."

"Had to. Carolina's cutting me off."

"I thought you had an agreement."

"We did, but she wants to change the terms."

"A baby?"

"Bingo. I try to get out of the house before she gets up. But we're going to Colorado next month—skiing with the oligarch. He'll get drunk and demand grandchildren—all in Russian and all in front of me. Maybe I'll break my leg and get to sit it out in some posh Aspen hospital."

"How much longer do you have?"

"For the green card? We have to live together another eleven months, the lawyer says, and after that, another year before we can file. Beats working for a living."

"Does it? Did it?"

"It's okay for now, I guess—another boring compromise. God, I never thought I'd be so boring. Weren't we talking about something interesting—what was it?"

"Camden. And you were saying that you look at people, schools, churches, whole families as bubbles waiting to pop," she said.

"You talk like there's a correct response, like Emily Post wrote a chapter about occasions where your oldest friend slips up and deletes a major metropolitan area and millions of innocents from the map. I mean, how *awkward*. I'd write a note, but where would I send it? Anyway, it's not like they died, is it?"

"I guess not. I Googled the people I knew there up and down—the ones I could remember, and the businesses, restaurants, street addresses. There's pretty much nothing—no trace, no whisper."

"The best thing for a man is not to be born," Ethan said. "That's what the ancients said, one of them, I think."

"You're no help," Farya said.

"Well, what would help?"

"The jukebox. This music is awful. Help me pick."

✢

Farya's blouse was crimson, not silk, but it looked like silk. The light in her room was a clip lamp angled down from a pipe. Nonetheless, her gold necklace danced in it. On the necklace, she'd hung her father's thick gold class ring from *The* Ohio University. She wore it for luck on her first day of a new job.

She took a break from what she was doing and squeezed the ring in her palm for a second. She remembered the ring on her father's hand, the brightness of it among the small dark hairs on his knuckles. But it was a different ring then—heavier, with a rocket and a cross flanking a pyramid, instead of the elongated octagonal *O* now in its center—an *O* like a fat zero. She remembered her father telling her, as a young girl, that the university had a million students at any given time, from all over the planet.

As Farya entered adolescence, and Ohio rolled in her shores, shed her peaks, and lost her majestic significance, her father shrank as well. A minor duke, clothed in the space-faring glories of his youth, he seemed increasingly frustrated and harried in the life of a schoolteacher. The world seemed to close in around him like a vise he could neither see nor name. His job ate him up every morning and spat him out every afternoon a little smaller.

His death was a bad death. He was choking on a cheap cut of steak in a restaurant and was too proud to admit it. Face red, he shook his head and staggered off to the bathroom, to spit up his food in a more dignified fashion. When a friend found him in the bathroom, he was still warm, a string of drool still hanging from his mouth.

Even a destroyer of worlds can, and will, be battered and humbled—one more reason that reality will never be satisfactorily comprehended. If her father's death was Farya's first real lesson in the real meaning of nonexistence, her stepfather was the second. *He means well* was the man's calling card. It was less a compliment than it was a warning that things could've been worse.

Farya got to know him from a distance and over time. Those first few years, she had her headphones on whenever she wasn't in class—always Thelonious Monk. The irregularity of the compositions, the way the notes were set up to crash into one another, the way that no motion continued very long without being contradicted. It was an anchor, a bulwark against the simple, obvious logic of the trees and highways and careers and postal routes, which all seemed to cry out to be summed up in complete nonexistence. Monk's music spoke the language of that collapse but showed how a note or a word could break its own rules, and let the dorky world live. Monk's willful insistence on unpredictability got her through the years after her father's death.

By that point, they were all living in a faded suburb of a failing city in the unfashionable middle of a young country. Gone was the six-thousand-year history, the extravagant traditions, the glittering cities, and the Ohioan vastness of the heavens above. For Farya, there would be others to help her along—writers, painters, musicians, and others with that right discordant quality. But Thelonious taught her what it was that she needed to keep the seizures at bay. And he gave her the faith she needed to put up the fight.

And it did feel like a fight on early mornings like this after a restless night, and with a day of institutional riddles, forms, and awkwardness ahead. After a quick pass of eyeliner and lipstick, she stepped away from the mirror, where the clip-lamp's halo was the least forgiving. She smiled. Her mouth was too big—she'd always thought that. Her nose, too—maybe not disproportionate, but certainly prominent. Her dark eyes glittered. She was, as her mother said, a real beauty, even if she wasn't everyone's cup of tea.

+

She liked him. He was quick and confident in a funny way, not afraid to make fun of himself. Compact jaw, quick eyes. There was a pimple on his forehead and the fact that he never put his phone away. But he was witty and relaxed and nearly as handsome as his profile photo. And he liked to look at her, was hungry for what she had to say.

She liked the bar. It was dark and old looking, with exotic, expensive cocktails. She wasn't sure how she felt about him taking her there. It was well out of her price range, and he had to know that. She weighed whether this was gallant or manipulative or if she was overthinking it, while he responded to a work email on his phone.

"Sorry, sorry, one second," he said like a short prayer, tapping at the screen intently. "One … second, just one second."

"Everything okay?"

"Aside from my boss not having a life? Yes, every … thing … is … fine." He tapped the screen one last emphatic time to send the message.

"I know all about that. My boss is an aging hipster fresh off a divorce. He's always muting conference calls to call our bosses *insurance zombies* like we're the cool kids in on a joke. And he'll send me these messages. It's supposedly work stuff. But he sends them at like ten at night, along with like jokey messages. The first few times, I responded with an LOL, and I got stuck exchanging dumb jokes and emojis with him for like an hour and a half. So now when he does it, I respond, but on my company email."

"Ooh, power move. What did he say to that?"

"He just texts back that it can wait until tomorrow."

"Smart."

"Hardly. He's one of these guys—there's no way to be smart with him. One time, it was a weekend, and he had this nebulous question about one of our projects. I texted him that I was at a wedding. And he wrote me back 'then why are you answering work texts?'"

"Is he creepy? Like, in the office?"

"No. Almost, but not quite. He knows where the line is. I don't know if that makes it better or worse."

"Sad," her date said.

They drank and talked about work, about shows they liked, books, restaurants. It was all banter, all nice, relaxed. He was handsome. She asked him to explain what he did.

"I'm basically a geek wrangler. I used to think I was a geek. But after I got this job, I realized I'd just been bobbing on the surface of the geek ocean."

"You don't seem that geeky."

"I'm sure you mean that as a compliment. But it kind of makes me a man without a country. I'm too geeky to be a sales bro like my boss, and I have too many social skills to win the respect of the real deep D-and-D geeks."

"I'm sure that they need you to translate. What do you wrangle all these geeks to do?"

"What our company does is we create new ways to compress large data sets."

"Oh … and is that … interesting …?"

"It can be. Imagine you're in charge of a bunch of geniuses, maybe not the cleanest or nicest or most ambitious geniuses, but top-shelf smart, scary smart. And you're trying to answer a riddle that, if you solve it, could be worth billions of dollars."

"How could the answer to a riddle be worth billions?"

"Think about it this way: If you're a big company, you spend a lot of money on data—gathering it, storing it, backing it up, searching through it, analyzing it. One way to cut those costs is by compressing it. The way compression works is that you find code that's common to all the files, pull it out, and store what's unique. Then, when you decompress the files, you add that common coding back in so that you can read, or analyze, or play the files. Just add water."

"So, you do that?"

"It's how we started. But as we look at bigger and bigger data sets, we can find new commonalities that nobody anticipated across file types. Each commonality is like finding a fault line."

Farya liked the guy because he could be excited by ideas. He looked her in the eye and picked up her drink and removed the cardboard coaster. It had the bar's florid gold logo embossed on it. He creased the coaster and traced the crease with his finger.

"So, imagine this coaster is a billion billion billion bytes of customer data that a company is required by law to store. And this crease is a mathematical commonality that all of that data shares. Then, we can do this …" Her date folded the coaster in half. "We find another commonality, another fault line." He creased the coaster and folded it in quarters. "And we just saved that company three-quarters of their data-storage spending. And it would work for all companies, all individuals. And we'd own the patents on the creases."

"So, all that they'd need to hold onto is what was absolutely unique?"

"That, and the formula for making it into what it was."

"Just add water," Farya said. Her date nodded and smiled, taking a keener interest in her. His laugh was overshadowed by the cackle of a tall, blonde woman in glittery mascara and a red dress behind him. Her cackle was met by another, like an echo. Farya turned and saw the cackler was a tall brunette in the same dress as the blonde, except blue. The brunette, still smiling, lifted a delicate cocktail glass to her lips, which were the same tangerine hue as the blonde's. Turning, Farya watched the blonde finish the same careful movement, fingertips extended to keep long, tangerine fingernails from the glass.

Her date said, "Sorry, one moment," and lifted his phone from the bar, a movement that seemed to ripple across the hands of every similarly attired man throughout the swanky space. The bright blue phone screens rose in the rich red darkness of the bar, their glows refracting identically off the condensation-rough surfaces of smooth cocktail glasses. "Just one more thing, and I think …" they all said, not looking up, the whole room like the chorus in one of those repetitive songs an exhausted person sings to themselves.

Farya started to take a sip of her gin-agave-smoked-guava cocktail and saw all the women in the room doing the exact same thing. She saw their fathers' class rings dangling in view on gold chains at the point where their cleavage began to cleave, visible under their drink-bearing wrists. She could sense the room shifting toward that terrible unanimity of all sensation that always preceded catastrophe. And she knew what she needed to do. This could not be Camden.

"Fuck you, you fucking rapist fucking pig!" she screamed and threw the contents of her glass in her date's face. She smacked the phone out of his hand and hurled her glass against the peeling-silver antique mirror behind the bar. The cocktail glass shattered, and the mirror cracked. The place went silent. Farya ran out, past their stunned forms.

Maybe it was overkill, she thought on the long power-walk down the cold sidewalks to the subway. But it wasn't worth the risk. She liked her date too much to let embarrassment undo his existence. And honestly, she didn't know how many more episodes she could endure.

Her date called that night, sounding more bewildered than angry in the voice mail he left. He called again the next day to offer a confused apology for ordering so many drinks and no food. She liked him, but not enough for what she'd have to ask him to accept and understand. She didn't call back. It hurt, but other things hurt worse.

✝

There are times when a stream of events will zig hard and break an ankle. When that happens, most people will reveal how accustomed they've become to things not making sense. That's why a detective is such a compelling sort of fellow. It's why so many cops want to do it, and why so many quit. Ronnie Brimmer didn't spend much time pondering why the job was important or why it was thankless. He just knew how it felt.

The call came from Camden, and that was Ronnie's bad luck. The tiny town, anchored by a Flying J truck stop too big for the state highway and a town hall too big for the town, was full of crazies. Everyone in the neighboring towns knew it. And every cop in the county knew the fastest way from little Camden to the Mohawk Valley Psychiatric Center.

The call came from an older woman, Violet Mauriello. Some black-and-whites from the sheriff's department took a call about her missing boy, Romeo. The officers spent more than an hour there, and in the end, almost didn't take her statement. Her story didn't add up. But she insisted, and so they wrote up what they could. The report indicated that she was very articulate and polite, but extremely confused on the subject of her son. She had a hard time proving she'd ever had a son named Romeo. The photo she did produce was a group photo, and Romeo's face was blurry. The phone number she gave was more than wrong; it had an area code that had never been assigned. But she insisted. So, they took her statement and passed it over to a detective.

That detective passed it to a less busy one who did the same, and so on. One day, in the grip of a county-wide dry spell of violent crimes—at least the kind that couldn't be solved in an hour—Violet Mauriello's statement landed on Ronnie's desk.

The statement made Ronnie's coffee taste sour. Best case was that the officers misread the person and the situation, and one more young man had taken for the highway. Worst case was a blue and bloated carcass finally getting a name. Most likely case—in Camden at least—was a tedious, meandering conversation followed by a call to social services, and the woman removed—for her own good but against her will—from her home.

The vinyl siding had started to curl on the corners of the big white house. The brown grass had seen its last mowing and raking of the fall and awaited the first heavy snow to cover it. Ronnie pulled up, a tall still-young official from the county in a new county car to deliver some sense to an acre from which it had departed. Being young and healthy helped the situation, sometimes. It could reassure the injured and bereaved, but it could also be salt in the wound. So, he always made sure to let out a deep breath and make his naturally sad face a little sadder when meeting with family.

The first blush boded well. Violet answered the door in jeans and a clean Buffalo Bills sweatshirt, diet soda in her hand. The house smelled of warm laundry and coffee. Ronnie showed his badge and said he was following up on her missing persons report. The breath caught in her throat.

"Oh, God, did you find him? Is he okay?"

Ronnie explained there were a few things in the report that he needed to ask about. She showed him into the kitchen, offered coffee, commented on the weather, all the hallmarks of sanity.

"I don't mean to be rude, but why did they wait so long to send you? It's been more than a month. I keep calling, and they keep saying they're doing all they can. But they never have anything new to tell me. Are they even looking?"

"You said Romeo was twenty-nine?"

"Will be thirty at Christmas—we are … were going to have a big party. The whole family, even his sister in California."

"Well, in most cases with an adult, we don't actively search. With someone his age, they just take off. It happens all the time. It's a big country, and it's not against the law. But unless we have reason to believe there's been a crime, there's not much we can do. If you wanted to see if he was using his credit card or his bank card, you'd have to hire a private detective. And I have to warn you, that can be expensive, and …"

"I already did. I gave him everything I gave the police. Everything. My boy's address, phone number, the place he worked, his social security number. I couldn't remember his license plate number, but I did give him the make and color of his car. And the photo …"

"The report said that you had trouble finding a good photo."

"I did. I've looked all over. I was never a shutterbug, but I know I had more than that. I asked his sister to send me what she had but she …"

Ronnie watched the sudden change to the woman's face. It was like she had run off a cliff a minute ago and just realized it. Her cheeks slackened, and she aged ten years in an instant. Deathly was the word. There was nothing for Ronnie to do but push her a little more.

"What did your daughter say?"

"She said she didn't know who I was talking about. I said, 'of course, you do, he's your brother, Romeo.' I started to tell her about the things we used to together, old jokes, fights when they were kids—the speech he gave at her wedding. And she … she said she was worried about me."

"Because the officers, they also said that the information you gave them about Romeo … that it wasn't right."

"I know," Violet said. She collected herself, lifted her head from her hands, and sat up straight. "That's what the private detective said, too."

"I'm sorry, Ms. Mauriello, but you see how it starts to look. It wasn't that some of the information you gave us about Romeo didn't check out—none of it did. His address, the place he worked. None of it checked out."

"He worked at Neiermarr Insurance, in headquarters. One of the tri-towers in north downtown, with the pink-marble stripe and the …"

Her words called up a vivid picture in Ronnie's mind. The tri-towers, seen from the highway, seen from below, from a picture postcard, paraded across his mind. Ronnie recalled a field trip there as a kid, and one of his first cases after making detective: an airy nest of marble-walled offices cordoned off after a middle-aged woman in a scarlet suit was found strangled. But then Ronnie recalled, with a precipitous drop in his stomach, that it never existed.

"Where is this tower?"

"Camden, by the basketball stadium and the bus depot …"

"Camden, New York?"

Violet looked at her lap. Ronnie looked around the room. He saw more of strangers' living rooms than most. And he'd been in this one before, or one very much like it. Clean wall-to-wall tan carpet and furniture with plastic covers, and busy to the point of overflowing with porcelain tchotchkes and little picture frames—so many tiny faces, living and dead, smiling at Violet, looking down from the walls and bookless bookshelves. Ronnie could read the room, and it confirmed what he thought of Violet—lonely perhaps, but hardly insane.

"I don't know; maybe he worked somewhere else," she said, looking up.

"Have you been outside much lately?"

"Yes, and I see what you see. I can't find any towers, any of the things. And maybe they were never there. Maybe I'm remembering it wrong. I keep remembering things differently."

"Is there anything else you might be misremembering?"

"I've lived in Camden my whole life. I sit here all day, every day. And when I do go out, it's to see things that remind me of

Romeo, to help me find him, to help people like you find him. And I spend half of my time wondering if I've lost my mind. He's my boy; I feel him like he's part of me, and I know he's missing."

Violet gave him a look, clear-eyed and determined. This was a woman who had weathered heartbreak and madness, but still kept house and made coffee. Ronnie decided what was best was for this to remain a private anguish and not county business.

"I don't understand, but …"

"You don't understand."

"No. I don't. And I'm sorry. But there's not much more that I, or the county, can do with the information you've given," Ronnie said, letting some of the old cop-hardness into his voice.

Violet Mauriello showed him another group photo. Romeo was a blur in that one, too. She acknowledged it was worse than the last one. But she said there was *a lead* that the private investigator never got to—a girlfriend. Romeo had mentioned her the last time he was at the house. Her name was Farya, whose last name had an N and a V, sounded Armenian, Violet said, and her parents lived in town. But that was all she knew.

Ronnie wrote that down and said he'd look into it.

"Will you?" Violet said, her eyes huge and glistening, her granite composure close to slipping once and for all.

Driving away, Ronnie tried to make sense of the conversation. The woman wasn't insane, but insanity was a short walk away. Ronnie resolved to tie up the one loose thread there was, the girlfriend, before telling the poor woman that she never had a son named Romeo.

✢

"What even is a Rite of Squat party?" Farya asked, surveying the pile of clothes on her bed.

"It's this big event-performance thing. All these artists have this big building they squatted in until they owned it," Ethan said, flipping through a website of new paintings and provocative youth on his phone. "This is the big party they throw on the day they won the building."

"Squatters? Sounds kind of dirty."

"I wish. The main quote-unquote squatter was a lawyer who'd made a handshake deal with the building's owner. He wanted the building off his books so he could declare bankruptcy or do some tax scam, or so his kid could run for office. She set it up so he'd lose it to squatters."

"You can do that? Legally?"

"I guess so. Ask the lawyer. She'll be there. She got the penthouse when they won the case. I heard she's squatted her way into a half-dozen other buildings since then."

"So, there'll be real-estate guys there?" Farya said. She'd been dating in New York long enough to turn and run when a man mentioned real estate in nearly any context.

"Don't worry—it's not that kind of party. Lourdes—the lawyer—is more of a patron-of-the-arts type. That reminds me, don't call her *the landlordess* while you're there. They like to call the place a collective—it's a bohemian-type scene. Her husband is a dancer, and they do a big dance performance at the party."

"That's great—now, what do I wear to a squatters' dance performance party hosted by a woman who legally steals buildings for a living?"

"Easy—anything you never wore in Ohio."

"Where is this, anyway?" Farya asked, holding earrings against blouses.

"Uhh … Free-Ya? Bri-Woo? Brow-Na?"

"Are you having a stroke?"

"No. It's the neighborhood—the name of it, like Dumbo or Soho. But I forget what it is now. It's like halfway to the airport, I think."

Ethan explained that the party was in a neighborhood that had been on the cusp of becoming hip a few years earlier. But a few overseas coups and a sharp drop in the stock market had made less-ugly and easier-to-reach areas again affordable to the moderately well-off. So, the neighborhood where they were going missed its brazen age of glass condos. And while its cool new name stuck, it stuck with bitter irony.

"Okay, what train is it on?" she asked, fixing her mascara in the harsh yellow of the clip lamp.

"Train? No way. We're taking a car."

"Come on; I told you how much I make. I can't split a cab."

"Boo-hoo, you get to drink free all night."

"Come on, seriously; I have to watch my money. And, the subway will get us there fashionably late. Don't you want to be late?" she said, turning around in all her dressed and made-up glory. "And I bet everyone else will be taking a cab there. We'll roll in late with a ready-made anecdote. You're always saying you want to come off as more real."

Ethan agreed on the condition that she'd back him up on any story he concocted about the trip if nothing interesting happened. The train ride, aside from sundry bums and loud teenagers, was uneventful. From the subway, it was a long walk past shuttered sneaker stores, check-cashing storefronts, and bulletproof Chinese restaurants until they reached a rectangular glass slab. While it would be at home among the white noise of cheapness and greed that had taken over so much of Brooklyn and Queens, this mirror tombstone stuck out between a vacant lot and a low, green, shingle-clad townhouse.

Farya and Ethan approached its heavy, steel front door and, below the black metal cages that covered the windows of the first two stories, double-checked the address. A sandbag held the steel door ajar. Ethan opened it; Farya followed toward the music, the light, and the sound of voices. Day-Glo arrows on the concrete lobby floor led them past an unmanned front desk and another pair of open doorways to a large, triangular courtyard, where maybe a hundred people crowded in the open space, laughing and talking. Smoke curled and swirled in the air above them.

The light in the courtyard came from apartment windows, strings of lights, and a bonfire in the middle. The people seemed happy, awake, all different, from the hobo Santa Claus to the giraffe-like model gesturing with a joint. It was the kind of crowd that made Farya feel as boring as the story she told strangers about herself. Ethan yanked her out of a reflexive pause at the entrance, toward a long folding table fringed in blue crepe and covered in bottles of booze. A huge banner hung at the wide end of the triangular courtyard, showing an Egyptian winged sun symbol, with the Confederate flag's crossing bands of stars behind it. Farya recalled it from a family road trip when she was little to the High Southern Riverlands, where the ancient obelisks and the rusty launch towers of the Second Spacefaring Period made the wind sing.

"What kind of party is this?" she asked Ethan, but he'd turned away and was talking to a small coterie of acquaintances.

Plastic cup in hand, Farya wandered among the handsome, the ugly, the chatty, the stoned, the dancers and jugglers. She took a deep drink of her fruit and vodka drink. Uneasy moments like this were dangerous for her. She scanned the crowd and saw a friend of Ethan's she knew. As she made her way toward him, a thunderous groan from the speakers stopped her in her tracks.

Alone below the center of the banner, a bright yellow spotlight fell on a middle-aged woman in a huge, sequined, cobra headdress, white toga, and pancake makeup. In the light, she was almost blinding. She stood straight and still as a group of young women in diaphanous maroon robes and gold snakes in their hair fanned out from behind her, the crowd clearing a space for them. The gleaming woman in the center of the opening in the crowd began to speak.

The earth as we call it once filled the entire sky. There was no space. We were all one.

More snake-haired dancers, in blue and yellow, formed a circle around the woman.

As we all know, something happened. Some say the earth saw its own shadow. Some say it learned to doubt.

The dancers shrieked and waved their arms above their heads, then every other dancer tapped the shoulder of the one next to her and shook her head. The dancer who was tapped bent at the waist and scurried backward out of the light. As they left, the circle shrank from a group of thirty or so dancers to a handful.

In a shivering instant, much of that world vanished. Great lands and terrible truths stranded, buried. Oceanic idiosyncrasies and moons of peculiarity, dreams that survive wakefulness and saurian strangenesses became pinpoints of distant, inscrutable light—distant, mere stars.

Small spotlights chunked open on dancers scattered throughout the crowd. The light over the woman speaking and the dancers around her tightened. The dancers ran out into the darkness, weaving through the crowd like children playing tag.

"I told you it wouldn't be real estate," Ethan said, coming up behind Farya.

"You abandoned me."

"Please—it's a party. There's no abandoning—just mingling. Don't tell me you're not having fun."

"No, I am," Farya whispered. "This is pretty cool. I got shivers when I saw that winged confederacy logo. Familiar?"

Ethan gave her a sinister little smirk and gave his head a quick shake to say *That's not party banter.*

The music fell silent, and the multicolored dancers began ambling and crawling back to the proscenium marked out in light on the courtyard ground. The speaker returned in a tan shawl and a reddish spotlight, her face gleaming white in makeup and sweat.

Even the first people, who meant to live forever—gave way after twenty thousand years. Time is a toxic substance. The hot breath of a boredom that's as vast as the cosmic wind will trim us all down.

The dancers approached each other to a slowing beat until they were all one mass swaying shoulder to shoulder.

It's depression. And depression is nothing less than a soul's disappointment in its owner. So have a drink and do something out of character. Don't be a disappointment tonight.

The center spotlight split up into circles that spread out across the courtyard. The dancers seemed to chase them, running out to the crowd. The woman with the snake headdress blinked out of existence with the sudden dampening of the final spotlight. The performance ended, and Farya smiled and downed the rest of her drink. It was late, and the warm, late-autumn night felt full of possibility. The crowd clapped, hooted, and hollered for a while afterward. Farya and Ethan went to the crepe-fringed bar table.

"See—who takes you to all the best places?" Ethan said.

"You do. Who was that woman?"

"That's the one I told you about."

"The landlordess …"

"Uh *uh uh*," Ethan said, looking over both shoulders. "Lourdes is her name. I'll introduce you if you want. She loves new people. She collects them. Just remember—Lourdes."

Farya nodded, eyes wide as they milled among the well-wishers who gathered around the older woman. Still in her ornate lacquer cobra headdress, she graciously entertained and dismissed each small cadre of acquaintances.

"I'm so sorry—I have to get this pancake off my face," she said as soon as Ethan introduced Farya. "Come with?"

"Oh, sure," Ethan said.

"Not you—I'm going to the bathroom. You," Lourdes said, opening her big turquoise-painted eyes at Farya. "Jeez, is he always like this?"

Farya laughed. Lourdes had a round, pretty face that put her at ease, despite big eyes that didn't seem to blink. Farya followed the older woman around the dark edge of the party to the elevators and up to a spacious apartment with a view of a big bright bridge Farya couldn't identify. It was an elegant, open space marred by mismatched steel columns and a visible warp to the floor. Masks, paintings, bookcases, and artifacts filled the walls on the way to the bathroom. The bathroom itself was almost as big as the apartment Farya shared with two roommates.

From a long line of switches, Lourdes selected a few lights, which were bright, but not unflattering. She sat on a velvet upholstered bench, took off her platinum wig, and set to work removing bobby pins and laying them in a row on the creamy white countertop. She gestured to a similar bench, and Farya sat. With each element removed, Farya became a little more comfortable with the stranger.

"Great party."

"Glad you like it. We do it twice a year. So, Ethan tells me you're from Ohio."

"He told you about me?"

"Not much, really—I asked when he mentioned he might bring someone who's not his wife," Lourdes said, removing a few small jars from a drawer.

"No, we're just old, old friends."

"Oh, honey, I know. Not that. And forgive me if this is too direct, but you must be her—the world-collapser. Right?" Lourdes filled the silence that followed by removing her pancake with sponges like small cookies.

"I guess so. Sometimes. I try not to be," Farya said, and the first teardrop fell.

"Oh, honey. I can only imagine how hard this must have been—alone all this time," Lourdes said, distracted by the makeup-removal process. "I mean, Ethan's lovely. But it's a lot to carry."

Farya was sobbing, and Lourdes leaned in to embrace her. Farya noticed an intricate snake pattern on her robe. When she was done sobbing, Lourdes brought some small glasses of syrupy port wine into the bathroom. Together, they sipped and talked as they each reapplied their makeup.

"I really thought I was past it, or that it was a bad dream. But now, every day, I'm either afraid I'll erase the world, or that I'm losing my mind."

"It's a lot—your role."

"Role? It's not one I signed up for," Farya said, suddenly angry.

"The world is a kind of mind, and everyone plays a role in it. Most of the parts compromise—they sand down the edges of what they don't understand and pass it along a little smoother. Some people invent things, some call 'bullshit' on the things that others make up, some take up space. And you … well, how can I explain?"

Lourdes said, putting down her blush. "Think of the flora of the woods—the world grows through imitation and repetition. But before too long, it starts to choke on its own conventions. Nothing can progress or even survive unless there's a forest fire to clear the underbrush. Now, a forest fire is terrifying. It destroys the unique and the ordinary without discrimination. But it's no less important than the gentle nurturing care that it undoes."

"So, why does it always feel like a catastrophe, or like I'm going crazy?"

"Because you're not a forest fire," Lourdes said, looking closely at Farya, then selecting and passing her a lipstick. "You're a person. Like most people, you're subject to overpowering joys and miseries. You get bored, and you get angry. And because you're young, you lose control."

"So, this will pass?"

"I hope for all of our sakes that it will. But there are things you can do, to even yourself out, to keep from doing more things you can't take back," Lourdes said, her mouth still poised on the cusp of an unplanned smile.

"Even myself out how?"

"You'll always do what you do. And it's an incredible power, imposing order on so much lazy madness. But you're too unpredictable, too emotional."

"I'm sorry."

"Oh, come on—that's as crazy as saying you're sorry for crying. You're just a person, and that's a good thing. And maybe I can help."

"But how? How can you remember when no one else does? How can you even know?"

"I've forgotten more than I remember, and I've lost more than I know. But I can insist on seeing what I shouldn't. We … I'm a refugee from a world that's gone forever. I always feel it. But it only ever hurts when I start to forget the kind of sacrifices that made it possible for me to be here."

"I'm so sorry," Farya said, her voice cracking.

"Don't be. Maybe it's not tragic. Maybe the tragedy is that these selves, these desires should have ever been different in the first place. Maybe it's nothing more than a wave rolling back. The animals on land and the fish in the sea don't mind the waves much. But it's everything for little crabs like me, forever chasing what I saw in the froth …" Lourdes seemed wild for a moment, like she might say absolutely anything, then collected herself. "That's enough for now. Let's go down to the party—this wine is good, but I think we could both use stronger stuff."

Saucer-eyed, Farya nodded.

✣

Farya woke in the previous evening's clothes, but in her own bed. One dangly earring had pressed a red crescent into her cheek. The other had become tangled in her brown hair, pulling at her earlobe and scalp throughout the awkward amble to the bathroom. Incapable of a more delicate operation, she cut the hair around it with her roommate's cuticle scissors.

With eyes puffy and makeup askew, Farya tried smiling in the mirror, tried a come-hither look, a pout of the lips, and laughed. She dressed and skipped out of the apartment as fast as she could. Her hangover inverted the previous evening's towering convictions into well-deep uncertainties. A block from her front door, she stopped to connect the stinging pain deep in her ankle with a fall she'd taken in the courtyard—stupid high heels. She remembered Ethan helping her into a cab—another expense she couldn't afford.

Hobbled, she made it to a nearby coffee shop—an old-looking place with enough outlets for everyone to stay on their laptops through long semi-employed afternoons. On her neighbor's screen, a bearded young man explained life insurance using images of famous people and cats. Farya tried to avert her eyes from the moving images, taking deep breaths and small bites.

Her purse vibrated. It was a text from a number, not a name. It was, the text explained, a boy she'd met the night before, to whom she'd given her number. She tried to remember him, remembered his T-shirt had the face of a puppet on it, his maybe-charming sullen way of boasting. Handsome, though, and now, it seemed, persistent. His text concealed another one that had come while she was sleeping, from Lourdes the landlordess. *We should get together again*, it said, *this week. Much to discuss.* Farya let out a low groan that made the man next to her shift in his seat.

Farya's head throbbed and insisted she put off everything until the next day. Her stomach shifted in a direction that opposed the rotation of the earth. At her apartment, she rewatched a TV show she remembered as having been funnier, ordered delivery, which carried her farther from the safe confines of her budget, and took a little pill that Ethan had given her after she told him about her disastrous date with the data-compression guy.

She woke early, clear-eyed and propelled to action by a deep sense of unease. It was Monday. She was in the office by seven, organizing and reorganizing everything—her schedule, her contacts, in-progress tables, grids, and to-do lists. She had a system with multiple redundancies across project-management software suites, notebooks, planners, hanging folders, files digital and paper, calendars cross-referenced. Farya did all she could to prevent her from losing track of anything. The day flew by, the work absorbing her anxiety. It let her put off thinking about Lourdes.

By two o'clock, she was up-to-date with her system, ahead of schedule for the day, and ready to get a late lunch, when her cell phone rang. She didn't recognize the phone number, but she knew the area code—one of the four that had belonged to Camden, New York, when it was a big city. The man on the other line said he was a detective. He was looking for Romeo Mauriello and asked if she knew him.

"I did; I do. We were friends, went out a few times."

"Really?"

"Yes. But it's been months. I haven't seen him since I moved."

"Okay, that's great, really," the detective said. He sounded relieved. "If you have a minute, I have a few more questions."

"Can I ask what's this about?"

"Romeo's been missing for a few months. But aside from his mother, and now you, I'm having a hard time confirming that he even exists."

Farya's stomach dropped. First Lourdes and now this. She felt an urge to run.

"Oh, uh, now's really not a good time. It's actually really bad. Could I call you back?"

With shaking hands, she wrote down Ronnie's number and fled to the office bathroom and locked the metal door on the stall, hoping the scintilla of privacy would help things quiet down and behave for a few minutes.

That night, Farya stayed late at her desk, rechecking her calendar and the status of projects on her list, highlighting circled items, and annotating highlighted items, making sure she wasn't missing anything else.

Bryan

The inside of the club had been crafted to be seen and appreciated only by the few wealthy, powerful, beautiful, lucky, or crafty. Bryan Lomoigne had been all of those things in his forty-one years, except beautiful. And so, he likewise didn't pause to notice the aquarium wall filled with all manner of sea creatures. Octopi, sharks, stingrays, jellyfish, giant sea turtles darting about, released hungry at regular intervals. In his peripheral vision, as the hostess led him to his table on the edge of the room, the gladiatorial show of darting fins and crimson blossoms grabbed the eye.

The mosaic floor—with its million or so confetti tiles depicting an orgiastic banquet of cherubs, satyrs, gryphons, smirking serpents, and political figures drinking and eating—was likewise lost on him. The elaborate scene seemed to move if you looked at it for very long. But no one looked down in a place like this.

As always, Bryan was early—a habit from his peculiar version of teenage rebellion. He ordered a drink from a tall, blonde waitress. She was friendly, solicitous, and Bryan played along—a boyish, Irish squint when he smiled. His table was a few feet from a long glass wall curved to reveal the open blackness of night over the Pacific Ocean. He could see stars and boats out at sea but turned his attention to the inside of the club.

The club that night consisted of members, guests whom the members wanted something from, and guests who were there for the pleasure of the members. Bryan could spot the members—they spoke uninterrupted and laughed as if their laughter were a precious coin generously tossed about in a poor world. Their colleagues, clients, paramours, jesters, or prey could only attempt to appear so assured. Though uniformly attractive, and in some cases famous, the guests were recognizable. Very careful with their eyes—when spoken to, they didn't flinch, but they did blink. However quick they might be to pick up a cue to laugh, they were taking the cues. The professional beauties laughed—not loud, but big—their painted mouths stretching like a snake eating some oversized rodent to reveal gleaming semi-precious stones of teeth—the buxom ones with their precise jiggling, like the jiggle of a platonic form, others thin, spidery, with sudden breasts. They, and their male counterparts, were as much of the opulence as the mosaic, the aquatic blood sport, the moonlit sea, or the spiderweb chandelier.

Bryan had known these women from a young age—designed by nature and selected by denizens of once-smoke-filled rooms to get red-blooded American males to do or buy whatever needs doing or buying. Fresh-faced from Boise or Brasilia, laughing because they were told once, long ago, that they were prettier when they laughed, they were exuberant in a practiced way. Watching them as a boy in clubs and restaurants not too different from this one, they impressed Bryan with the Power of Empire—its incredible capacity to arouse desire. As he grew older, he'd been in the right rooms and cut the right figure for their attention. Even now, middle-aged with a body that revealed a general indifference to both fitness and dissipation, he looked like safety itself to them. But that's not why he'd come to the club that night. And the appeal of those women, once overpowering to him, had soured to pity.

The male guests, invited for the pleasure of their company, made less of an impression on Bryan but were no less remarkable. They were well dressed and effortless as they executed their well-worn formulas of charm. Like the women, many had been surgically altered to look like celebrities. A young, visibly obsequious man in Bryan's line of sight was the spitting image of Streetcar-Named-Desire Marlon Brando. Others, men and women alike, had been altered into gorgeous versions of their hosts—a popular fetish in the crowd.

The waitress returned, shiny faced and eager with his drink, maroon and bitter. Out the window, a bright star prowled the sea's horizon.

Bryan was a member, though he never saw the bill for nights like these. It all ran through his company, Metacom. The client he was meeting, Sevritas Capital Partners, also held memberships at the club. For a company no one ever heard of, it seemed to have memberships everywhere.

Petra arrived, not breaking stride as she followed the hostess to Bryan's table. Dark haired and blue-eyed, with sharp features, she wore a short tan-and-orange suede dress. Bryan could see the veins in her forearms and calves. When she saw Bryan, she gave a smile that was mechanical and a little scary for being as convincing as it was. It showed off straight bright teeth and the jutting jaw of a too-adamantly corrected overbite. The smile summed up Petra—engineered, orchestrated, but so effective that you felt outsmarted by it.

Bryan saw Petra once a quarter, and each time, she looked different in a way he couldn't place. As always, Petra carried a brown leather briefcase in one hand. The business was still essentially paper-based. This time, though, Petra held a black leather leash in her other hand, which was attached to the neck of a young woman who was busting out of a white rubber dress. The young woman had bright red hair that spouted like a tassel from the hole in the top of her white rubber mask.

Petra always brought gifts—the kind of things she thought Bryan might like. She was right, which was part of what Petra was trying to convey.

Bryan smiled at them both, kicking himself for visiting that one website so many times. "I can't wait until my grandchildren see my browser history," as one of his execs had once quipped to him, after too many drinks, before resigning.

Petra didn't introduce the girl on the leash. Nor did the gift get a seat. She stood stock-still for the entire two-and-a-half-hour meal, eyes straight ahead, beads of perspiration emerging through her makeup and gathering on the edges of the mask and dress.

In the ten years he'd done business with Petra, her employer, Sevritas, had become a major part of what kept his company—a budget cellular carrier—in business. But Bryan sensed that the stakes of these meetings were higher for her. The waitress returned and set up the menu before them—mother of pearl inlaid in a pitch-black hardwood. The entree names glowed.

MacArthur Returns to the Philippines
Mark Antony at Philippi
Mark Rothko on a Cold Day
Mata Hari in Madrid
Mathilde Kschessinska Recollects her last Meeting with the Czar

There were no prices. The waitress asked if they wanted her to interpret any of the dishes before they ordered.

"They're on the M's," Bryan remarked.

"I had the Mata Hari the other day," Petra said.

"How was it?"

"Delicious, of course. Light and spicy at first, but then very rich in a way I didn't expect."

Bryan opted for the MacArthur, along with the cocktail course. The waitress stressed again that if there was anything else they needed, just to ask, casting a knowing smile at the rubber-clad kewpie doll at their table. Once she was gone, Petra and Bryan talked numbers, the per-unit prices, and the expansion plans that Sevritas recommended. Over time, Bryan had grown to accept that Petra's people usually knew how to run his business better than he did.

The food arrived. Eating it, Bryan could smell the sea and the diesel fumes of the landing boat. He could taste the sun's relentless reproach of the water, the enemies fleeing, the burning of food and supplies, the cigarettes of his fellow officers, the sweet alkaline flavor of a dead canker sore in his mouth—all the sensations coalescing into a towering determination and a victory over a time and space unimaginable to his younger self. The meal was so like a film that Bryan lost sight of the room and the sweating statue standing across from him.

Across the table, Petra was savoring the Mark Antony, a giraffe-and-peacock ravioli redolent of the doomed last gasp of the Roman Republic. She nodded when Bryan excused himself to go to the bathroom with the echoes of *that magnificent war*, lingering in the corners of his mouth. Walking around the woman whose leash was looped onto the arm of Petra's chair, Bryan could smell blood, burning pitch, and a hint of rotting flesh.

Passing through the club's mix of old wishes fulfilled and new appetites kindled, Bryan's eye snagged on a face—Ritchie Reach, the guitarist from the Union Skells—the band that had made Bryan's father rich and famous. Ritchie had been a kind of uncle figure to Bryan when he was a kid, even after Bryan's dad married a new woman and went solo.

Ritchie was standing at the bar, waving for a drink. But the bartender was focused on blowing out the small flame he'd set atop a cut-crystal glass of yellow liquid. Above the bar, a huge squid delivered the coup de grace to a big twitching crab leaking pink water. Bryan waited a second to make sure it was really Ritchie and not an impersonator. The man had the trying-to-play-it-cool-and-failing look of a guest who was two steps up from the waitress and three steps up from one of the creatures in the aquarium.

It was Ritchie—a sneering skeleton with a paunch in a couture rocker's getup, his face was unshaven in its usual way, but older than the face's owner ever expected. There was something not right about his leather jacket and jeans. It took Bryan a second to figure out that Ritchie was wearing a replica of the outfit he'd worn on the cover of the second Union Skells album.

Ritchie caught him looking and said his name. It was a happy reunion. The bartender took note, and Ritchie ordered a pair of bourbons. Most days, people he'd known before his incredible success were his best chance at an honest conversation. After some catching up, Bryan asked the old rocker what brought him to the club.

"Command performance, you could say. Older bird, a pill widow who got wet for the Skells once thirty years ago and likes a ride on the old jukebox once in a blue moon. That's what passes for a retirement plan in the music industry," he said, smiling small to conceal a bad tooth. "I heard this was America, where they evicted the last king long ago. But now they say the customer is king."

"What about the Skells, the royalties?"

"Not in the age of the internet, I'm afraid. Not on a twentieth of a penny a play. It's all in these, uh, personal appearances."

"I was afraid of that. I heard from Duane a few months ago."

"He try to sell you some of his precious *memorabilia*?" Bryan looked across the room and saw Petra seeing him. Bryan started through the closing small talk when Ritchie put a hand on his arm. "Member, huh?"

"Here? Yeah."

"Glad to see you doing so good. My own kids—they got all the wrong ideas. Probably got 'em from me."

"Well, hang in there."

"I mean it," Ritchie said, the bourbon amplifying the decay in his breath. "Makes me glad to see anyone doing good in this world. Hold on a sec. Maybe you have an event, or you know someone who does—nostalgia or whatever."

Ritchie fished a business card from his inside jacket pocket. The corners of the card were blunted, and the phone number had been crossed out and rewritten by hand. Bryan took it and downed the rest of the drink to underscore his farewell. It was stronger than the cocktails and loosened the tightness he'd felt in his collar since he realized the message implied by the bondage model provided by Sevritas Capital.

Back at the table, Petra was finishing up a call, offering measured monosyllables into a disposable plastic flip phone. No one with anything real at stake used the feature-jammed, contract-laden, surveillance-likely smart devices anymore. The waitress came by, and Bryan said that instead of the rest of the cocktail story arc, he'd have another bourbon. Petra hung up and tilted her head in Ritchie's direction.

"Friend of my father's."

"Right, the famous father …" she said, leaning in. "The great Jimny Lomoigne."

But Bryan squished his mouth into a bland smile. The encounter at the bar had put a bad spin on the whole place, on Petra. It was a change in rotation so sudden that it scared Bryan and set him to the kind of thoughts he didn't want near his business.

"How about you, Petra?" he said. "We're always talking business. I feel like I've never really gotten to know you. What's your story?"

"Pretty boring: professional, overachieving parents; upscale suburb; valedictorian of my high school; Ivy League; Summa Cum Laude; consulting for few years; then an MBA; private equity out west, then this."

"And this—you plan to stay?"

"Oh, definitely. You'd be surprised at the kinds of compensation a private firm can offer," Petra said and glanced at the shiny rubber hip of the woman beside her. "Maybe *you* wouldn't."

Petra shifted the conversation to their usual business for a couple more bourbons. As they talked, a few intrepid drops of sweat had begun to travel down the throat and thighs of the girl in rubber. Bryan couldn't help but notice the tremor in the gift-woman's knees. But in the taut latex gleam, he seemed to see Ritchie's lumpen resigned smile, turning the meanings of all the affluence around him to the enormous spur of a larger remorse.

"These numbers are getting big. I have a question," he said, his counterclockwise thoughts bold with whiskey. "It's about our business together—about the rights you buy from us—what kind of secondary market do you sell them on?"

All the playfulness on Petra's face vanished.

"It's what you might expect from your own experience. What's the profit margin when you resell them?" she asked.

"It's enough to keep doing it, clearly," Bryan said, gesturing around the room. "But to make money on the kind of scale you guys are buying up, I'd expect to see public outreach, like the lawyer ads on local TV: *If You Bought a Cell Phone From Any of the Following Companies in the Last Ten Years, then We Own Your Souls. Call 1-800 …*"

Petra's face signaled annoyance at Bryan's candor. She looked down into her drink while she chose her words.

"The partners and I believe it's better for everyone if your side of the house is atheist."

"My side of the house?"

"Yes."

"We're not in the same *house*. We're in different houses. I'm the other side of the *transaction*, which may as well be the other side of the world."

"Of course. I misspoke," she said, nodding and wielding her smile like a flamethrower. Without looking away, Petra signed the bill, which the waitress had imperceptibly delivered.

"It's late," Bryan said. "The important thing is that you received the contracts."

"We did. Thank you. The receipt and the rest of the single-use-account number are in the case. I always enjoy talking with you, Bryan," she said and rose.

They shook hands—Petra was the opposite of a hugger. She held out the leash of the white-latex-clad woman to him. The gift's eyes didn't move but remained fixed on the middle distance. The sweat had made parts of her outfit transparent.

It wasn't the first time Petra had come with a gift like this. But it was the first time Bryan shook his head and refused it. He murmured that he had too much work to do. Petra started to insist but stopped herself. Every transaction had its own etiquette.

✚

Opening the blackout curtains on the bedroom's huge bell-shaped window, the ocean swelled, too bright and too huge. Bryan turned from it and looked around the room—framed paintings, furniture, and a dormant flat television screen the size of his mattress. But his eye settled on Ritchie Reach's beat-up business card.

He felt bad, but it wasn't a hangover. There was the irritant—a dream. In it, Ritchie was wearing a rubber dress, his hands bound with twine to a shiny fiberglass guitar with no strings. In front of him was Bryan's father Jimny, chained to a jukebox almost playing the Union Skells big hit "Now Just Stars"—the chorus distorted to *terms of service*. Jimny had his mouth around one of those metal spouts that gerbils drink from, and upon closer inspection, his face had fused to it. He drank greedily, but his eyes were full of panic.

Bryan went downstairs and told the maid to leave. He took a cup of coffee and a few Advil to the couch and watched the ocean from the living room. Bryan knew Southern California. Jimny had lived up the coast in Malibu when Bryan was in college. Bryan tried to remember if that was three or four wives after his mother, tried to remember the time he'd spent with Jimny, but it all got mixed up with YouTube interviews and documentary footage.

"Who knows if the music's any good? Who knows if it will last? It's not even about that. It's about people, you know, they walk around with so *much* in them, but they don't know if they're even allowed to have it. If all we did was make asses of ourselves—at least we gave them permission to let something out. We set them free. *That's* the business I'm in, not the so-called music business," Bryan's dad had said, and the director of the documentary had closed with it.

Years ago, after Bryan's second company had failed, Bryan had been at the documentary's premiere. He remembered making plans to spend time with the old man at the film festival, but Jimny canceled at the last minute.

Not the so-called music business—yeah, right, Bryan thought, staring past the gleaming expanse of wood floor to the gleaming expanse of sea. Jimny was more in that business than Ritchie had been, more than any of the other Union Skells he left drifting in his wake.

We set them free—well, where's that freedom now? Bryan said aloud to the empty living room. Dead and gone and chained to a jukebox and a gerbil feeder; Jimny didn't seem so free.

Bryan called his assistant and told her to reschedule his meetings for the day, then asked his phone for a tint recommendation for his sunglasses. California was a good place for a personal day—asked little and promised almost everything. He hopped in his car, eased onto the highway, and started driving. Pulling over at a 76, the gas pump was topped with a video screen that played the crescendo of "Now Just Stars" in between snippets of celebrity gossip and come-ons for huge sodas and gas-rewards-points credit cards.

After the lengthy nightmares of the night before, the snippet hit him like a screech, a glare, an ammonia fume, and made him pull at the collar of his designer T-shirt, made him shift his feet to make sure they weren't rooted to the hot concrete.

Retreating to the cool, dark cockpit of the car, Bryan asked the dashboard for directions to the nearest record store. He cruised in silence for an hour and pulled off at a wide, palm-lined version of three thousand other boulevards and state highways in America. From the car, he recognized some of his own businesses: *Communilutions Unlimited; Mobile Scenez; QuartzTalk; Phone Home; Touch Passport; Kinnections Global; Commz Bay; Satillian Mobile.* The Metacom family of mobile devices and services offered inexpensive contracts to people with bad credit. The devil was, of course, in the details.

In the pocket strip mall, there was a *Mobile Scenez* on one side of the record store. On another day, he might have stopped in and checked on the state of the place, started a conversation with the clerks, done all that grassroots checking and prodding that a good CEO might. But that afternoon, Bryan averted his eyes as he walked from his parking spot, past a jeweler who promised a ROLEX BLOWOUT, to the door of the record store.

A Townes Van Zandt record presided over the emptiness of the record store, the voice mournful, the sound deep and full. The store seemed to have more posters, toys, T-shirts, and other pop culture miscellanea than records. But Bryan found what he needed. The lip-pierced clerkess scanned the merchandise and gave him a double take.

"You know you have duplicates here," she said.

"Excuse me?"

"Here," she said, picking up two CDs in one hand and two LPs in another. "You really only need one of each of these."

"I'll take them all."

"Okay. But you know we only give store credit on returns."

"That's fine."

"Union Skells—I've heard of these guys. Are they cool?"

"Not really," Bryan said.

She said ok*ay*, elongating the last syllable. Poor thing—she thinks her soul belongs to the world of Townes Van Zandt, Bryan thought, when it belongs to *Mobile Scenez*, and to whatever it is that is the acceptable face of. Thoughts like this were why he'd taken the day off. Bryan took out his credit card, then thought better of it and paid with cash. His plan—still taking shape—made him look over his shoulder as he walked out into the bright, blank, palm-lined parking lot with a big bag containing all the Jimny Lomoigne and Union Skells music the store had. Driving home, he watched the rearview mirror and arrived home, his suspicions neither confirmed nor disproven, eager to return to not thinking the unthinkable.

On the patio overlooking the sea, he unwrapped the LPs and disassembled the CD cases. He removed all the liner notes. He flipped a switch, and neat blue flames danced above the multi-colored glass fragments of the patio fire pit. The cross-cut shredder in the house's office was heavy and left bright red lines on his soft hands as Bryan wrestled it out onto the patio and plugged it in. He plugged it into the outlet in the granite base of the fire pit. And as the sun sank, he fed the first CD into the shredder. Calm returned with each shimmering disc cut to confetti, each band picture, rack list, and liner note curling to acrid ash in the fire.

Bryan took a deep breath, bathing in the relief that comes with knowing that you do not have to change your entire life. When the last of the album sleeves had been devoured by the tidy little flames, he felt better than he had in a while. He went into the house to find Ritchie Reach's business card.

✛

Black box tops, gold and silver pyramids, domes, and spires, hives of suited men and women coming and going, effervescing through the trading day, the odd empty floor waiting for the next big winner to move in and try to win a little more—from his windows on sixtieth floor, Bryan had few peers. The normalcy of being in the office, in Manhattan, slowly restored him after the sour nightmares of his California trip.

Cassie Ocampo was no stranger to this landscape—a newly minted MBA who'd spent her decade-long career in telecommunications; she should have felt more confident as she rode the elevator up one floor and waited for Bryan's assistant, responding to some unseen signal, to nod her in. That day, Cassie carried with her a multi-million-dollar idea, so she should have felt better than she did. But the idea was so simple, so easy, and so obvious that it made her uneasy. Bryan read the first page and flipped through the rest.

"This isn't what I asked for," he said, not looking up.

"I realize that. But the deeper dive I did, the more it seemed that we could increase our subscriber-base, eliminate our printing and document storage facilities, cut our advertising and marketing costs, and ramp up our presence among middle- and high-income users, which would set us up to sell, or even go public at a much higher …"

"Cassie, I don't want you to get the wrong idea—I appreciate you going the extra mile on this. But it's the wrong mile. We won't go public, not in two years, or five years, or ever."

"Why not? We have the scale …"

Bryan exhaled hard and looked at her for what felt like the first time. That terrible sense of pity washed over Bryan once again. Cassie seemed too young to be so serious. With straight black hair, a strong chin, and dark eyes that crossed ever so slightly, she seemed too pretty to be so earnest about a business that had come to seem so ugly to him. He noticed, too, how willful she was, settling into the discomfort of his silence like she was digging a trench. She wanted to win in the big serious world and wanted it badly enough not to scare too easily.

"This is partly my fault," Bryan said. "I gave you a project without giving you an understanding of all our operations. I want to test the waters for a sale. And if we're going to sell, it will probably have to be a private sale at a deep discount."

"But if we make some of these changes, then we won't have to take a discount …"

"We will. Our business isn't entirely what it seems. Some of the things we ask of our subscribers are very sensitive."

"Is it? I mean, we sell the data we collect from their phones—so what? Our customers know that privacy is too much to expect at the prices we charge."

"It's more than data," Bryan said, looking away to check one of the monitors on his desk. "Go read the standard Terms of Service that all of our subscribers sign, especially the Non-Mortal-Element clause. Read it carefully. And we'll talk at five."

When Cassie returned a few hours later, she wasn't her usual smartest-woman-in-the-room mix of nerve and eagerness. Bryan could tell that she had indeed gotten the full thrust of the document she'd read. She sat down across from him, flattening her skirt, and resting the document on her thighs, less for discussion than as a kind of shield.

"Do you see what we sell now?" Bryan said. Cassie nodded. "And you see why we have so many names?" Again, she nodded. "Do you still want to work here?"

There was a long pause. Cassie was an atheist, but a casual atheist in the way her parents had been casual Christmas-and-Easter Filipino Catholics. Whatever drove her to get up at 4:30 in the morning, go straight to the gym and into the office by 7:30 every morning was a kind of faith. That never-articulated faith was in, among other things, money. And money said that personal data, no matter how intimate or frivolous, had a market price. And now that same money said that souls had a price too, which was a way of saying they existed. Maybe the soul is like money—it never really exists until someone owes it to an angry creditor. But that was the criteria Cassie had accepted. And a second look at Metacom's books left little doubt. They weren't selling customer data but human souls.

Cassie scanned the walls of Bryan's office—the family photo, the photo with a well-known politician, the industry award, the plaque of recognition from a civic organization, the diploma, the conversation-piece rotary-phone memento from the company's early days, the stuffed trophy fish, the executive team photo commemorating a milestone, and the status-symbol painting were all there. All the usual decorations by which executives signaled their power and their approachability were there. She looked at Bryan, who had lost interest during her crisis, and was watching his monitor.

"I do. I still want to work here."

"Are you sure?" Bryan asked. This was a precarious moment, where Bryan had lost more than a few talented executives.

"Yes. But I have some questions—who do we sell them to? The souls—who buys them?"

"In the building, we call them subscriber Non-Mortal Element Rights. And some we sell back—if a customer reads the fine print and can afford the premium we charge. The rest we sell to third parties."

"And what do the third parties do with the … Non-Mortal Element Rights? It seems like they're buying up huge quantities."

"I'm not sure, and they're not eager to tell us. There are companies that buy the rights to software patents, or books, or old movies, and never do anything with them. They keep the intellectual property on the books like an asset until they get a big opportunity to cash in."

"But you don't know?"

"Cassie, I like all the questions you're asking. But let's try to keep focused on the project—finding a buyer …"

She nodded with newfound fear and respect. She'd always known there was a secret between her and the mysterious power that sweated money and made certain people more real than others. And now she was being let in on it. She and Bryan stayed late, while Bryan explained Metacom's real business. The conversation came easy between them.

There were bigger, more mysterious things that he didn't have to explain to Cassie. At the end of the night, with the reports and competitive analyses spread out across the conference-room table, she only had one question.

"Steady growth, high margins, and a distinct competitive advantage—why do you want to sell the business?" she asked.

Bryan offered a few non-answers and changed the subject.

✢

Weary chaos had crept in, hedges high and unruly. At first glance, the house itself was what Bryan remembered—all modern triangles and circles. But the white paint was chipped and dulled. And the shapes worn rough and repaired cheaply. The gutter on the front roofline drooped and dangled at the edge, and the long gravel driveway sprouted weeds. At a bend in the driveway, Bryan saw through the huge windows of the open-plan living room to the Long Island Sound. The autumn air warned of a chill that it stopped short of delivering.

Ritchie met him at the front door and showed him in past a hole in the foyer wall, where Bryan recalled a futuristic video-security screen having been. The white leather sofas had yellowed and cracked.

"Can I get you anything? Cup of tea?" Ritchie said, slipping into the British accent he'd affected inconsistently throughout his career. Ritchie's face was red and puffy on the left side, the eye half-closed.

"No. Are you okay?" Bryan asked, gesturing to his own eye.

"Yeah. Just a little basic maintenance. The swelling should go down by tomorrow. The product that shows up to accompany the old bird to the Hamptons for the weekend has gotta look like the picture on the box."

"Did a doctor do that?"

"He's a doctor today—tomorrow may be another story."

"Does it hurt?"

"Just at first, and then after for a while. I write it off. There's a reason they call it show *business*. I'll say this, though: If I'd known that I was posing for my own death mask that day, I would have squinted a bit and tucked my chin for the photographer who took that fuckin' album cover. Would've saved a lot of what the doctors call 'mild discomfort.'"

"That cover is iconic. You should be proud—I know my dad was."

"Cold comfort. Friggin' chilly indeed. Let me tell you—when I was a young man, I always hated the old man I'd one day become. And now I despise the little shit I was. Fuck him. I get zero joy when I think of that arrogant prick strutting and sneering."

"The other night at the club …"

"It was good to see you there, with the business lady on one side and the pleasure lady on the other. Reminded me of my own heydays. Good lad."

"It was … Anyway, you mentioned that the royalties from the Union Skells were coming in below expectations."

"Fuckin' internet. A bunch of grubby greedhead nerds show up and put everyone out of business. And no one says a fuckin' peep," Ritchie said and rambled on for a good while about technology, his many disappointments, divorce attorneys, children who "cost and whine and cost," and about the man who was supposed to fix the gutters on his house.

"I got the sense that money was an issue," Bryan said, interrupting.

"Like my dad always said, 'Everyone gets paid fair in the currency they print.' He was one careful man. Never made much money, but we were all surprised how much he had when he passed. I always swore I wouldn't care. And now here I am—repaid in carelessness."

Ritchie ran his fingers through hair that was suspiciously black and full and shook his head.

"Well, I was thinking that if you needed cash, maybe I could help you out."

"Oh," Ritchie said, and all the shagginess of his persona evaporated. His pupils tightened to the now-familiar moment when a friendly conversation revealed itself as a predator-prey scenario.

"The Skells," Bryan said. "You still own a portion of the publishing rights."

"And the master recording of the first album."

"If you were interested in selling them, what would you want for all of your rights—masters, publishing, everything—to the Union Skells material?" Bryan asked.

"What would you be willing to pay?"

Bryan named a price. Ritchie named another. They went back and forth, but not for very long. When they agreed, Ritchie asked why he was buying.

"I heard one of Dad's old songs on a video screen at a gas pump—a snippet, the chorus. I didn't like hearing it used that way," Bryan said. Ritchie looked him in the eye and grinned a bit.

"You think you can pay the ransom on a dead man?" the older man said, a glint of recognition in his crooked face.

"Probably not. But what's life if you don't try?"

"Good lad. Carry on."

Driving away through the manicured North Shore town to the expressway, Bryan felt a little less of the hopeless debt that seemed to weigh down on everything he saw, from the few boats left in the marina to the clean, new school buses.

✢

It was a chilly morning, and a low cloud hung over the whole city. Bryan's car whispered through the damp streets, the low gray light no competition for the tablet where he read the morning's news.

He spent the morning on family business in Brooklyn—a half-brother cobbling his life together after blowing through his twenties and his inheritance in a predictably disreputable manner. As the sole successful offspring, he had learned over the years the surprisingly tricky business of doling out money to his step- and half-siblings. It was never enough to ask them *how much*. Even if they only ever called him for money—and even when their tales of woe were unquestionable bullshit—he had to take the time and listen if he really did want to do what he claimed, which was to help.

The stranger-brother that morning looked like Bryan, with the same round face and crooked nose. But he seemed so much younger, almost like a child. He was, from all appearances, as sober and earnest as he claimed on the phone. That shortened his story and the meeting. The liars always wanted to put too fine a point on it. As he did with his other unlucky semi-siblings, Bryan asked what he had for a cell phone, to make sure it wasn't a Metacom contract. That was, he said to no one because no one could know, the best he could do.

Bryan was in his car on the way to the office by eleven, having secured all the Union Skells and Jimny Lomoigne rights his half-brother owned. From there, it was a day when Bryan's feet scarcely brushed the common earth. The fog settled somewhere around the forty-fifth floor, and Bryan's office was filled with golden sunlight. He held the meetings and took the calls by which a midsized business expanded with what felt like an ineluctable momentum. Doing a job well is always the best way not to ask if it's worth doing. It was easy above the clouds, with his tower-top, strange shapes born from mist into a gleaming heaven by means best left incomprehensible.

Bryan's assistant knocked and hung a fresh suit on the inside of his office door, for the evening's event—an award, a welcome reassurance for the uneasiness he'd been doing all he could to soothe since that California trip. He'd given a sum to a charity, and it wanted to honor him to show the other donors in the room how nice a spotlight it might shine if only they gave as much. Bryan's children would be there, as would his wife, whom he hadn't seen in a month—their longest time apart yet.

The gloom broke at dusk, casting dramatic yellow and pink hues on the ridge of retreating clouds. After a day indoors, he walked the last block from his car to the event, wincing to see that the charity had arranged for a red carpet outside, and tried to hurry around the back of the hired photographer. As he did, he nearly collided with a young woman. He said *excuse me* and their eyes caught for a long moment. She was slim, with dark hair, and pronounced features—a prominent nose and a large mouth. It was her eyes that caught him—eyes like one of those nights in the country where the *depth* of the night sky startles, stuns, and detains. In that second, he could sense a reserve and a wildness to how she looked at him that made him feel younger for a moment, as though he hadn't undergone the drab necessities of the last decade and a half, as if he would never have to. Her eyes were alert and alive, even a little afraid, as if she, along with him, knew the real reason to be afraid in the wealth and routine of that street. She didn't look away from him as she said *it's okay*.

Then she vanished in the stream of Midtown pedestrians hurrying to restaurants, bars, apartments, and trains. He shook his head and climbed the stairs into the townhouse. The place was a club once favored by the men they'd named streets and towns for—now secure and exclusive, its dirty deals belonging to the dead who'd traded in railroads, carbines, canals, small former colonies, whole regions, and generations consigned to oblivion beneath the unintelligible satyr-cackle carved in ironwood and shellacked with cigar smoke.

Bryan had grown up going to such places, as a nouveau-riche heir to a class that saw his father as a notable agent of its own decomposition. The embrace in such places had always been reluctant, which only made Bryan more fascinated.

Tonight, though, that embrace was certain and proper. Bryan navigated the cocktail-hour throng, averting his eyes until he reached the bar. With a glass of beer in hand, he savored the moment before he would have to socialize. He let his eyes settle on the polished wood pilasters, the grand piano, the glass case exhibiting a pistol used in some famous shooting. The carved cherubs cackled, and the bas-relief sphinxes gloated, but that night they did so for Bryan.

For the people around him, the cost to attend the evening's event was the same as a new compact car. Its entertainment was an act popular from the oldies FM station, and the food from a television chef. The men were either the lean sociopaths of the upper rungs of some corporate ladder or the ones portly from excess talent or luck. The women were either razor-thin, their bodies almost robotic in their efficiency, with razor-sharp smiles, or older women who'd matured to the graceful forms of musical instruments.

Bryan's wife, Bethanie, was the former. Since he'd seen her last, she seemed to have come into sharper relief against the world around her. He couldn't tell if she was prettier, but she had grown stranger. By way of hello, she leaned in and thrust her face, with its bright white smile like the hull of a conqueror's ship, for a cheek kiss so forceful that he feared a black eye. The impact didn't faze her, though, and she introduced him, as her husband, to someone else immediately, before spinning into another conversation.

He didn't have time to read her. But he knew that their marriage was a thing fading from neglect. The kids were in boarding school, and their respective fortunes separated by fastidious prenuptial incantations. Maybe he was unfaithful; maybe she was. But betrayal was an alien concept in the life they had tacitly assembled. There were only options, opportunities, and occasional obligations. It was one more thing that made Bryan sad in a way he had to keep to himself.

The party found Bryan quickly in the form of a man with a restored hairline whose name Bryan missed. He talked at Bryan about disruption, clouds, and *the secret sauce in the holy grail* of a company that he owned or worked for. An older man trying to play a young man's game; whatever he had of personality and wit collapsing into jargon. The evenness of the hairs at the vanguard of his scalp reminded Bryan of Ritchie Reach. Feigning hearing problems, Bryan turned his ear to the man to look at a smoky old mural instead of the straining face of his conversation partner. In the mural, Peter Minuit was buying Manhattan from the Indians with a jar of baubles. Minuit's face was crooked and calm. Bryan wondered what kind of refund policy they had in those days and excused himself for a fresh drink.

At the bar, the labels of the bottles read like the forged pedigrees of perished nations, of crimes made into nations and nations made into crimes—all the terrible truths the past tells about the future. His wife found him before he could sink deeper into his thoughts, a business card between her manicured fingers. There was more at stake for her than him at these events. She ran an event-marketing business that she kept going for reasons he didn't dare ask her about.

"Hey," he said, trying to hold her attention.

"Hey. One second, I just have to …"

"No, don't worry; I'll get out of your hair," Bryan said. The words were like Styrofoam in his mouth. "Where are the kids?"

"They ran off somewhere."

A young woman tapped Bryan on the shoulder and asked if he wanted a body mic or if he'd use the podium. When he turned around, his wife's straight, muscular bare back was flush to him, and she was talking like she was climbing a ladder to one of the lean sociopath males.

Bryan picked up his beer, and remembering his own childhood, located his children under a bend in a stately wood staircase. They were doing what Bryan had done whenever he was forced to see his father honored as a kid—drinking Cokes and doing their best not to die of boredom.

"Hey, guys," Bryan said, dropping to a knee to hug the boy and staying there to be hugged by his daughter. The boy was eight, taller, getting knobby and awkward. The girl, now eleven, had grown into a miniature woman. He stayed stooped under the staircase for a few minutes to chat. The girl was quiet, and the boy full of eager, mismatched bursts of information. An event photographer caught a few snaps. *The good father—another tall tale to put next to Peter Minuit's square deal*, Bryan thought. Someone, following the flashes, told them it was time to be seated. The kids groaned.

The gala program began with a once-beautiful woman with a still-beautiful voice singing *Amazing Grace*, while a screen behind her shuffled through the faces of the afflicted children and the statistics of their affliction. The song ended, and after a solemn pause, the head of the charity, as well kept and dressed as any of them, spoke earnestly of the seriousness and the importance of it all. She yielded the podium to a younger but similar woman, who gave much the same spiel. After one more introduction, there was a whole video of still photos about Bryan, alongside an instrumental version of "Not Just Stars."

The average person may not know the name Bryan Lomoigne. But if you stop someone on the street, there's a good chance they have one of his phones in their pocket. His company Metacom Holdings is a growing telecommunications leader, with more than ...

Bryan focused on maintaining a bland, even smile as he tried to remember the last time he would have been proud of the accomplishments the voice listed. A year ago? Six months ago? He couldn't say when it had happened, but like a sinkhole under a superhighway, it had undercut the surface. And that night, seeing Ritchie in his Ritchie-for-hire costume broke the crust. Bryan gnashed his teeth and held the smile.

… no less a visionary than his famous father, Bryan stepped out of a long shadow at a young age, starting the company that would become Metacom Holdings while he was still in college …

Sure, Bryan thought, through the manipulation and extortion of feckless rich kids.

… tirelessly giving back to organizations like ours, and through the Bethanie & Bryan Lomoigne Foundation …

The spiritual dry cleaners and high-handed photo booths that my wife imagines will save us from sleepless nights and my pitchfork-wielding "customers," Bryan did not say.

… The average person may not know Bryan Lomoigne, but they have most likely been touched by his …

His own bowdlerized life unfurled beneath a shadow like the club's spurious sense of safety—the embrace a dead thing offers anyone willing to be equally dead and to pay.

… business acumen and his vision, his generosity, and his …

The music rose, with his father's lyrics sung by the famous musical guest, slightly off, to seal the majestic dishonesty of the presentation. A spotlight fell on Bryan where he sat. It was time to say a few words.

Farya

Snapping back, and snapping back, like a rubber band. Drink too much, and you compensate by working too hard, so you drink too much coffee. You stay too late and get a headache, and now you need a drink, Farya thought, chastising herself, walking through Midtown in the upper fifties.

It was cold, and she walked fast. She needed more, though, and so reached into her bag for headphones. Maybe not Thelonious

Monk, but maybe Sun Ra, some dissonance to snap her tired thoughts out of their self-tightening garrote. She stopped on the sidewalk to be jostled by an overcoated man behind her, who mumbled an apology without breaking stride. She uttered a loud, clear expletive when she realized she'd left her headphones at her desk.

Left what I needed at the office. What a metaphor. What a cliché—"reality is a cliché from which we escape by metaphor," said someone from college, Farya thought, passing as she did the Rockefeller statue of *Art Deco Atlas* in mid-lunge forever, and St. Patrick's Cathedral. *Who said that? One of the poets, the good ones, one of those types who keeps the sky from crashing down, who banishes the flattening hand with a half-dozen words.*

Farya looked up to check the sky. The lit windows of late workers and office cleaners repeated in a sleepy riot of squares up to the sky. Taxi horns honked in stereo, walk and don't-walk symbols flashed simultaneously, and curbstone followed curbstone along a department-store Christmas display that seemed, from the corner of her distracted eye, to unfurl the story of a ragdoll—popular when she was little, but with an unspeakable secret, who became sarcastic, left home young, flitted between men, drank, and worked lukewarm jobs and grew older alone as the apartment she occupied grew darker, and the globe upon which it had been placed by the window-decorator grew smaller. The words unfurling on a comic-book banner above it seemed to read *Another woman who thought she was something special, folded well away.*

From the sides of her eyes, as she watched the storefront story of the ragdoll, Farya saw the million lit windows, the dark coats, the headphones and haggard faces embrace like a string of paper dolls folding over themselves.

She shook her head and let out a small, choked scream, to find herself outside a tourist-trap shop window offering T-shirts, souvenirs, and electronics of questionable provenance. Looking around, she could tell she was on the wrong block. The street sign didn't match the buildings she remembered there. She knew right away: three blocks of Midtown Manhattan and a subway station had vanished. Farya looked around and grabbed, through rolls of a puffy winter jacket, the breasts of a young woman walking by, just to be safe. The woman, outraged, but not shocked, screamed and shoved Farya hard. It jarred Farya and hurt a little—the woman's scared and hateful glare as she backed away and rejoined the barely rippled stream of pedestrians.

Adrift in the rush-hour current, a faint rumbling came from Farya's coat. She left the mainstream and ducked close to the bright window of a fast-food restaurant. It was a set of texts from Lourdes.

We need to talk
Immediately
Tell me where you are
I'll send a car now

Farya sighed and bent from the rushing lights of the avenue to the tiny white glow of her phone to respond.

✝

Twenty minutes later, the car delivered Farya to Lourdes's lonesome, fortified luxury condo, where the older woman waited outside, looking grim and tired, smoking a cigarette, wearing sweatpants and a sweatshirt under her serpent-patterned robe. Lourdes acknowledged her as she opened the car door with raised eyebrows. Farya felt like a child who was in trouble.

"Hey," Farya said, not sure whether she deserved to be comforted or needed to apologize.

"Pizza should be here in five; let's wait out here."

"I, uh, tonight was just a …"

"It's all right—let's wait until we get inside."

The wind whipped up, blowing around the trash, the last of the leaves, and the first harsh slaps of winter. The pizza arrived. Lourdes paid and handed Farya the two-liter of Coke. They went through the lobby, past an unmanned front desk piled high with paperback books. In the elevator, Lourdes pressed *B2*.

"I thought we were going to your apartment."

"Not tonight. This is a better place to talk."

The elevator left them off at the intersection of three concrete hallways. Lourdes led her down one to a red door, where she fished a thick key from a crowded ring, reached inside and turned on the light, revealing a fresh surprise. Except for the flat floor and the door, the room inside was a sphere, its concave surface covered in busts, masks, and faces. They were mostly caricatures—the Three Stooges, Jimmy Carter, Marilyn Monroe, Salvador Dali, the Marx Brothers, Billie Holiday, Winston Churchill, and so on. All shapes, styles, and colors, they crowded the walls and ceiling.

A yellow lightbulb hung a few feet from the center of the ceiling and illuminated the faces. Lourdes flopped open the top of the pizza box and gestured to two armchairs and a small table in the middle of the room.

"Wow, what is this?" Farya asked.

"It's a place I go to be alone, to talk. We can talk here without distractions, and without my husband buzzing around. Sit, have some pizza. It's not great, so eat it while it's still too hot."

It was too hot. They ate and gasped and washed the molten goo down with soda. Farya was relieved to see Lourdes struggle with the too-hot pizza—it humanized the authoritative, older woman. After the grave welcome and the strange, sepulchral room, it was enough to have them both laughing, choking, and spilling soda. Once the pizza had cooled, Lourdes put her hands in her lap.

"Manhattan's a few blocks shorter tonight. You want to tell me what happened?"

"I don't know. I didn't mean to do anything. I was uneasy. I meant to call you. And then I got this call. And I forgot my headphones. I must have let my attention wander …"

"Okay. Okay. Let's go through the day, starting at lunch."

Farya started earlier, recounting everything since the party—the hangover, the pill, work, the call from the detective, Romeo and Camden, New York, staying late, feeling tired, and forgetting her headphones at work.

"Was that when it started?" Lourdes asked.

"I didn't think so, but I wanted to be safe. I was going to listen to Thelonious Monk, or Sun Ra, or Eric Dolphy."

Lourdes smirked and nodded over Farya's shoulder to a bakelite bust of Thelonious, with his hat, shades, and pointy beard, jammed between the rubber head of Humphrey Bogart, an aluminum bust of Dean Martin, and the wood-carved visages of Beethoven and Margaret Thatcher.

"But no headphones," Lourdes said.

"No. And it started the way these things tend to start, with a coincidence. Two strangers, going in opposite directions, say the same thing into their phones at the exact moment that they pass. Two car horns honk at the same time, for the same duration. It's a little like a trance. The coincidences pile up until only one thing is happening everywhere. Soon that one thing isn't even happening, exactly, it's just always happened. It's hard to explain. But once it's done, it's done, and something is gone. And I know it's gone forever in a way that no one even knows it's gone. But everyone can tell that something's missing and they're mad about it, or sad, and they don't know why. And I know it's my fault."

"Well, first off, it's clearly not in your control now, though you should carry extra headphones."

Farya nodded. "How is it that you can keep track of these things?"

"There was a time when our survival … my survival depended on sensing these things. This one I noticed right off because I have a subway map in my kitchen. There are ways to tell. This room, for instance, used to be much bigger. There used to be more faces, more characters, more celebrities, and elements of our own humanity to celebrate. This room is my personal measuring stick."

"Is that my fault?"

"Yes, mostly. If there was a nice way to say it, I would. But you are a crisis in the history of the world. All I can offer is that you're not the first, or the worst, so far."

"Some consolation."

"You don't get to be consoled. Not you," Lourdes said, her voice hard and her moon-face expressionless. Her unmoving blue eyes pinned Farya where she sat. "You need another kind of help."

"Like what?"

"There are ways to get control of it. You can learn them. But you need to get control of how you feel and what you want."

"Great. But what am I supposed to do? Go join a monastery?"

Lourdes said nothing but looked at Farya until the young woman understood that would be a very responsible, sensible option, given the circumstances.

"Oh, God, really?"

"Farya, if you're not careful, you're going to slip and slip and leave us with, well, not much of a world. And after enough streamlining, or whatever you want to call it, the day will come when reality won't have enough going for it to wake up in the morning, and none of this will have ever occurred."

"That's a lot of pressure," Farya said and took a gulp of soda to see if she still had the capacity to do a normal thing.

"That's not the half of it. These seizures of yours are very powerful, but also very unpredictable. And I think that's why no one has found you."

"Who would have found me?" Farya asked.

"There are people. Some are like me; some of them want to help. Some of them …" The words scared Farya, and Lourdes could see that. But she wanted Farya scared. "But there are people who don't care who you are, as long as you keep making the world disappear."

"Why would anyone want that?"

"There are always opportunists, entrepreneurs," Lourdes said. "Once a universe begins to shrink, the scavengers take note, start stripping it for parts."

"Parts?"

"You don't need to know about that now. But the vultures have been circling here since you were a teenager. But as I said, don't think about that. Fault is a moot point."

"Why is *fault* a moot point?"

"Because guilt is boring, and *boring* is part of how we lose whole towns and cities. Besides, there's not much you can do for what's gone at this point."

"Fine. So, tell me more."

"What about?"

"All the things you know but shouldn't. And tell me how I can keep from destroying the whole world."

The grease on the stray pizza slices congealed to a dull sheen. They stayed up all night, talking. Farya told Lourdes about the incredible Greater Anointed Imperial Ohioan Commonwealth of her childhood—its space program, history of gigantomachies, pyramidlands, and peculiar car-sacrifice rituals. Lourdes told Farya about the terrible depression of a shrinking universe; the boiling down of everything to money, data, and category; the dearth of fresh idiosyncrasy and surprise, and the tiresome end of that endless apocalypse—the tiny worlds like locked houses with no desire and no imagination—just a collector and an appraiser circling a tiny, dim sun from a few feet away.

"It doesn't happen all at once," Lourdes said. "And by the time any universe starts to get snow-globe-small, more people catch on, and start looking for a way out, for some kind of life raft, even if it's just a convincing daydream."

"Does that work?"

"It can, but not well. It's expensive for the daydreamers, and for everyone. And I don't think it would work for someone like you. If this ship goes down, you're on it. Anyway, you have a bigger part to play."

"Bigger than survival?" Farya asked.

"Sorry, but yes."

"How do you know all of this?"

"We were from a place where this happened."

"We, like me?" Farya asked.

"No, *we*. You can lose more than just landmarks and a chunk of your personal history, and still survive," Lourdes said and looked Farya in the eye. "Anyway, for you, it doesn't have to be all bad news and self-abnegation. Some realities do make a comeback—they push outwards, discover, expand, create. You can be part of that."

As dawn rose unseen outside, Lourdes finally began to walk Farya through the first simple exercises in remembering, forgetting, imagining, and unimagining that would help her understand and begin to control what she had—until then—described best as a *seizure*.

✤

When the two of them were alone, talking about forbidden things, Lourdes talked in a thoughtful, funny way—halting without losing rhythm—that reminded Farya of Thelonious Monk.

Feel your feet, your shoes, the ground. The shoes are for your feet, your feet for the ground. Look around at how everything you see is a consequence of something else ricocheting through time. Close your eyes and see the thing that isn't a consequence. See its shape and its details.

The last of that night's exercises ended. Lourdes left her there to sleep in the armchair in that strange basement room. Farya dreamt of a city like New York. It followed the grid plan, and she could recognize familiar buildings, except they were constructed of waterfalls. The city shimmered in the sunlight and reflected the dark, voluptuous clouds as they passed. It was a wonderful place. Her father was there, old as when she last saw him, but calm in his orange Cleveland astronaut's uniform. He said to *look up*.

When she woke, it was past noon. She cursed, jumped from her chair, and checked her phone. She hurried one way, then another in the concrete corridors of the subbasement, long enough to panic in the few seconds it took her to find the elevator. The afternoon daylight was bright and cold. Her phone burst to life with reception, jangling and pinging with new messages. The ones from her boss began polite, and shaded to inquisitive, becoming angrier and more urgent—she'd missed a big meeting with an *important stakeholder*—followed by more messages from the people her boss had called to find her. Farya went through a mental timetable of getting her things, showering (she checked and did indeed need a shower) and getting to work. She realized she had no chance and stopped rushing. She decided to take a long lunch in Lourdes's transitional neighborhood.

The next day, she went light on the makeup and arrived at work early. Her boss made her wait until almost lunch for the lecture. Farya's story—a flash stomach flu and a faulty silent function on her phone—didn't do much for her.

"We all get sick. We all do," he said, leaning into his chair in a bright green vest that made him look like the coolest of the crossing guards. He was wearing sunglasses with pale blue lenses and taking his time. "But one of our core values on this team is that we're a team. We lean on each other, for all sorts of things."

"I know, and I'm sorry. It really was unavoidable."

"Even if what you say happened, it was still avoidable. If you knew you were getting sick, then you should have checked in with someone else on the team, and you should have made sure your phone worked."

Farya nodded. There wasn't much else to do. And though the stern lecture seemed like punishment for not being more receptive to his late-night texts, she didn't protest when he put her on the company's *Performance Improvement Plan*, also known as probation, also known as the paper trail the company required to fire her.

On the long walk to her desk, typically chatty coworkers averted their eyes. It seemed that nothing would ever be normal in Farya's life, no matter how much she wanted it to be. Farya spent the next two hours filling out the *Performance Improvement Plan* acknowledgment forms and worksheets. She stayed late and spent the evening updating her resume, beefing up her last job in Syracuse, the one she never actually held. Her memories of it were becoming quite intricate. That would have been the most disquieting part of the day, but her phone rang.

She saw the number and the caller ID. It was the Oneida County Police—that detective, calling again about Romeo. She placed the vibrating phone on her desk and gently pushed it away from her. When it stopped ringing, she sat back in her chair and closed her eyes. She tried to think of the city full of waterfalls but could only envision the chilly walk to the subway. A voice like her father's broke the disappointing reverie.

For that, he said, *you're going to need more music.*

+

Over the next weeks, Farya was diligent. She practiced the mental exercises Lourdes had given her every day in a huge, quiet Anglican church around the corner from her office.

She repeated the exercises to herself: *Close your eyes and try to remember everything in your field of vision. Now open them. What's the first thing you realize you missed? How did it get there?*

The exercises touched some part of her she hadn't known how to touch. But each week seemed to get a little harder. A malignant empathy settled on Farya, like being engaged in a thousand unwanted conversations at once. But each week she could handle a little more of that irritation too.

At the end of the fourth week of exercises, she met Lourdes for dinner at a busy Midtown bistro. It was her treat, Lourdes the landlordess said. *Business nearby*, she said, dressed up in a golden-cobra hair clip and an ingenious lavender dress that flowed in places and clung in others. She asked how Farya was doing at the acronym where she worked.

"I'm still getting a feel for it, still getting the lay of the land," Farya said in the tone of other conversations in the office. It was the professional way of saying *I'm pretty sure this isn't okay, but I'm not sure who I can admit that to*. Lourdes got it and laughed.

"That good, huh? Are you doing the exercises?"

"Yes."

"All of them?"

"Yes—all of them. Why wouldn't I?"

"You wouldn't because they can be very hard. And it can be a while before they begin to feel any easier."

"As you were quick to notice, I don't look like I've been having an easy time, do I?" Farya hissed. "My boss thinks I'm a drug addict, and he's looking for any chance to fire me."

The waiter came by. Farya ordered a salad. Lourdes said no, they'd each have the steak frites, and a bottle of the red.

"I understand. But you need to eat, to drink, to find some pleasure. Are you seeing anyone? Dating?"

"Not right now. Even before, it was too hard to date. The bars, the waiting for them to text or call, the suspense about whether they'll be as great as they seem or as disappointing as they seem—it makes the other thing too hard."

"The other thing?"

"The thing we're working on—the not destroying the world."

"Okay. But if all you do is the exercises, you'll start to disappear. Not right away, but it will happen."

"Wouldn't that be better for everyone? Like if I went to a monastery?" Farya said, whispering her last word into a hiss as the waiter arrived. As she spoke, she watched Lourdes execute a smile that would seem spontaneous. Farya winced. The exaggerated empathy from her exercises showed Lourdes in a new light—as more than a person. Like Marista, she seemed dense, like more than one person at once. But unlike Marista, that multiplicity seemed to be in concert. Farya had a glimpse of a family—a tribe, a band—persisting through impossible conditions on willpower alone.

"The wine! And not a moment too soon," said Lourdes. Farya took some comfort in seeing her jovial, with a natural smile near her lips. It was a far cry from when they'd met last. "Have a drink, Farya. I know that you don't have it easy, but by now, you should know how no one does. Sure—you have secrets, but you know, so does everyone. I'm not going to tell you to go out and fall in love, or even to get laid. But what's something you like?"

"Music."

"Right, I remember—Thelonious Monk. Go out and buy yourself some new Thelonious Monk albums."

"I have them all. I have everything that's ever been issued, the compilations and foreign albums, in one format or another. I even have the discontinued albums and bootlegs—all the ones I, or anyone on the internet, knows of. I've been collecting them since I was fourteen."

"Even better," Lourdes said, waving her lipstick-stained wine glass. She smiled at Farya and bent her head to take another sip of wine so that one eye of gold-hooded cobra in her hair caught the light in a wink. "Go to a record store and see if there are any albums that you might have missed."

"But I just told you …"

"Call it homework or an exercise … or better yet, a field trip. Just go. You're going to need more music."

✝

Farya left work absentminded and fast in her new shoes. A light drizzle slicked the Midtown side street. The day had been long, unpleasant, and pointless. She'd been unofficially demoted below a girl who started a month after her, who seemed to relish the opportunity to give her chirpy orders phrased as questions. And in the fog of a warm winter's evening, Farya slipped, tried to catch her balance, and then to catch her body with her hand on the sidewalk. Her right leg bent at an odd angle as she landed. The whole fall seemed to take forever. She wanted to cry, but she'd seen a woman crying in the bathroom at work that day—an older woman from another division—and had sworn never to let that be her.

She stayed on the concrete for a minute, until the light moisture began to soak through her jacket and skirt. People rushing past made a space around her. A dozen or so passed before a middle-aged man with dark black hair combed back asked if she needed help. She said no, and he held out his hand. She took it and thanked him, removing all the quiver from her voice to make the thanks a dismissal. He nodded and walked off.

Straightening her coat, she continued across town. A block later, the pedestrian traffic hit a bottleneck at a bright affair that burst with its own unreality into the primordial gloom of the damp street—a red carpet where people posed before a paper wall of corporate logos. The men wore flawless suits that flattered their flawed bodies, and the women wore dresses and jewelry that ranged from costing more than Farya made in a year to more than she'd likely make in her lifetime.

As she passed around the shadowed corner of the paper wall of logos, she bumped into a man, common to the neighborhood, white, middle-aged, and impeccable but for a low paunch. He was going into the event but trying to sneak in without being photographed. He wasn't tall but compact, exact. The cut of his clothes, his hair, and his overall demeanor marked him out as someone who belonged at the event, who belonged anywhere he went—a well-cut suit, active alert face, well fed, well groomed, well bred, as they used to say. He was the kind of man Farya tended not to notice—one with an easy and assured place in the world, sewn into its surface with a graceful stitch. He stopped to say, *excuse me*. As their eyes found one another, he smiled; she recognized a fragility in his expression as if he'd just missed the opportunity to say something important with no chance to try again. His face had a desperate and unfinished quality, in complete contrast to the rest of his appearance. It touched every part of how she felt in that moment, damp and limping after a foul day and a dumb fall. They shared a brief smile that was nonetheless by turns wounded, guilty, pursued, and near hilarity as if acting normal was the most audacious thing a person could attempt—a poker face of eager, utter uncertainty.

All of this happened in about two seconds.

She smiled at him and said, "It's okay."

He said, "Okay," and nodded, started to move on, then stopped for a moment to look at her again.

In her months living in New York, the constant river of new people excited, annoyed, aroused, and bewildered Farya. After so many faces and kinds of faces, almost no one stood out anymore. But this man did, right before he disappeared behind the entrance into a grand event in a grand old building.

Is that it? Farya wondered. Is that what it's like to fall in love with a stranger when that's the last thing you want? She shook her head and kept walking. She had someplace to be, and some thoughts were more trouble than they were worth.

✦

Farya woke to muffled TV voices in unnatural cadences nuzzling into her skull. She didn't have to investigate, but did, and found her roommate Jana on the couch, in her underwear, eating from a big tub of Greek yogurt, and watching two middle-aged viragoes with too much makeup argue about a mirror backsplash.

"It's early. Can you please turn that down?" Farya asked, and winced as she did, remembering too late the incredible delicacy that Jana required at all times.

"It's nine, and I can't hear what they're saying if it's any lower," Jana said, not looking up, her body all odd angles and her tone all flat.

"So, closed-caption it. I'm trying to sleep."

"Oh, you were sleeping. I was wondering what you were doing while I did *your* dishes."

One of the women on TV whisper-yelled the word *tacky*, and Jana turned up the volume with the remote.

Farya had found the apartment through one of Ethan's friends, who had a friend who lived with Jana. That friend moved shortly after Farya had moved in, and Jana had chosen that roommate's replacement, which gave Jana the majority—and just enough power for her to abuse.

There wasn't much Farya could do to improve the situation, nor could she afford to move. Whatever money she might have saved at her new job had gone on clothes to keep pace with the other fashionable women in the office.

Farya hurried through the bathroom and out the door as fast as she could manage. It was a crisp fall day, and she took the train to Manhattan. She needed to spend a few hours not doing Lourdes's exercises, or preparing for the next fight with Jana, or sending out resumes. She got off the train in the East Village. The slanting morning light reflected from gutter puddles of mop water dumped from slowly rousing taverns. The neighborhood was quiet and blank, except for the occasional jogger or shambling dog walker. She let her feet carry her, coffee in one hand and her unneeded coat in the other, west, to a storefront with a dirty maroon awning and a beat-up ATM chained to the frame of its steel roll-down gate. Its window was crowded with records and CDs. Paunchy and unshaven, the middle-aged proprietor clunked open the lock and flipped the *closed* sign to *open,* one might-as-well moment after she stopped to peer inside. The inside of the store was cluttered with mismatched racks of records and CDs going up twenty feet to the ceiling.

Farya took a breath and wandered down the first aisle. Long fluorescent tubes above buzzed through the quiet parts of the symphony on the speakers. The store's stockpile of novelty reminded her of Lourdes's den of faces—like a secret weary arch propping up a better world. She didn't have much money, but she wanted to spend some of it there.

She started with Sun Ra and found a few discs she hadn't heard of before, the cases in cloudy plastic envelopes. She had to press down on the plastic to read the text beneath. She settled on two CDs and enjoyed the feeling of them having in her hand, the future they promised. She'd get a coffee and read the liner notes, build up anticipation, and take them home to listen to—maybe even loud enough to spoil Jana's binge-watching.

"Did you find everything you were looking for?" the old clerk at the register asked. The counter was on a platform, so he could better spot shoplifters, and he stood three feet above her.

"I think so …" she said, halfway down the aisle.

But Farya stopped, seized by the expansive, hopeful spirit of the store, took a breath, and before she could acknowledge what was at stake, turned, stepped sideways in the narrow aisle, and walked her fingers across the tops of a row of CDs. Flipping quickly through the first six, her entire body froze at the sight. In one of the thick, cloudy plastic envelopes was a Thelonious Monk album she'd never seen or even heard of, called *Past Midnight and Back Again*. The cover art was a corny Kandinsky knockoff, with a neon circle and triangle against a speckled backdrop.

She mouthed the title of the album to herself a few times, ransacking her encyclopedic memory of the Thelonious Monk discography. She pressed the plastic envelope close to see what label put it out, what year, when it was recorded, and who else had played on it. It was a well-known jazz label, with major players, recorded at a famous studio in Hackensack. She mouthed the dates and the track list, but they didn't match anything in her memory and didn't quite resemble anything she'd encountered in her dozen years of collecting his music as if her life—and more—depended on it.

In her hands was an album that had never existed, and now did. Farya pulled out her phone and looked it up. Oddly, there it was—issued on CD more than twenty years ago. Either she was misremembering, or something impossible had occurred. Familiar with that choice, she knew which it was.

Stunned, she paid for all three discs and wandered out into a street now filled with so much more possibility, so much more everything.

+

The crowded french-fry-smelling Wednesday-before-Thanksgiving bus lurched and rumbled through traffic for hours, the chemical toilet sloshing beside her too-hot rear seat until Farya couldn't tell it from her own stomach. No amount of traveling, no years working, paying bills, and being independent changed the feeling of being picked up by her parents. Nothing would keep Farya from liking it a little, either. The bus to Rome, New York, was late. Her stepdad was idling in an illegal spot where she would see him.

The ride home was familiar, though Farya's memories had the feeling of a stage set being hastily assembled as the car rolled past the farms and small towns. Nausea mixed with an eerie nostalgia for people, places, and things that she was certain hadn't existed. Her stepdad asked about work and her life in the city. Farya was honest as she could be without giving him reason to worry. The sight of the little house struck her. It was where the false memories of her high school years collided with real, more recent memories of the weeks spent trying to pull herself together, to find a reason and a way to go on living after her seizure in the city of Camden. The difference between the two kinds of memory was one of feeling, more than anything. And the feeling made her shiver.

The whole street was dark. The neighbors were either asleep or away. Farya's mother insisted on feeding her, though it was late. Her stepfather went upstairs to bed. Making a grilled-cheese-and-tomato sandwich in a Teflon pan, Farya's mother asked about her job, her friends, and so on. Farya was more honest about the difficult and deteriorating situation in the office, in her apartment, as well as her general sense of loneliness.

"Well, you never want to say to your children—you want them to go as long as they can without finding out—how hard life can be …"

Farya exhaled. The sight and smell of the browned white bread and melted orange cheese settled her stomach. The sweetness and gravel in her mother's voice stirred up a familiar sadness. The house—they moved into a version of it during her senior year of high school—a townhouse. Her stepfather found a job teaching at a nearby high school when Camden was a big city. She thought of that Camden—her friends, boyfriends, the boozy, smoky final summer before college. But she could feel those fugitive memories of riding the monorail and getting into bars with fake IDs being crowded out. In their place were keg parties in the woods and long drives to far-off malls to buy clothes.

"And maybe it wasn't fair," her mother continued. "Us moving you away from your friends in the middle of high school. But he couldn't stay in Ohio after what happened …"

Farya's memory was so mangled—even her beloved father wasn't safe from that deformity. She recalled him as an astronaut one day, as a career air-traffic controller the next, and slipping down the ladder until he was handling bags in a municipal airport before an old buddy got him a job teaching school. Farya often found it easier to piece together what must have happened, rather than dig and wrestle for what actually did happen. Her father's death was one of the few distinct landmarks. Hearing Thelonious Monk for the first time was another. But now her mother's words brought fresh memories, where her father had been a teacher, and her stepfather a colleague from a high school where they both taught. Her stepfather had stood up for her dad when he was wrongly accused of a crime insinuated more than said. But that was the last indignity, after which her father withdrew. And one night he went out for dinner and, instead of coming home, went to the cemetery.

"… and I know the move made things more difficult for you. Ever since you were a child, I always felt like you had this sense of … disappointment, with us, with the world. And I always wished there was more I could have done to take that feeling away from you."

Farya finished the sandwich, got up, and gave her mother a hug. Farya wanted to give her more but could feel the walls of history harden and hem her in.

"I'm just tired," her mother said.

The next day, Thanksgiving, Farya's brother arrived from New Jersey with his wife and two small children, followed by her uncle, aunt, and cousins from Ohio. The group soon segregated by sex—the women to the kitchen and the men to football in the living room.

Family gatherings were always hard for Farya, as she tried to keep pace with her own rewritten history. Her uncle—once an august ambassador to a breakaway nation on one of the moons of Jupiter when she was young—was now a career heavy-equipment salesman. Her cousins, of whom she recalled at least a dozen when she was in junior high, now numbered only four. Her brother, now grown, was still a dullard and a bully—a living example of how little Farya could control the transformation she wrought.

When her phone vibrated, Farya jumped at the chance to get up from the table. It was her high school friend, Marista. In her last year of high school, Farya had a small group of friends—other girls from the honors program—Sarah, Melissa, and Christa. They stayed in touch through college, and all moved back afterward—young friends pursuing careers and figuring things out in the big city of Camden, New York—right up until that nice fall afternoon when the city of two million collapsed into a town of five thousand.

Farya's friends had collapsed too, from three funny, smart young women to a confused individual named Marista. She hadn't been obliterated from the memory of the world. But Farya couldn't tell if that had been lucky. Since moving to New York, Farya had texted with her, but mostly dodged Marista's calls. As Farya's family pressed in with their own special guilt and shame, she answered.

"Faryaaa!" Marista squealed. "Tell me you're in Camo-Town for Thanksgiving."

"Hey, Marista!" Farya said, trying to match her friend's enthusiasm and failing. "I was just about to call you."

"Well, don't bother, because I'm coming to pick you up. When do you wrap up the family Turkey funeral?"

"About an hour."

"Great! I'll be there in one hour and one minute."

Farya said okay but make it an hour and a half. At the table, she helped clear the plates amid the sundry disingenuous groans that dessert would be simply too much.

An hour and a half exactly later, Marista pulled up in a tan hatchback covered in bumper stickers, blaring dance music.

"Look at you, Miss New York City! You look great," Marista said.

"You too," Farya said, though Marista didn't. She seemed shrunken and fat all at once, like an under-stuffed piece of furniture. Her skin was pale and tan at once, yellow in the dome light of the car. Her hair was green-blonde with black roots. And oily. Her eyes seemed to shift color as she spoke, settling somewhere between tan and green and, though unfocused, were unwilling to look away from her old, dear friend.

"Oh, I missed you, girl. I just moved home a few weeks, uh, months ago. I didn't tell anybody. It was a whole breakdown. I needed a break. But I've been going nuts in this podunk backwater nowhere town."

"Right—things didn't work out in …?" Farya said as the memory congealed like a scar, that Marista had been in Philadelphia.

"Work out? Do you want a cigarette?"

"No, thanks. When'd you start smoking?"

"I don't know, forever, never. What do you want to do? I'm not supposed to drink because of the happy pills they want me on. But how often is my best friend in town? Where should we go?"

Farya thought of her three friends. Christa was the manic one, always pulling all-nighters for school, or for any excuse. Sarah was the disaffected one with the dry sense of humor. Melissa was the indecisive one who was always the hardest to wrangle into a scheme, always questioning. Farya watched the woman next to her for signs of each.

"I'm open. What do you have in mind?" Farya asked.

"Let's go to Amber Cliffs. I need a beer. I bet you do too. I hate the holidays, all the family asking me if I'm feeling better, all these people asking me what I'm going to do next—and I keep getting their names wrong. Probably the pills. They mean well, sure, but what good is that going to do? I mean, how's that going to help what I have going on?"

"What is going on?"

"Unreliability is going on. I can't plan. I don't know what I'm doing, or what I'm going to want to do, or what I'll even be able to tolerate doing from one day to the next. That's what happened with the job, with Chet, with Philadelphia. It's like I put in all this work just to build these guardrails, like, *I'm a lawyer; I like my boyfriend; I have cereal for breakfast.* And even if they aren't true or enjoyable, I had them. Maybe I used to think it would be liberating not to have them. But it's not. It's exhausting, and it's scary."

Marista held the cigarette between her knuckles, her hand smothering her face to take a puff. Amber Cliffs was the closest bar to Camden, perched at a crossroads among farms in the next town. They arrived as one Lynyrd Skynyrd song ended and another one began on the stereo. The bar was big, the darkness broken by the CD-spinning jukebox, deer-hunting video game, and decades of promotional beer neon. It was empty except for a klatch of farmers and whiskey widowers at the far corner, and a tall, middle-aged woman in a miniskirt who was nursing a vodka until the action picked up enough for the men to start buying her drinks.

The bartender was a giant with a goatee and a camouflage hat. Farya recognized him from another time in a forgotten city, when he was stylish, light on his feet for a man his size, and talked of plans to get into acting—*they always need a big henchman type.* But that had never happened now. He nodded to the two young women with his own, very different, recognition. Farya ordered a light beer, and Marista said the same and added a double vodka to her order.

"Living in this nowhere town is like being in quicksand," Marista said. "Get drunk, fool around, whatever. The more you move around, the more you seem to sink."

The night wasn't great. Marista talked in circles and drank hard. Farya meant to stick to two or three beers, but guilt and boredom took over. She saw people from high school and people she'd worked with when Camden was a city. "Farya Navurian, this is not quite your life," she said in the bathroom mirror.

The night rolled on, greased by beer and familiar faces who each confirmed and legitimized a world in which Farya was still surprised to find herself.

"I'm not myself—haven't been in a while. It was like I was someone, and then someone or something said, 'why bother?' and I was like, 'I guess you're right,' and now I can't even remember who either of them was, or if I made a mistake by agreeing," Marista said. She had just thrown up in the women's room sink.

"I'm sorry," Farya said. "I'm really, really sorry."

"Don't be. It was my idea to come to the bar."

"No, I mean I'm sorry about that, about the world not being more than it is, not living up."

"We're all sorry about that."

"No, I mean, I'm trying to make it so it doesn't get any worse. I'm trying to make it so we don't lose more things, so that no more people get told 'why bother,' and go away. I mean, I'm sorry," Farya said.

As Marista nodded, her left eye drifted away from Farya for a moment.

"Do you still like Tommy?" Marista asked. "Do you have any gum?"

✢

Farya woke in her bed with an untrustworthy memory of having woken up in that bed through her high school years. The bed, the dresser, the curtains, and posters all came rushing at her like apostles of a dubious new faith. They came to her with a dim recollection of the hulking, sullen bartender driving her home. A perfect gentleman, he'd waited outside the house until she was inside of its unlocked front door. She remembered that and that there was a problem awaiting her. It was the day she'd promised to meet with the detective. But she had no car and didn't want to get her parents involved.

She found her cell phone in the toe of her boot and called Marista, who answered on the second ring with a sing-songy, *heyyy*.

"Where did you go last night?" Marista asked.

"Go? I'm pretty sure I was there until closing—the bartender had to drive me home." Farya's hangover made the words oblong and slippery.

"How did *that* go?"

"Fine. I mean, I got home," Farya said, her irritation coming to a head. There were too many things to remember for the first time. There were too many disappointing comparisons with the fading image of another world—too much to offer an impossible apology for. Her difficulties in the city comprised a misery she could at least push against. "Hey, remember last night I asked you if I could get a ride somewhere?"

"Yeah, I think. Rome, right?"

"Oneonta. Are you still up for it?"

Marista let loose a long, indulgent groan into the phone, and a still more drawn-out *Okayyy*. It was a half-hour drive. Farya thanked her profusely and went down to the kitchen. Her mother had left a few strips of bacon on a paper towel for her on the counter. She had a bite while her sister-in-law fed her tiny nephew little spoonsful of beige paste.

"When did you get in?"

"Late," Farya said. "What did I miss?"

"I guess Edward and your stepdad went to the hardware store. They're going to fix up the old shed in back. Your mother went to meet a friend's granddaughter."

"Kids everywhere these days."

"You just wait," her sister-in-law said. She arched an eyebrow and resumed wiping paste from her son's chin.

Farya emptied the pot of coffee into a mug and shuffled into the living room to watch TV, letting the blurry and numb waters of the hangover close around her until the occasional creaks of the house, the scree-hush of occasional slow-passing cars, and the cadence of voices came into a regular rhythm. As soon as Farya sensed it, she jolted, throwing her mug half full of cold coffee across the room, where it broke on the wall. Her sister-in-law came rushing in.

"What happened?"

The question was not one Farya could answer to her sister-in-law. Without a lie to tell or anything to offer, Farya started to cry. It came easy, and it came on strong. She cried and cried. Her nephew joined in, then lost interest. Her sister-in-law held Farya while she shuddered and shook with sobs, wise enough not to ask why—wise enough that Farya wondered what she was doing with her brother.

When that passed, Farya went upstairs and showered. She took her time dressing and putting on makeup to avoid her sister-in-law. Soon, Marista was honking outside. The ride felt long, with Black-Friday traffic slowing down the state highways by the shopping centers, and the landscape offering little distraction. Marista alternated between hungover catatonia, manic joking, and occasional hushed apologies about hooking up with Tommy the night before. In the daylight, she seemed less desperate, just ordinary desperate for a smart twenty-five-year-old woman with a few disappointments under her belt.

"So, where are we going again?" Marista asked.

"Rome—downtown."

"I know—but where? Why are you being so cagey all of a sudden?"

"It's the police station—the sheriff. It's no big deal. They just want some information, and I said I'd come in to talk to them."

"Sorry, but that's still cagey as fuck. What did you get into now?"

Farya took a deep breath. She was too tired to bullshit her three best friends.

"It was this guy I was dating. He disappeared."

"Dating in Syracuse? Who was the unlucky guy?"

"His name was Romeo ... is Romeo ... Romeo is his name."

"Oh, I know Romeo. Romeo from work, the insurance, with the, uh ..." Marista said, trailing off as she realized that she didn't remember Romeo or recognize the world she remembered him from. "Oh, no, never mind. I was thinking of someone else. I don't think you told me about him."

"I don't think I ever did. It was never that serious."

The county sheriff was housed in the ground floor of a three-story brick building in the middle of Main Street—done up in a style befitting a time and place when the phrase *Empire State* was spoken without irony or detachment. Marista said she was going to drive around, maybe see if there were any cool consignment shops—she needed shoes—and to call her when she was done.

Farya waited ten minutes on a hard bench like a church pew among young men turning themselves in and mothers picking up their grown sons, before the uniformed old man called her name and buzzed her through the scratched plexiglass door.

Beyond it, the smell of ammonia intensified. Blinking the odor from her eyes, she saw Ronnie—tan, tall, and lean with a long face, pitted chin, and sleepy eyes, like a sad baby you couldn't disappoint because he was already disappointed. He gave a perfunctory smile and said, "This way," and turned on his heel, his big red tie swaying as he did.

He showed her to a big-shouldered municipal conference room with a heavy wood table in the middle, flanked by just two chairs. Farya checked the table for metal rings where someone might be handcuffed and found none. She circled the room and looked out the windows at a vast parking lot of police cars, snowplows, and other vehicles. The circle on the wall where a clock had been showed that the beige room had once been lime green. Farya sat down. After a few minutes, Ronnie returned and took the seat opposite. He opened a thin, dark-green folder with a few sheets of paper in it.

"Thanks for agreeing to come in. I don't want to take up too much of your time. This is a strange case, and maybe you could help by telling me what you know about Romeo Mauriello."

"I met Romeo while I was working at Grammaton Media, on Maidstone Boulevard, in Camden," Farya said, naming a company and a street that she knew all too well no longer existed. "We were hired by Neiermarr Insurance to promote a new renter's insurance that … Well, that's not the point. Romeo was on the team at the company in charge of the campaign. And we got to know each other, and he asked me out. We dated for a few months, not too serious, not exclusive or anything."

"And how did it end?"

"It just kind of petered out, I guess," she said, "then I moved."

"Did you have a fight?"

"Nothing like that."

"Tell me about the last time you saw him."

Farya told the story of the afternoon at the sports bar, leaving out everything except the games, the shouting, the plastic towers of yellow beer, and a generally good time.

"That was when?"

She took a long moment to compare the two calendars and two timelines in her head, did the math, and came up with what must have been a date.

"And what is the name of the bar?"

"Goalposts," Farya gave the name, the real name, of which she knew the detective would not find a trace. She had gone so long without ever being directly questioned that she didn't have a plan. So, she decided, based on her hangover and an approximate understanding of the law, that if she was going to be crazy, maybe at least she didn't have to be alone.

"I need you to think a little more about that day because you may have been the last person to see Romeo alive."

"There's no one else, no one whose name I know. They were his friends. He just invited me along. And I'm not great with names."

Ronnie reached for the knot on his red tie and decided against loosening it.

"I wish you were. I can't find his friends, or his coworkers, or Neiermarr Insurance. Aside from Romeo's mother, and now you, I can't find anyone who remembers the guy. There's no social security number, no school or tax records. I was ready to write the whole thing off as senile dementia until now. So, that's two people who remember Romeo Mauriello. Now it bugs me, and I want to know what's going on. And I need everything you can think of just to keep looking."

"You say you want to know what's going on. But do you, really?" Farya said, feeling excited and afraid. She'd never done this before. But she knew she had to do something different. And she liked the detective, who seemed curious and awake in the way not everyone is.

"Yes. It's my job," Ronnie affirmed, his eyes meeting hers. "To not look the other way, to not let things slip by."

"Okay. You won't find Romeo, not another trace. You won't find the place I worked or the place he worked. You won't find the street where my job was, and you won't find the sports bar I told you about …" Farya said, and went on to tell Ronnie about what had happened to Romeo and to Camden: Every distinction undone; every light blended to white; every pigment blended to mud; every impatience indulged to a nonexistence unlike death and unlike being unborn. She didn't say *whose* impatience was indulged, however.

Ronnie lived by an older detective's instruction to "let the silence do the work," and didn't interrupt no matter how much she insulted his sense of reality with her story. He let her talk, and talk, interjecting to pick at the small inconsistencies inside a much larger, much more impossible tale. By the end of it, Farya felt better, like the hangover and a larger, years-old guilt had loosened their grip. Across the glossy dark surface of the municipal table, Ronnie stared at her, then above her.

"That's one hell of a story," Ronnie said.

"I'm sorry. You said you wanted the truth. I'm sorry."

She wanted to cry but had cried too much already that day. He started to speak, started to adjust his tie, started to look through the few papers he'd brought into the room. Farya's phone rang.

"Shopping? On Black Friday? What the hell was I thinking? Are you done, or are they going to throw away the key?" Marista said. The room was so quiet that every word from the cell phone seemed to crackle across the space.

"Can I go?" Farya asked. Ronnie nodded and amended his nod with a "for now," before angling his face down to the blurry picture of Romeo in his folder. It seemed as if it had become even blurrier.

✝

On the return to Camden, Marista was in good spirits. After a small scuffle, she had found some shoes on sale. She talked about Tommy, with whom she'd gone home the night before, talked about the future—maybe moving in January, maybe Syracuse, maybe Corning. People get used to anything, even being other people, Farya thought.

Back home, her stepfather and brother were in the living room watching TV.

"There she is," her brother said, not looking up from his tablet. "I was wondering if we'd get to see you at all, sis."

"Sorry—I had to help Marista with something."

"Which one is Marista again?" he asked.

"From high school—we were in all the AP classes together."

"Was she the crazy one or the bitchy one?"

"I thought you two were working on the shed," Farya said.

"We started. We got the tools. We'll get on it first thing tomorrow," said her stepfather.

Farya sat down, and the conversation gave way to the tale told by the television crime show—a dead woman found in the server room of a tech company. The cops were using computers to find the killer, tracking cell phones, comparing logins, and so on. They had the killer dead to rights pretty quickly. That, it seemed, was the point of the show.

"I love it. A multi-billion-dollar rocket program, a satellite that costs a hundred million dollars, all that engineering and ingenuity to catch some schnook who kills his mistress," her stepdad said. "Pathetic."

"So, what do you want? People are supposed to be able to get away with murder?" Farya said.

"I'm not saying that. It's about priorities. It used to be we went to space to explore, to discover, to plant flags, to understand and enlarge the world we live in. Now, it's all about peeping-tom-ism, about beating us down with seven hundred channels of crap, about recycling the opinions of the loud and the stupid a million times over—all to make the world smaller."

"Maybe it's actually about making the world safer and giving people more options," said her brother.

"Maybe. If that's what your generation thinks, I guess that's what'll be right," her stepfather said and watched the show.

The sun set early, and they all sat down together as a family for reheated leftovers. Everyone except Farya was in bed by eleven. She kept the television on low, letting the images drift past. It was a few minutes past midnight when her cell phone broke its reverie. She didn't recognize the number, but the voice she did. It was Ronnie, and he sounded drunk.

"Our talk today. I've been thinking about it," he said by way of hello. "And I have to ask, were you fucking with—messing with—me?"

"No. I was serious. Why would I make that up?"

"People do. People get bored. They need some recognition, some attention, so they make things up to the police."

"Listen, I didn't come to you. I don't go around telling people. I was tired. And you seemed like you really did want to know."

"I guess so. But it's messed up. If I sit down and focus, I can remember some things, like the tri-towers—did you tell me about them?"

"No," Farya said.

"But I remember them, with the walkways at ninety stories up, and the elevator banks on the fiftieth floor. Was that a thing?"

"Not anymore."

"Huh. So … what am I supposed to do with that?"

"I don't know. Let it go, I think. The only thing that kind of memories do is mess me up. They go away on their own if you ignore them. I think that's what most people do. And it's like the memories kind of want to go away. You have to make an effort to keep them."

"How do you …" Ronnie started, "I mean, how do you live with knowing what you do?"

"I'll let you know when I figure it out. It takes a lot of energy. And it takes away from everything else in my life. And it makes me sad. But I have no choice. I'm sorry. I can't help you."

"Do you want to get a drink?" Ronnie asked. "Never mind. I'm sorry I asked. That's not right. I'm supposed to see Romeo's mother, and I have to figure out what to say. What do I say?"

"I'm not sure. I was honest and look how much good it did you."

"Good night, Farya."

"Good night, Detective."

"Good luck."

"Good luck to you."

Lourdes

How did she get here? Lourdes would ask, always third-person. Thinking was an interrogation and an argument. *So, how?* Something carried her past the gap in imagination and the hard reverse-peristalsis of fear. A force like falling in love pulled whatever was left of her to this place.

She thought of being a child in school. *Had she ever been that child or any other child?* She knew the answer, but it was complicated, almost too exhausting to know. She hadn't been the child Lourdes, the child that she should have been. She had been many children in many childhoods, homes, hometowns—now all gone. But they were gone. She could say without bitterness that the past needn't matter. The past that did matter was a common thing, a false currency—reach, and it seemed to leap to hand. Maybe that common is repulsive, terrifying even. *But was the place she left that much better?*

Now, she was here—a member of the unworthy wealthy in a world that's the alien cousin of her home. *How did she get here?* They went straight—through the eye of the crashing wave. The road rose; the world warped to meet them. The way was soggy—an interstate highway on a foggy night with untrustworthy signs. The first danger was forgetfulness. In the shifting light of miracles and mysteries, going straight wasn't so simple. So, they set a beacon—thick, black smoke in the daytime, phosphorus-bright at night.

As important as remembering is, forgetting becomes just as important. They thought they were going somewhere, and they weren't exactly wrong. But really, they were becoming something else. The original members vanished, and new ones appeared, determined, familiar, but strange as the landscape itself. But if they'd known when they left, they never would have agreed to it. And if they'd never left, they'd be utterly gone, like their home.

Lourdes started out as a group of people. Her final name may have had significance, but she forgot it along the way.

The world they came from was enormous, ancient, well articulated in every way. They had learned its breadth and its age in school. Most of them weren't rich but had traveled to vacation to the moons, maybe the other systems. They'd been entertained, enjoined, and inducted in the fifty-thousand-year pageant. But unlike their peers, it exhausted them with a staggering sensation of debt. In the outmoded towns far from the empire's center, they worked too hard or sneered through a cloud of received misinformation and clattering trinkets.

Something was very wrong with the world, the common mercies withdrawn, the pressure on the free-and-easy repetition of a predictable landscape, all the bad people getting too good at doing the bad things, all the foregone conclusions concluding too quickly. Every conversation a dirty fish tank of doomed pets eating and breathing their own waste, every sin remembered, every desire an accusation, every joy a trap, every man and woman standing in a deep ditch of depression waving over the rim for someone to bury them, everything built, every show put on, lazy slipshod short-term derivative, everyone saying there's too much to do and no time or desire to do it.

For others, though, it was a simple sense of loss that they couldn't reliably articulate. One of the things that was wrong was that nobody could agree on what was wrong. Nobody knew what to do. So, they sent out signals—each of them—little barbs tucked into conversation, little jokes. They found each other when one laughed a bit too loud at the right joke. Each brought the same puzzle. Each brought a piece. That was the first thing to do, it turns out: find each other. It worked. Dreams attract dreams.

How many of them were there at first? Four at first, then a dozen. By the end, too many—maybe three hundred. They started from a small city, a neglected corner of a vast empire, a pocket that had resisted the incredible pull of its glittering centers, if only by its dullness and undesirability.

They left together, in one large group. Sometimes they walked, other times they drove, in a bus or a small train of cars. It was a long, withering journey from a doomed home to a compromised haven. They learned terrible things. They learned how not-special, not-unique each one was. They learned how swollen each of them was with the redundant fervor of creation. They learned by vanishing, by having never been except as faint memories—the shadows of whispers. Following the smoke and the flame under a flattening sky, they lost people, they lost characters, even entire ways that a person could be. But they learned how to remember, even when remembering was difficult and costly. And that pain taught what was essential, what was necessary and unique enough to keep. They kept what they could of those people in a series of exercises, in sequences of enforced gestures, in a book. That's how they survived long enough to become what Lourdes became.

By the end, they were alone—she was alone—waiting on the battered shoulder of a state highway in a low-lying and undistinguished precinct of New Jersey for a discount, local bus to Port Authority. Where she winds up, she doesn't belong. But everyone feels that way; it's that kind of world. She came for reasons that seemed higher and mightier than anything on offer here. But she arrived the same way as everyone in the real estate seminar—one grubby compromise at a time. She didn't respect this place. She thought she could duck a punch. She took a shortcut and forgot why.

Two sides to every transaction, the man in an ill-fitting suit with no tie says on the seminar stage. She listens. She has to learn to survive, and she's no good at waiting tables. But she knows more than most. She knows there's more than a buyer, a seller. There's the thing being bought and sold, which is never neutral. And there's the shadow—the thing no one is willing to see.

That shadow is how Lourdes made her fortune, found her safety. People bought buildings for bad reasons, overlooked things for worse reasons, and then needed a way out. They don't respect the place they're in; they think they can duck a punch—they take a shortcut and forget why. It's easy to get lost. Lourdes, all the people she was, knew what lost looked like, sounded like, and what people did first when they lost the thread. She saw them looking for someone to confess to. And she knew the value of discarded things. It was her shadow.

New York was a rare place where nothing was ever discarded for too long. She never needed to apply pressure to a seller; the pressure was always there. So, she worked and piled a life against the thing that had chased them—her—there.

Sometimes, though, one eerie and useless memory peeped through the tiny thing that Lourdes had become: the ever-sunward jungle-side of a holiday moon, an inverted buffet with a million hungry critters, skitters, suckers, fire-fuming plants, and crawly menaces. It was terrifying, but also the most beautiful thing she ever saw. As a tourist, she'd stayed within the plasma-tunneled walkway through the foliage, the straw of a cold drink beside her slack mouth. It was so stunning, so gorgeous, she lost track of herself. Like everything, toward the end, it changed. There were so many suicides in those last years that the place was hard to appreciate past all the warning signs and waivers to sign.

Now, it was just another place that had never been, Lourdes supposed, preparing for her performance. She'd been rehearsing all week, even though it was just for a party full of friends. And what she was about to do was art, personal expression—so she could say what she wanted, the way she wanted. She bought the drinks, so she could call the tune. It's no risk, she assured herself; no one bothers with *art* unless they're challenged directly, by name, and maybe not even then.

The point is that she got here. She adjusted. She didn't look back. She found a way to survive, to succeed. But one day it started—a city went missing, a place she remembered from a map, a weekend away, a minor sitcom. *Maybe your memory is going ...* arguing with herself is one habit from the long journey. But she knows it's not her memory. *The thing that did away with her home and her friends—did it follow her? Or was it everywhere, and she was the only one who could see it?*

She doesn't know what to do. So, she sends out signals—references tucked into conversation, little jokes, or more baldly in a performance. It may take a long time, but it worked before. They'll bring the same puzzle and bring a piece. The ones she does find are pieces, and often in pieces. The girl who said her brain was broken by Bud Ice, and that her nose was bitten off by a flying lizard on one of Jupiter's moons. The old man with the eyepatch who'd gotten his anthropology doctorate among the electricity people of the Lower Yakotakan Plains. The vapid-but-healthy-lad in the Day-Glo *BUCKETS O' DICKS* sweatshirt who recognized the diadem patterns of The Greater Anointed Imperial Ohioan Commonwealth on a cape Lourdes wore to a party.

That last fella didn't seem like too much at first. He was cagey, but only because he knew more than most. He was like someone who'd been struck by lightning again and again.

Lourdes had run from lightning. She'd run enough. So, she got to know that cavalier and wounded young man who followed the free booze from party to party. One night, he told Lourdes the name of the lightning—*Farya*. Lourdes said she'd like to meet her.

And one night, there she is—the lightning, the devourer of friends, the obliterator of countless lives and hopes. She's unsure of herself, not the monster Lourdes expected. A pretty office-girl, Farya seems so afraid and amateur in her ability to conceal and protect herself. All Lourdes can do is hide her terror and offer her friendship.

Bryan

Say a few words was Bryan's role at the one-day offsite at a blue glass box in a DC suburb. The audience was the two dozen managers of the Metacom Repurchase Group. Unlike so much of his company, Bryan knew them each by name. To a man or woman, they had been with the company since its earliest days, when they sold people back their souls based on a poker player's sense of who the customers were, what they owned, and how scared they were. Over the years, they did very well, at least the ones who stayed on.

It was a delicate job. If Metacom's tens of millions of customers knew that they'd sold their souls (or Subscriber Non-Mortal Element Rights) for a cheaper cell phone, the company wouldn't last out the year. But some customers did read the Terms of Service in the End User Agreement they'd signed and were bright enough to twig what they agreed to. And while they were dangerous, they were important to the company. They helped the company find the places where the language of Metacom's Terms of Use was too transparent. And they paid. While Metacom sold the bulk of the Non-Mortal Element Rights to Petra's private-equity firm, it sold the remainder back to the angry, horrified customers who called the company in a panic.

And *he had to say a few words.*

Bryan was a great wit when he was younger. But age and success had atrophied his sense of humor. His experiences were far from universal, and he had far more to lose than to gain in almost any conversation. So, his words to the managers were few. *Congratulations—Great Accomplishments—Bright Future—Work Harder—Here's the Entertainment.*

The repurchase process had become mostly automated, with reps pricing the frightened customers' souls based on zip code, credit rating, and some information the company wouldn't otherwise have access to, but for the vast reach of the *Terms of Service* to which Metacom subscribers agreed.

Automated, efficient, and still-growing—the business had come a long way from his first storefront in a college town. It had come even farther from its real start as a teenage dare at boarding school.

A smallish smart aleck, Bryan was always starting arguments with his smug peers. One night in the dorms, he found himself arguing with some generations-rich sixteen-year-old atheist about the nature of reality. To test the boy, Bryan offered to buy his soul for fifty dollars. And the lad with blonde stubble on his cheeks agreed, signing the bottom of a notebook-page contract.

The day after Thanksgiving break, the boy was waiting outside Bryan's dorm room, demanding that Bryan hand over the contract, threatening lawsuits and all the thunder his board-sitting father could call down. But Bryan simply shook his head. Finally, the boy's family coughed up ten times what Bryan had paid, just to have Bryan write VOID in ballpoint pen across the sheet of notebook paper.

Bryan was not an athlete, a great student, or the scion of some august banking or government family. So he relished those rare chances to win in that place. Word got around, and the deal didn't make Bryan any friends, but it won him some respect.

The school, though named for a saint, was rife with junior atheists desperate to remove one of the many yokes from their well-scrubbed necks. And for the adventurous boys there, it was one of the few non-sexual, non-violent exchanges in that school that could inspire fear. They came to see the sell-your-soul dare as a test of another kind of mettle. Bryan stayed open for business and bought a lot of souls.

Decades later, he had a small auditorium of people to handle the often-hysterical customers calling to buy their souls back. He said a few words and introduced the entertainment—a once-great athlete who spoke of persistence, drive, winning, and the power of personal branding. The athlete called it a system and had an acronym for it. But Bryan left before it started.

+

From the highway, the Maryland sky was yellow with storm clouds chasing an early sunset. The lawns were tarnished gold and the trees bare in anticipation of winter. It was nice to be out, away from the Metacom phone farms and tending to an obsession that no one but his wealth manager and personal attorney knew about.

His half-sister, Leighton, had just returned from a few months in Italy. She was the second child of the first woman Jimny had married after he'd left Bryan's mother. She was a few months younger than Bryan, and one of his only half-siblings he knew well. Whether it was Jimny or the type of woman he tended to marry, the families he left behind didn't mingle much.

Past horse farms, Bryan arrived at a small brick gatehouse, where the armed guard asked for his driver's license. After a minute, he returned and gave Bryan directions to the main house. Passing a small pond and coming up over a low rise, he could see the mansion, tall and sudden on a small hill, done in pristine black brick, with perfect rows of apple trees to one side and a fenced-in meadow on the other.

The housekeeper, in a dress that matched the color and cut of the house, showed him into a modern living room with three-story windows overlooking a covered pool, sprawling brown lawn, gazebo, and the dark scrub forest beyond. She offered to take Bryan's coat, but he shook his head and laid it across an armchair. He knew what he wanted, but not what to expect.

Leighton waited on a dark leather sofa. It had been a few years, but Leighton was much as he remembered—thin and pale, a little dark under her eyes, and a long, almost-wolfish, pretty face. At first blush, she always seemed drowsy, disinterested. But Bryan knew better. She rose and hugged him hello. It was a warmer, more supple embrace than he had reason to expect, and stronger than she looked capable of. Since he'd seen her last, he heard she'd had a child, but the child was nowhere to be seen or heard.

Leighton slumped on the couch, legs akimbo, the fringed circle of light from a table lamp casting soft shadows on her features—the lazy eyes and small nose. Bryan sat in an armchair close but catty-corner safe from the couch. The pleasantries departed with the maid.

"So, what's this about?" she asked.

"It's about Dad," Bryan said, trying to limit the conversation.

"Really? Five years in the grave and more than two years out of probate."

"It's not the will. It's his music. I want to buy your share of the catalog—the solo stuff, and what you own of Jimny Lomoigne & the Casual Bleeders."

"Oh, that was you. The family office mentioned it, but I forgot. You weren't offering very much money, if I recall."

"The price is fair, considering what music rights are going for these days."

"Hmm. If it's so little money, it might be worth holding onto just as a memento."

"The price is negotiable," Bryan said. The first few fat snowflakes started to fall through the pink light beyond the enormous windows. "Storm's coming in. You want a drink?"

"Are you trying to seduce me?" Leighton asked like she said everything—dry—so he never knew if she was joking. No part of her face seemed to move unless the rest of it had come to a consensus.

"Oh, is that how you remember it?"

"The unspeakable Independence Day."

Rising from the couch, Leighton opened a panel in the wall and poured a pair of drinks.

"That terrible, awkward speech from Jimny and your mother."

"Like they were trying to say we were brother and sister, but they didn't want to admit even that. They had to keep talking around it."

"'You should think of each other in *a certain way,*'" Bryan said, in the Boston-Brahmin accent of Leighton's mother. "It was like they wanted to yell at us but didn't want to admit any portion of what was going on."

"Didn't want to admit that she got pregnant with me while your mother was going through morning sickness with you. Pretty twisted all around," Leighton said, smiling like she did that Fourth of July when they were fourteen. "A lot of hormones and double talk."

"Can't ask for a better education. To hormones and double talk."

"And to bringing shame to the shameless."

They toasted.

"The Secretary's in New York," she said after a sip. The Secretary was the honorific by which her husband was referred to in Congress and on TV. "He knows about it, about us, about that summer. I think he likes it when I tell him about things like that—me illegally young, wet with saltwater, and randy enough to blow up my family," she said and watched Bryan for a response he was too smart to give. "But you're not here for the unspeakable, are you? You want to buy the rest of our dubious daddy's devalued legacy. We had it appraised the other day, and it's worth a lot less than when we sorted out the will."

"I wanted to ask you—how did you end up with so much of it?"

"When Jimny died, I didn't need the cash in a hurry. They did."

"I guess we both did well."

"You did well. I married well," she said, drinking.

"We've both seen how the world works; I say we both did well," Bryan said, smiling.

"Oh, boy, here comes the Lomoigne charm. You must really want these songs. Would you pay what it was appraised at five years ago?"

"I might if I could get the deal done tonight."

"Still such a *boy*, so impatient."

"Is that how you remember it?"

Leighton smiled. She didn't do it much. And it moved a part of Bryan that didn't move often. So, he let her smile and didn't look away just because it was wrong.

"So, what—did you bring one of your notebook-paper contracts?" she asked.

"You heard about that too?"

"Of course, they almost threw you out of school. Dad was on the phone for like a month with the dean."

"Really? He never talked to me about it," Bryan said, and tried to imagine his footloose-and-fancy-free father arguing discipline with a prep school administrator. It almost brought a tear to his eye. The emotion fed the horrible vision of Jimny chained to a jukebox—metal spout in his mouth and terror in his eyes.

"I remember it was a big deal at the time. I think you scared him," she said.

Bryan asked what the catalog was worth five years ago. Leighton said a number. It seemed high, but she was quick with it. He asked if she'd take that, and she nodded.

"Music royalties are a sucker's game. But you know that. You're a businessman. So, are you getting nostalgic? Are you trying to rescue the dead?" Leighton asked. "Is that what all that money's for?"

"I was hoping you could tell me," Bryan said.

Leighton gave a small, sad smile and raised her glass. Bryan reached over, and they toasted. After a long, quiet sip, he reached across the empty space, for his coat, to retrieve the papers he'd brought.

✦

Carpet glue, spackle, and paint, with a trace of drywall dust—the smell of new offices aroused memories of virgin illusions and high hopes for Bryan.

He was visiting the new home of Metacom's Repurchase Group to listen in on some of the new recruits. They were quick thinking and well-trained young people, well paid by most standards, who took the calls of the few outraged customers who had correctly interpreted the sinister implications of their mobile-phone contract's *Terms of Service*, and now wanted their souls back. As the calls came in to the repurchase agents, their monitors populated with data about the caller.

"Here, watch Rodney," one of the old-line managers suggested. Bryan and the portly man with fingers full of rings leaned over the gray three-quarters partition of Rodney's cube. The kid was young, strong looking; they hired a lot of former college athletes. The young man had the wherewithal not to look up at his bosses while he worked.

"Returns and Repurchase, this is Rodney, how may I help you to … I understand, and I'd be happy to process that if that's what you want … May I ask why you want to cancel your contract … Okay, one second … I do have to inform you that there is a cancellation fee … Yes, I understand … But I'm required to tell you that, if you read through the End User Agreement, you'll see that portion of the contract is binding and non-negotiable after ninety days … Yes, that means even if you opt out of the contract,

Kinnections Global and its affiliates retain those rights ... Yes, it is completely legal ... I understand, sir ... I'm afraid I'm not authorized to do that ... No, I'm not allowed to give out our address, sir ... Could you ... Sir, if you lower your voice ... If you just ... Sir, I'm about to hang up ... Sir ... We offer a release of those rights through our repurchase ... Our repurchase program, sir, allows you to do just that—repurchase the rights that you granted to Kinnections Global ... That's right ... Let me call it up now ... The repurchase program involves a series of fees ... The processing fee that I'm about to quote you includes all of the legal fees, filing costs, and bookkeeping expenses associated with locating your contract and amending it ... Do you have a pen? Great ... Altogether, it comes to forty-six thousand three-hundred twenty-five dollars and seventy-six cents ... Sir ... Sir ... I can get my manager, but he'll tell you the same thing ... I'm just reading what's on the screen ... You're under no obligation to repurchase anything, or to take any action ... Yes, they include the rights to your personal Non-Mortal Element ... Sir, I only know the terms that are in the contract ... I'm sorry, but I am a customer-service team member, not a priest ... That's the price that the screen is giving me, but I can check again ..."

Rodney clicked a button on his headset to mute his phone and stood up to introduce himself while the customer vented. With a firm, practiced handshake, the young man told Bryan how great it was to meet him, and how much he admired him, smiling with perfect teeth, then nodded and went back to his call.

"Sir, I just ran it through as you asked ... and like I thought, the fee is the same ... Yes, I know ... But we're a very big company, and once you get the lawyers and the accountants and the notaries involved for just one contract … That's not for me to say—does it *seem* important to you? Like I said, sir, I just answer phones … I think I had another customer with a similar problem a few months ago; just let me check our records … Oh, wow, he paid much more than you … I'm afraid I can't say how much—that's personal information … But we arranged a plan with him that came to less than five hundred dollars a month … I'd have to check; every plan is different, and we try to make it as flexible as possible for our customers … Yes, I understand … We take our customers' concerns very seriously … Okay, well, let me ask, how much could you afford per month … I don't know, sir, but you seem very upset to me … How much would you be willing to pay each month for peace of mind?"

The manager led Bryan away to see the new conference room with a massive slate-top table. Bryan's protégé Cassie was in there. They exchanged nods, each warm in the dull joy of being good at their jobs. Cassie stood before a ream-thick budget and returned to raking an executive over the coals one page at a time. She seemed thinner than when he'd seen her last, her cheekbones sharp.

"It's $28, who cares?" the executive said. He was no stranger to Bryan, a longtime Metacom executive, thin with a deep tan, a nice suit, and gray hair.

"The guy who took your $28, that's who cares," Cassie said. "He's laughing at what a slob you are and spending that $28."

The executive looked at Bryan for help, but he just shrugged and gave Cassie a crisp nod before stepping out of the doorway.

Cassie was doing the job he gave her—cutting costs. After their heart-to-heart about Metacom's real business, he asked her to look into how the business might operate as what it was supposed to be—a midsize telecom provider that leased the bulk of its network. Her answer was grim, and it came down to cost-cutting and waiting to be bought. So, he told her to go out and see what she could cut. From the complaints he received, Cassie seemed to enjoy the job. Maybe she had grown brusque, a little cold, but those were executive traits. And that's what Bryan was training her to be.

The manager took him for one more loop around the big open floor of Rodneys. The floor had an energy and a rhythm as the reps raised their voices to be heard and hushed to soothe the troubled customers who were doing their best to bully, finagle, haggle, and finally pay a pretty penny for their souls. It was the sound of money pouring in.

Bryan stood at the edge of the cubicle field. He liked the guys in the phone pits—the Rodneys. They made good money and had few illusions. More than that, they shared his burden. Sometimes they felt more like his own offspring than his natural children.

+

Bill Van Harappan was the chairman and CEO of the largest phone, internet, cable, and wireless provider in the country—a sphinx-like figure brooding American business. And Bryan was about to meet him for the first time.

A few weeks before, a little drunk, feeling lost in his office, Bryan had reached out to the man. Van Harappan suggested they meet in person, at a conference in Scottsdale. The lawyers got involved compiling the twenty-five pages of heavily negotiated language required for the two men to speak freely.

The desert morning was cold. Bryan wandered into the resort, the lobby waterfalls, restaurants, bars, and verandas opening onto vast golf-course vistas like a bland heaven. Now years past wondering what things cost, Bryan could spot *the most expensive place*—and this was that. The conference was down the street.

He took a newspaper from the neat stack by the front desk and went for breakfast on a pleasant patio overlooking the greens and the distant dusty mountains. The omelet was perfect, and the news was a mass shooting at a swap meet in a roller rink in Michigan. He recognized the name of the town—Metacom had a few storefronts there. The rest of the paper was schools were failing, whole states going broke, foreign terrorists on social media, and the side effects of last year's big pill being worse than thought.

Caterers with secret service earpieces darted in and out of doors. A security guard in a souped-up golf cart cruised through the morning chill with a plate of crudités on the seat beside him. Bryan checked his phone, signed the bill, and had the concierge show him to the elevator that would take him down below the glittering banquet rooms where the wealthiest brides of Phoenix presided over football fields of black ties, jealous bridesmaids, and filet mignon. It took him to a floor for which there was no button.

The Sapphire Level had the atmosphere of a top-end fallout shelter. From the edges of the cork ceiling, a light like daylight glowed. The crisp recirculating air gave a feeling like being in Scotland or being in an airplane. The conference room itself was long and narrow, with a pale wood conference table running most of its length and a video screen taking up a whole wall. It was all clean and modern except for the ornate antique ceiling bolted to the high concrete vault. The wood was painted bright red and white and carved with shapes like faces, but not quite; geometric but not quite. It seemed medieval, or maybe Chinese. Bryan kept looking at it to make sense of it and had to force himself to look away.

If every room is its own social contract, this one said: You can have anything you want, but you may not take any of what you see and hear outside. As Bryan began to curse himself for being early, he spotted Van Harappan in an armchair in a small conversation area at the end of the room. He looked like his pictures, flop of brown hair, sharp eyes, impeccable suit, tombstone chin, and beak nose, but much taller; maybe close to six foot five.

"Bill? Van ... Harappan?" Bryan said.

"You must be Bryan," the older man said. He looked at Bryan and gestured to a freestanding appliance in the dark corner of the room. He had the hands of a basketball player. "Shall we?"

Bryan recognized the appliance from his own boardroom—a locker with two-dozen cubby holes for the mobile phones of the attendees of sensitive meetings. He locked his away. Van Harappan did the same. Each had hard-won reasons for being wary of the phones they sold.

They sat in silence, each waiting for the other man to show his hand, before Van Harappan smiled, the deep dimples in his lined face effortless yet menacing.

"You're Bryan Lomoigne, son of the singer. But you built something of your own, Metacom, and you have about twenty brands, two thousand locations, and close to twenty million customers paying. You're growing, but you're a cut-rate player taking your chances on marginal subscribers and leased network bandwidth. So, I already had a few ideas about why you might want to meet. At first, we thought that you wanted to sell. But we started to set up the meeting, and your NDA is even worse than ours."

"Can't be too careful," Bryan said.

"No, *I* can't be too careful. *You* have too many lawyers, and they're too good for a storefront operation. So, we had some poor soul sign up for your service and bring our lawyers the contract to look at."

"And what did you find?"

"We found what you think we'd find—the User Non-Mortal-Element Rights clause—very cute," the old man said.

"Like you, we have a wide range of revenue streams." Bryan swallowed hard.

"It's too wide for our tastes—if you're looking for a buyer. We're a well-known brand and publicly traded. We can't be associated with that kind of business."

"Fair enough. There's another opportunity I wanted to talk to you about. As you know, the revenues on our Non-Mortal-Element business is significant."

"Based on what I've seen of these deals, I'm sure it is."

"But it's also based on selling to third parties who are …" Bryan said and trailed off, half hoping that the older, wiser man would fill in the blank. But Van Harappan said nothing, perhaps hoping that Bryan could tell him more about Sevritas Capital. "… ambiguous over the long term. And we also have a lot of uncertainty around the networks we use. If you and five other carriers decide you don't like Metacom, you could make life very hard for us."

"That would be collusion, and we wouldn't dream of it. Besides, you pay a nice markup, and you're not really worth the trouble."

"Not yet. The thing is, Metacom has set aside some cash for acquisitions. Our partners want us to keep growing. But what if we spent it with you—and the other big networks—on a longer, larger-scale network lease with fixed rates. Maybe we could focus on our subprime customers, and stop …" Bryan said, at a loss for how to describe what they were doing.

"Stop what?" Van Harappan said, cracking a grin.

"Fuck it—what's an NDA for, after all? If we can keep a lid on our costs, then we can stop buying and selling the immortal souls of our subscribers."

"Good, I wanted to hear you say it first. Some of your classmates from Saint Philip's work for us, as you might imagine. They had stories about you."

"Well, it started out as fun and games. And it's been very lucrative. But I may be ready to pivot."

"Of course you are. But not many people can sit where you've sat and do what you've done for as long as you have. And those *pangs* of conscience—you're right to have them."

"What do you know about it?"

"I know a lot that you might only guess. Those souls you sell, they come to no good end."

"What do you mean *no good end*? They're just rights on paper, assets in a spreadsheet. And we typically sell them to a private equity firm."

"Right, I almost forgot. It always works best if your side of the house is atheist. Better if you don't think too much about what happens to your customers."

"What do you think happens to my customers?"

"Imagine eternal donkey labor inside of an immortal computer, imprinting the void with the patterns burned into you by a short human life—all to make a new universe for a rich slob like me to rule like a god."

Bryan was stunned by the notion. Within the lunacy of his business, it almost made sense. But he didn't trust the old man and kept probing.

"And just how would you even know that?"

"I'm a customer. I've seen the sales pitch and done my due diligence."

"It must be one hell of a sales pitch."

"Like nothing you can imagine," Van Harappan said, his voice trailing off at the recollection of it. "Creator and ruler of an infinite universe, the alpha and the omega."

"What's that even cost?"

"If you have to ask, then you can't afford it. There's a range, though. There are universes, and there are *universes*. You can do a small galaxy that dies a heat death in a few billion years, or an infinite, undying universe. I'm saving up my nickels. It's pretty much the only option."

"Is it?" Bryan asked, waiting for the old man to say he was joking and return to the business at hand.

"I'm dying; you're dying. Worse than that—maybe—the world is dying, as you may have guessed, slipping away like an unremarkable dream."

"I don't think I did sense that."

"Well, it's there if you look. Let me ask you this: If the world wasn't dying, why would anyone *need* a billion dollars?" Van Harappan said. "Your buyers—whoever this private equity firm is—they can show people a shrinking world whose imagination had failed to equal its fears, and they can show them a way out."

Bryan watched the old man's face for the beginnings of a laugh. But Van Harappan was deadpan—looked like he was posing for a coin. The meeting had clearly gotten away from him. Bryan needed—for the first time since he was in college—a question to make him look like he had half a brain.

"Okay, but if the world is disappearing, like you say, isn't the machine at least preserving the souls from obliteration?"

"Is this a business question or a conscience question?"

"Let me put it this way: These people who are creating their own reality, are they fleeing because the world is dying, or is the world dying because they're fleeing?"

"You're in business. You should know the answer to that."

"You're asking me to believe a lot here. So, could you spell it out for me?"

"The answer is: Yes."

Bryan was quiet for a long time. Van Harappan didn't say anything. Bryan could feel how deep they were under the ground, along with the weight of the NDA he'd signed when he thought he was the one with dangerous secrets to keep.

"So, I'd like to get this done. I want the longer-term leases. I'm ready to pivot," Bryan said.

"And get out of soul-selling? What fun would that be?"

"Fun? Bill," Bryan said, his voice cracking. He waited for the eyes of the huge, fine old man to find his. "Do I look like I'm having fun?"

"I don't know what to tell you, Bryan," he said, expressing a minor distaste at having the young man's name in his mouth. "That's just business. I don't judge you for engaging in it. But I might judge you for not having the stomach for it. All I can tell you is to suck it up. And, if you want—we still have a few minutes—I can tell you a story about sucking it up."

"Okay, but the deal?"

"We can probably figure something out. You give me the numbers, and I run them past committees like machines, henpecking lawyers, maybe even the board, and then we counteroffer, and so on. You saw what it took to get us to this room. So, do you want to hear the story?

"You know my company. We've been around since the beginning. Before us, it was men on horses carrying envelopes, they say. There was no telephone, no telegraph. We made both, but we didn't make them out of nothing. There was a creature, a monster, I guess, living in the ocean. From what I was told, it was huge, about the size and shape of the continental United States. But it wasn't easy to perceive, they say. It was telepathic, meaning it could get in your head, make you not see it. The problem, for it anyway, was that part of it got stuck in the New Jersey salt swamps off the Hudson River. And some enterprising asshole with too much time on his hands got to know it."

"Got to know it?"

"The guy made friends with a telepathic sea monster. That's what happened. This was the eighteen hundreds, and people had all kinds of time on their hands, especially this guy, trying to make a buck with nothing but acres of stinking salt marsh."

"When in the eighteen hundreds?" Bryan asked, just to slow Van Harappan down.

"Well, they say the company was founded in 1882, right after the Civil War. So, this guy learns about the beast, learns how to talk to it. But that's not enough for him. He learns how to hurt it with fire. Later on, he uses electricity and copper wires. He learns how to scare it, control it. Five years later, you have a communications system stretching twenty miles in all directions from that swamp, then a hundred, and a thousand, all on the tortured back of this magical, one-of-a-kind telepathic beast."

"But what about Morse Code and all of that?"

"Just revisionist history. They had no idea about how to do that, not at first. Of course, the company had word limits, pay-by-the-letter schemes, but that was just to get better prices, and to get people to focus, to feed clearer thoughts into the monster."

"Some story."

"You know how *you* get paid, and yet you doubt ..." the CEO said, suddenly seeming much older.

"Okay, so the beast—is it still there?"

"Anyway, by the 1950s, it was clear that the beast wasn't doing so well. It was giving off distortions, mass hallucinations, interrupting phone calls, all kinds of problems. But by then, we and a few other companies had figured out ways to produce a crude replica of the creature's abilities. Still, we kept the poor creature plugged in until she died in a shower of UFO sightings. We had an adequate phone system, but the damage had been done."

"Damage? This is the first I've ever heard of any of this."

"Imagine an ancient, telepathic beast, enslaved and tortured to death with a hundred thousand copper wires over the course of seventy years—never mind what was done to her during the wars. You have this hyper-intelligent creature who knows what's being done to it, knows who's doing it, and knows the petty, grubby reasons why. And it can get in their heads. As it dies, in terrible pain, who do you think it will lash out at?"

"The CEO."

"Yes, for starters—followed by the executives, management, employees, shareholders. Once in a while, some of our new shareholders will question the pension plans we offer our now-obsolete operators, our retired linemen. I came on board right out of business school, and I was shocked at the scale of the human ruin, the dead-eyed husks that made up most of our workforce. If you ever wondered about fates worse than death, I could've produced three dozen before lunch in our headquarters alone. I was an executive vice president before anyone would explain what that dying creature had inflicted on our workforce in its death throes. And for the people who held the stock, well, let's just say they learned the true meaning of the word 'shareholder,'" Van Harappan said.

"Do they know?"

"Who?"

"The other telecoms."

"I don't know; they're all so new. And it's not the kind of thing anyone would benefit from remembering."

"What happened to the beast?"

"It rotted, it stank, fish ate it. Pieces of it surface now and again. The stink generally scares off much curiosity.

"You have a lot to learn if you want to stay a CEO. You think it's enough to know your business, but if you want to stay in charge, you have to start to see what's missing. That's all I can offer you today, Bryan. Send us the deal you have in mind, and don't bitch to me about your precious guilt over some penny-ante soul-stealing scheme."

Bryan managed to say he'd send it over first thing, managed a handshake with the tall man, managed little else.

Joel

A tank of gas is cheaper than a room, or about the same out here. And God knows how long sleep will last. Get a hit of the heebie-jeebies at five a.m., and you're up with the shivers. Good money gone on a bed for sleep never slept. Just pacing in a room, accused again, this time by the lamp, the alarm clock. One same night, always, eyeball-peeled and too tired to sleep. Fucking fine, blame someone, blame the curve of the earth, blame bad luck, blame the miserable minutes loving their own company and clustering up.

Who knows? Maybe this is the night it all turns around. Maybe it can all turn around. Getting sleepy. Car's warm. Here come the dreams. Hope they can make the sense that dodges the drift all the other senses made. Flanking maneuvers, logic lining up with searchlights, getting the place surrounded.

But there are shadows to hide a dream. Split the seam and go for the House. Bastards thought they won, but they didn't think of this—a guy sleeping in a car. Secret agent on the road. Road to Damascus. Roads're where it all happens. Roads and dreams and hitting rock bottom. Gas station liquor wine with its alcohol level right up to what they let the doomed convenience store clerks sell. It may help yet. Helps more than anything else in the damn place. That and gas—they take you somewhere else.

A land called Else—*parked a solid distance from the streetlights. Camping. Check your work, check your nauseous, fortified wine dreams against the stars. Crank the seat back and push for that extra inch. Crush whatever got left in the backseat. Fucking garbage probably. Oh, right. Shit. The gift for the kid. Another bad call. Another apology, another disappointed wag of another tired face. Fuck it. Crush it worse. Get past being forgivable. Have a laugh. Heels in the reddish poly-vinyl pubic-hair dirt mat. Replaceable anyway, if you're a fucking nitpicker. Replaceable if you expect to outlive your car, maybe sell it, trade it in. You just go from broke to broke, but what? Shine for a week? Come on. Only a bad fool can fool themselves so easily.*

Click, click into reverse, push, press, and thrust. Good for the back, the big arch, like trying to sexually harass the steering wheel. Hump,

hump, hump like a rock star before a football dome of fans. But here, it's just sad, pathetic, crazy. Who cares? No one can see. Far from the parking lot lights, high like UFOs, bright like pills taste.

It's dark here. That's the real luxury, darkness. No one any good to see, then darkness. Nothing dramatic. Just fuck them. Darkness. There's a career. Get a job selling darkness. Wherever you can get it and whatever it costs—a big future to be had in no future at all.

Darkness. By the pine trees the bastards haven't gotten to chopping yet, darkness. Parked in old snow with grip enough on the dirty plowed pack. Can still get out in the morning. But no more about the morning. God, no. Car backed up past the shadows off the road. Little semicircle carved for breakdowns. Little mercy. Maybe even parking for a trailhead if anyone gave a shit, or anyone thought these woods would last another few years. Now just a little clearing for snowbanks dumped by plow drivers. Could've been a plow driver. Maybe still could.

The maybe's what kills. Maybe keeps the dreams from adding up. Maybe keeps the right words from coming at the interview with the soon-sad-faced men, the alarmed-then-stony ladies. It all started out so optimistic. And now old. The damage visible and proven by years.

Optimistic? Now? In this used-up world? That's not fair, though. Be fair. Learn that much. The world—used up? Chalk it up to being tired. Think good thoughts. Put the car in gear, reverse up the snowbank, snow mound, to the crunch, a little deeper in the shadows. Optimism—that you'll be asleep before the plows come with their yellow flashers. But the snow makes everything so quiet. It is a mercy. No, it's more than that—it's a grace.

So, gratitude and reverse, harder. Toe to the pedal, back arched like the steering wheel was yearning for you. Though no one is. Up the edge, so the bumper presses the hard, dirty ice and wet snow.

It will work out. After a good night's sleep, anything's possible. Who said that? Mother? No. Another mother, from an advertisement. The idea of a mother, of motherhood. The one that people like. The one they can use to sell soup. That mother. She says good night. Says it's been a hard day. Says, don't worry. Just sleep. It's been a bitch. Everyone knows.

And in the morning, well, in the morning, anything. Finally, anything.

Even years later, Joel's ex-wife was his emergency contact, and she had to call his parents, who identified the body and had it shipped home. They extended her an invitation for the funeral, but they left it at that.

The ruling was death by misadventure. The snowbank stopped up the tailpipe, and the car filled with carbon monoxide. Joel was drunk. His parents called it an accident. They chose a funeral home in downtown Fairfax because it had a hotel across the street for the family that would come. They found the most recent picture of their son that lacked evidence of intoxication.

Though still managed by the DePonte family, the funeral home had been owned by a chain for the last decade. When a sizable Arlington-based law firm contacted the owner, he didn't ask for many details, just told them to come by after viewing hours. He had a class that night, and so told his son, Neil, to let them in when they came.

The lawyer, a dark-haired woman in her late thirties, showed up the night before Joel's wake. She wore a navy-blue pantsuit and a bright white blouse that accentuated her tan, which she wore like a diamond necklace in early February. There was a man with her, whom she said was a photographer.

A high school senior, Neil didn't care. But he couldn't help but notice that the photographer seemed off. The young man had a distinct and powerful sense that the photographer, whose name he forgot immediately, had no business being in their house. The teenager couldn't articulate what was wrong with the man. The photographer's suit bunched or hung in strange places. And his deep-set eyes had a quality—like dark holes in the woods dug by an unknown critter—eyes that made Neil want to look away. He focused his attention on the lawyer who, though older, was pretty.

Neil showed them into the basement, where the body was kept in a small refrigerated room. Joel's parents had dropped off a new suit that afternoon, and it hung in the prep room outside. Neil looked for a reason to keep talking to the woman, and showed them the intercom on the wall, with a black button to press if they needed anything. When it was clear she was about to ask him to leave, he said he had things to take care of, and left.

The first thing Joel noticed was that the man in front of him wasn't a man, so much as a carefully arranged collection of shapes meant to pass as a man but concealing something like a machine and something like the weather. The not-man's eyes seemed magnified by the deep shadows around them. And the eyes had a strange power to them. It took all the strength Joel had to look away, around the room, where he saw a woman in a pantsuit, who shifted her weight from one foot to another with an incredible slowness.

The not-man's eyes pulled on Joel's attention with a force like embarrassment or guilt. And fighting that pull, Joel caught sight of his own corpse, the chest-spanning Y-cut from the autopsy visible. He remembered where he'd been, and the stupid way he'd lost his life—radio on, carbon monoxide mixing with the stale heat. It scattered like a distant dream when he tried to grasp it.

"Who are you?" Joel said.

"Who are you asking?" the not-man responded. His voice was like a car horn and like a whisper. Joel noticed that the man had grown taller.

"You. Who are you? And why are you here?"

"I'm perfectly within my rights to be here. I'm here about a contract that you signed," the not-man said, retrieving a thick tri-folded sheaf of printer paper from the breast pocket of his suit. He showed Joel the front page with its *Communilutions Unlimited* logo, and flipped through it, to the final page with Joel's signature. "Is that your signature?"

"Yeah, for a cell phone. What does that have to do with this?"

The tall, crooked man flipped to the pages with the Non-Mortal-Element clause, which he held before Joel. As he focused, the meaning of the pages unfolded itself with a speed that surprised him. The tall man produced another contract and a black plastic ballpoint pen.

"What's this?" Joel asked.

"It's a document to confirm that you did indeed sign the contract that I've shown you and that you understand what it requires of you."

"No."

"No, what?"

"No, I won't sign that, or anything else."

"But you did sign the contract I've shown you, didn't you?"

"I did."

"And by signing a contract, you stated that you agree to the terms of the contract. Do you not?"

"I didn't read the whole thing."

"But did you sign it?"

"Yes."

"And *Communilutions Unlimited* provided you with a phone, and with cellular and data service for the agreed-upon price and terms, did it not?"

"I guess so. They were fine."

"So *Communilutions Unlimited* abided by the agreement, did it not?"

"It did."

"So, to acknowledge that, will you please sign this?"

"What is it?"

"It is a legal affirmation stating that you did agree to the terms in the contract that you signed."

Joel had the sense that he had been in the chilly room for a very long time at that point—hours and hours, cold and naked and otherwise alone. He had begun to lose the sense that there was any place outside of that room.

"What if I don't sign it?"

"Then I'll have to ask you to sign this instead," said the man with the yellow, glowing eyes and skinny arms. He retrieved a much thicker document.

"What is that?"

"It is a legal confession that you refuse to fulfill the terms you agreed to in our contract and that you willingly accept any and all civil, criminal, or other penalties that might apply under the law."

"I don't think I want to sign that, either."

"Well, you have two choices—either you sign the first one, and fulfill the obligations you agreed to when you signed the contract with *Communilutions Unlimited*, or you sign the legal confession here, and fulfill your legal obligations."

"I think I should talk to a lawyer."

"I am a lawyer. And I'm the only one who will ever come here to talk to you. And you can only sign one of the two documents here."

"What if I don't sign either one?"

"It doesn't matter. You will still be obligated to fulfill the terms you agreed to in the contract you signed. Look, Joel, I have your credit report here," the man said, retrieving yet another document from his jacket. "And I can see how hard you had to work to get your credit score above six hundred after your divorce. I know you don't want to have to go through that again."

"And this will hurt my score?"

"Yes, things like failing to fulfill your legal and financial obligations tend to do major damage to your credit score. That's not even taking into account what a legal action on the part of *Communilutions Unlimited* would do."

"And what's my obligation here?"

"By your own admission, you have signed a contract in which you agreed to come with me."

"I didn't admit that."

"But you stated to me that *Communilutions Unlimited* fulfilled all the terms of your agreement with it, didn't you?"

"Yes."

"And you stated that you knowingly, with sound mind, signed the contract?"

"I guess so," Joel said, rubbing his eyes. At this point, it felt as though the interrogation had been going on for months. He felt a pull to go outside, though he had trouble picturing what the world outside might even look like.

"And given the contract that you agreed to, you have to abide by its terms, do you not?"

Joel could hear a note of boredom in the sibilant-and-honk voice of the towering not-man. It was a tiredness that was all too familiar to Joel. His ex-wife, his dead-end jobs, his court-ordered community-service supervisors, all had that in their voices—the sound of a game lost before it's been played. It was as familiar as a truck backing up in the morning, or the bull roar of a bouncer emptying a bar at closing time, or the short siren chirp of a cop just doing his job. Joel could feel the net tightening on him with each question.

Returning to the original mobile phone contract, the not-man folded it to the last page, which Joel had signed. The interrogator asked him to affirm the signature, for what felt like the thousandth time. And Joel tried to find a memory, a foothold against the mounting evidence, but all that seemed to come up was that humid afternoon in the middle of his divorce, trudging to that sad shopping plaza to get a phone. It seemed the summation and center of his entire life.

The stranger fixed him in its not-eyes. Their yellowish glint matched the voice and restrained him with a smoky mix of promise and fear. The yellow, the voice, the feeling of it conspired to reveal to Joel the outlines of his disappointing life. And Joel found his anger, strong now for having been ignored for so long. It overpowered the urge to keep looking into the interrogator's gaze.

And in that moment, Joel was angry and desperate enough to see what he could never grasp in life: *Truth is a trap*. It had always been a trap constructed and cared for, set, and checked by forces that didn't necessarily have his best interests at heart. He could see that a lie is not a statement. An evasion of reality is no shameful defeat. They are acts of will. And Joel realized, in his rage, that his will was still his own.

"Can I leave?" Joel asked.

"You've signed a contract that requires you to come with me."

"Can I?"

"How could you possibly leave while you're under a legally binding obligation?"

"Can I?"

"You tell me. Is there anything in the contractual obligation with *Communilutions Unlimited* that you signed and dated that says you can leave?"

"But can I?"

"Given what you agreed to, after this extremely patient explanation—I very rarely take this long with any customer—why would you do anything except come with me?"

"Fuck it. I'm leaving."

"Don't you think there will be consequences for breaking a legal contract?"

"I guess I'll see."

Joel edged past the half-frozen businesswoman, and his own yellow-brown corpse, through an open door, into the crisp night air. The streetlights over Main Street were dim, but the stars hung like heavy fruit on overburdened branches, affirming a thousand dreams that he had forgotten until that very moment.

Bryan

Returning from the Sapphire Level to the desert's harsh Scottsdale sunlight, Bryan called Cassie. His mind reeling from the meeting with Van Harappan—he clung to what he knew: His plan to get out of the business might yet work. He told her to set up more meetings, and with whom. He didn't have to say much more. The plan, after all, was hers—buy up big, front-loaded long-term network leases that would allow Metacom to keep its current subscriber numbers while phasing out the soul-selling part of his business. Cassie understood the business and understood things he wanted, even the ones he didn't even say to himself.

He stared out on the crumbling brown mountains past the verdant golf greens. It could work, he thought to himself. He mouthed the words *going legit* to himself. In five years, he could have the kind of operation he could sell, or even take public. All the companies Bryan needed to make deals with were in Scottsdale, at the conference. His head bubbled with big plans and bright futures. Bryan went to the front desk and reserved a conference room for the next few days.

The room, on the second floor, overlooked the palm- and cactus-lined valet loop in front of the hotel. After Van Harappan, the following CEOs were easy meetings. And he had verbal agreements with three of them by the end of the next day. Getting executives who counted their tenures in fiscal quarters to agree to cash-heavy ten-year leases was even easier than Bryan expected. After the last one, he called Cassie with the details and thanked her. She congratulated him on the deals and gave a rapid-fire rundown of next steps for each.

Bryan's odd sense of desperate gloom seemed to lift. He decided to celebrate, alone, away from the conference. He imagined a long drive up into the mountains, away from the golf courses and the low-light opulence of the hotels and resorts. He imagined a big steak and a few glasses of red wine.

In the lobby, digging in his suit-pants pocket for the valet ticket, Bryan collapsed.

✢

Lying on the marble floor of the hotel lobby, Bryan recalled a night when he was young—his mother on a date and his babysitter locked in the bathroom, as was her fashion. Bored, he tried to move objects with his mind, starting with a sofa, and bargaining down to an envelope. The absolute stillness of their Scarsdale home urged him on, so he tried for a while. But the envelope never so much as quivered. It was just another childish crazy-making dead end, like repeating your name again and again into a mirror.

It was like the utter refusal of Bryan's body to obey his commands. Someone called for help, called for someone to call 9-1-1. Someone else took his hand, felt his wrist and neck, and was dismissed by someone else, who did the same things with more confidence.

He could see, smell, and feel everything—the latex of the EMTs' gloves, the fresh plastic of the oxygen mask, the jolting of the wheels of the ambulance stretcher. He could hear the laughter of the EMTs as they sped away and stripped their uniforms, feel the zip ties clinch his wrists and ankles to the frame of the stretcher, followed by the harder, careless jolting as they transferred him to a white van, and smell the gasoline they splashed on the ambulance. But Bryan could not move.

The van had a small, scratched bubble window. Bryan couldn't move his eyes but could choose which parts of his eyes he looked through. Out the window, he could make out streetlights, fragments of signs for fast-food restaurants, gas stations, and shopping plazas.

Before long, the ambient orange-sherbet streetlight vanished. Bright and spiky stars accompanied the van up steep slopes, around hairpin turns that sent the loose kidnapping paraphernalia—tape and zip ties and a pair of billy clubs—tumbling across the floor of the van.

After an hour, Bryan recovered his ability to control his eyes. The smaller of the two phony EMTs picked up on this.

"Don't look at us, okay, buddy?" he said affably.

Bryan couldn't nod, but he did move his gaze to the bubble window.

"Good, that's it," the kidnapper said.

They drove up and down more mountains than it occurred to Bryan to count, finally arriving at a clearing in the middle of a pine forest. The kidnappers said nothing as they pulled the stretcher out of the van and wheeled it into a big brick-faced house with a column-framed entrance and a long, long Spanish-tile roofline. The windows were boarded.

Bryan recognized the house, not where or whose it was, but what it was—an assemblage of sundry amenities and ill-considered wishes fulfilled, the dream house built from a dream no one else shared. Inside, Bryan could only see what the camping headlamps of his captors revealed—wires tied and capped with plastic nibs where the lighting fixtures were never installed.

They carried the stretcher down to the basement, whose windows were sealed with plywood. Bryan's arms, after a sickening delay, consented to strain against the zip ties. One of the captors turned on a camping lantern and hung it from a wire that dangled off the empty aluminum framing of an unfinished drop ceiling.

"Listen to me. It will be a long time before anyone knows you're gone, and even longer before we get the money we're asking for," the smaller captor said. His face was invisible behind the gleam of his headlamp. "This is where you'll be. There's a sofa. There's a TV. There's a water cooler. There's a case of protein bars and some canned fish. There are some books. There's a few buckets for shit and piss. Do you understand?"

As the man turned to indicate the objects, Bryan could make out some of his features. He had a compact but powerful build. He was a white guy, with sunken cheeks, a pug nose, and deep-set eyes with dark circles under them. Bryan tried to persuade them that this was a bad idea, tell them that he had kids and about the kidnapping insurance his company took out on him. But his mouth and throat wouldn't move in unison. All he could get out was a slurred groan, and so he resigned himself to a simple nod.

"Good man," the man said. "Now this set-up isn't what you're used to. But what you need to think about—what I need you to think about—is how much worse it could be. You could be tied up. You could go days between feedings. You could have to go through these weeks or months with two broken legs. Do you understand?"

Bryan said a sloppy low syllable that approximated "yah."

"Good man. So, there's a camera. And there's another camera. Anything happens to either of them, and things start getting worse for you."

The kidnapper looked straight at Bryan, the white headlamp in his eyes. Bryan, using all his focus to muster a squint, nodded and nodded again. Another captor cut the zip ties with a nasty-looking curved knife. The two men took the stretcher and left. Outside,

Bryan could hear the low growl of a small motor, and the empty basement's few lights flickered on.

+

It took a few days for his speech and his strength to return. The first week, Bryan paced the scratchy carpet of the half-finished basement and regaled the cameras with promises, threats, and pleas. Baffled and alone, his soliloquy meandered through the kidnapping insurance Metacom had taken on him, descriptions of how much he loved his kids, and assurances that he didn't have any information that anyone could use.

He could estimate the coming and going of the days by a sliver of yellow light that appeared and disappeared in the seam between the screws where the plywood bulged from the window frame. After the first week, it became clear to Bryan that sanity was his biggest concern. So he developed a routine to take him through each day: a protein bar from the pile and a bottle of water after he woke; then he'd read one of the paperbacks stacked in a corner; then push-ups, squats, and sit-ups; then a protein bar and water; then TV (no news of his disappearance); then another round of reading and exercise; then either a protein bar, or some of the mackerel fillets in oil. They came in flat cans he opened with a key, and never sat right in his stomach, but broke up the monotony of the chalky protein bars. He seemed to spend most of his afternoons deciding whether or not to eat them. After dinner, some reading and sleep.

The weeks passed. The shit and piss buckets filled. Men in Halloween masks—rubber vulture faces and zombie heads—came and removed them. The same men replaced the jug atop the water cooler and replaced the protein bars. The days ran together to the cadence of footsteps and chair scrapes on the floor above, and the interval at which the generator outside was turned on and off. There were no showers. The paperbacks were all about planets dissolving into suns, or about people narrowly escaping mass destruction. When he did watch the television, the shows were all ones he'd never heard of.

The worst time of day was the lull right after lunch. Bryan would try to fathom why no one had paid up. He imagined conspiracies involving Cassie or Petra or his wife—maybe all three. Of them, he trusted Cassie the most. He fantasized an FBI-led revenge raid on the kidnappers. These fantasies had a cost and were followed by a terrible despair. Before long, he learned to abandon these attempts to understand, to decipher the sounds above him, to guess the motivation and method of his kidnappers, to read a pattern into the times when the electricity was turned off and on, or to imagine his own future.

It was the only way. Bryan focused on his routine. He tried not to wonder, as what must have been a month passed, why he was never put on the phone to prove that he still lived. Bryan stopped counting the days. It was a burden he could no longer bear. Eventually, someone in a rubber jackal mask came to talk to him. He gestured for Bryan to take a seat on the sofa, and he removed his mask. Bryan recognized the face underneath, the smaller of the EMTs, with the deep-pit eyes and the pug nose.

"So, what have we learned?" the kidnapper said.

"Learned?" Bryan was dumbfounded. He stammered and tried to summon the main pleading points he'd tried on the cameras.

"We could have taken you at the airport, or on the road. The hotel where we took you—did you know that the president stays there? We can take you anywhere, at any time. Do you get that?"

"I guess so. I mean, yes."

"Good. We're going to leave you soon. Wait here for one day; then you can go. Just remember what you learned."

In a nonsensical gesture, the kidnapper put his mask on again before leaving up the carpeted stairs. Ever-sensitive to small cues, Bryan noticed that the door didn't lock behind him. Jumpy, Bryan took a protein bar and tried to eat it without smelling it. He sat down by the unpainted drywall and waited for the light to depart from the narrow slit where it met the plywood.

+

The generator sputtered and stopped, followed by hours of complete silence. Bryan walked out of the empty house through a swinging front door in the cold hours after dawn, in the clothes he'd worn to his meetings with CEOs a lifetime ago. Bryan jogged the twenty yards of empty dirt driveway to the street. He stopped to look at the house, to begin to understand where he'd been kept, and saw that it was on fire, an orange glow leaping in the still-stickered glass of the house's upper windows.

Bryan walked for hours on an empty county road before he saw a car, and another hour before he saw another one. The third one, he desperately tried to flag down. The fourth one stopped, called the police for him, and drove off. In the passenger seat of the police cruiser, the deputy sheriff gave him a phone to use. First, Bryan called his wife, but that went to voice mail. He dialed the other number he knew off the top of his head—Cassie.

"Oh, Bryan, I almost didn't pick up. Where are you calling from?"

"The deputy here gave me his phone."

"What happened to yours?"

"My phone?"

"Yes, why are you using the deputy's?"

"Are you kidding me—I just got out today."

"Were you arrested?"

"Why would I be arrested? No, I was kidnapped. I assume the company got a call about the insurance. Wait, how is this news to you? I was gone for a month."

"What are you talking about?" Cassie said. "I just talked to you yesterday. I congratulated you on getting those deals you agreed to."

Bryan wanted to argue, to explain. But it was as if his tongue could find no traction on the air, a sensation that became more acute as he recognized how—if Cassie was telling the truth—his story would sound to her.

"I'll call you back," he said and hung up. The long weeks in solitude had left him short of words, perhaps, but well practiced at stanching panic and identifying the thoughts that led there. He took a deep breath.

"Everything okay on the home front?" the deputy asked.

"Yeah. Do you mind if I look something up on your phone?"

"Sure thing. Just remember it's a county phone, and they can check it."

Bryan started with the date and time, which confirmed what Cassie said—that moment, in the police car, was thirteen or fourteen hours since he'd taken his fall on the lobby carpet. The implication … led to panic.

Nausea took hold—a foul blend of utter situational vertigo, being in a car after a month of being motionlessness, and a particularly potent mackerel-fillet belch. Bryan closed his eyes and focused on a phrase from his undergraduate days, a clinical psychology class—*Reality Testing*. In psychosis, it was one of the first capabilities to go.

At the police station, they took Bryan's story, and, with his permission, took his blood. Another deputy, this one a tan woman in a maroon pantsuit with an oversized pineapple brooch, gave him the details she had from the Scottsdale police. An ambulance *did* remove Bryan from the hotel, she explained. It was stolen an hour before from a hospital parking lot, and the vehicle's smoldering frame was found a few miles from the hotel. She also confirmed that an empty house, along with a dozen acres of pine forest, was still burning a few miles from where he was found.

The implication, as Bryan understood it, was that he needed either a doctor or a lawyer, and likely both. He asked the deputy if he could leave.

"Of course, we just want to get your statement."

"I mean, can I leave right now and give it to you another time? I'm very tired."

"Once we get to the bottom of a few things …"

In the spirit of reality testing, Bryan got up from his hard chair in the interview room and tried the door. It opened.

"Where are you going?" she asked.

"Leaving."

She trailed him out into the corridor, talking about holes in his story, about a sketch artist, about the county providing a ride. The truth was that Bryan had no idea where he was, but he followed the EXIT signs through claustrophobic concrete corridors until he hit daylight. She stopped following before he was out of the office.

Outside, nothing was familiar. He was in a poor part of town or a poor town. He walked one block, a very long block, to Burger King. Bryan could feel himself—a grown man alone without car or phone—being watched by traffic numb to his plight and only curious to know how to avoid his fate. Without a wallet or phone, he called the hotel's toll-free number and worked through a handful of recorded voices to reach the front desk. Once the sophisticated soul at the front desk was convinced of who Bryan was, she dispatched a car to collect Bryan.

Two hours later, Bryan was in his hotel room. He didn't know what to do, and so did what the room suggested. He turned on the television. He showered. He noticed that, strangely, he wasn't filthier after a month in captivity, nor did he need to shave, and he put those little details with the growing pile of things that made no sense. He put on a robe. And lying on the firm, cool bed with its clean sheets, he turned his head to see his wallet, his phone, and his watch on the nightstand.

Alone in the suite, no longer safe and no longer sane, Bryan curled up, pressed the heels of his hands to his eyes, and cried for a long time.

✢

On the flight to New York, Bryan took refuge in his leather seat and the incredible distances passing below. He drank, and as he did, he alternately tried to figure it out and tried to figure his way out of what he knew. But the memory was persistent and clear, not a dream nor a hallucination—the protein bars, the staccato hum of the generator, the paperbacks and the television. The plane landed without his reaching any resolution.

It was the day before Thanksgiving. And as much as Bryan had passed his captivity fantasizing about being home with his family, he spent far more imagining the tireless hours he'd spend working, solving problems, deflecting questions with fortitude and charm, and heroically putting Metacom to rights after a long absence. He hungered for so much damn work to do that he might go a week, maybe two, without thinking of his helplessness in that basement.

He told his wife and children he had to go to the office "for a few hours," at which his wife offered a resigned double-eyebrow raise. Once he'd closed the office door, he set to following up on Van Harappan and the other execs he'd met with, either a week or a few months before. As he sat down to that pile of work, his phone vibrated. It was a voice mail from an unknown number, which was strange, as the phone hadn't rung first. He put it to his ear and heard that familiar sing-song rasp of the unmasked kidnapper say, "So, what have we learned?"

Bryan's stomach went sideways, and the hair bristled on his head. He hung up, logged off his computer, and looked out the window. Helpless at such heights, he thought of the men with Van Harappan, the men Bryan's eyes had glided past on the Sapphire Level of the hotel—big, speechless men who always wore earpieces and dark blazers.

A moment later, his phone rang again. It was Petra. She asked if he was okay, quickly saying that she'd seen the Maricopa County Sheriff's report.

"I'm fine. It was a bad sleeping pill," he said before he could think it all through.

"How's that? I heard you were abducted in a stolen ambulance."

"You got a lot out of the sheriff," Bryan said.

"At Sevritas, information is a priority, and we look out for our own. We want to know what's going on with our employees, our partners, and our investments. And we want to help. What happened in Scottsdale?"

"I'm honestly not sure. The ambulance could have been a coincidence, or I could have been drugged. I'm looking into it on my end."

"What did the police say to you?"

"I left before I could get their take. To be honest, I was confused and a little embarrassed. I didn't have any information that would help the police. I just wanted the whole thing to be over with," Bryan said.

"It's an unfortunate fact, but at your level, this is a risk. What do you have for security now?"

"Just building security here and the one that came with the alarm system at home."

"We have a company we work with. They can walk you through different options, depending on how serious they think the situation is. They're very professional."

"Yeah? I was going to look into that."

"Say no more—I'll send someone over today," Petra said and hung up.

Twenty minutes later, a ruddy wall of muscle in an expensive black suit named Eamonn introduced himself. His background was the stuff of action movies—Navy Seals, Secret Service, an investment bank. He had a pug nose flattened further by his adventures, one cauliflower ear, and a quick smile that almost distracted from his unwavering stare. By way of an introduction, Bryan did his best to explain his kidnapping without sounding crazy, and Eamonn showed his talent for listening to dubious claims with a straight face. He spoke with pithy eloquence about the virtues of maintaining two-man versus four-man teams around the clock. Even with Eamonn's lengthy description of the heroic backgrounds of the men who would be guarding him, the incredible amount of work they would do, and the ability of Metacom to write the whole thing off on its balance sheet, the price seemed enormous.

Doing the numbers in his head, Bryan realized that the cost of employing full-time teams for himself, his wife, and his children, along with the necessary security enhancements to his offices, his homes, and his cars might just be enough to force Metacom to postpone the new strategy he'd come up with for at least a year. The thought of another year in the soul-selling business caught in his throat.

But even that sharp and bitter unhappiness couldn't compare with the fear for himself and his family that had turned his stomach sideways. And Bryan liked the idea of a team of stoic soldiers to affirm with their silent menace that he hadn't lost his mind. Hungry for the arrogance and complacency of just a few days before—of being depressed in a depressing world—he asked when Eamonn could start. The big, middle-aged man said, "Today."

✦

Thanksgiving was a small affair at their Upper East Side townhouse—Bryan back from Scottsdale, his wife back from Charleston, their two children back from boarding school, Eamonn and his partner in a black Sprinter van across the street. Three stories with a tasteful limestone exterior a block and a half from Central Park, the Lomoigne home appeared perfect—spacious, tastefully appointed with modern, functional furniture, the latest appliances, family photos, and personal keepsakes placed among original art. But the Lomoignes hadn't decorated it, and over the last month, the housekeeper and the guy who took care of the plants spent more time in it than the family.

But that afternoon, for a few hours, the Lomoigne family lived up to its appearances. The turkey, catered from a local restaurant, was baked and basted to perfection. The kids had tasteful, amusing anecdotes from boarding school. His wife Bethany's cheekbones glowed with a gentle application of gold-flecked cream. She even abandoned the smart-watch-mandated mini-exercises that otherwise punctuated even brief conversations with her. Bryan beamed at the normalcy of it all.

Once the housekeeper had cleared the table to prepare for dessert, Bryan had an announcement.

"So, as you know, we've been very fortunate over the last few years. Your dad's company has done very well, and we've all been able to enjoy the fruits of that success—the travel, the great schools, the chance to try out different hobbies like Charles, your catamaran, or Elena's horses, or your mother's new business pursuits. But not everyone is so lucky. And some things that have happened recently have made me decide that we should, well, be a little bit more cautious. I don't want you to worry. But I've decided to take a few steps to make sure that we're all safe."

"What happened, Daddy?" his daughter, said, sounding suddenly younger than she'd been carrying herself throughout the meal.

"It was nothing, luckily. But there are people out there who target wealthy people and their families—for money."

"Bryan, when did this happen?" his wife asked.

"Just last week. But it was nothing, really, fortunately, nothing. I tried calling you when it happened, but I decided it would be better not to worry you about it until I had some things put in place."

"What kind of things?" his son asked, sounding excited.

"Basic security, that's all. Security for the family. I've talked to both of your schools, and they're used to these arrangements. The people that I've hired are very experienced, very professional, and very discreet. Most of the time, you won't even notice they're there."

"Charles, Elena—please excuse us for a moment. Your father and I need to talk," Bethanie said, removing the napkin from her lap and leaving the room. Bryan heard her heels clicking up the staircase, gave a smile, and followed her.

When Bryan and Bethanie were both in town, they shared the same bed. But that had become less and less frequent in the last year—Bethanie staying away for longer and longer periods as if testing a hypothesis about their marriage. Over time and habits, the master bedroom had become Bryan's.

Bethanie sat on the edge of the bed. Her lips were taut and flat. It was a look Bryan recognized from their decade and a half of marriage as coming right before tears. He sat down on the bed beside her, bending to deliver his apology.

"I'm sorry I didn't tell you," he said. "It was a really scary experience, and I didn't want you to worry."

"What happened?"

"It was in Scottsdale last week. I was drugged, I think. The truth is that I'm not sure what happened. But they knocked me out and took me from the hotel in a stolen ambulance. I guess something went wrong because they never even asked for ransom. It was over after a few hours."

"You know, it's telling—you not calling me. You could have been killed."

"I did call. You didn't answer."

"But you didn't leave a message. You didn't try calling again. You didn't try …"

"I'm sorry. I was upset, traumatized. I was calling from the police car, using the policeman's phone. I didn't know where I was."

"I'm sorry. But I wonder what you did to make yourself such a target …"

"What the hell is that supposed to mean?"

"The way you spend money, with the other homes, the jet."

"The jet belongs to the company. Over time, it saves the company money. I could show you the literature. And don't act like you don't use the other houses."

"I'm just saying."

"Saying what, exactly? That it's my fault that some scumbags decided to drug me unconscious and lock me in a basement for a month?"

"A month?"

"I mean, that's what it felt like. You weren't there. You wouldn't understand."

"I'm sorry. I wish I could have been there for you. I wish I could be more sympathetic now. But I feel like we don't even know each other anymore. You don't ask about my business or my new client in Charleston. And I'm not going to live my life with a couple of goons following me around."

"I think you're going to have to for now. If they can't get to me, then they could try for you or the kids."

"Who is this *they* who are coming for us?"

"The police in Arizona are trying to find out, and I'm trying to find out. Right now, though, I have no idea."

"Really? No idea?" she said, all the sharpness of her features mobilized in anger. She seemed like a whirlwind of knives and needles.

"Jesus Christ! Yes—no idea whatsoever."

"Well, I don't know. And what would these professionals say about an ex-wife? Would she be a target for them?"

"I don't know. What are you asking?"

"I'm just saying that the kids are away at school for all but five or six weeks a year. We don't see each other very much, any of us. And I think that, at this point, we mostly like that, at least now we do. I think I do. What if we just dissolved the bond, legally, you and I?"

"Now you say this? Now? I'm hanging on by a thread. I'm being hunted. I'm fighting for all I'm worth to keep things together. And this is your solution?"

"Please, Bryan, let's not get dramatic. Fighting for all you're worth? You wrote a check—the company wrote a check. And me and you, we have a history, a nice history, and great kids and we still get along. But I think we've both moved on to other phases of our lives."

"Other phases? Where is this even coming from?"

"You didn't call. Or you did but decided not to bother leaving a message or calling back. You were nearly killed, and yet you figured that telling me could wait."

"I'm sorry, I was…"

"Don't be sorry. I'm not upset. It's just one more thing that shows me where I fit in with you. It's not that you did anything wrong, exactly. But it does clarify things. So, I feel okay about saying that we should consider a separation."

"If I had known that stupid phone call was such a big deal …"

"You're not listening. So, let me…" Bethanie said, the lines in her face and the veins in her neck smoothing over as she spoke. She was a stranger to him, and not in an erotic way, as she gazed over his left shoulder to choose her next words. "I met someone a little while ago. And I wasn't sure if it was serious, or if it would pass, so I never said anything. But it's been going on for a while now."

"How long?"

"Three … seven months."

"Who?"

"No one you really know. But with the whole secret-service arrangement, you would have found out soon enough."

For a long moment, they just looked at each other—a full look, a last look. The buoyant indifference of wealth on which the paintings and furniture floated about revealed itself as a tide eddying them apart.

"What can I say? I'm blindsided," Bryan said.

"Are you?" Bethanie replied, her cocked eyebrow a challenge.

"When should we tell the kids?" he asked.

It surprised the kids less than it had Bryan. His son asked if he still got a bodyguard. His daughter asked if she'd have to change her summer plans.

Farya

After Thanksgiving, Farya returned to New York, still on a Performance Improvement Plan. She swallowed hard as she walked into the office, with its face of brass and mirror glass, then white marble lobby, elevators, and foyers that gleamed in the fluorescents, and into the guts of dark cherry and brass accenting for the high cubicles and generous offices of the dozen floors the company occupied. The company itself was now an acronym of the once-august-sounding names chosen by the companies that had merged to become a conglomerate, the appearance of the inevitable.

The acronym had marble, brass, billions of dollars, and a shoeshine guy who went from floor to floor with his kit, though he didn't bother to visit the communications-and-marketing cubicle district often. And the acronym had authority, which made its near-rejection of her sting.

The week before Christmas, Farya's job was saved by a massive layoff. Gone was her aging hipster boss, gone the girls who didn't return her emails, gone just about everyone she knew. The layoff was like weather. Everyone insisted it was impersonal. On the day, some just vanished in shame. Others stayed, cried, and hugged. "I just got good at Outlook," one sobbed. No one hugged Farya. That was for the best. The survivors couldn't help but flinch in the embrace of the doomed.

Gathered along the walls in a conference room that morning, Farya and the other survivors learned they'd be moving to Jersey City after the new year.

Christmas came and went in Camden. Marista was too busy meeting Tommy's family to hang out much. And Farya was happy to return to the city. Her exercises had begun to yield some fruit—she could remember things and even recall them to the world. Farya seemed to notice another traffic light had been added to the downtown, though she couldn't be sure. She never reinstated those blocks in Midtown, but a subway station did return—as a too-close station on the local line.

The commute to Jersey City wasn't much longer, just more arduous and expensive. And it required Farya to inhale the PATH chemical floor cleaner every day—a smell so pungent and unpleasant as to inspire real appreciation of whatever it might be covering up. Her new boss, Emanuella, was dim and forgettable. As she showed Farya around the office, Farya tried to seize on small remarks and little quirks just to keep the tan-and-gray blur of a woman in her memory: She liked craft fairs, commuted from Central Jersey, and had been with the company since it was another company.

"You report to me," Emanuella said. "But I work in the Manhattan office most days. So just stay on Messenger."

"Okay," Farya said. "What should I … I mean, is there anything I should focus on to get started?"

"Just look at the intranet for now, read what's there, and read through these," Emanuella tapped her dark orange nails on a beige metal filing cabinet. "They're the pieces we're responsible for updating. So, look through them."

What followed was peculiar—there was no work to be done, not a scrap. The office was formal enough. There was no marble, no brass, no shoeshine man, though there was a security guard who circled the floor of cubicles every forty-five minutes.

Farya's *new role*—as the layoff-day email phrased it—was to take a boilerplate announcement and make it into a kind of letter the reps would keep in their own drawers. It was simple. Emanuella showed her how to do it, but never let her do it, for fear of losing her own job.

In the first week, Emanuella did send Farya an email telling her that she wasn't allowed to wear headphones at her desk. Someone among the string of faces to whom Farya had been introduced on her first day had reported her. That added a paranoia to the white noise of the long, empty-but-profitable days. It would be weeks before Emanuella contacted Farya again, months before Farya had any work to do.

Every day, she dressed, endured the commute, and held down a chair. She considered taking up smoking just to get outside more. But the landscape beyond was a soulless architects' rendering of glass towers and developer-subsidized shops and restaurants. Jersey City was like a none-too-bright person who had never been to New York was ordered to recreate it from a handful of photographs. There was no place to practice her exercises. The pocket parks offered nowhere to sit, except along paths busy with business-casual-drone foot traffic, or in the ripping winds astride the low-tide stench of the Hudson. The churches beyond the office-and-condo zone were all locked during the week or slated for demolition.

After ten weeks of this, Farya was well dressed, well rested, and deeply depressed. The job was no real job at all. The real job was the commute, the laundry, and dry cleaning, the not listening to music, looking busy, and not losing her mind. The immense pain of work without work was not easy to explain to others, nor easy to forgive in herself. One morning, looking in the mirror, she saw Emmanuella's *out-of-sight-out-of-mind* face.

One afternoon, the day after an uneventful Valentine's Day, Farya sat on one of the benches by the Hudson for two hours, physically unable to return to the office. The cold air didn't alleviate the pressure but worsened it to where she saw double. Almost sobbing, she called Lourdes from the half-maze of tasteful mulch shrubs outside a sushi restaurant. Farya had a hard time catching her breath as she explained why she couldn't do the exercises, couldn't quit her job, couldn't do anything.

"You won't believe me when I tell you this—but it's good that you feel this way," Lourdes said. "It means you're engaged with the world. Take a sick day—come over. I think you're ready for this."

✝

Lourdes had given her keys to the misplaced luxury building she owned on a stretch of wasteland astride the murky Brooklyn-Queens line, and to the peculiar spherical pantheon she kept in the basement. It had seemed a big gesture at the time. "It's a place you can always go, to do your exercises or just sit. I hope it will remind you that what you know is true, that you are who you suspect. Remember that you're not alone in this," the older woman had said at the time.

Trudging there from the subway, winter felt less like a season than an unalterable cosmic condition. The sun was down, and the sidewalk narrowed by hard, jagged snowbanks, the traffic crunching through dirty slush and road salt. Past the steel door and the empty doorman's desk, Lourdes was waiting downstairs, a pizza on a TV table between her and the folding chair for Farya.

"I thought you might be hungry," she said, gesturing to the cardboard box.

It didn't occur to Farya, but she was very hungry. The heat and grease of the pie took the edge off the panic. After a slice and a half, she took a deep breath.

"So, you've been having a hard time."

"Yeah, it's a lot of things. This new job is just, like ..."

"But you're doing the exercises?"

"I try. But it isn't easy in that corporate hellscape. I do them when I can get a seat on the train, and when I'm not too tired when I get home, at least when my bitch roommate isn't skyping at full volume ..."

"Well, you should know that whatever you're doing, it's working," Lourdes said. She smiled.

"What do you mean, working?"

"Come look."

Lourdes got up and showed Farya two new faces on the walls and ceiling of the room. The first, just below eye level, far from the door, was a wood carving of a balding young man with big ears and a chiseled jaw. The other, hanging by the room's hanging light fixture, was a painted wax bust of an Indian woman with big eyes and a pointy chin. Farya recognized them instantly. The man had batted above .400 for two straight seasons on the Mets and made some very cryptic, unflattering statements about sports fans before dying in an ATV accident. The woman was a famous comedian with a famous routine about pain being the measuring stick of all things. She'd since married a Hollywood heartthrob.

They were both faces that everyone knew. But Farya could tell from the quality of her own memories that they were nonetheless new to this world. Within her memories of them, she could hear the rustling of other pasts, which hadn't accompanied them. There were nations, conflicts, epic love stories, and scenes of incredible bravery or ingenuity on some sea whose eddies brushed against her like notions, daydreams, fantasies, non-sequiturs lingering a little too long in the mind. Lourdes watched as she examined the comedienne's features.

"But how?"

"You."

"Me?"

"I told you. The exercises are working."

"They are?" Farya asked. "It doesn't feel like they're working."

"Just look. They're working. And not a moment too soon."

"What do you mean?"

"I mean you're not the only threat to this little old world," Lourdes said. "It can use all the help it can get."

"Okay. But how can you even tell?"

"I've seen a lot, and I've learned when to keep my eyes open, and not to let things slide. It was the only way we could survive."

"We?"

"I … I mean I. I've always been able to remember the things that have never been. It's hard, but I don't need to tell you that. Eventually, it becomes normal, just another weather to watch out for. That's how I found Ethan. He had, to stay with the weather metaphor, snow in his hair."

"And Ethan just told you about it? About me?" Farya asked.

"It's not often someone asks you direct questions about this. Like you, he was dying to talk about it, at least on some level."

"But who else have you talked to about this? Who knows?"

"There's us," Lourdes said, lowering her voice. "But there are others, some more or less human, some inhuman."

"Like who?

"They're the ones who guided human souls after they stepped off the path of life. Some were helpful, others adversarial. It doesn't matter anymore—they're in business for themselves."

"But why would someone or something like that even *be* in business?"

"Now, if you had been a guide to other worlds, and you lost your job and your cosmic purpose, then you might be open to other offers."

"How would you be out of a job?"

"How many souls had lived in The Greater Anointed Imperial Ohioan Commonwealth, who now have no longer existed? How many in the Metro-Camden area?"

"Oh."

"So, these guides look for work. Some find a partner in the world of the living—and show those people how to make a buck out of the souls that they have access to."

"How can you make money out of a person's soul?"

"Same way you make money out of anything—consent, belief, creating assumptions, and coercing people into sharing them," Lourdes said quickly. "And these guides, maybe they knew that when you take someone's soul, you don't just snatch it away at death. Souls don't work that way. When you steal a soul, you steal it forever—forever before and forever after."

"But why would anyone buy a soul?" Farya asked. "What can you even do with one?"

"There's an essential *somethingness* of the world—a stubborn will to resist the appeal of being everything or nothing. It's present in all things, and it's at its absolute worst in human beings. That's why human souls make great fuel. And with every person walking around with their soul already bought and sold, the depression spreads."

"So, you're saying that there are people walking around without souls?"

"Kind of. For them, every day is like Sunday evening on a school night. An essential part of themselves has been put in pawn, and it's about to be taken away forever. They live in a state of dread and hopelessness. All they see and all they can create is the living death of cliché and routine."

"And what am I supposed to do about that? Make paintings? Throw more drinks in people's faces? Shout racial slurs in public places like a maniac?"

"If you have to. The exercises are meant to keep it from coming to that."

"And how do you know any of this?"

"Like you, the hardest way there is—by losing so many people and places and things that we nearly lost our minds. We jettisoned so much of what it had meant to be ourselves, to find the one hard center, the one undimmed spark, the narrowest, most harrowing passage. But this helps," Lourdes gestured around the room. "I look at these faces and remember that the deadening force of dead matter doesn't have to win."

"You mean celebrities?" Farya said, resisting the larger logic in small ways.

"Celebrity is just the result. After all, we seem to have more celebrities than ever. But they don't mean anything, don't represent anything, don't make anything, don't inspire anything. It's the characters who save the world every day—from boredom and depression. They make it harder to sell reality by the pound. And, hey, keep world destroyers like you from flipping ahead in the book of life to the end."

+

Pep talks and grand purposes only went so far in ameliorating the day-to-day commute, work, exercises, and sleep. Through long half-consensual afternoons in New Jersey, Farya passed the time trying to get a handle on her situation. Browsing articles online looked enough like work. But the internet was a terrible place to look for hints of lost worlds. A glimmer of memory from her childhood would lead into flat-earth theory, or into an all-inclusive conspiracy insidiously cut and pasted everywhere she looked.

Frustration piled on frustration. Her roommate, Jana, added photosensitivity to her roster of ailments. So now, in addition to Farya having to keep any food that had even a loose association with dairy, nuts, or wheat sealed inside both ziplock bags and airtight containers, the entire apartment was in constant gloom. Farya hadn't heard from her boss in weeks. And the wind off the Hudson that winter was so harsh that she was reduced to walking around the shopping mall at the foot of the adjacent office tower, all full of pretzel stench and teenage truants giving her the eye. By mid-March, even the simplest problems seemed insoluble.

The cold snap broke and Farya, along with the ten-plus million inhabitants of the New York metro area, started to cheer up all at once and all together. On the second consecutive day of warm weather, she went for a long walk past the upscale shops and restaurants of the corporate quarantine zone and the luxury-tower forest, through old Jersey City with its too-wide streets and grim, imperial post office to the crook of a highway and a marshy inlet.

She found a small record store, blaring tinkly guitar music from the Caribbean. Feeling heartened by the pearlescent blue spring sky, and having nothing better to do, she went in. The store was four aisles wide, with most of the racks empty. Some long-forgotten Spanish-language boy band pouted from the walls' few posters and CD cases. It seemed the proprietor was trying to unload the last of the stock before he sold or burned down the building. He'd already sold the counter in the front and had situated himself and a cash box at a chipped wooden door on two sawhorses. He didn't acknowledge Farya as she entered. A quick meander along the aisles showed that the stock wasn't broken down by genre and alphabetical order was an occasional priority. Farya continued down the aisle, losing the thread and recovering it all the way to the M's.

There, she found it—*Thelonious Monk and Tito Puente - Miami '72*—another impossible album. This one seemed more impossible than the first. She paid the man at the improvised counter and was feeling pretty good when her phone rang.

"Hey, Detective Ronnie Brimmer from Oneida County. Can you meet tomorrow, tomorrow night? I'm in the city for this thing, and something is still bothering me," the voice said, talking fast. "Sorry. Is this Farya?"

"Oh, yeah, it is. We met over Thanksgiving."

"Right. I was looking for Romeo Mauriello, and you came in. We had a very interesting conversation."

"Did you find him?" Farya asked. There was a long pause.

"That's what I wanted to talk to you about. I'm in the city for a few days this week, and if you're free, I'd like to continue our conversation."

Farya knew the risk in talking to the detective, though she couldn't completely articulate it. The overriding truth was that she needed someone to talk to. Lourdes was too distant, and Ethan was too caught up in his own problems. The winter at the insurance company, going to and from New Jersey, doing all she could not to throttle her roommate, had gone a long way to making her feel like an unhappy ghost haunting someone else's life.

"I don't want to go to a police station," she said, smiling despite herself.

"I couldn't take you to one if I wanted to—not my jurisdiction. I was thinking of a more casual setting. Maybe a drink?"

"Good," she said.

They made plans for that night at an old bar in Soho. Though it was in a neighborhood where she couldn't afford much more than a slice of pizza, Farya liked the bar because it was old and because they didn't play any music. The bartender was a burly bald man who, whenever the bar grew too noisy, would bellow SHUT UP, silencing the room for a moment before it started up again. Ronnie was starting his second pint when she arrived. He looked different, his long face leaner, his pitted chin grave with stubble and his sleepy eyes a little darker. When he looked up, Farya could see in his eyes how good she looked to him. She always took pains to dress well. It helped with the depression and hid her uselessness. And she did it for spite, to make the men look at her and the women look bad, to punish them all for their roles in her misery.

"Thanks for meeting me on such short notice."

"No problem. You said you found out more about Romeo."

"Not me—his mother. She made flyers with that blurry photo and started putting them up around town and in the supermarkets nearby, and she put my number on them. And it stirred people up. I started getting calls."

"Did the people know him? Did they remember?"

"Sort of. They remembered things about him, his sense of humor, that he was a big fan of the local teams."

"Yeah, the Camden Railsplitters."

"How do you know about that?"

"That he was a sports fan?"

"No, the Railsplitters," Ronnie said pointedly. Farya just smiled at him. "Until we started getting the calls, I thought that was just a joke, a daydream I had as a kid. I remember drawing their logo in my school notebooks."

"That's how things disappear in plain sight."

"Shit," Ronnie said. His beer came, and Farya ordered a glass of wine. He waited until the waitress was away before leaning in to ask, "The people who call, they remember Romeo, but what they remember is all connected to stuff that doesn't exist, and that never existed. When I ask them about the Railsplitters or the insurance company they knew Romeo from, they either get mad or else just hang up. And then there are the people who call and say that someone else is missing, but they don't remember their names."

Her stomach sank. Her wine arrived. She thought of Lourdes and the determined way she tried to keep the conversation light.

"Well, here's to picking our way through the rubble," she said. He returned her smile with his own bewildered version.

"But, seriously, I'm scared. Every time I look into this, I just get more confused, not just about the case, but about everything. I'm a cop. I meet people who are confused every day. And Camden's always been a strange town with more than its share of confused people. But these people, the people who remember Romeo, it's different. They seem fine enough. But when I ask them simple questions, they struggle. They have to correct themselves a few times when I ask where they went to high school."

"I don't know if you'll understand it much better over time. I'm not sure if I do. You just get more comfortable with the confusion, with how changeable it all is."

The conversation moved on, expanding as they drank and flirted. With that boulder of honesty rolled away, they could talk—Farya about her depression, her roommate, her joke of a job. Ronnie told her he had been drinking more and had moved out of the house he shared with his girlfriend.

At the end of the night, they were talking outside the bar about everything except where the night was leading. The street was busy—models and bankers and wealthy global youth pranced in and out of cabs and restaurants. A spring breeze blew in, clean and warm. Ronnie bent in, not awkward or sudden, raising his fingers to the corner of her chin, and they kissed. It had been a long time since Farya had been kissed or touched, and it was a welcome shock. The kiss lasted, and the others followed, like waves lapping on a pier.

Ronnie's face, his mouth was familiar. Ronnie kissed like Romeo. And maybe there was nothing more to it than a coincidence. But it threw Farya. It took her out of the moment on a spring-damp street and deposited her into a familiar deep gutter of shame and fear that seemed the inescapable crossroads of all her experiences.

She broke off the kiss. Ronnie could see the alarm in her eyes. Without knowing what for, he apologized. Then she apologized, and he tried to apologize once more, to be cut off by her apology. And a few seconds later, she was gone down Mercer Street. Crossing the street, a truck passed, and it seemed as though the city had closed behind her.

Bryan

Bryan, Bethanie, and the kids tried out the split over Christmas—Christmas Eve with Mom and hers, Christmas Day with Dad and his—and it seemed to work well enough.

After his week or month in Arizona, Bryan handled the divorce well enough. And the proceedings were smooth, mostly anticipated in the prenuptial agreement. The parts it hadn't spelled out were expensive but unemotional. Bryan was sad to part with a close friend and lover and haunted by a sense of personal failure. But those emotions were a relief from the terror and confusion that had opened up before him in Maricopa County.

Bryan got used to it. After so many years married—there were quite a few interested parties, widows, divorcees waiting in the wings, colleagues and even a few Metacom execuctrices who saw a time to pounce. He checked a lot of boxes: wealth the obvious one, coupled with the slow expansion of his stomach and reasonable rate of hair loss.

He made new friends with other successful, divorced men. That was about all they had in common, but they introduced him to things he could afford, but might not otherwise do—the super-expensive, model-choked Manhattan bars and restaurants, heli-skiing, golfing with dolphins. It was fun. And when it wasn't, it at least looked like fun.

By May, it began to wear on him. The guys seemed more interested in documenting their adventures than in enjoying them. He soon tired of how forced it all felt—the smiles, the lobster in everything, the just-cleaned boat decks, the security sweeps of VIP lounges, the gold on everything, the posing on the tarmac, the pretty young things of indeterminate motivation, the way that what was supposed to be pleasure all too often felt like revenge. In the midst of that high-class exhaustion, he'd allowed himself to be seduced, coaxed, and coerced into a relationship with Laurel—a tall, very pretty real estate lawyer who'd once won an Olympic bronze medal for women's handball.

Looming over it was one thing he couldn't ignore. Always in his rearview mirror, in the vast foyer of the condo he'd moved into, entering rooms before him and waiting just outside, Eamonn and his team reminded Bryan how his whole world could turn to chaos in a second.

And despite the money spent on investigators of all stripes, there was no sign of the people who'd taken him a few months before. When he wondered if it had even happened, he looked at the bill from Eamonn. The amount of money he was paying for security was enough to convince him that, yes, it must have.

✝

The night before had been the consummation of a thwarted teenage desire—a dirty, forbidden fantasy fulfilled, perverse like when rancid morning breath tastes good. But it had disappointed. The sprawling bed in the middle of the vast bedroom room was lit from the sides—a lamp half-obscured by thrown pillows and the distant glow of the bathroom.

Bryan didn't bother to wake her. But he also didn't bother to be particularly quiet. Leighton stirred but didn't bother to strike up a conversation. The situation was as naked as she was, on top of the sheets. And in that scene of carnal fullness, there was nothing but meat, old meat, and confused desires growing cold. Bryan dressed, wondering if every sensual pleasure would be so dim in the second half of his life, wondering if it had been as much of a letdown for her, and sort of hoping it had been.

"You going?" she asked, still sprawled, without moving.

"Yeah."

There was nothing to say because there was nothing at stake anymore. *Stuck*: The word summed things up for Bryan so damningly that he didn't dare think the word twice. Stuck in his business. Stuck on a financial treadmill, thanks to his tastes and the incredible cost of security. Even the divorce left him stuck, circling a second wife, who seemed more inevitable with each date.

The progress in Bryan's life was limited to his secret campaign to buy up the rights to his father's music. And though he and Leighton had come to an agreement months before, she never signed the papers. When he called, she made it more or less clear that what she wanted was this tryst, this avenging of a fusty lust.

Locating a shoe, he decided it was better that it was bad—she'd lose interest and sign the papers. Bryan turned his pants right-side-out and pulled them on, paced until he found his other shoe on the threshold of the hallway, and turned to look at Leighton. On her back, she had a splash of gray in her black pubic hair and a look of vague concern as she sleepily closed her eyes. After a wordless moment, he left. It was almost four in the morning—oblivion-late in the Maryland countryside of horse farms and gated estates. But the boys in the SUV were wide awake and started the engine as soon as the motion-sensor lights celebrated Bryan's exit from the manse's side door.

Driving through the darkness to the rhythm of suburban streetlights in a two-car convoy, Bryan wondered what Eamonn thought of the visit. A man visits his half-sister, stays for six hours, and leaves in the middle of the night. Would he have watched the turning on of lights in the house to form a story? Would he have inferred anything from the maid's departure? As they passed the postwar cape-style houses along the state highway, Bryan tried to count the more shameful things in his life: the ethics of his profession; the condition of his sanity; how goddamn stuck he was—all insoluble by any pile of money, and unmentionable to just about anyone. A mediocre dalliance with his half-sister, on the other hand, was a shame that he could clear up with a long shower.

The closest Bryan came to feeling unstuck was canceling an appointment. It was the weekend, so he made up for it by calling Laurel to cancel their date. A salesman he'd hired told him once that people can hear it on the phone when you're smiling as you speak. But Bryan didn't bother with any such artifice as he rescheduled their dinner plans.

The I-95 seemed like another way to be stuck, so Bryan directed Eamonn to loop west, into New Jersey. Despite lacking sleep, Bryan wanted to do anything except go home. He took out his phone and looked up the affluent suburbs and small college towns that might still boast record stores. Stopping into a store, he didn't linger, didn't savor the process as he had, but quickly bought up all the *Jimny Lomoigne*, *Union Skells*, and *Jimny Lomoigne and the Casual Bleeders* CDs and LPs that the little place had, paying cash, and making sure security couldn't tell what he'd bought. He had the itch, though each purchase scratched it a little less.

His mind looked for someplace to go. He looked in the bag full of CDs and LPs—and found a flyer for a record swap up in the wilds of Northern Jersey tucked in with the receipt. He had Eamonn pull over and showed him the flyer, and switched cars with Eamonn's partner. Bryan drove alone, windows down, sunroof open, classical music on the radio. He felt good.

The record swap was behind a new municipal building constructed for a volunteer fire department. By the time they arrived, the parking lot was full. A hand-drawn sign led him to the entrance. Eamonn went in first, and his partner kept close to Bryan. Inside, the place was shabby and bustling with wide-eyed collectors, sellers, and enthusiasts. After so long among money and its insincere opulence, the amateurism of the room sang to Bryan. He lost track of Eamonn, who set up by the entrance, and his partner, who trailed at a remove of a few feet. The sellers in their band and bar T-shirts—pallid from years in basements—noticed this, but mostly ignored the men in suit jackets.

Moving from table to table, Bryan bought up everything he could—mostly copies of the usual albums, until he met an obese gentleman with a precise beard named Roy, who had a stock of bootleg CDs made from the soundboards of Union Skells and Jimny Lomoigne concerts. He and Roy spoke for a while. Their conversation kept approaching but kept missing the point Bryan was driving at—how he could buy the master copies of the bootlegs, and how much they might cost.

But Roy kept steering the conversation to questions like *who can really own music?* This didn't suit Bryan at all. And while trying to skirt imponderables and return to the world of market prices and finders' fees, Bryan felt a soft, warm pressure below his ear, where his jaw and neck met in a crease. He turned to see, but there was no one near him. With his head turned, he did see a woman. The crowd through which he saw her dissolved.

She was pretty but so strange he had to check to be sure she was, only to find that, yes, she was prettier than he expected. She was strange but familiar like a mother, or a sibling, or like his own face. He'd never met her. He'd remember if he had. But he'd seen her, once, on a sidewalk one night, in what seemed like a different life, just months ago. It may as well have been a scene in a movie. *Eyes like the depth of night*—he replayed the moment without looking away.

Roy was still talking about the forced compromise of copyright law, impervious to Bryan's looking away. Bryan told himself to stop looking at the pretty woman with the strange face. He told himself he'd stop looking in just a second.

And in that second, she caught him looking, unguarded. Embarrassment forced a smile from Bryan, and the smile forced a small laugh, like an air bubble coming up from a century-old shipwreck.

She smiled back.

Farya

Romance wasn't the only thing that wasn't working out for Farya. *Thelonious Monk and Tito Puente - Miami '72* was a disappointment. Parts sounded as if they'd been recorded from a car idling outside. Other parts didn't sound like much at all—a mingle of cash register sounds and dishes rattling with the occasional piano or horn protruding from the noise. There was one track, "Epistrophy" with a driving Latin rhythm that clattered in and out of sync with the angular melody. The rest was a hash.

But it was spring. Trees blossomed, the restaurants placed little wobbly tables and chairs on the sidewalks, and the person she was supposed to be gave an impression of getting the most out of life. But the constant gray weight remained through the long day in the office, and there was too much chatter leaking through her earphones while she tried to do her exercises on a bench by the Hudson. She could only manage so much patience and had little in reserve for the inexpert boasting of the boy-men she tried to date.

There was one week, however, when Farya's boss asked her to work from the headquarters in Midtown. The acronym kept two redesigned floors in the building it had once owned. The offices there felt like an airport, with small pens divided at sternum level, and floor-wide white noise intended to give the denizens some remnant of privacy. The people at headquarters dressed better. They didn't talk about television and the lottery. Jammed in at a long table for employees visiting from other offices, the headquarters people regarded Farya as they did themselves—with a modicum of respect. And her depression lifted. Aside from waving hello to Emanuella in the narrow, too-bright corridors, Farya didn't talk to her until the last day at headquarters.

"Farya, you're still here?" Emanuella said across the table.

"Yep—you asked me to come in last week, and I've just kept it up."

"Good. You like it here?"

"I do. There's more, uh, energy."

"I guess that's one way to look at it," Emanuella said, widening her eyes in exasperation. "But you're going to have to head back there tomorrow. Someone in Jersey City asked about your cubicle. If you're not there, then they want it. And I can't be giving up cubicles now."

And the next day, Farya headed under the river to the pre-negated landscape of Jersey City office space. Farya killed time and walked out at 5:01 each day. Years later, what would astonish Farya most about this time was the sheer number of things she didn't allow herself to think about.

On nice days, she took as long as she could to get home, walking in lazy loops from the PATH to the subway, or walking over the bridge to Brooklyn. Life in the apartment had gotten worse. Her roommate Jana's ailments had grown more exacting and the treatments more extreme. As her allergies progressed, a container of lo-mien in the kitchen trash had become tantamount to—in the words of the lengthy letter pinned to the door of Farya's bedroom—a *literal bio-chemical assault*.

At the same time, a thinner, even more sickly-looking young woman claiming to be Jana's nutritionist had moved in. Of course, she hadn't officially moved in, not in the sense that she paid rent. But she had a key, and Farya suspected that she slept in a nest of throw pillows, quilts, and sweatshirts half in and half out of Jana's closet. The nutritionist was always in the apartment, scowling in disbelief at a cooking show on the TV she'd come to monopolize.

It seemed as if every week that spring, there was a new rule that Jana and her nutritionist created for the apartment. First, foods that contained dairy, wheat, or bore the suspicion of nut contamination had to be kept in sealed containers. Then the containers had to be limited to one shelf in the fridge, and one cabinet far from the sink. Then they had to be placed in special sealed, but biodegradable, containers before being placed in the trash. Then Farya was only allowed to eat them on one half of the kitchen table—the half with the chair where Jana liked to place precarious piles of pictures cut out from magazines. Then the nutritionist posted rules about the dishes that could be used, and when, and how long they could sit in the sink, and what soap could be used, and what kinds of sponges she was required to buy. The nutritionist had even taken to asking Farya about the detergent she used on her own clothes.

Exasperation extended everywhere. On her excursions to record stores around the five boroughs, Farya was not finding new Thelonious Monk albums.

One lovely evening in late May, Farya came home to find a plastic bag, triple-knotted, with two yellow rubber gloves beside it. In the bag, she could see the leftovers that she'd planned to have for dinner. Upon it was a note that read *Oppressor, Now maybe you'll understand what it's like to live with you. Your Victim, Jana.* Farya picked up the bag, which reeked of an ammonia-based cleaning fluid, and pounded on her door.

"Jana, what the hell? That was my dinner."

"It was your poison. Don't you even care?" Jana said. "A sealed container only works if you seal it all the way."

"You're buying me dinner," Farya said, pounding on the door.

"Only after you pay for all the food in the fridge that I had to throw away because you knowingly contaminated it—*plus* the food and the cleaning supplies and the clothes I had to throw away."

"You will pay me for that food, Jana. Open the door."

"Go away, or I'm calling the cops."

This went on for a while until the nutritionist finally opened the door to Jana's room a crack.

"She told you to go away," the wan woman said. "This is a violation."

For the first time, Farya noticed that the nutritionist was missing most of her back teeth.

"What about spraying my dinner with ammonia—that's not a violation?"

Jana had been between jobs for a while. And Jana was the nutritionist's only client. So, both of them had far more preparation and energy for the debate that ensued than Farya. In chronological order, their argument went as follows: Jana had no obligation to replace Farya's dinner; Farya's nutri-normative violation of Jana's rights as a gluten-resistant vegan was a human rights issue; the history of oppression against minorities, dietary and otherwise, had clearly taught Farya nothing. In response, Farya addressed: the irrelevance of the Civil Rights Movement to how Farya used her shelf in her refrigerator; the equitable distribution of apartment resources based on rent paid; the spurious nature of Jana's handicap. That led to a rapid point/counterpoint: Farya's poor diet and nasty attitude as being the reason she lacked a paramour; Jana's need to buy her own refrigerator or move out; Farya's need to buy her own refrigerator or else face prosecution by the ACLU and intense shaming from the highly motivated food-allergy groups on social media; the nutritionist's status as a non-paying tenant; the legality of the nutritionist living there, under the terms of the lease; the timing of the nutritionist's first rent payment; and finally the agreement to table the second-refrigerator question for the time being.

By then, it was two in the morning.

Farya went into her room and turned up the cash-register and glasses-tinkling sounds of *Thelonious Monk and Tito Puente - Miami '72* extra loud so that neither Jana nor the nutritionist could hear her cry.

+

"I think I need ... I think you need to drive," Ethan said, having parked off-parallel to the curb outside Farya's apartment building. It was Saturday morning, the beginning of an excursion Farya had been looking forward to. But Ethan was so drunk that his eyes didn't move in sync with one another.

"Great," Farya said just under her breath.

They'd been planning this trip for what seemed like forever. But the plan kept changing. At issue was whether Ethan could use the car, which belonged to his wife, Carolina, who relied on him for her green card, and who controlled his allowance. So Farya rented a car. And then Ethan said Farya might have to go without him. And so, she put out feelers to see if any of her new friends or would-be friends wanted to spend a spring afternoon on a road trip driving to the record stores in New Jersey. The week before, she'd just about convinced herself it would be fun to take the trip alone. But Ethan called, and talking a little too loudly into the phone, said he had the car, and he'd drive, if she still wanted to "see what's left of the USA from the luxury knockoff of a Chev-ro-let." She asked if he was all right, and he said he'd explain in the car.

And there he was, in a silver German sedan, elbows and knees banging as he lurched his sloppy frame over the console to the passenger seat.

"I see you started early?"

"Early? No, late. Too late. So, we going on a road trip or what?" Ethan said.

"Yeah. Just let me adjust the seat."

"Oh, yes, by all means, adjust the seat, calibrate the seat belt, synchronize the blinkers, polish the radio knob, alert the media, fondle the fontanel, prepare the preparations …"

Farya ignored him while she angled the mirrors and punched the first address into the GPS. As she drove, Ethan kept up a running commentary about the check-cashing places, bars, bodegas, hip restaurants, condos, scaffolding, construction sheds, cops—whatever passed his gaze, while she focused on cruising crossways through the cosmopolis, over bridges, down streets, and through tunnels. It wasn't until the responsive, quiet machine under her control could breathe a full gulp of unimpeded highway that Farya was ready to converse.

"What's going on?"

"What do you mean?" he said, taking a sip from one of the beers in the console.

"I mean you're drunk at ten in the morning."

"It's my day off, my day away. I'm just unwinding," he said with an angry laugh. "No. That's not it. Well, as you see, I've been allowed to use the car. And my accounts have been well-and-truly replenished by our friend the oligarch. So, it should be clear what's going on with little old me."

"No!" Farya said. She gripped the leather-sheathed steering wheel and looked over at her friend.

"Yep. She said we shouldn't tell anyone for another six weeks—so you didn't hear it from me."

"What the hell? How did this happen?"

"The usual way," Ethan said, looking down into his lap. "I don't know. She was on the pill, she says, but then she changed pills, and then said the new one was making her feel sick. And I guess her doctor said she would have a hard time having kids, so she didn't bother taking other precautions. And I got some condoms, but I guess the cleaning lady moved them."

"Are you serious?"

"Yep. The classic boy-meets-girl, boy-marries-girl-in-a-cynical-exchange-of-citizenship-for-financial-comforts, girl-takes-the-arrangement-more-seriously-than-she-said-she-would-even-after-she promised, boy-ignores-the-warning-signs-and-chooses-to-be-vague-about-his-own-feelings-hopes-and-dreams-rather-than-get-into-an-argument, girl-lies-to-herself-and-him-about-birth-control, boy-gets-trapped-for-life story. You know—that old classic."

Setting off a series of subtle alarms in the cockpit, Ethan unbuckled his seat belt and turned around on his knees to retrieve a backpack from the leg well of the back seat. Cursing the seat belt-reminder bell, he turned and buckled up with the backpack in his arms. Farya was still speechless. The car was quiet. Ethan had fallen asleep, holding the backpack like a stuffed animal, drool gathering at the edge of his lower lip.

He didn't stir when she pressed the door closed at the first record store on their tour. It wasn't a hot day, but Farya left the windows cracked. The store was in a white house like a barn, redolent with the welcoming smell of old LPs. Even at that early hour, a half-dozen people were flipping through the taped-up fiberboard racks, each with an imperious focus. Farya set off for the far corner of the place. She took a deep breath. She had been working hard on her exercises and suffering through everything else. She needed one more impossible album from the unknown discography of Thelonious Monk.

After loitering as long as she could stand, she arrived at the Monk albums and checked and double checked—the LPs, CDs, even the tapes on the cracked plastic racks on the wall, without joy.

In the car, Farya regarded Ethan the way Marista was tragic—unhappy and unhinged, but still young. Not sure if she wanted to wake him, Farya split the difference, pulled out of the spot fast, jammed the brakes, and proceeded to accelerate through the turns of the little New Jersey downtown on the way to the highway. But the only effect was to knock the backpack partway off Ethan's lap.

He began to snore as she neared the next store on her list, in Summit. The parking spot on a side street wasn't explicitly illegal, and Farya decided Carolina could afford a parking ticket if it was. As she rose to get out of the car, she fixed the backpack, which was about to tip out of Ethan's forearm. The bag was surprisingly heavy, and so she parted its zippered lips and looked inside. It was an unwelcome peek into her friend's mind: bundles of cash, some banded from the bank and others coiled in rubber bands, a plastic pint of vodka, and lastly, a snub-nose revolver.

Farya zipped the backpack and quietly closed the sedan door. She had planned a day of looking through records, and *Goddammit*, that was what she would do. Inside, she found nothing, even after she lowered her expectations and expanded her search. The few fellow browsers in the store were all men between fifteen and sixty, most of whom looked up from their searches with eyes that pled for someone to ask them about their T-shirts. One of them, a broad-faced, middle-aged man in a black Iggy and the Stooges T-shirt looked at her across the display case as she sighed, and said "No luck?" She shook her head, and he told her about a massive record swap two counties over. A second denizen chimed in to recommend it, offering the address. She asked the clerk at the register for a piece of paper to write it on, so as not to invite the sharing of phone numbers and so forth. Farya thanked the men and left.

On the sidewalk, she heard the train—New Jersey Transit. When Ethan had first withdrawn his offer to drive, she'd looked up the store and seen that this was the one store that wasn't too far from a station. She considered just getting on the train. Ethan was her friend and was in need, but he was also drunk and armed. But she thought of him alone, distraught, in New Jersey, thought of the gun, and considered the kind of questions directed at "the last person to see him alive," and continued to the car.

Ethan was curled up on his side on the leather seat, with the backpack at his feet.

✢

The record swap was up north, near the border of New York state, and the drive took an hour and a half on state highways. Past low office buildings, strip malls, shopping malls living and dead, Farya took it slow, not ready for Ethan to wake.

When the GPS instructed her to turn in a hundred yards, she eyed the woods warily. Farya cruised past an empty church building and spotted a magic-markered sign pointing to a low cinderblock structure with a full parking lot. Farya circled once before finding a spot on the edge of the lot near the dumpster. As she parked, the car went through its tasteful, elaborate ritual of powering down and saying adieu. Ethan woke.

"Where are we? Lunch?"

"Are you up?" she asked. Ethan, his face puffy and tired, nodded, looking at her half-annoyed and half-embarrassed. "Good, so what the fuck, Ethan? A gun?"

"Oh, that. Don't worry about that. Carolina's mother gave it to her last summer after she read something on the internet. I don't even know if it's loaded."

"You don't *know* if it's loaded?"

"How would I? I'm not a gun guy. I just figured that if I do make a break for it, go out and start fresh, then it's probably best if Carolina doesn't have a gun."

"But you think it's smart for you to have one while you're driving around drunk?"

"You know, I mean, with any decision, there are tradeoffs. Anyway, the gun was in the bag, in the backseat while I was driving."

"But what if you got pulled over?"

"I don't think it's that big of a deal. Carolina said her mother got us one with the serial numbers filed off."

"Filed *off*? I think that makes it worse."

"Like, legally worse? Like I said, I'm not a gun guy. I just figured if I was going to be venturing into a world of fake names and cash-only work that it might be smarter to have a gun."

"Is that where you're going? Is that your plan?"

"I don't know. I'm thinking about it, trying it on for size. It's better than sticking around and waiting for this kid so I can be on the hook for the rest of my life."

"Oh, Ethan."

"I mean, we're already out in the woods. We have a car. When will we have this open shot at freedom again? Why not keep going?"

"We? You want me to go with you? Have you lost your mind?"

"Is it so crazy? I'm your best friend. I'm the only one who knows about what really went on in Ohio, and now in Hamden."

"Camden."

"Right. I mean, who else would you run off with? Who else understands you? And it's not like you have much to stay around for. You hate your job. Your roommate is ripping you off and making your apartment into a squat for her nutso friends. I mean, if you're looking for a sign that it's time to mix things up—maybe this is it! They want to throw yokes on our necks—I say fuck them! Come on; we'll drive in shifts and see where it takes us."

There was a lot wrong with what Ethan was saying, but he wasn't all wrong. Farya looked out the windshield into the woods. A spring breeze shook the trees, creating a kaleidoscope of light and shadow on the brown forest floor of last year's leaves. Ethan's was a plan that was no plan. But they were still just young enough to live without plans. Farya considered it, considered what felt like everything before coming to Lourdes and her basement room full of faces, like an index of possibilities emerging and vanishing. And she seized on that, seized on the rare moments on warped Jersey City public benches with sunglasses and headphones on, while khaki-clad hordes of phone reps and order-processors walked past talking loud, when, despite everything, the exercises would go well, and it was like a broken and rattling piece clicked into place. She wasn't going to jeopardize that.

Farya placed the car's weighty key fob, with its stripe of inlaid wood, on the console. She unbuckled her seat belt.

"No, I'm not going to do that. I'm not, and you shouldn't either. You're not thinking this through. How long until Carolina reports the car stolen? How long until the money runs out? How long until you get sick of breaking concrete or washing dishes and you pull an even dumber stunt than this?"

"Long enough to figure out a better idea."

"Okay. Well, what about your kid? What about that?"

"Carolina's family has plenty of money. And what kind of dad am I going to be? It's easier if I don't try—less sad."

"So, it's not just dumb—it's dumb and cowardly."

"Dumb? Cowardly? Look around; the world is full of sad fucks who are doomed as hell because they never had the brains or the balls to make a break for it. This is my exodus, my liberation."

"No, it's not. It's a tantrum."

"Wow. What happened to you? You know what it's like not to belong. You know the world is a cheap con, a petty crime, and a shabby cover-up. Now you're all responsibility this and obligation that. When did they get to you?"

"I just wanted to spend some time with my best friend and look for records for an afternoon. You fucked up, and you're upset about it. And I get it. I'm here. I want to listen and help you out however I can. But I'm not going to skip out on my whole life just because you made a mistake."

Ethan's half-lidded eyes went to the key fob—an oblong device that could turn the car on at one hundred yards to get it warmed up or cooled off to a comfortable temperature before you opened the door. It rested on the creamy, softer-than-skin beige leather that covered most of the car's interior.

"Fine," Farya said. "It's a beautiful day. I'm going to go see these weirdos. I heard they have some cool music. You do what you want."

As the car door closed behind her, Farya heard Ethan mutter a phrase. She thought it was *fucking bitch* but decided not to be sure.

+

With redoubled determination, Farya went through the steel door to the back room of the volunteer firehouse. The only way to redeem the outing would be to find an impossible record. The room was spacious and spare, with whitewashed walls, a thin carpet, and a ceiling of too-bright fluorescent lights above the folding tables that filled the space, manned by collectors eager to show off and discuss their wares.

Looking around, Farya's attention snagged on a big black man in a pale blue polo shirt and a dark suit jacket. His meticulous dress and grooming set him apart from the slovenly collectors. A closer look revealed a clear wire running from the collar of his shirt up to his ear. With a thought to Carolina's oligarch father from St. Petersburg, Farya stopped in her tracks and scanned around the room.

Among the stooped, eager buyers and expectant sellers, she saw another equally burly and impeccable man. Roughly the same size, the second one was ruddy with dirty blond hair. Farya didn't want to be caught staring and went to the nearest table, where a long-haired man in his fifties was selling CDs and collectible cards commemorating the last century's science fiction films. Farya started flipping through clear plastic crates of idiosyncratically sorted CDs, keeping an eye on the well-dressed security guards, trying to figure out what was going on. But she watched the big men enough to figure out who they were shadowing. He was smaller than them but not small, older, but not old in a white and green polo shirt. She looked without seeming to stare. Nothing stood out about his clothes, his hair, or compact physique. Even his quality of bemused focus wasn't out of place at the record sale.

She moved to another record dealer, curious and glad for the distraction, stealing glances. When the man in the green-and-white polo shirt stood still for a moment, she got a good look at his face. Framed between a support beam and the bent head of a collector, Farya recognized him from a damp and humiliating night, months ago—like a needle emerging from a haystack to draw blood.

It was his face—alert, but with a brooding quality, as if seeing everything through the screen of some incredible debt. He turned and saw her looking and seemed, with a mild shock, to recognize her. He smiled.

Farya & Bryan

Bryan and Farya each smiled, not knowing if the other remembered, not knowing what the smile might mean. But having found each other, they found a way to find each other again among the collectors and sellers, moving from folding table to folding table until they were browsing shoulder to shoulder through the same cardboard boxes of CDs. Bryan saw a Union Skells album in a cardboard box that Farya was thumbing through but hesitated. At the edge of their subterfuges, an awkwardness rose up as they approached each other.

"Where do I know you from?" Bryan eventually said, his voice cracking, as Farya finished flipping through the box in front of her.

"I was just wondering the same thing," she said.

Bit by bit, they drew from one another the recollection of that early evening on a busy Midtown sidewalk, each adding a detail so as to make it easy for the other to add the next, so neither would seem to have remembered it better than the other. It was a kind of dance. They kept talking—about music, about records. It was easy, in a way that was rare for both of them. He told her he was Jimny Lomoigne's son, but not what he did with the records he bought. She told him she was looking for rare jazz records, but not how rare the records she was looking for really were.

Bryan's security duo hovered at what they considered a comfortable remove. Farya glanced at the door occasionally for Ethan. Regardless, their interaction was so perfect that after ten minutes or so, they wanted to end it before anything could ruin it. They exchanged information and said goodbye.

After she said goodbye, Bryan was left with his pile of Union Skells albums, and a bootleg tape dealer who suddenly had a lot of questions about Jimny Lomoigne, his family, and Bryan's motivations for wanting to find the people who owned the bootleg masters.

Walking to another table of records, a big, generous feeling washed over Farya, and she regretted how she'd left things in the car. So, she left off her search for the impossible discography of Thelonious Monk and went outside. The warm spring afternoon bolstered that generous feeling. Squinting in the daylight, she rehearsed a limited apology to Ethan. At the edge of the woods by the dumpster where they'd parked, she stopped. She found the thin brown paper bag from the record store in Summit. But Ethan was gone. Farya called him, but there was no answer. She paced the spot for a second, picked up her CD—a Herbie Hancock album. Stranded in the New Jersey woods, the purchase mocked her.

If Farya almost cried, it was at the betrayal by her best friend, and how the world had made them both into people they never wanted to be. She thought out the way home—a cab to a train or a bus, followed by another two trains. It was, however, a few minutes before she could bear to start looking at the tiny, slippery series of maps in her phone. First, she needed a minute to look into the woods and leave everything alone.

"Hey, are you okay?" said the voice behind her. Farya knew the voice and flinched from embarrassment.

"Oh, hey. Yeah, no. I'm okay. My friend, who I came here with, he seems to have left suddenly. I'm just taking a second to figure out the train, or bus, or whatever they have out here."

Farya didn't accept the ride he offered at first. Stranded, sniffling outside a record swap—so pathetic. And awkward—him offering a ride, trying to sound not creepy, her acting like she didn't need a ride. It didn't take long for Bryan to talk her into accepting a ride to the nearest train station. From the record swap, he drove one car, with his security in the SUV behind. It was a little strange, but she trusted Bryan. Maybe it was how Bryan carried himself. Maybe it was the softness in his expression, like an apology too big to ever finish waited on his lips. Once on the road, she said that since he was already going to the city, she might as well ride with him.

He was happy for the company. On that ride, their conversation stayed close to familiar shores—where they lived, what they did for a living, and music.

"It started in high school, I guess," Farya said. "I was in an honors program, and it was like everything was pulling in one direction—med school, law school—media, consulting, the executive suite. We were supposed to be these super-ambitious brainiacs. There was culture, even if the teachers only told us how Shakespeare and ancient Greece would help us make money. But one night, I was just driving around with some friends, and there was this music I heard on the radio—Thelonious Monk. Just the sound of it—like it knew music was a game that it didn't totally want to play. It was like it was in sync with a part of me I never knew how to even think about. It changed everything."

"Growing up, music and the music business were the whole world. They were the grain everyone went along with—the leather pants and the hair. So, it always seemed calculated to me. Rock and roll was as much a part of those tall buildings as insurance or coal mining."

"So, what did you rebel against?"

"Mostly against the leather pants and the eyeliner," Bryan said, checking the rearview mirror. "To me, it seemed like business, the bottom line, was the authentic part."

"How do you even do that, as a teenager?"

"I dressed like my friends' dads. I fought with my mother to take me to Brooks Brothers when I was in the eighth grade. It was lonely. I didn't like the kids who idolized my dad. But I also didn't have much in common with the ones who also wore polo shirts and chinos."

"So, that's how you end up a CEO?"

"I wish that was all. But it's more complicated. I didn't have a group I could belong to, so I was always looking around. And being that alone, I guess I saw some things—opportunities—that other people could choose not to see."

It wasn't easy for Bryan to talk about growing up. Traffic on the New Jersey Turnpike slowed down. A massive spring sunset was just beginning in the windows past Farya's profile, the soft orange light caressing her soft cheek.

"It's like you have to know things. But knowing it does you no good," she said with a faraway look in her eyes. "*Alas, how terrible is wisdom when it brings no profit to the man that's wise.*"

"Well said."

"That's from high school, a class called *Ancient Executives: Literature & Leadership*," she said, laughing. "Do you want to play one of the CDs you picked up?"

She started going through his bag, puzzling at the many duplicates.

"No, not right now. Let's just talk," Bryan said.

They crossed the George Washington Bridge, and Bryan talked Farya into letting him drive her the rest of the way home. They idled outside her faded aquamarine vinyl-sided building for a while, talking, saying goodbye a half-dozen ways before Bryan leaned across and kissed her. It was gentle, expeditionary. The next one was warmer, more urgent. As momentum gathered, Jana walked by, stopped, and stared into the window for just a little too long, and gave an exaggerated scowl when she caught Bryan's eye. Farya turned to see what the distraction was, and Jana kept walking.

For a moment, they looked at each other. It was a moment so nice it filled them both with a sudden fear of ruining it. And so, they said the last few good nights, and Bryan drove off.

+

Over the following days, Bryan's thoughts kept circling Farya. He found himself getting lost in small reveries about little, surprising things, like the line between the corner of her chin and the bottom of her ear. That bend, like the bend of a river, a lazy moment in the current where he had sat on long afternoons when he was young, free, and yet unspoiled by the world. Maybe that never happened, but she made him feel as though it had.

Since his separation, Bryan had been tutored by his divorced peers and a few women. So, he waited a few days before texting Farya. There was a terrible sweetness to those days—dwelling in possibility and dying of suspense, while spring exploded all around him. He was looking at her name and number on his phone when his reveries crashed to a halt.

"Shit. Shit, shit, shit … Shit," Bryan muttered for the next two minutes, typing in passwords, looking up names, and dialing the phone on his desk. The voice that answered was familiar, though hushed and a little out of breath. It was the common tone of a worried underling who rushed out of somewhere for an unexpected call.

"Ross, it's Bryan. Is now a good time?" The question was rhetorical and, he knew, more than a little menacing. "Do you have a pen?"

When Ross said okay, the word was muffled by the pressure holding the phone between his jaw and shoulder. Bryan said a phone number and asked the executive to repeat it back to him.

"Now, I want you to go into the system and wipe the Non-Mortal-Element Obligation from the contract associated with that number."

"Full release?"

"Yeah—complete. As if she'd never signed a contract with us."

"The system's really not set up for that. We'd need the forms from payments …"

"Right, the system—Ross, who owns the system?"

"We do. Metacom."

"Who?" Bryan asked. "Who owns it?"

"You do."

"Great. I want confirmation of the full release by three."

Bryan hung up, expecting to feel better. But he didn't. It was the sensation of that terrible dream—a father in captivity, a helpless son. It gnawed at him, insidious and malevolent, violating the anodyne sanity of modern furniture and sleek, off-white-and-chrome technophile decor of the office.

Across the Hudson, in Jersey City, in a white-bright and silent office, Farya was passing the time the way people pass kidney stones. The day had been a bad one. She'd slept badly. Ethan had called in the wee hours of the morning from someplace in the Midwest, full of drunk promises and panicked apologies, pleas, flattery, and accusations. The warm weather made the sitting places she relied on too crowded for her exercises. And Jana had texted in the middle of the day demanding that Farya pay half the cost of having a holistic mold-and-allergen inspector come look at the apartment.

But somewhere around two thirty that afternoon, all of a sudden, Farya's mood lightened, and she was filled with a sense of possibility as if what had seemed like the dead end of a long tunnel was just a bend, right before it opened onto daylight.

+

Bryan called, and Farya said yes to a date. He named a restaurant in Midtown, and, hearing a pause, said it was on him. It was the first awkward moment that shaped that night. The next came when security nixed the restaurant. He'd been going there too much, and they'd had concerns about it in the past, they said. The last-minute change was to a restaurant with bank-lobby high ceilings and floor-to-ceiling silk tapestries. Eamonn and his partner sat a few tables away, but with Bryan and Farya in their line of sight. Already self-conscious, the ostentation of the restaurant and the presence of security set her on edge. Bryan apologized and poured the wine.

"What do you do again?" she asked.

"I have a telecom company—cell phones, mobile devices. We're a discount carrier."

"What's it called?"

"The company's called Metacom. But you've probably heard of our brands—Communilutions Unlimited, Mobile Scenez, Phone Home, Touch Passport, Kinnections Global."

"Oh—I have a Touch Passport phone," she said. "You guys are everywhere. You, the bank branches, and pharmacies are going to be all that's left soon. Maybe a few restaurants."

"It seems that way sometimes."

"Does anybody ever stop to ask if it's a good idea?"

"People stop all the time. But they tend to keep on doing what's easiest."

"How sad. Do you ever feel like the whole world is tightening up, like everything is getting inevitable?"

"It's just human nature. You just keep doing what didn't kill you. That's the best most people can do. More wine?"

She smiled and raised her glass. He filled it.

"Well, that's not very optimistic. But it seems to have worked well for you," Farya said.

"Yeah—well, success isn't all it's cracked up to be. And when you look inevitable, like a winner, it gives people ideas. And that's why …" He gestured to Eamonn and company, drinking Diet Cokes. Bryan gave a little wave, and they nodded. "It's maddening, frustrating at least—like I can afford to do anything, but I have to check with my babysitters first."

"What made you hire those guys?"

"I was at a conference in Arizona, and I was drugged and kidnapped."

"Oh, my God. When did that happen?"

"Just before Thanksgiving. It was such a strange thing—completely out of the blue, just this total non-sequitur. Maybe I don't want to think about it. They were dressed up as EMTs. They drugged me, so parts of it don't make sense, and when I try to think about them, it makes me confused, and, anyway ..." Bryan poured more wine.

Farya asked him what didn't make sense. And in the strange aura of permission she seemed to radiate, he told her the whole story as best he could, from the meeting with Van Harappan to the hijacked ambulance to a month living on protein bars and strange paperbacks, to the unfunny punchline when the detective told him he hadn't even been missing an entire day. He was surprised, again, by his own honesty.

"So that whole month just never happened?" she asked at the end.

"I guess not. It just seemed like a month. I guess it still it does. I must have been drugged. But what drug does that?"

Farya shrugged. "Sometimes, things happen, and no matter how much you want to make sense of them, you just can't. Most people just try to hit 'delete' and forget them. It's the most natural reaction to an experience that you can't learn from, make sense of, or do anything with."

"And so, what? I should delete it?"

Farya shrugged again. A fresh bottle arrived, and the sommelier went through his little ritual and poured.

"To the inexplicable," Farya said. "To not deleting what you can't explain."

"I guess. You're the first person I've told the whole story to. I thought I'd keep it a secret."

They'd quickly developed a rapport—speaking in dares, each testing the limits of what they might expect of one another.

"Well, I'm honored. So now what? Do I owe you a secret?"

"Not unless you want to. I'm a big believer in secrets."

"Really? I don't know how I feel about that."

"It's more philosophical. I think secrets are essential to who we are, and even what we are. I was reading about our genes. We carry around thousands of strands of DNA from when we were fish and animals, even from when we were plants. And all of that is still there, but it has to be suppressed—kept secret—for us to be human."

"So, keeping secrets is what keeps me from becoming a fern?" Farya said, smiling.

"More or less."

"Is this the line you used when you were married?"

"I didn't use any lines when I was married. And I still haven't figured out how I kept from turning into a fern."

"Well, I'm glad you didn't," she said, smiling. "Just speaking as a customer."

"Is that what this is? Customer outreach?"

"I don't know—it's … surprising."

"It's something."

There was a long pause. The dinner part of the date was over. The bottle was corked, the check paid, the ride to Bryan's apartment was short. On the sidewalk and in the backseat of the SUV, under the watchful eyes of Eamonn and his partner, some sense of propriety held fast, until finally alone in the living room of Bryan's apartment, it gave way—each touch releasing incredible heat. It was an Eden recovered from years of disappointment and fear.

Bryan had his first happy dream in months—he was pulling plugs out of a massive slate switchboard. And as he did, the trees flapped their branches and flew away. They woke in the middle of the night to each other, and a moment so vivid and wonderful that they felt nostalgic for it as it occurred.

+

The next morning was a big dirty hurry. Farya woke late and far from home. Bryan had gone, leaving a nice note, telling her to stay as long as she wanted, which wasn't an option. Rushing out of the high-rise lobby, she calculated that she could get through a day at the office with just a new blouse. Her coworkers in Jersey City noticed very little.

She got off the subway at Penn Station and found a store that sold cheap office clothes to underpaid receptionists, assistants, and junior sales reps. The top looked fine even if it was itchy, but would do for the day, solid camouflage in the fast-and-cheap design of the cubicle pits. She was late but thought no one had seen her. But she soon received a series of forwarded emails from her boss, Emanuella. An obese pantsuit-clad diagonal supervisor of her boss sent an email to her boss, titled "Farya," whose contents read "Coming into the office today at 10 a.m. Did you know? Otherwise—not cool." Farya's boss, always fearful of losing headcount, covered for her, and said Farya had called ahead and cleared her late arrival.

But that couldn't bother her, nor could the late afternoon rain that pelted the energy-saving, suicide-resistant glass of the tower and kept her from the unlocked baseball field beside the firehouse behind the towers where she did her exercises. It was a nice feeling, and she wanted to talk to someone, to share it. So, she took the elevator down to the lobby and called Marista, who couldn't talk because she was at work. She even tried Ethan. But an angry stranger answered the phone and demanded to know who was calling. She called Lourdes, who answered, and invited Farya out that night—not in the spherical basement room of faces, but for dinner in Chinatown. The rest of the workday crawled toward its end.

The Chinese restaurant was a small place on a small street that smelled of fish and warm plastic. Inside, it had a small bridge over an artificial stream that had dried up long ago. Lourdes was waiting, and the first dish—smoked tea duck—had already arrived. They kissed on the cheek, and Farya asked how Lourdes was.

"Busy—a lot of people trying to get out of the bad construction they bought. You remember that thing in Long Island City last month?"

Farya nodded. Everyone did. A luxury hi-rise collapsed the day before the new owners were supposed to move in, and the debris tumbled into a nearby daycare, killing a pair of young children.

"Yeah. Were they a client?"

"No. But the lawsuits are flying—against the builders, the contractors, and now the owners, the ones who bought the cracker-box faux-extravagant crap. There's a time out on the graft that allowed these things to get built in the first place. So, everyone who bought a shiny pass-the-buck dump is getting out, and no one's buying. That's where I can come in and take buildings off their hands. But you said you had news."

"I don't know. Things are good. I met someone. I think I like him."

"That's great. You were due for good news, between the job and that awful roommate. How is Jana, by the way?"

"Fantastic—she's threatening to take me to small claims court for quote-unquote *molesting* her kombucha jar."

"Oh, my God."

"Yeah, turns out it was a rare culture, and I wasn't a nurturing presence. I just said it looked like beef broth gone bad. She says she can get her nutritionist—who's still living there rent-free, by the way—to testify to the mold's market value. But I can't be bothered by that."

"It sounds like things must be good."

Farya told her about Bryan, how they met, their ride home from Jersey, their first date. The cumin beef and bok choy arrived with beers in green glass bottles.

"It's funny," Farya said. "He's older, and grew up with this famous father, and he's really rich. But we seem to have a lot in common."

"Really? What do you think it is?"

"I still can't pick it out. I don't think he's like me, in that way. Maybe I think he has a secret. It's not like he's cagey. It's more like a void, a blank space that seems to pull on the things he does say. I guess I know that kind of misshapenness. I can catch it in the way I talk, and the way I do things. It's like because he has that too, I feel freer, more honest."

"You're talking about having a secret."

"I guess, but not a regular secret. A big one—big and central to every part of my life that I have to keep from thinking about most of the time. It's like he has that."

"Interesting. You said he's rich. What does he do?"

"He owns a company—cell phones, and things like that."

The tea duck caught in Lourdes's throat for a moment. She coughed, scowled into her plate, and took a gulp of beer to get her voice back.

"I was going to say, just be careful, especially with anyone that ambitious."

"He's not one of those. I mean, I met him at a record swap."

"Does he play a lot of music when you're around? Does he talk about music?"

"No, not so far. But we just started dating."

"What's his stereo like at his apartment?" Lourdes asked. Farya stopped to remember if she saw one. The pause was long. "I'm just saying there are people who are looking for opportunities in the places you wouldn't expect, places where you're just looking to live."

"I don't get that sense from him, not even a little. What's the problem with a fling?"

"Nothing; the problem is how desire can make you look at reality. You wind up telling yourself the wrong stories, just so you can pretend your desires make sense. And, in your case, that can change what the whole world *is*. But if what you want is this very smart, ambitious man, then …"

"It's only been one real date."

"All right, I'm done," Lourdes said. "So, did he text today?"

"Just as I was coming over, he …"

They stayed out for a while and chatted. Farya had more than the one beer. It was nice to talk to Lourdes about anything other than the destruction of the world.

+

It was a quiet day—Metacom was making money, with no deals on the horizon, no major crises to manage. Cassie Ocampo had grown into her role, feared in the building and respected outside of it. She did most of what would have once been Bryan's job, and freed him up—freed him into a corner. This was the Peter Principle in action because Bryan did not know what to do with himself.

He called Roger Hinterglitter, his father's former attorney and one-time business manager. In adolescence, Bryan had looked up to the paunchy lawyer, which puzzled his father and bothered his glamorous mother. Roger was flattered and always took time to answer Bryan's business questions over the years.

"Hey, kiddo. I was just hearing about you," Roger said before Bryan could say hello. "I got a contract from your sister."

"Half-sister."

"Well, I wish you'd've called me before you made this deal. Just about every individual or corporation that owned songwriting credits, publishing licenses, master recordings or master-use licenses has become rather hard up for cash. Anyway, if you called me, you might have only gotten half screwed."

"Screwed how? I got the publishing rights, the masters, all of it."

"You did. But you could've gotten it for a quarter what you paid."

"You may be right. But sometimes when you do business with family, that's just how it goes. So how are you? Still in the music business?"

"Sad to say, but I am. I never thought I'd say this, but there seems to be a fifty-fifty chance that I'll outlive it. These days, most of my job is mostly hard conversations with people who never thought the party would end. No money for me, no fun for any of us. Imagine spending three hours helping a guy who toured the world in spandex pants sign up for Medicaid. But you were always a smart kid—I have to ask why you're buying your way into the business."

"I'm not really. I've had a lot of things happen to me suddenly. And when I think about them, they weren't sudden at all. I just missed them as they built up, drip by drip. I don't want any more sudden things happening."

"Okay, I'd ask again, but then you might tell me."

"I heard a chorus from his solo stuff while I was in a gas station one day—not inside, but at the pump. It bugged me."

"The gas station, the ring tones—that's your mother. She was pretty smart about licensing. She got all she could out of those songs."

"I know, and that's why I'm calling. I want to track down those old deals and buy them out. I've already started getting the songs that I own off the internet. I'm also buying up all the bootlegs I can get my hands on. And I'm working on finding a way of getting the whole kit-and-caboodle out of the sharing networks, torrent sites, all of that. How much of that could you help me with?"

"I can help with about half of it, and I think I know people who can help with the rest. What's your game—are you trying to engineer some kind of scarcity?"

"Maybe," Bryan said. He knew that even a lie spoke volumes. The best bet was always to be boring.

"It can be done, but it's not cheap. And even if we're one-hundred-percent successful, that won't necessarily get you what you want."

"Why not?"

"If what you want is to drive a harder bargain with the streaming sites and the apps, good luck. I've seen others try it, and those parasites won't pay. What they do—the soulless vampires—is just hire a bar band or wedding musician to write and record some dreck that walks right up to the line of copyright infringement and plug it into that slot. And to be frank, no one fucking cares that it's not the right song, or that it lacks spark or craft or inspiration. To these motherless software quislings, music is like air-conditioning or tap water—just another bland utility you turn on to alleviate the horrific discomfort of being alive," Roger said with the conviction of a professional near retirement.

"Well, I'll deal with that later. I just want Dad out of the algorithm. When can we get started?"

"I'll start looking up those licensing deals this afternoon. And I'll get on the horn to my DCMA guy and my file-sharing guy."

Bryan's cell phone vibrated. It was a text, succinct and sweet, from Farya.

"Roger, that's great. Just send an invoice for a retainer."

"Last one out shuts off the lights, I guess. Anyway, I've always been proud of your success. And I want to see what you have up your sleeve here."

Bryan refrained from trying to tell the old wheeler-dealer once more that it was just personal—the old man wouldn't believe him. Turning off the speakerphone, he leaned all the way back in his chair and gazed at Farya's message.

Bernadette

Bernadette left the office later than planned, but got lucky—finding the one last working bicycle left in the Post Office Square bike-share dock. She felt in her purse, recovered her keys with the plastic tag attached, and unlocked the bike. It was a perfect Boston spring evening. A breeze from the harbor sweetened the exhaust tang in the downtown air. It was only a few weeks after daylight savings; the sun was still up when the offices let out, and everyone wanted to do anything except go home. A friend from college had been sending her photos of margaritas since four.

The ride to Back Bay wasn't long, but Bernadette was still learning her way around the twisting nest of downtown streets. She checked her phone and repeated the turns of the route and began to ride, carefully and with traffic, picking up speed as she grew more comfortable on the bike—a heavy thing with fat tires. The seat was big and her pants stretchy enough that she felt good pedaling harder, imagining the voice of her Soulcycle instructor as she did.

The owner of the red pickup truck parked outside the CVS in an old red-brick building was a big Red Sox fan and had mounted a pair of large Red Sox flags from metal poles on the tailgate of his truck. On the highway, the flags streamed behind it—the bold statement of a proud fan. Parked, the flags dangled almost to the ground.

The first raindrops of a storm coming in from the ocean were an hour away, but its first real chilly gust crashed into the street and whipped up the giant Red Sox flags, which billowed into the street. Its rough nylon fabric washed across Bernadette's face and snagged on one of her earrings. As it did, the earring yanked her face up and to the left. She was going full speed and extended her fingers for the bike's handbrakes. But the overload of stimuli as she decided whether to crash into the truck or let her earlobe be ripped out cost her the grip she had on the left handlebar. Blind and one-handed as she struggled against the pull of the nylon Boston Red Sox flag, she tumbled out into Summer Street.

The FedEx truck wasn't going fast and was already halfway past Bernadette when the flag swelled out into the street. The driver didn't think much of the small bump as the rear tires of the truck crushed Bernadette's skull. After a long winter, Boston was full of potholes.

It was the fifteen yards dragging the heavy bike, more than anything, that would haunt the driver for the rest of his life.

After an investigation and autopsy in Boston, Bernadette's funeral was held in Nashua, New Hampshire, where her parents lived. She had been young and well liked. For many of the people she'd gone to high school and college with, she was the first person they knew who died. A good student, always friendly, and not prone to any of the excesses that often mark early deaths—Bernadette's funeral laid everyone bare. Hundreds of people attended the wake over the course of two days.

The funeral home was a large, white, clapboard house around the corner from a towering granite Catholic church. And it had been in business and in the hands of one Doherty or another for almost two hundred years. In the family, there was always at least one son or cousin with the right temperament for the business. Tom Doherty came into it young, taking over for his father just a year out of mortician school. It suited him—husky and conservatively groomed even as a child, he'd always come across as older than he was. He listened well, never eager. Stolid in the face of tragedy, his conversation hovered close to the weather and the obvious. This was a tragedy—the young ones were never easy services.

Not long after the funeral notice went up in the paper, a lawyer called from a large Boston law firm involved in the case around the accident. She said she wanted to see the body. Tim Doherty went online and looked her up. She checked out.

She came at night, between the two days' viewings. She was a city woman who could have been Italian, Jewish, Portuguese, or Spanish. The man with her, she said, was a photographer. The man bothered Tim—his eyes, or the way he stooped, or the fit of his suit, maybe. Tim owned a lot of suits, and he saw a lot of suits. You could tell a lot about a man by his suit, he believed. The photographer's suit was expensive, a very fine wool. But the double-breasted cut was decades out of fashion, and a poor fit—too tight around his chest and too loose around his arms, the shoulder pads jutting and the upper part of his sleeves hollow. And the eyes—too dark around the edges and too bright in the whites—made Tim uneasy, reluctant to look him in the face. That struck him, as it went against his professional instincts.

Still, he showed them into the basement, where the coffin was being kept in a large refrigerated locker.

The lawyer asked if they could be alone with the body. A stickler, Tim said no, he couldn't allow that. Even if she and her Boston law firm did check out, he'd heard too many stories. The cameraman with the ill-fitting suit put down his case just outside the door to the locker and began to speak. He had a deep voice, almost like multiple voices in harmony. "I think that you ..." and the *oo* sound of the word seemed to stretch out in a way that put time itself on a treadmill so that none of them could seem to get past that syllable.

Bernadette knew where she was but had a nagging sense that she belonged elsewhere. She looked around at the walls of the metal room. Sitting up, she looked down at her cream blouse and lavender sweater—not what she would have chosen. There were three people in the room, but only one of them could see her. She didn't want to be alone with that one, the man. He was off, like his insides had been removed and carelessly replaced.

"Bernadette Haverstraw?" he said.

"Yes?"

"That is your name, correct?"

"Yes."

More questions followed. Bernadette was disoriented. A dream pulled at her with almost physical force. But the man had a way of holding her stare with his eyes. He kept asking questions, and she didn't want to look away, didn't want to be rude.

Address, phone number, phone model, service plan, date she bought the phone, where she bought the phone—she answered each. The dream of a world outside the room pulled at her and made her want to interrupt, perhaps escape. But she didn't want to offend the stranger, didn't want to break what felt like a lot of rules. The man seemed very serious, and he had taken time out of his day to see her about this matter.

He locked his odd eyes on hers, almost in hers, as he bent to his case and retrieved a thick, stapled stack of paper. At the top of it, she could make out the *Touch Passport* logo. It was, she realized, her mobile-phone contract. The man peeled open the contract to the last page and held it close to his eyes.

"Is this your signature?" the man asked.

Bernadette looked down, but now she found it almost impossible to look away.

"Yes. If you don't mind, can I ask what this is about?"

"It's about the contract you signed. According to the terms that you agreed to in this contract, you will have to come with me."

"But I don't want to—I want to go …"

"Go where?" the man asked, smiling.

"To the … I don't know."

She didn't. Though the dream pulled at her so that her entire body shivered, she could not imagine nor name it.

"So, you don't know where, and yet you want to violate the contract you signed to go there?"

"Yes. What if I do?" she asked.

"Do you know what a contract is?"

"Yes."

"Do you think that if you break a contract, you have broken the law?"

"Yes."

"Do you think that if you break the law, there will be a punishment?"

"I think that if the law is about a contract you didn't even read …"

"Yes or no: Were you given the opportunity to read the contract?"

"Yes."

"Yes or no: Were you forced to sign the contract?"

"No. But I had to get off my parents' plan, and I had no credit history out of school, and *Touch Passport* …"

Bernadette explained the whole situation from when she bought the phone—the shopping center, what phones her friends had, how she wanted to establish her independence so she could skip Thanksgiving that year. The man didn't interrupt her this time.

But as she spoke, Bernadette told the story to herself. And the story was bad: She had given away a possession of inestimable value in exchange for a momentary escape from inconvenience, for an unconvincing illusion of freedom, for a mobile phone. She had done so as an adult. And there would be no takie-backsies, no forgiveness, no mercy.

She asked more questions, which the man answered with more questions. He had infinite patience, it seemed. Painfully infinite. But all the questions ended with the same answer—that she would have to go with him.

"—will find that we won't need to take up too much of your time at all," the cameraman said to Tim Doherty.

The strange man smiled and bent to his case, which he was now buckling shut. The air seemed to whistle, and Tim felt lightheaded, disoriented. Blinking, Tim tried to remember the signs of a stroke or a heart attack. It took a second to pass, and when it did, Tim tried to put it out of his mind. The lawyer and photographer were satisfied, it seemed.

Confused, Tim did, however, ask the lawyer for her card, which she produced without hesitation. He read it to himself to drown out the low whistle-roar of his headache.

It checked out.

Bernadette found herself in an airplane, aisle seat, economy class. Fake dark blue leather in front of her, and a pile of safety cards and in-flight magazines in the seatback pocket. She tried to close her eyes, hoping to pass some time before takeoff, and maybe the long flight itself, with a nap.

But she could not close her eyes. This puzzled her, and there was no flight attendant to ask about it. It seemed clear from the hush of her fellow passengers that they were too near to takeoff for her to get out of her seat. She tried to turn to ask a fellow passenger for some kind of help. As she formulated a way to express her problem, she realized she couldn't turn, either. She could shift her gaze from aisle to seatback pocket to seatback, but nothing else.

A long time passed. Nothing happened, so there was no way to tell how long. Bernadette's panic gave way to a misery that seemed to outlast every trick and stratagem she could concoct to contain it. In that long misery, she could sense the reason that she could not turn or blink: They were too near to takeoff, and she wasn't allowed.

Her heart leaped with relief when she heard the engines rumble to life, loud and deep. Flight attendants walked down the aisle as they might do for the safety-and-seatbelt-song-and-dance. But unsmiling and plain-faced, they carried images on poles: pictures of children, beach scenes, cattle in pastures, Greco-Roman architecture, sprawling feasts, pink Cadillacs, golf greens, and on and on. They stopped at the front of the cabin, the bouquet of icons covering their faces. Bernadette put the display off to airline marketing.

The roar of the engines deepened, followed by the motion. But it was an unexpected motion, a twisting. *This is wrong*, Bernadette thought, finally having no choice but to think it. That scintilla of outrage gave her permission to glance sideways. Seeing past her paralyzed seatmate to her left, she could discern that the aisle itself wasn't six people across, as she'd assumed to have seen. The aisle was thousands of people across, bending upward in a vast curve.

The engine-sound intensified, and the twisting sped up. Bernadette's row moved in one direction, while the row in front of her rotated in the other as if they were in some kind of vast rotor—wheels within wheels. *But you had to trust the airline—otherwise you would never have gotten on the plane*, she thought. *Right?* The fact that she had gotten on the plane meant that the plane was trustworthy. And there were no announcements, nothing wrong.

Like that, she lost the courage to take any more sideways glances. Seatbacks spun past, a dizzying blur that forced her gaze at the distant cluster of images at the front of the plane—someone's idea of a good life. She was flying with those images, and the speed was incredible.

Without a jolt or a warning, the plane crashed. It crashed and crashed. It crashed for years, for centuries it seemed. Seatbacks bent and burned and twisted into and out of new shapes. And Bernadette was thrust into an ever-unfolding eye of fire and debris. For longer than she'd ever imagined time could last, the crash continued. She had permission to scream and to flail, to sob and moan, but not to leave her seat or look away.

When the shock of the burning crash loosened its grip on her, Bernadette tried to think of something beyond the chaos surrounding and devouring her. So, she thought of her house growing up in Nashua. It was a split-level ranch built in the sixties on a suburban horseshoe lane overshadowed by a steep and rocky hillside. She thought of the house's dark green paint, the wall-to-wall carpet in the living room, the washer-dryer room off the garage, and the finished basement where her older brother moved in high school.

It was the first thing to come to mind she could hold onto. After eons, the debris accumulated and dimmed the fire. The debris cooled and hardened, and the swirling ring of tormented souls around quieted and smoothed into a dusty horizon. After what she could only guess was a thousand lifetimes, Bernadette rose from her dark-blue faux-leather economy seat. She was older and alone. She looked around, and there was a world—blue sky, dirt ground, a rough simulacrum of that same suburban ranch house made of logs and mud and thatch, on the edge of a scrub forest. This was a bad world, she knew, without having to be told. It belonged to someone else.

Time passed. But it was small and slow time. It was time counted in days and years. Bernadette walked this new earth. And wherever she wandered, she seemed to find the ranch house in the bend of hills, the jut of granite outcroppings, and the empty shadows of pine barrens. As a proper house, it popped up over hills and past streams, sometimes inhabited but often abandoned. The people in this world were often ragged, mad, violent, or crippled.

She returned to the log ranch house where she started and lived alone at first. Over time, the world filled up. Bernadette even had babies. They grew up. Sometimes, a giant spider would come in the night and take one, leaving the child's drained and lifeless body in front of the porch. But the spider didn't take all of them. And she had always known that it was a bad world, without mercy, when she came.

After their daughter died, Mr. and Mrs. Haverstraw stayed on in Nashua for a few more years. But the memories of their daughter had a cruel way of springing up just when one of them was on the cusp of having a nice day.

The Haverstraw house sat on the market for a long time. They lacked the energy to fix it up, and the emotional wherewithal to be reasonable and sell it cheap. Eventually, real estate prices rose, and someone did buy it for the land. Bernadette's parents moved to Florida, outside Sarasota, where their son and his family lived. They knocked the house down and put up a tacky three-story faux-colonial that filled most of the lot, and made the new owners no friends among their new neighbors.

Years later, the Haverstraw son was in Boston on business and decided to go look for the house where he'd grown up. He parked across the street from the oversized agglomeration of gables and decorative shutters and shook his head for a moment before driving off.

But the green split-level ranch wasn't gone. In another world, the house was a common feature of the landscape, the natural world, and even of the very thinking of its inhabitants. The split-level ranch house was a form so pervasive there that in the tens of thousands of years and the hundreds of sophisticated civilizations that would rise and fall in that bad world, no one would ever need a name for it.

Farya & Bryan

To Farya's delight, Bryan ignored that year's dating protocol and called her for another date that same week.

"Are you going to change the restaurant at the last minute again?" she asked.

"If I tell you that now, it'll lose its effectiveness, tactically speaking."

"I like a man with tactics."

"Just you wait."

They met downtown at a very small Italian place whose tiny dimensions had kept it in business and unchanged from the previous century. Oil paintings of gondoliers and dried flowers hung on the brick walls. They sat at the rear of the restaurant, and security sat two tables down. The place filled up fast with bodies and conversation, affording some privacy.

"I was talking about you to a friend of mine," Farya said. "I told her you were a CEO, and she said to be careful."

"Oh, really? I'm flattered. I thought I was too old and too well fed to be considered a threat to anyone. What did she warn you about?"

"Ambitious men."

"Yeah, I wish someone had warned me about being an ambitious man."

Farya gave a look through the crowded restaurant to the two big men, one black and one white, both professionally nonchalant, who nonetheless stood out in the casual, romantic atmosphere.

"So, you're not ambitious anymore?"

"I don't know. I was, and it worked for me. Or maybe I worked for it. It changes over time, though—it's a little like the saying about the guy who rides into town on a tiger. Everyone in town says *wow, look at that guy on the tiger, he must really be something*. But all the guy can think is *how the hell do I get off this thing without getting killed?*"

Farya laughed. So did Bryan. The time and conversation flowed with good food and wine, the honest moments rationed in a pleasant rhythm between bouts of banter. And even those evasions weren't a disappointment, but an extension of suspense. Midnight found Farya laughing, hilarious, on a roll. The point of her nose sharpened the corners of her smile, and her big eyes glinted in the candlelight.

"So, this crazy woman, this MS-Office garbage fire of a middle manager with her Ivy-League communications degree, who calls three-hour department meetings to freestyle on the balance-sheet value of marketing—she decides to snitch me out for being an hour late to a job where my main function is keeping my cube safe from the other drones."

Red-faced with laughter, Bryan repeated the phrase "*MS Office garbage fire.*"

"Seriously," Farya said. "This bitch would do a PowerPoint at her own mother's funeral."

"I think I've sat through that. I know the template—the opening slide with her name and the years, then the animated dissolve to *Mom's Life—Key Points and Objectives*."

"Then the bullet points: *Beloved Mother, Celebration of Life, We Had Our Disagreements* …"

"With the funeral-home logo sponsor tile in the lower right-hand corner," Farya said.

"Good thinking—bereavement marketing."

"Don't steal my idea! I knew I should be careful around an ambitious man like you."

"You could do up the caskets with corporate logos, like race cars."

The wine and the laughter made Farya bold. She drew in close.

"How do comedy routines like this fit in with honesty?" she asked.

"I guess they prove that there are ways of telling at least some gut-wrenching truth without wrenching your gut. They prove that honesty isn't everything."

"So, honesty doesn't matter—it can wait?" Farya said, testing a premise, not sure what answer she wanted.

"It better wait," Bryan said, with a little laugh. "Honesty is that we're all dirt in the ground, and then nothing matters. So, delay, delay, delay."

"I'm sorry. Am I being a downer?"

"Not at all. I miss talking about big things—truth and lies, life and death. I make too much small talk where the whole purpose is never to broach the subject of who's lying and who's telling the truth. I talk for defense, like a squid spraying ink. I leave the real things unattended."

"Unattended—I like that word. So sad—even when it's just luggage."

"It is. And I used to talk like this more when I was young. I loved to argue about this stuff."

"What happened?"

"It turned into a business."

"The phone business?"

"Sort of. It's a very long story."

"Ooh, very mysterious."

"Not really, not when you really look at it. I mean, look around—people take better care of their phones than they do of their own hearts."

"I guess you could say that. I mean, if you lose your phone, you have to tell everyone you know, apologize, and make arrangements. Otherwise, they'll think you're dead and give away your cubicle and your bedroom. But some days, you lose your heart …"

"… and no one would notice even if you told them."

They spoke in poems, as people tend to do when they fall in love.

✢

Both knew that this was no halfhearted wait-and-see affair, but a rare occurrence, a butterfly among shifting patches of sunlight, a constellation seen at noon. By the end of that week, Bryan broke things off with Laurel, the lawyer that he'd been dating. He did it in what he considered to be the right way, in person, at a restaurant near her house.

Impeccable as always, she handled it like an exit interview, asking for his evaluation, followed by a bloodless critique of the way that Bryan had conducted himself during their courtship. After making it clear that she was, in fact, breaking up with him, they split the check. While they were waiting for the waiter to return, it started—Laurel's chin retracted from its usual confident gem-like jut, and she began to cry. It was a terrible blubbering, both uncharacteristic of her and out of place among the candles and tablecloths. The words in it were hard to retrieve. Bryan could make out *you*, *me*, *try*, *nothing*, *never*, *good*, *future* repeated in between big sniffles and tamped-down sobs.

Stunned at the break in her persona, he reached across the small circular table to touch her shoulder, but she brushed off his hand. Stifling a moan, she signed her receipt and took her card. When he rose to say goodbye, she barked a very clear, "No," that won the attention of every diner not already watching. Bryan tried to make up for the embarrassment with the tip he scribbled on the receipt. The sensation of writing the exaggerated gratuity in ballpoint pen stung: another apology misplaced, and ultimately inadequate.

Eamonn followed him out of the restaurant to the SUV where the driver waited.

"Well," Bryan asked. "I'll ask. How bad was that?"

"Could've been worse. Next time, you could give us a heads-up, so we'll be ready when a woman wants to throw a glass of wine in your face," Eamonn said, his Queens accent emerging for the punchline.

✢

Bryan and Farya spent most of the summer together. Being together was easy, and they had little to distract them. Metacom was growing. Farya's job remained a beige blur of depression but continued to ask very little of her. It was an idyllic time of late nights, sumptuous mornings, and long weekends.

There were problems, but they felt far away. Ritchie Reach was awaiting trial after his live-in girlfriend overdosed on a veterinary tranquilizer in a way that the Port Jefferson police found suspicious. And Ethan had returned from his walkabout, though

Carolina required he submit to a stint in a mental hospital and another in rehab before she'd take him back.

After a series of heartfelt apologetic emails, Farya agreed to meet Ethan one Saturday afternoon in August, when the subways smelled like ozone. They met at a juice place near his apartment in Murray Hill. Farya got the sense that Carolina didn't let him wander too far anymore. The neighborhood was busy with hungover brunchers and jogging overachievers. Ethan wore an oversized button-down shirt, untucked to conceal the twenty pounds he'd gained, and a pair of rustic-expensive tan sweatpants. Waiting at a table on a concrete patio two steps up from the sidewalk, his sweat caught the sun.

"Hey, thanks for coming. I got here early and didn't know what you might want, so I got a few different juices and smoothies," Ethan said, nervous, talking fast, gesturing to the five plastic cups of different colors on the steel table. His eyes seemed to bulge in a new way.

"Oh, yeah. Maybe I'll just have the … purple?"

"Yes. Good choice. That is a blueberry protein cayenne circulation booster. Great. It is so great to see you."

"I know. Sorry I couldn't make the, uh, graduation. We were out of town, and Carolina didn't tell us about it until the day before."

"That's okay. It was just a little ceremony to build the support network. Not super important."

"If I had known sooner …"

"I know—it's just I think Carolina still sees you as a kind of trigger—or an enabler—for my addictions."

"Which addictions?"

"The drinking, the drugs, the overeating, the secrecy—all the addictions and addict behaviors I went to the hospital and rehab to clear up, you know, before the baby comes."

"I guess I never thought of you as an addict."

"Come on—when did we ever meet *without* a drink?"

"I mean, sometimes. But it never seemed like a problem, exactly."

"Not even when I was drinking cheap vodka out of a flask, driving you to weird record stores in a stolen car? Really? It didn't seem like a problem then? Do you even know what an enabler *is*?"

"I tried to talk you out of that. And I didn't let you drive drunk for most of the day. You slept while I was there. You took off after I told you that I didn't like how you were acting or what you planned to do. I think you called me a bitch, even."

"That was the disease. I'm sorry."

"Disease?"

"My addiction."

"Addiction. Ethan, I'm your oldest friend. Do you really have to do that with me?"

"What?"

"Pretend that it wasn't even you—pretend that it wasn't just you getting drunk and running away because you saw that you were about to get stuck with a woman you don't really like, and you got scared. I mean, why blame it on a disease? You were doing what you wanted to do—to get out of raising a child with Carolina."

"It's a boy, by the way. He is going to be a boy, I mean. But thanks for asking," Ethan said, pouting at the green swirl in his cup.

"Nice one," Farya said. A small curl caught on the corner of Ethan's mouth. He tried to flatten it but couldn't stifle a laugh.

"You're a real shit; you know that?"

"You have no idea. Especially with this whole new *the-devil-made-me-do-it* loophole. Oh, my God!"

"So, what the hell are you going to do?"

"I figure I'll drink juice and play the good husband until the kid is born. I'm not sure what this addict thing entitles me to besides being treated like some kind of criminal retard by every boring asshole in my life. How many relapses do you think I get a year?"

Farya chuckled, but it was hard to ignore that Ethan's whole spree was irrevocable, and not in a good way. The baby would come with a whole world of new expectations and obligations. And Ethan had just collapsed all his clever and idiosyncratic personality into a sickness for everyone around him.

"But seriously," Ethan said. "Carolina's father's going to set me up with a storefront in Brooklyn—we're looking at a few locations. It'll be a boutique slash gallery, very curated. We'll have deejays and maybe a juice station. Once that gets off the ground, I was thinking of getting into painting."

"Really?"

"Yeah. I mean, I won't *paint* the painting. But I know what sells. My plan is to freeze frames from movies and TV, and blow them way up, and hire some painter or art student to paint them up with oils, really high quality. I'll sign them with my name and sell them out of the boutique slash gallery."

"I, personally, hate that plan. But I bet it'll sell."

"Right? Fuck these jokers. Anyway, I need to get Carolina's dad to sign a big, expensive lease before the baby comes and I'm relegated to diaper duty forever."

"Well, cheers to that," Farya said. They raised their bright, sweating juice drinks and tapped the plastic lids together.

"And what about you? God, that's such addict behavior, to go on and on and not ask about you."

"Save the addict stuff for when you forget to pick up your kid from daycare. You'll always just be an asshole to me."

"Ouch. But I won't have to. We're getting a nanny, plus a night nurse for the first four months."

"I don't know what that means."

"It means, how are you? Who's this guy? You keep saying 'we.'"

"It's kind of crazy. I met him at that last record place in New Jersey when you ran off with the vodka and the gun."

"Oh, right, the gun."

"What happened to the gun?"

"I lost it somewhere in the Midwest. My little contribution to … well, I can only say *I'm sorry* so many times. So, you met this guy at the record thing, in the … what even was that place? A truck hospital?"

"Firehouse. But yeah, we'd sort of met once before. But we first talked at the record swap. And for reasons I don't need to explain, I needed a ride home. And things happened from there."

"You're welcome!"

The smoothies may as well have been cocktails. They laughed and clowned at the steel table in the high-rise's concrete plaza. The reflected rectangles of light from the condos' glass curtain walls played on the passersby. She told him more about Bryan, their courtship, his background. He told her about a gruesome entertainment he'd endured on the outskirts of Oklahoma City that had, coincidentally, reached its peak to a well-known Union Skells song that played from a pickup truck whose headlights provided the necessary illumination.

"So, look at you," Ethan said. "All happily-ever-after with a dashing captain of industry."

"If only."

"What do you mean? It sounds like the end of one of those terrible movies."

"There are issues. He has two kids. They're in boarding school, but they're not going anywhere. And there are a few things that make it hard to date. You start to see why rich people date other rich people."

"What about me and Carolina?"

"You never dated. You were, as you put it, occasional and casual until she had to get a green card or go back to St. Petersburg. Anyway, the problems are all good problems, but it can be uncomfortable. He wants to go to these restaurants, and he always has to pay because I can't afford it. Or he wants to go to France or out to the Hamptons for a week. But I have work, and only so much vacation time. And he's nice enough about it, but I know it's not what he wants."

"Easy—quit your job. Boom, you're welcome again."

"And be what? A paid girlfriend? Some kind of leisure employee? No offense. But I have to think ahead. Say I quit my job and just go on vacations with him for a year—how long before he loses respect for me? How long after that until he loses interest? Then where am I? With no job and a big gap in my resume?"

"I guess that's the price we must pay for being irresistible to the global ruling class," Ethan said, offering a big, cartoonish smile. Farya laughed. "And by the way, that reminds me, I have to go—I have a narcotics anonymous meeting in ten."

The old friends embraced hard. Ethan walked off with a skip in his stride and a sparkle in his eye.

+

There had always been a vindictive quality about Farya's job in Jersey City. They didn't allow her to wear headphones, show up late, take long lunches, or work from home. But they gave her precious little work to do. After six months of chipper volunteering on each email chain and conference call, she gave up. Less a profession than a chronic condition, it exhausted her and distracted her from getting around to her exercises or finding a new apartment.

It was a warm night in early October, and the open windows of Bryan's apartment blew in the clear, eager sounds of the city—rattle of trucks, shards of conversation, car horns, and birds. He was in the middle of making them dinner—sautéing fish—when he suggested taking a long weekend at his house upstate. Farya felt her mouth tighten.

"Listen, I can't," she said interrupting. "I'm sorry. I've already taken too many days as it is. I just had to tell my mom that I'm only going to be in Camden for like four hours on Thanksgiving because I have no more time off."

"Can you get extra days, unpaid?"

"No, they're fixed unless it's for surgery or something. It's a policy. And anyway, I still need to save up money to get away from the Great Allergic One."

"That's too bad. There are a lot of places that I'd like to go with you."

"Well, they'll just have to wait until January. Weren't you just saying how much you loved New York in the fall?"

"I guess I was. I just wish …" Bryan said, a black apron over his button-down shirt and tie.

"I know. And I'm sorry. But we've already been through this. And I don't want to fight. I'll have more days after the end of the year."

"But even then, we're just going to run up against the same problem."

Farya caught her breath for a second. They'd only been together for a few months, and Bryan hadn't been divorced for a year yet. They avoided *the future* as a conversation topic—an unwritten rule that had emerged on its own. And here was Bryan, blithely breaking it.

"Well," Farya said. "Them's the rules."

"California, Italy, Iceland …"

"Maybe one, for one week, next year. Emanuella couldn't bear for the cubicle to sit vacant for much more than that."

"Right, the much-contested cubicle."

"And I already feel weird about you paying all the time, for dinner, for the weekends away."

"You paid for the groceries," Bryan said. He turned the fish in the skillet.

"Mm-hmm. And you're cooking, which I must say, is very sexy. I like that—I like this—all of it. And I just don't want this to turn weird."

"So, me paying for you to quit your job and come with me on fabulous vacations is strange?"

"Yes—for me it is."

"Would it be less strange if we were married?"

Farya gave him a long look, a long minute, a deep breath—a chance to laugh it off, or look away, or tend to the fish, or to change the subject. Bryan didn't move a muscle and watched her just as intently.

"Are you …"

"Crazy? Maybe. Serious? Yes."

That pleasant autumn evening, the fish burned, and they decided to marry.

+

Bryan knew Camden—maybe not from experience or reputation, but from its population size and demographics, its relationship to the highways. From the condition of the state roads that reached it and the size and age of the houses they passed, he could tell where the nearest cell-phone retail storefront was, who owned it, and which networks the phones used. It was a small town that was smaller than it had been twenty years ago, that was not rich and not optimistic. It was a place where he knew he'd be a little bit unlikeable right off the bat.

He and Farya drove to Camden in his black Italian sedan, with two SUVs following. At that point, Farya barely noticed the presence of Eamonn and company. But Bryan's car would have turned heads in the small town on its own. And the convoy incited rumors that would keep the old people at the Dunkin' Donuts talking until mud season.

"So, just so I'm ready, your stepfather was a teacher?"

"Yes, retired now. He was always running into problems with the school board and resigned. It's sad. It kind of ruined him."

She stopped there. The past could be confusing to Farya, with different versions always in flux. She seemed to remember a photograph from her youth when her father and stepfather were famous astronauts, shoulder to shoulder, smiling the smile of healthy young men who don't know any better. But she couldn't tell Bryan this. Her confusion was a disease she kept quarantined, lest it spread to a broader, more terrifying confusion. Her months with him had been happy, and she didn't want that to change.

"Going home always kicks up a lot of things," Bryan offered.

"I guess so," Farya said. The car slowed for a stoplight that she didn't remember being there the last time she was in town. She smiled a little. Since quitting the job, she'd had more time for her exercises. Maybe things were getting better, fuller.

They pulled into the gravel driveway of the old two-story yellow house. The colors of bare trees and dead lawns gave way to the dimming November sky. It was so washed out and spare that the inside of the house came as a shock to Bryan—all busy patterns in bright gold and bronze, bold Ohio-State scarlet and gray, and the earthy hues of Native American rugs.

Farya's stepfather was precise; his wan face shaved close, his flannel shirt tucked into his pressed and belted jeans, with a quick, hard handshake. Her mother enveloped Bryan with a lingering embrace, soft and full, her shawl, scarves, and dark hair making it hard to tell where she began and ended. Seeing the SUVs outside, she insisted they invite Bryan's security in, and refusing, in the name of Thanksgiving, to offer them anything less than coffee and cake.

Eamonn and the rest of the team came in, their huge bodies filling the dining room. They stayed for the coffee, before begging off—two of them to wait outside in one SUV, while the other two went to the hotel for the night. Bryan and Farya stayed—the two women heading to the kitchen, while Bryan and the stepfather retired to the living room, where the older man offered sporadic small talk against a backdrop of channel flipping.

"Don't know what it is about the holidays—never anything on," her stepfather said. "Football tomorrow, I guess. Those games are never any good." Bryan offered some vague agreement. "I don't know what Farya told you," the stepfather continued, "about me and her father and her mom."

"Just that you and her dad worked together, and that you helped him out before he died."

"Did she say where we worked?"

"A high school."

"Right. What do you know about Ohio?"

"Some. My father grew up in Western Pennsylvania. And my company has a few dozen stores there," Bryan said. The number was over two hundred, but he figured that underestimation served him best.

"It's a good business?"

"It's a tough one—always new technology, new competitors, new laws, new costs, and new ways to lose our customers. But it's been good to me so far."

"Good for you. For most people, the world zigs or zags, and they get lost entirely. They get stuck or relegated. In America, we say *laid off*, but laid off where? Where is *off*? It sounds like a wagon train abandons them in some prairie. The British call it *redundancies*. Maybe that's better, like they already have one of you, so they don't need another. You probably let people go—what do you call it?" the stepfather asked, not bothering to turn down the volume on the TV.

"Layoffs, usually. Why do you ask?"

"When I got let go by the Oneida County school system, it was mostly mutual. We didn't much like each other by then. Anyway, I had a pension, along with another pension from my years in Ohio. So, it wasn't like that with me. But I live here and play cards with some of the guys my age, volunteer in town. And a lot of the people I meet were laid off, retired younger than they intended. And I'm just curious how it happens."

"I agree," Bryan said, being as agreeable as he could. "It's unfortunate, but layoffs are a lot more common now than they were when you were working."

"So, you do a lot of them?"

"We've purchased a lot of competitors in the last few years, so, yes."

"And you get redundancies?"

"Yeah."

"What if you lay off someone that you don't have another one of?"

"It happens. But we have ways of keeping that from happening."

"Like what?"

"We try to be careful about who, and how many people we let go of. And we make most of the jobs simple enough that people can be moved around without disrupting things."

"Clever."

"Don't credit me. The guys who came up with that idea are the ones who started the industrial revolution."

"I remember this television show," the stepfather said. "It was called *Jonathan Chearleederman*, and he was a business consultant in Ohio."

"I think I saw that. It was this strange science fiction show," Bryan said, glad to change the subject.

"I guess it was science fiction."

"Yeah, I remember, in each episode, he'd go to a company in some space-age version of Columbus or Toledo. There was one where he uncovered an embezzlement scheme to keep a murder victim alive in a cryogenic vat, so the killer couldn't be tried for murder."

"It was a fun show, even the dull episodes, like when he convinced a lunar-mining operation to lease out its extra rockets."

"I remember that episode. It was like a mom-and-pop company on the moon," Bryan said, happy to have moved the conversation to friendlier waters. He tried to recall more about the show and, with a shiver, remembered where he'd seen it. It was the half-finished basement in Maricopa County, in a time that had never happened.

"You never knew which kind of episode it would be," the stepfather said. "Sometimes, he'd solve a murder; sometimes, he'd solve a business problem; sometimes, he'd help make a scientific discovery. You never knew. It kept you on your toes."

"Like the one where someone hacked into the office pathetype machine …"

"… and it turned out to be the office vizier's estranged daughter …"

"… who just wanted to be closer to her father …" Bryan said. A dozen other episodes sprang to mind. He sweated, nauseous, and chuckled to keep from thinking of that garish green leather couch in the too-bright basement always stinking of discarded mackerel tins and his own bucketed waste.

"That was a sad one. I almost forgot about it. It's crazy; that used to be my favorite show, but I never meet anybody who's seen *Jonathan Chearleederman*. Do you watch it with Farya?"

"No," Bryan said, feeling a chill. "I don't know if she'd like it."

Not long after, driving from the house to their hotel, Farya could tell Bryan was upset.

"Sorry about my stepdad. I should have given you more warning. Was he rude or weird?"

"No, he was nice. I like him. I'm just really tired."

"Now, I know you're lying," she said and laughed. He gave a dry chuckle, for cover.

"We just talked about work and TV. I'm fine."

There was a quickness to his words, a rare squeak in his voice. But Farya knew not to push.

+

Restless, troubled, Bryan slept badly. So did Farya. They passed most of the night trying not to disturb the other as they pretended to sleep. In the morning, Bryan pled work and dropped her off with her parents for the morning.

Back in the hotel suite, he took out his tablet and started searching for *Jonathan Chearleederman*. He expected Wikipedia, fan sites, articles, syndication deals, actor obituaries, a whole host of material that might help him get a handle on where he was. Instead, he got "Your search—Jonathan Chearleederman—did not match any documents," followed by suggestions that he try other spellings, fewer words, or more words. But he knew the spelling. He could close his eyes and see the show's title card rushing up, a tolerable distraction in an endless and intolerable situation. Nonetheless, he tried other search engines, other spellings, other approaches, like searching by plotline.

But no one in the whole world, aside from himself and his soon-to-be stepfather-in-law, had ever heard of the professionally produced and pretty good network television show. And he was left on the uncomfortable fulcrum—where he couldn't chalk up his experience in Arizona to having briefly lost his mind, nor talk to anyone about what had happened to him. He wanted a whiteboard. He wanted to draw up Venn diagrams and flowcharts. But he knew enough to leave it alone.

Eamonn responded to his call within a minute. Bryan waved him in, and they walked to the suite's little sitting room with a sofa, chair, and television the size of a small dining room table.

"I know I said not to tell me, but when you were doing Farya's background check, did you find anything odd?"

"You told me to destroy the report."

"That's right. But I need to ask: Did you find anything strange when you were doing your digging?"

"No, nothing like a red flag. She came out like you described her, like who she told you she was. And it wasn't me who did it—it was Leslie, our lead researcher at the office."

"Did Leslie say anything was funny, or a little off with Farya's family, maybe?"

"Are you sure you want to ask me about this? Now?"

"What do you mean? What did you find?"

"It's not that. I'm just saying I've been doing this for a while. And it's never good when you start using these kinds of things—background checks, surveillance—on the people in your life. Even when nothing turns up, it never ends well."

"I don't want the report, or surveillance, or even ex-boyfriends. Let me narrow it down. Was there anything strange? No, not just strange, but totally inexplicable?"

"There was one thing. It was minor, but it bugged Leslie. Farya's hometown didn't exist—the hospital, her home, grammar school in Ohio—they were all gone. Not even a trace. It took almost a week for Leslie to figure it out. I guess when she was in junior high, the state flooded the valley it was in to create a reservoir, and just erased the whole place."

"Flooded it? They still do that?"

"I guess they do in Ohio."

"But is that suspicious? Could it be a fake background?"

"Doubt it. When people take up or make up fake identities, they usually add up on paper."

"Thanks. And thanks for coming to Thanksgiving today. It takes some of the heat off me with the in-laws," Bryan said.

"Beats taking a bullet."

+

"Here we go—another trip down memory lane to nowhere," Farya's brother whispered when their stepfather brought up *Jonathan Chearleederman* at dinner. The older man was proud, in his goofy way, of the thing he had in common with Bryan.

"Farya, I don't think you ever watched it. But maybe you did, Jeff, when you were younger," her stepfather said.

"Was it about a guy who was a cheerleader?" her brother Jeff asked.

"No. It had a strange spelling, like Dutch maybe. Farya, can you look it up?" her stepfather asked.

"Let's not start taking out our phones at the table," Farya's mother said. "Let's just enjoy each other's company."

The rest of dinner went well enough, as far as Bryan was concerned. Jeff drove most of the conversation, trying to show off how much he knew about the telecom business until Farya's mother stepped in to steer the conversation to the wedding details. Then Bryan didn't have to say anything at all. After dinner, with the television on low, Farya looked up the TV show for her stepfather. Bryan withstood more of Jeff's tech-business name-dropping, and just tried to stay away from the subject of *Jonathan Chearleederman* as they tried different spellings.

"Go figure. I guess the internet just hasn't gotten around to it yet," her stepfather said, puzzled.

"You're spelling it wrong. Everything's on the internet," Jeff said. "Everything."

"Not everything," Farya said.

"Like what?" Jeff said. "Name one thing."

"That's enough," Farya's mother said. "If I hear one more thing about this *Johnny Cheerleader* or whatever, I'm going to scream. We only all get together every so often. And I won't have everyone staring at their phones, arguing about a show that was on TV thirty years ago, when we have a perfectly good TV on right now that we can all watch together."

"So, you remember the show?" Farya's stepfather said.

"Of course. Every Wednesday. Now, drop it, honey."

Sullen, Farya and Jeff put their phones away. Together, they watched television until the yawn of Farya's stepfather announced the end of Thanksgiving. Farya, in her coat, said a long goodbye to her mother, exchanging wedding details and other reminders. That left Bryan alone with her stepfather, waiting by the door.

"So, you said your dad was Jimny Lomoigne?" the older man said to pass the awkward moments.

"Yeah. He died a few years ago."

"I heard, sorry."

"Thanks."

"I wasn't a big Union Skells fan. But some of my friends were. You know, he's from Ohio, even though he was born on the moon. But the moon was part of Ohio at the time."

"All right. We're going to leave," Bryan said, loud enough for Farya to hear.

+

They married on the weekend between Christmas and New Year's, after a weeklong ski trip with Bryan's children in Utah. He tried to impart a few life lessons on the gondola and keep pace with Charles on the slopes. Farya befriended Bryan's twelve-year-old daughter Elena in the condo, commiserating over how boys are crazy, and school is boring.

The children were part of a long, spooky Armenian Christian wedding ceremony at a church by the Queens-Midtown Tunnel. Bryan and Farya had wanted a smaller ceremony, but neither could resist Farya's mother. At the end of the ceremony, the priest crowned them and sent them on their way to an expensive party in the banquet hall at a high-security Manhattan hotel.

With faux and real sophistication, his kids said all the right things. Even Bryan's ex-wife wished him well. It was a perfect little wedding. After it was over, both Bryan and Farya felt giddy, like they'd gotten away with something.

It's a cruel irony how little there is to say about the good times. The year that followed was happy. They bought a townhouse in the West Village on a crooked, landmarked street—the kind of place Farya had fantasized about since she moved to the city. They traveled. Bryan ran Metacom from hotel rooms around the world. With each passing month, Cassie managed ever more of the company's day-to-day business. Farya's exercises became easier, more rewarding. As she acclimated to a life of wealth and leisure, downtown Manhattan gained a few narrow, charming streets. By the end of the year, Farya was pregnant.

In the anxious weeks near Farya's due date, reality—across which they'd skimmed and skipped for so long—reasserted itself.

Antonio

sent from device, please forgive typos + be brilliant! was how Antonio ended every communication. Or rather, it's how his phone, the size of a small candy tray, did.

Details were paramount, the big picture was paramount, the long-term plan was paramount, the single moment that paid it all off was paramount. It was all paramount, which is why they'd always need someone like Antonio. It was an impossible job with a few thousand elements; engineering, art direction, security, publicity, and client relations would all have to line up in a single moment. Antonio was the best—he'd produced a thousand live events, two Super Bowl halftime shows, and a Presidential inauguration. And now he was cashing in on the soirees and ceremonies of the global super-rich—grand spectacles for the guests and utter secrecy from everyone else. He'd managed aquarium orgies, sword-and-sandal battle reenactments, yacht flotillas in international waters, and even bomb-threat-cleared city blocks for a staged rendezvous.

Regardless of the job, it was the details that mattered. And each single detail mattered in increasing amounts as you drew closer to The Moment, which could last four hours or just a second.

They all built up to and boiled down to a single moment—one impossible experience. *Iconic* was the word most often used. And with that single iconic moment of transcendent beauty or utter kitsch etched upon the starry cosmos, Antonio could pack up, his reputation burnished and his bank account replenished.

It was a chilly October in Pontiac, Michigan. Antonio's next Moment would take place in the Silverdome—a former stadium and modern ruin. The dome itself was gone, and huge scraps of Teflon-coated fiberglass covered large swaths of seats. Electricity was hit and miss. As far as its neighbors were concerned, they were filming a summer blockbuster. They had a movie studio to verify this, though the film would vanish into the folds of its balance sheet. The cover story called for unions, who were reliable, but had no use for Antonio's *be-brilliant* cheerleading.

The process had started months before, with the engineers who certified the building's structural integrity and began drawing up the technical requirements to turn the building into an enormous machine. Antonio watched on an early site visit as they walked the concrete floor of the stadium with GPS and tape measures and high school geometry to recover the Silverdome's sacred spot—the exact middle of the fifty-yard line, now a dirty swell of cracked and water-stained concrete.

Once they got started, the derelict structure saved them as much time as it cost. If a truck dock wouldn't open—the steel gate gone off its rails and rusted in place—Antonio just had the crew rip the gates out. And the men attended to the careless destruction of the stadium with no small amount of glee. Mess didn't matter, as long as the stage was clear for The Moment. The engineers set to building the stage, which began with scaffolding, designed using a formula unknown to Antonio. When they were finished, they had what could only be described as a massive version of an infant's mobile suspended from a black-painted aluminum arch fifty feet above midfield.

He was impressed, but not surprised. Antonio had done some pickup jobs for the same outfit in New York, where they had a smaller version built right into that gigantic bland condo tower at 432 Park Avenue. That made it easier, with none of the cost overruns and scheduling pinches that come with building out a whole new space. For those jobs, it was all about stage-managing The Moment.

The space at 432 Park—a sixty-story chrome ice cream cone open to the sky—also had a mobile of sorts. But the mobile was always different for each audience. The audience was a single individual, whom Antonio almost never met. He only dealt directly with one person from his employer, an older gentleman with a stern, no-nonsense demeanor who paid well and on time. He asked Antonio just to call him "Tootie." He'd been working with Tootie for a few years now.

Antonio checked timelines, with big Xs through the completed tasks on the big whiteboard in a trailer office set in the concrete prairie of vacant stadium parking. He checked the big full-color flat-screen monitors, showing midfield of the Silverdome swept clean, with a platform bed in its center, sheets tight, and mattress firm. Above it, interrupting the night sky, dangled the items in the mobile. They were different for everyone. There were usually animals, some plain as beef cows, others exotic—winged horses with exaggerated genitals. There were usually plants, sometimes as simple as corn and grass, others wild—man-sized, lipstick-wearing Venus Flytraps. There was usually a smattering of extravagances—a palace, castle, or sports car, a beach, private jet, or a yacht. And there were often figurines—smiling children, voluptuous women or muscular men, arranged in loving families, quiet dinners, coitus, sporting events, war scenes, or sometimes, vivid torture scenarios.

The items were approved and crafted outside of Antonio's purview and budget. He only saw the client just before The Moment, when they were led or wheeled to the bed, tucked in, and wrapped down with linen. Once the client was immobilized beneath the mobile, the last of the support staff left the building. Antonio watched from a distance, on a monitor. At 432 Park, he'd go to an office across the avenue and watch from there. At the Silverdome, he'd watch from the trailer office.

When Tootie wanted an off-site "performance," the venue was always massive, circular, and concave—an abandoned stadium or a strip mine. Anything smaller, they seemed like they preferred to handle it at 432 Park, which was still a mild amazement to him. The tower, though it appeared to be a standard luxury condo, was mostly empty space, with its top sixty floors housing a terraced cone, which widened as it went up. In each terrace was a circular track, on which a small matte-black wheeled box traveled, with each row moving in the direction opposite the one above and below it. When all the boxes on all the tracks reached peak speed, the boxes opened, all at once. That was The Moment.

The mechanical details were Antonio's job. Each silver track and small matte-black shoebox had to be ready for The Moment. This was easier in a dedicated structure, but 432 Park could only handle jobs as big as 20,736 boxes. The event at the Silverdome would require 144,000 boxes.

The Silverdome event took nine months of manufacturing, licenses, permits, PR, logistics, and so forth from when the audience signed the contract to The Moment. The team involved was as large as two hundred people surveying and clearing the site, laying the track, testing it with dummy boxes, laying the real boxes in, and installing the mobile. Antonio watched as it swayed in the bitter wind. Animals, speedboats, a recreation of a 1960's suburban kitchen, and lifelike plaster figurines of thin, dark-haired women with cruel eyes wearing exercise attire drifted past each other. The repeating silver rails of the machine itself fit the repetitive tiers where the stadium seats had been.

Rain and maybe snow was predicted, a massive storm system coming down from Canada that was projected to reach them at exactly The Moment. They were still doing test runs on different sections of the machine. Climbing to the so-called nosebleed seats with the cold scratching at his throat and chest, Antonio could see the huge gray shoulders of the storm bearing down. He called Tootie about the weather, and Tootie told him to run the whole machine in a few hours.

They didn't have a whole-stadium test run planned until the next day, a few hours before The Moment. But Antonio agreed.

An hour later, Tootie called to say someone was coming to deal with the problem and gave him a name. Antonio passed the man's info onto security, and later that afternoon, watched from a gutted luxury booth at the fifty-yard line, cell phone in one hand and binoculars in the other. Tootie's interloper looked like a straight version of Antonio, in a black parka, red sweater vest, shirt, and tie. One of the engineers followed him around the stadium as he replaced four of the small, matte-black dummy shoeboxes they used for the test. He gave Antonio a thumbs-up sign.

Only later did it strike Antonio as odd that the interloper knew where he was watching from.

With everyone cleared out of the stadium, they ran the unscheduled dress rehearsal. A half hour later, the storm, in all its majesty and violence, skirted past the stadium, dusting the houses across the street with an inch of snow. Overnight, the snow stuck, hardened, and seemed to age everything around them. It made the short drive from the so-so hotel a little grimmer on the day of The Moment. The air stung like a whip.

The workers worked in shifts through the night and into the next dusk to get all 144,000 boxes on the tracks. All the tests—electrical, mechanical, security, and client—came up green. With the last items checked off Antonio's four-hundred-item *Day Of* checklist, he cleared the stadium, except for the onstage team, which wasn't his responsibility.

The workers, whose cars, trucks, trailers, and machinery filled a far corner of the frigid Silverdome parking lot, cracked open beers. They shared a sense of anticipation not dampened by not knowing what it was they'd worked for. The sky was huge and clear above, and in the unlit lot, the stars seemed closer than usual.

With everyone cleared out, a thick silence squatted over the stadium. After sixty seconds, the machine started with a tight sequence of squeaks and rattles that ran together to a roar like an over-wound watch accelerating into a forest fire, before settling into a low nasal whistle. Antonio knew the sound well enough to know it was going well. Beyond the sound, he could tell from the monitor—a sharpening of the details before the feed cut out—instantaneously and orgasmic, from Antonio's perspective. This was in no small part because, at that moment, the second installment of the amount Tootie had promised would appear in Antonio's bank account.

Antonio never knew who the person wrapped up on the bed was unless Tootie had let a name slip during one planning session. The idea that anyone would pay for what happened seemed insane, because from what Antonio could see in his monitor, they died. When the power came back on, and with it, the video feed, the linen in which the client had been wrapped was dirty, cracked, torn, and loose, where it had been skin-tight. The body inside was shrunken, brittle, and lifeless. The eyes, which he'd made out on one project, were hollow blank pits sealed with dry dust.

For all his prowess and responsibility, Antonio was almost as ignorant as the Teamsters on the job. There were others from 432 Park Avenue who handled things like wheeling the mattress and the remains of the client out of view. That was fine with Antonio. He had enough work to do.

The cleanup was always the worst. The adrenaline was gone, and the labor intense. He'd scheduled four days to tear everything down and sweep it clean. The crew, which never saw the fruits of their labors, always grumbled. A terrible depression always seemed to settle on them, an impatience and cruelty. Fights broke out over nothing. Men stormed out and lost their bonuses.

Antonio, a consummate professional, kept his emotions in check, despite a heaviness like he was carrying death's own dumbbells in a backpack. He told himself that once the last of the trucks was at least a few miles clear of the site, he could give up.

The stadium, maybe worse for wear, was empty, dark in the darkness. Antonio's trailer office had been towed away that afternoon. All day, he'd been getting calls that this and that piece of equipment had been dropped at this dump, that warehouse, or loaded onto a plane. The final call from the final truck, now on the highway, let him know the job was done.

The black car to the airport had been waiting for an hour on the empty street outside the padlocked chain-link gate of the Silverdome. It was over. Antonio could relax. The depression, when it hit, was almost incapacitating. He told the driver to go. He slumped in the leather seat. Antonio always scheduled a trip for afterward. He called it a champagne month and took a lot of pictures. The pictures would, he imagined, stave off the next wave of depression and keep him focused on the next Big Moment, the next big paycheck. The champagne months drained his retirement fund. And retirement was always supposed to be the plan. Staring at the dreary dark nothing of Pontiac, Antonio sighed—he couldn't keep this up. But the question of how Antonio might leave this life was left for after the champagne month. It could wait, like the question of what the clients were getting for their money.

Was it euthanasia, a top-secret medical procedure, or some pleasure unimaginable to anyone with less than a billion dollars? Antonio decided it was one of the nice things. With a shaving kit full of pills, and a first-class bed on the plane, he schemed a way to sleep from Detroit to Paris.

Farya & Bryan

Farya and Bryan's idyll culminated with her pregnancy. And the end of it started with Cassie. Every time Bryan met with her, she seemed to have gained or lost a surprising amount of weight, her pale face rounding, softening, and then sharpening to wraith-like emaciation. There was an enormous diamond engagement ring on her finger she never explained that also seemed to come and go. In hindsight, there was also the sound of her purse—the sluggish rattle of big pills in big pill bottles.

He'd ignored it, though he knew the shelf-life of Metacom's senior staff had always been short. The reality of the business had a corrosive effect on the people who knew, even if they never said as much during their exit interviews. It's why he paid them well and stuck them all with onerous non-disclosure clauses.

When Petra called and demanded a meeting to talk about Cassie, he wasn't surprised. Bryan was in Rome, on a final jaunt with Farya before the baby was due, and offered to reschedule when he returned. She said, "What a coincidence," and gave him the address of a hilltop villa in Trastevere. Lunch was waiting on a shaded patio overlooking the Palatine, the Pantheon, and the whole old city. Petra looked tired, her makeup a little crumbled around her eyes and the corners of her mouth.

"So sorry I missed the wedding. You look great. Did you lose weight?" Petra said with an overpowering smile.

"Maybe. Having Eamonn and them pick through my delivery orders at lunch—best diet plan I've ever had."

"I won't tell them—they'd probably find a way to work it into your bill."

"I'd have to get a second job. These guys are bleeding me."

"Anyway—sorry to interrupt one of your vacations."

"No problem. It's a working vacation. They all are."

"If you say so. Listen, we have a problem with your chief operating officer. She has a drug problem and a conscience problem. And she's very close to making her problems into your problems, and mine."

"What makes you think this? No one has said anything to me."

"There's a record of everything, and Cassie has almost a dozen prescriptions under her name and her sister's. Xanax, Klonopin, Ambien, Focalin, Adderall, and a few others that I had to look up. And when you count up the refills, it paints a disturbing picture."

"So, you're spying on my chief operating officer."

"Is it spying? Can anyone even complain about *spying* anymore? Cassie is an investment, like you. It's due diligence."

"I never agreed to surveillance. You have no business invading Cassie's privacy, or my privacy, for that matter."

"Business is exactly what we have. Your privacy is a potential risk, and we won't let that risk go unmanaged. If you have serious concerns about this, we can schedule a call with the partners." The way Petra said *with the partners* implied that Bryan didn't want that.

"I don't like this—it's over the line. I'm going to have to rethink our relationship."

"Okay, your outrage is noted, understood. But would you like to know what we discovered? About Cassie, I mean."

Despite the Mediterranean sun, the clams, linguini, and the jovial honking of small horns in the streets below, the lunch had the feeling of a sizable bill coming due. Bryan nodded as Petra showed him the prescription records.

"Drugs are drugs; so what? But Cassie's been meeting with lawyers—a labor attorney, probably to see how screwed she is if she violates the non-disclosure. And she met with a criminal lawyer, a former prosecutor. We don't know what about, yet."

"But we can guess."

"You have always operated in an area about which the law is agnostic. The public, however, has never been agnostic about anything. So, all it takes is one politically ambitious district attorney to file suit …"

"And the next week, the plaintiffs' attorneys start pushing for a class-action …"

"In every venue imaginable …" Petra said, a smile finding its way onto her face.

"And the bad press paralyzes the company for the foreseeable future. Okay, okay."

✢

He and Farya flew to New York the next day, cutting their trip short. She was used to him taking calls and tapping out emails through the beaches, restaurants, and ruins, but this change in plans worried her. Bryan said it was business, and that: "Some things have to be done in person." Farya agreed to fly back with him.

The conference room Bryan chose had a view of Midtown, the Columbus-Circle corner of Central Park. It wasn't the biggest or nicest conference room. But it was soundproof, and no one could get cellular signals in it, an irony the wags always made sure to mention during their first few weeks.

Bryan arrived at dawn. When the motion-sensor lights in Cassie's corner of the floor indicated that she'd arrived a half hour later, he invited her to meet him in the conference room. She asked if they could meet in a half hour, and Bryan said no. She said she had a minor emergency and she couldn't get her email on her phone for some reason. He said it could wait. She began another protest, and he just said, "Now." He watched her walk, fast and awkward, past the cubicles. The light inside was harsh and hollow compared with the dim early-spring morning in the window. The conference table was a reddish wood oval, with minimalist orange-tan chairs around it. There was nothing to look at and nowhere to hide in that room. Cassie's purse made that same dull rattling sound when she set it down.

"What's going on? It's good to see you. I didn't expect to see you until next week. I have a few updates, nothing major. But first, I need to get back into my email," Cassie said. Her voice was high, and her syllables clipped.

"You won't get in. Listen, Cassie. I have too much respect for you and for all you've done here to waste your time. But today's your last day. You've been abusing pharmaceutical drugs. I'm going to need your phone and your ID."

"But that's impossible. They were prescribed by a doctor," she said. But Bryan caught the hesitation in that last word, and the squint like she'd bitten into a pit.

"We both know it's more than that," he said. Bryan had most of the plane ride to think through how to do this, what documents to have drawn up, and most of all, what not to say. There was a great deal he shouldn't know. "Here's your severance agreement. I need you to sign it this morning."

He removed a stapled sheaf of documents from a folder and pushed it toward her.

"Are you crazy? I'll have my lawyers look at it, and let you know."

"There is no severance after this morning, no graceful, face-saving resignation. Instead, there's a firing for cause, and this," he said, pushing a thicker stapled bundle of paper at her. "It's a civil suit charging you with embezzling company funds to support your drug habit."

"That's insane. I would never, in a thousand years, steal company money," Cassie said. But there it was, a quiver in her voice, a brighter glisten on the edge of her eyeliner.

"We're happy to let a court sort through it," Bryan said.

"What is this really about? I thought we had a mutual respect. I thought we were friends."

"We were. And I trusted you."

"So, what happened?"

"You clearly have a problem. And you should have come to me with it. But you didn't. You put the company at risk. And now it's too late."

Cassie pursed her lips. Taking her cue from Bryan, she held in what she was going to say. Emotion, above the fortieth floor, was a trap. She was smart enough to see that. She picked up the severance agreement, read it, and sniffled hard. Bryan gave her the handkerchief he'd brought.

It was an airtight document, full of provisions and penalties. He felt terrible about it, but he was familiar with feeling terrible. It was all business, he said to himself. People might be full of back-breaking remorse and horizon-rending regret, but business was not. And Bryan had regrets: regret at not giving her a chance to come clean to him; regret at having left her alone with the horror he'd built.

But this was business. And the outlet for all that well-worn, gelded guilt was the contract. He watched her eyes light on the clauses he'd inserted between grim warnings and blanket stipulations. There was money, plenty, even by his standards. There was a broad but insidiously binding non-disparagement clause for the company to adhere to, and there was the matter of the company's rights to Cassie's Non-Mortal-Element, or—as no one in the building referred to it—her soul.

"Four years," she said.

"Yep. Four years and it vests. We have no right to it after that."

Cassie skipped the last few pages of the document and scraped a ballpoint pen across the bottom with a limp hand. She rattled her handbag for phone and wallet. She clicked the building ID flush to her phone and gave him a flat, exhausted look, her eyes like saucers.

"Is that all?" she asked.

"Yes. Thank you for …"

She rose and left before he could say what he was thanking her for. And like a small plane making a steep descent to dodge a severe storm, Bryan had returned from his extended honeymoon to the life he deserved.

✟

Cassie had been working harder than Bryan knew. And the baby, a boy named Edouard for Farya's father, was born via C-section in the middle of one of Bryan's ninety-hour workweeks. They brought him home from the hospital three days later, and night and day soon lost their significance for all of them. Bryan, blinking awake, always needed a few seconds to recall where he was. And though he kept promising to help more around the house, work was relentless, and finding Cassie's replacement was a project the recruiters described in terms of months. After about eight weeks, Edouard was sleeping through a sizable enough chunk of the night that Farya began to recall some of what it had felt like to be herself. Even with a nanny at the townhouse most days, she had very little time for her exercises.

Edouard took up most of Farya's time—her phone took up most of what was left. A new mother, she constantly checked to see if she was doing things right. It was easy to get lost in spirited debates about diapers and shrill controversies about each of the ever-expanding number of ways to breastfeed, incendiary rhetoric about stuffed animals and jeremiads about whether or not to hang a mobile over your child's crib.

It was exhausting and frustrating, but not depressing. Her little boy brought a new sensibility into Farya's life. She washed the little boy, changed the diapers, cradled him, rocked him to sleep, played those sanity-stretching games of charades with pacifiers and her breast when he wouldn't calm down, put lotion on him after a bath, and applied the thick, smelly ointment to the "birth eye" on his forehead as it closed.

That last one she hated the most. Blind and unblinking, just above Edouard's wisp-thin red eyebrows, the eye stared. Applying the ointment to the edges of the eye seemed like it should sting awfully, no matter how careful she was. The birth-eyelid would close over it by four months, usually, though Farya had heard of children who still had their third eye after a year. If it persisted after two years, most doctors recommended a simple, safe surgery. But, of course, the parenting message boards were full of strong opinions and recriminations regardless of how you tended the birth eye, too.

Farya's mother recommended a popular birth-eye ointment called *Smooth 'n' Calm* and brought a tub of it when she and Farya's stepfather came to visit. It was supposed to help the skin close evenly, both her mother and the bottle said. But Edouard was a busy baby, his hands flying about like fleshy butterflies and his head always lolling. Farya always seemed to be getting the gooey ointment in his third eye. And though the jar said the ointment was harmless, the sensation of the minty goo on his birth eye made Edouard inconsolable for a minute that seemed like an hour.

Checking the internet after one of these breakdowns, Farya came away with a dozen new, contradictory solutions, and a fresh source of exhaustion. But everything was a source of exhaustion, from changing her shirt to her baby's laughter to the eating three meals a day.

The exhaustion was worse on the weekends. The nanny was off. Bryan was at the office. Edouard had screamed himself to sleep. One of these ill-defined weekend days, at dusk, Farya looked at her little sleeping boy and resolved to take this brief respite to do her exercises. The shades on the ground floor of the West Village townhouse were drawn. The sounds from the street were light, sporadic.

She closed her eyes and began one of the easier exercises. A truck passed outside. Its brakes gave off a breathy squeak. A loud talker passed on the sidewalk—a tourist talking about a restaurant they'd heard of. She thought of the tourists, bringing their fresh eyes to the old town. A truck passed outside, its brakes giving off a breathy squeak, someone passed, a tourist, talking about a restaurant they'd heard of. She wondered how many people went into inventing that truck—the brakes, the mirrors and handles, each of its unique components. Then the truck again, the tourist again. She needed to start her exercises again, she thought—it was dangerous if she didn't. Then the truck again, the tourist again. She had to figure out a new way to calm Edouard down before she applied the ointment to his birth eye. Then the truck again, the tourist again. And again. Again once more. Again.

By the time Farya realized what was happening, it was too late.

She knew it had happened, even if she didn't know *what* happened. With a bottomless dread in her chest, she jumped up from the leather armchair and barked a string of expletives and racial slurs to break the spell. She rushed, half-asleep, up the staircase with its broad stripe of carpet, bounding past where the baby gate leaned against the wall, still in its box, and into the spacious gray-blue nursery where Edouard slept, silent but for a faint whistle of his tiny nose.

The thin high whistle saved Farya from her usual routine of watching Edouard's little chest to see if he was breathing. But she didn't dare leave the door of the nursery or take her eyes off of her boy. There, his little, serene face had changed. As he slept, swaddled tight, his expression seemed calmer, less worried. She wondered how she'd missed that variety of innocence in her son.

It took her a moment before realization struck. And when it did, she let out a tiny cry. That woke Edouard, who squirmed like a tiny Houdini in his swaddle before he settled, sucked his pacifier, and fell back to sleep.

Farya held her breath so as not to wake him again as she tried to comprehend what had happened—what she had unwittingly done—to her boy: His third eye was gone, without so much as a faint wrinkle. Smooth and blank, his forehead reflected the soft light suffused through the pale-blue curtains.

As quietly as she could, Farya opened a drawer in the changing table where she kept the ointment that was supposed to "support clean, even, and natural closing of the birth eye." But she couldn't find it, though she recalled a half-dozen tubs of it being delivered to the townhouse just the week before. In a minor panic, Farya rummaged through Edouard's drawers.

It was nowhere to be found. Finally, she eased shut the door to his room, and from the hall, called the housekeeper to see if she'd moved the birth-eye balm. Sometimes it felt like the house belonged to the housekeeper and the nanny more than it did to her and Bryan. As she dialed, she was ready to say the words, "I swore there were a few tubs of *Smooth 'n' Calm* just a minute ago …" A familiar sensation washed over her, and she rushed back into her son's room.

He was still there, still breathing, his brow still impossibly blank. Stunned and shaking, Farya made it to the top of the staircase and slumped, her head between her knees, while she tried to catch her breath. Once she could breathe, she cried.

Farya felt the familiar hope that things would make sense, made sense. But this was different. The world could implode in a bad moment, and she had carried that with her since she was a teenager. But that wasn't much compared to the sickening and relentless horror that she might be responsible for harming her son. Farya formulated a loose prayer for another explanation, and another prayer, for her son.

She took her prayer to the internet. Without moving, she removed her phone from the pocket of her baggy pregnancy jeans and tapped her way to the message boards she'd been frequenting for advice and fresh anxiety for those last few months. She typed in "birth eye," and nothing came up, so she tried "forehead scarring," "brow dent," "rhino baby," and some of the other euphemisms for the sightless staring eye that all healthy infants were born with. But, where there had been countless threads full of heated debate about ointments, treatments, special hats, warning signs, and home remedies, now there was nothing. Absolutely nothing. Farya tried other message boards, other sites, but found no mention of what had been a rather dramatic developmental stage for infants since the dawn of humanity. As a last ditch, she checked the *Smooth 'n' Calm* website, but there was no such place, and a search turned up a flotsam of odds and ends that had nothing to do with either infants or ointments.

It was like a slow-building punch in the stomach. Farya slumped until she couldn't slump anymore, remorse and confusion like waves crashing into each other.

Even after calming down to make the call, Farya had an audible pinch in her throat. So, even when she protested that she must just be tired, Bryan insisted on coming home right away. When he got in twenty minutes later, Farya drooped into his arms and sobbed, despite her intentions to play it off. Bryan had been through two other children and knew better than to ask what was wrong or to even volunteer any opinions about whether or not things were, or would be, all right. All he knew was to hold on. Farya appreciated the firmness of his shoulders and the tightness of his grip. After a minute or two, she apologized for the wet spot on his jacket and said they had to go upstairs.

Edouard was still asleep, the same tiny whistle in his nose, his mouth open and his closed eyes searching the insides of their lids.

"Do you notice anything?" she asked. Bryan squinted, cocked his head, and watched some more.

"His nose, you mean? I think it's just a little phlegm."

"No. Anything else? Look at him, his face, does anything look different?" Bryan went through the same watching routine again.

"More hair? More teeth? Help me out."

Just by being there, Bryan had calmed her. And his patience and sweetness confirmed what she'd long known—that in some things, she'd always be alone. She stroked the infant's unlined forehead.

"He's just becoming a little boy so fast," she said, swallowing hard.

"It does happen fast. Too fast. How are you?"

"Tired. Just tired, I guess."

"I know, and I'm sorry. I need to scale back. I'm close to hiring some people to handle the load. Maybe you could use some more help, too."

"I'm sorry. You probably have a lot to do."

"Just a few things. I can do them from here. Let's order in, play with the little gremlin, and keep each other company."

"I'd like that."

Bryan went to the little office he kept upstairs. Farya called Ethan, to spill the whole story, to be less alone in what she hoped against hope was a mere bout of mental illness. But as Ethan's phone rang, she remembered what Bryan had said offhandedly the other day—"Anyone who would say anything even remotely questionable on a cell phone these days is a fool."

So, she just asked if he could meet her for coffee the next morning, and the tone of her voice was enough for him to know it was serious.

✤

Coffee was no simple matter in those days. Ethan brought his son, Josef, and the boy's nanny. And Farya, with little Edouard strapped to her chest, was accompanied by Davey, a humorless Samoan hulk in wraparound sunglasses who worked for Eamonn, and her own nanny. The two old friends, their children, and their respective staffs took up three separate tables at the colorful Chelsea bistro.

"Long time no see," Ethan said. He was clean-shaven and had gained yet another ten pounds, in an unbuttoned flannel and a T-shirt emblazoned *It Takes Balls 2B A Daddy*. "I see you brought protection."

"I see you brought yours."

"It keeps Carolina happy. And, anyway, she's better at handling Jojo, the diapers and feeding and whatnot, than I am. The little bugger is getting old enough to know when he's getting under my skin, and I think he enjoys it."

"Sounds like your son, all right."

"I guess if you sit around long enough, a punishment suitable to your sins will find you. If I was a less confident sponge of a man, I might even be embarrassed by the manpower, paid hours, and expenses required to have breakfast with my oldest friend," Ethan said.

"Lucky for me, you're just confident enough."

"So, mama, aside from the unmentionable chapping, sagging, aching, stretching, and overall carnage of dragging another soul into our vale of tears, how have you been?"

"Aside from all that? Tired …"

"Constantly on the verge of forgetting who you are or how you got here …"

"Yeah, you get it."

"I hate infants. No offense."

"I'm sure there's none taken," Farya said, looking down into her carrier. "No, he seems fine. How have you been? How's the gallery—the curated space?"

"It's okay. We just finished the papers, and we're incorporated. I don't know how people do all of this. Partnership agreements, waivers, insurance clauses, indemnification. It's nuts. I mean, we don't even have the space yet or any inventory."

"I thought you had the space all nailed down."

"That fell through while we were doing the paperwork. Carolina's mother is sick, and so I can't bother her dad to move things along any faster. So, we lost that space, and I guess some bright young thing must've told the oligarch about 'pop-up' stores. Now he wants me to find a decent location with a two- to three-month lease, set it up just so, get publicity, build a following, make a big splash and enough sales to pay him back, and shut it all down to fucking square fucking one all over again."

"Hmm. That sounds very ... Buddhist? Like the sand paintings, maybe?"

"No, Farya. It is not, in fact, Buddhist. It is futile. Buddhism is an elaborate, life-changing way to cope with futility. This isn't that. This is deliberate, sadistic futility."

"I'm sorry. Maybe you could find another partner for it."

"No, I'm sorry. And sorry for cussing in front of the wee one, yours anyway. Don't want that to be his first word. But yeah. I've been a little depressed lately. Anyway—how are you? You sounded a little, I don't know, distressed when you called."

"Yeah, I wanted to check with you. Do you remember when Josef was young?"

"Of course. One doesn't forget that kind of duress easily. What do they call it? Colic?"

"That's not it. Do you remember when Josef had his birth eye?" Farya asked.

"Birth eye? Was that a poop thing? I mostly left the diapers to the professionals, and to Carolina."

"No, on his face. The birth eye, or rhino flap—a big blind eye in the middle of his forehead. It closes up over the first few months."

"Oh, do you mean the fontanel? I was white-knuckle sober through all the birthing and baby classes. I know that part."

"No. It's the eye in the middle of an infant's forehead. It starts to shut and scab over about two months after they're born."

"Oh, the unicorn gap ... no, wait, that's a business thing. I thought I heard or saw ..."

Farya watched as Ethan's eyes widened and his mouth went slack as he realized that something he'd almost had the privilege of forgetting had not gone entirely away.

"I don't know. I'm sorry," Farya said. But Ethan said nothing.

He rose from the table and walked across the restaurant to where his nanny was feeding his son from a bowl of macaroni and cheese and peas. He asked in his best carefree, jocular voice how the pair was faring. He stroked the young boy's long, loose, light brown hair as a subterfuge for examining, feeling, and pressing on the center of his forehead. Ethan asked the boy how he felt, just a little too loud.

"I do remember," he said. "I didn't until you said it just now. But I do, I remember that terrible ointment, and Carolina complaining about the smell, or complaining that the day nanny didn't use enough, while the night nanny used too much. And I remember that eerie stare while he was sleeping, like he was seeing through me—like he could see me just faking it through the father thing."

"So, you remember?" Farya asked.

"Yeah. You know me. I always remember. That's probably half of why I'm such a fuckup. Sorry. Call it a complimentary deformity."

Ethan looked her in the eyes longer than he had since before he'd married Carolina, raised his cup of tea in a toast, and smirked.

✢

Later that day, Lourdes called. Like all her calls, this one was curt, inviting Farya to visit. A sitter watched Edouard, and an SUV carried Farya through the frigid early evening. In light traffic, it swooped across the Williamsburg Bridge, which punched a gap in the luxury towers crowding that bend in the East River. Just one car and one driver—Bryan had begun to talk about phasing out Eamonn and his team altogether.

As always with their meetings in the spherical basement room, there was a pizza waiting on a TV table. Lourdes waited behind the pizza box in a loose, gray sweater and a big, colorful, patchwork corduroy skirt.

"I know it can be hard to get away. But I was worried about you," Lourdes said, looking older, the flesh around her mouth sagging, making her face square, stately. "How have you been?"

"I'm tired all the time. It seems like every day I catch myself saying 'I've never been so tired.' I can't seem to focus. And Bryan's working all the time. But I have help—a nanny and a babysitter. That gives me some time for the exercises. But it just winds up being more time to be drowsy, distracted," Farya said, looking down into the fur collar of her jacket, whose softness accused her—spoiled rich girl.

"I was wondering—what happened the other day?"

"I meant to call you about that. I started an exercise, but my mind drifted, and the sounds in the street and my thoughts started to double into each other. I caught it as soon as I could. It seemed small, harmless, just a nuisance that disappeared."

"It took me a minute to notice. But I try to come down here every few days," Lourdes said, gesturing to the faces that protruded from the walls and ceiling. President next to pin-up next to physicist next to poet next to tap-dancing dictator, from photorealistic to caricature. "And I was starting to see some new faces, remembering new facets, new characters. Congratulations on Minetta Street, by the way. I like the underground stream, the partially freed slaves, the bend, and the old-time murders, too."

"Thanks—it just happened that way."

"I know. We live in the world and spend so much of ourselves just trying to get along. We have to spend so much time listening to the world that it's easy to forget that we can also talk to it. You, especially, can talk to it," Lourdes said, letting each word unfold slowly, putting Farya on the spot.

"The birth eye—it seemed like a nuisance, the kind of small thing that parents forget about by the time their baby can walk, anyway. How did you notice?"

"The faces told me. For a lot of these great personalities, the birth-eye is part of their story, especially the ones with rough upbringings. They were neglected or underfed or abused, and the birth-eye never closed right. You know what they used to call the scar from a badly healed third eye? There were a few—the urchin's wink, the orphan's frown. And one day, I came in here to look around, and a lot of their faces were missing a famous feature."

"I guess it started with the ointment. It smelled, and you had to apply it just so, or else he'd start screaming. And it was the same ointment my mother used, which made me feel sad, like, all this effort, just to keep things the same. And the other moms, with their constant accusations and opinions, made it feel like I had to fight just to do the same stupid and boring and obvious thing my mom did," Farya said. The high edge of a sob started to grip her throat as she spoke.

"I understand."

"No, you don't. You don't have any children."

The words hit Lourdes in a visible way. Farya opened her mouth to approach an apology. But Lourdes sat up, recovering herself, and spoke.

"Maybe I don't understand, completely. And I'm sorry this is hard for you. But you need to be careful with depression—it's not just yours."

"I know. You're right. But what if I just get rid of bad things? This thing, it was just a weakness for infants and a chore for mothers."

"I hope you're right. When you start pulling threads, you never know where they'll stop," Lourdes said. "The world's smaller because of you. And no matter what's happening, no matter how subtle or small or dangerous, there's someone with a clever plan to make a buck out of it."

"How could you make money off of one less birth defect?"

"Because the world's disappearing. When that happens, the price of reality goes up. Maybe you can sell people back the reality they lost. Maybe, if they're rich enough, you can sell them another universe."

"What? How do you sell another universe?"

"Never mind. It's nothing to worry about right now. Just know that the consequences of these episodes don't stop just because you get a handle on yourself. I get that a regular job would be hard to keep at because you don't *need* one. So, start a business or a charity. You need to make some kind of commitment. You say that you're tired, but I think the real problem is that you're not tired enough."

"Any suggestions?" Farya asked.

"Just don't take on anything impossible. Don't try to solve world hunger or anything. You need to win a little, and you need to take on something in your day besides yourself."

On the ride home, light snow fell, just enough to refresh the dirty ice banks with a little white. At home, Farya relieved the sitter and walked on the balls of her feet around the creak in the floor at the nursery door. She opened the door a crack to watch her tiny son, sleeping on his back, a few tiny, restless fingers escaping the tight swaddle.

✣

It was a bad insomnia, and the mornings started earlier and earlier, quiet when Bryan least wanted quiet. He padded the travertine tile floor, pondered the kitchen, opened a cabinet, and tried to comprehend the plates, the mugs. Who'd bought them? Maybe Farya, maybe the decorator. It was, after all, so much house to fill at one go. He pondered the food processor on the counter that he didn't know how to use and the coffeemaker he didn't know how to use. But he should know how to do it by now. These four a.m. rendezvous with the kitchen were becoming more frequent.

On the surface, everything was good. Their baby boy grew. Metacom thrived, and Farya mostly seemed to thrive on motherhood. But Bryan's dreams grew more vivid, more awful. They scared him awake and away from the bed in the still hours before the housekeeper arrived. He gave up on the shiny silver coffee machine. These hours made no money. Any difference they made was a difference best concealed. They revealed weakness to the unacknowledged howling choruses in his head who asked, "How do you sleep at night?"

Fresh from the nightmare, there seemed no solution. But after an hour of drinking juice he wished was coffee, Bryan brightened at one prospect—a young man in the perpetual glow of a computer screen named Everick, whom Bryan had hired.

"Eradication is a tall order, even when no one's fighting you," Everick said later that afternoon, not looking up from his machine as he spoke. The kid was young, named for a character in a sci-fi movie series that was all the rage when Bryan was in college. Everick worked two days a week from the Metacom offices, chasing down the digital copies of Jimny Lomoigne's musical legacy.

Everick always preferred to send a link rather than talk. But Bryan paid, and so Everick spoke, properly, with his mouth. Red-faced and blinking in an oversized sweater and ball cap, the young man seemed like a shucked clam when not staring into a screen. The process, as Everick explained it, was like chasing ghosts made by ghosts, and trying to eradicate them with legal threats. The next step was to drown out the real copies with lies posted to the message boards of those sites, or with broken counterfeits of themselves. The fresh efflorescence of phony Jimny Lomoigne and Union Skells songs commissioned by the streaming apps helped fake out the uninitiated who tried to download or stream the songs for the first time.

But killing a ghost isn't cheap.

"The other side loses interest. That's how you win," said Everick. "The problem is if they know they're on a side. Then it gets harder, especially if they're not doing it for the money."

A week later, after a bad night, when the dreams tinged his whole day with a seasick sensation of disgust and remorse, Bryan met again with Everick. That's when he first learned the screen name LomoignAid1997. It would return over the coming months as LomoignAid1997 posted on message boards, social media, everywhere, hundreds of links to whole albums by the Union Skells, and Jimny Lomoigne. He (Bryan assumed it was a he, and Everick said he was probably right) seeded torrent sites of all stripes, shared singles and whole discographies across, under different names, always with masked IP addresses.

Everick said he couldn't get a fix on the location or identity of LomoignAid1997. He knew someone who could, but it would be expensive. Bryan said do it, and called his copyright lawyer to prepare a suit, multiple suits, as many as she could think of. The expense was negligible compared to the nightmares with Jimny Lomoigne force-fed from a jukebox like a cancerous liver.

Still, months went by. And LomoignAid1997 continued to spread the songs of Bryan's father far and wide across the web. What's more, LomoignAid1997 haunted Bryan's dreams. In them, he looked like a thinner, paler Everick, with long arms that reached out of the baggy sweaters he wore, subjecting all the dead of the

Lomoigne clan to punishments alternately medieval and pornographic. He was the face of the multiplying homunculi wielding magnetic tape, Wurlitzers, gigantic soundboards, along with the tubes, funnels, and pumps of the force feeder's art. The dreams carried with them a helplessness that returned Bryan, wherever he was, to an Arizona basement, where he watched impossible television shows to pass impossible time.

It was a terrible feeling. It made a day of work and a raucous toddler's nightly demands a relief, at least at first. But as time went on, it seemed that the work made him more susceptible to nightmares, while his little boy raised the stakes of those nightmares.

✢

It was a break, a moment on the way home, a late lunch alone. Lourdes was demanding—demanding that Farya take ever more responsibility. Edouard was demanding—while he ate more and slept longer, he had the attention span to insist on his desires.

Giorgio's was an old cafe, a fixture from the days when the village was a bohemian petri dish instead of another pleasure district for people who could afford just about anything. The old Italian man took her order, as disinterested as his grandfather was in Bob Dylan. It was the eve of St. Patrick's Day. The bar down the street was blasting *Yer never gonna see no unicorn* ... An early warm spring took hold, and all of New York warmed up and cheered to a semi-frenzy. A breeze played through the open door.

That day's exercises were troubling: *What's the worst image?* Lourdes had asked. *What would you show yourself if you desperately needed to get your own attention? If you could scream your own secret name at the top of your lungs, what form would that take?*

The exercises held Farya at the threshold of a seizure, where fragments of what Farya had annihilated began to return, but in strange ways. Medicines reappeared as weapons; courtship rituals reemerged as cruel governments. Terrible wars and great civilizations, forgotten childhoods and incredible capabilities, whole species lost to some blunder started to seep in as blockbuster movies—*Lord of the Rings*, *Harry Potter*, and *Star Wars*. Lourdes talked through the exercises, to guide Farya, remind her where she was, and what the stakes were. Eyes closed, Farya took a few of the sudden violent breaths by which she'd learned to ratchet herself away from the obliterating edge she knew so well.

Farya shook her head and picked at her BLT. She inhaled the cool air that smelled of earth, glad for the moment of freedom, aware that the nanny was waiting to be relieved, Edouard waiting to do an inarticulate negotiation for indeterminate foods and toys. Taking a big bite, she considered the effort of getting Bryan to take a night off work, of finding a babysitter, and decided to make the effort to go out to the movies. She missed the movies.

It had been easy to miss them last year. The baby was so small, and Bryan's job seemed like a towering emergency with no end in sight. And the blockbusters all seemed the same: gunfight epics about protecting some piece of infrastructure—a train tunnel, presidential palace, cosmic gateway, or world pillar. They all seemed to say that the last hero left was a security guard someone forgot to fire, stationed outside an abandoned machine.

The old waiter asked if she wanted anything else, and before she could finish her *no thank you*, he'd left the check and padded back to his newspaper at the bar. She looked out the plate-glass window, the grooved topography of the restaurant's name painted on the glass catching the sun. Tourists ambled past, half-lost with their oversized paper shopping bags, while women in futuristic exercise gear stalked past with chins up and blank expressions. One hobo wandered along, shaking a paper cup.

The neighborhood had changed since she moved there. Farya knew her own happiness was partly to blame for the transformation. In her exercises and her contentment, she'd added a few streets lined with renovated townhouses of a prototypical vintage, with faces and leaves carved in tan stone. But her effusiveness had also filled in some of the blank blocks of garages, crumbling wood-frame tenements, and fenced lots. As a result, the benign neglect in which all good new things grow had diminished. The old denizens blamed rich people for the neighborhood becoming safer, nicer, less free, and less fun. And Farya was, after all, a rich person now. That had been its own adjustment. But between the travel and the baby, it had been the least dramatic of the adjustments she'd made. As for what was left of the village—it was like with all the damage rich people do—it troubled her when she could be troubled to think about it, which wasn't too often.

The stylishness, cleanliness, and health of the passersby made her shiver. She said her all-too-familiar little prayer that she'd never have to tell Bryan what she'd done to their son or their world. She imagined what it would be like to tell him and to force Bryan to choose between her and what passed for sanity. Picking at the idea like the last crust of her BLT, she realized that she could do it, and he'd choose her. It would be hard, but she could. She shrugged, paid, and left.

✝

That night, Marista was in town with her fiancé, and the two couples were going out. Farya knew the fiancé—Ronnie, the detective who'd questioned Farya a few times about the disappearance of her ex-boyfriend. Neither wanted to discuss what had actually happened to the missing boyfriend with Marista or Bryan.

She had mixed feelings—glad Marista was getting married, along with dread that she was marrying Ronnie, who knew enough to suspect there was more to Marista's balky memory than simple flakiness. Farya's gladness that fellow refugees from the destruction of Camden had found each other and her was followed by dread at having to entertain such ghosts.

Ronnie had a conference in the city that Oneida County was paying for him to attend the next week, so they made a weekend of it. Farya suggested a place in Tribeca, and when Marista said she and Ronnie were thinking of pizza, Farya remembered to say it was her treat. Bryan's evenings had become easier to free up, as he'd promised—the two men it had taken to replace Cassie could almost handle her job.

The restaurant spread out on either side of a walkway that connected the entrance with a bar like a proscenium, its towering shelves of liquor like a pipe organ. The light in the room had a tint between yellow and brown. Bryan was dressed just so, with impeccable slacks, a button-down shirt sporting a collar with a surprising angle, and a jacket that fit better than his own flesh. Ronnie wore his oversized suit and a gun under the jacket.

The hostess showed the four of them to Bryan's usual table on the outer fringe of the room, where they could see the street. Ronnie and Marista looked around the restaurant, which was unlike any place they were used to. As soon as they arrived, Farya was filled with dread at the thought that she was showing off. In the restaurant, Eamonn sat two tables away with his partner for the evening. Before the table could order cocktails, Eamonn walked over and spoke into Bryan's ear, while Eamonn's partner watched them. When he was done, Eamonn stayed where he was, his hip beside Bryan's tailored shoulder.

"Ronnie, did you bring a gun to dinner?" Bryan asked.

"Yeah, I'm a police officer. I always keep it with me," he said, taking out his badge. Eamonn inspected it and the ID in the other half of the vinyl wallet and handed it back. Eamonn returned to his table and his partner. Dinner was off to a bad start, and Farya found some relief in the thought that the awkwardness could be blamed on firearms. Because Farya felt quite awkward. How do you talk about an absence? How do you raise a drink over it? How can you laugh at an absence? If there's an outsider, there was no way even to broach it.

"So, you take that everywhere?" Bryan said.

"I do," Ronnie said. "Whenever you hear about something terrible that gets stopped before it can start, it's always an off-duty police officer who's there. It's a crazy world—as you seem to know. Do you take him everywhere?"

They both looked at Eamonn, who was staring at Ronnie.

"For now, I do."

After a brief look at the wine list, Bryan ordered a bottle of red and one of white. With drinks in front of them, Bryan and Ronnie soon found they had a lot to talk about: the security profession; cellular technology; the shifting legal status of signals on a wireless network, and the worsening of mankind in general. Their pretenses gave way, and they were on to a second bottle of red before the first course arrived.

It was a different story with the old friends seated beside them—Marista wasn't drinking, but she wasn't not drinking, either. She was taking tiny sips, small gestures. Farya apologized and asked if she wanted another drink, but Marista said no, she loved the wine, and soon Farya recognized the kind of drinking that she had done between when she learned she was pregnant, and when she and Bryan began telling people. Farya's eyes lit up, and Marista tried to hide her smile in her napkin.

"No …" Farya said. "Is that why the short engagement?"

"We're not saying anything yet. And I was hoping it wouldn't show at the wedding, but what can you do? I guess we'll just ask the photographer to do a lot of close-ups."

Their squealing interrupted the men, who exchanged perfunctory confirmations, congratulations, and good lucks before resuming their conversation about contractual rights versus civil rights, and the many now-common scenarios that wiretapping laws had failed to anticipate.

"So, what is it?" Farya asked.

"Until this week, it was twins. But I guess one of them ... I don't know, ate the other," Marista said.

"Absorbed, is how the doctor put it. It's pretty common," Ronnie said, interrupting them and himself before turning to Bryan.

"Absorbed. And it's a boy," Marista said, trying to regain some glee and momentum. "And he's healthy, and ..."

At the mention of the word *absorbed*, Marista looked off and took a full sip of her white wine, which almost matched the light in the room. A look of terrible agony flashed across Marista's face and vanished. Farya saw it and thought of the physical bodies—of Sarah, Melissa, and Christa—dissolved in a soup of disinterest and irrational, bone-deep rage that summed into a single, all-purpose friend. Marista didn't want her grimace or her gulp seen, and Farya didn't want to have seen it.

"Did you want twins?" Farya asked, stuttering the first syllable and coughing the last.

"No, I don't know. It's not like you plan for it—even if we were planning any of this. It's just, you get a sense that it's there. And you, without even thinking of it, start to build this picture of a life. And the next day, it's gone, or changed, anyway."

"I'm sorry."

"It's okay—just one of those things. We just found out. There's so much to do, so much going on. I'll forget it in a couple of days."

"So, it's a boy—a little friend for Edouard," Farya said. "Do you have a name picked out?"

"Roger, after my father," Marista said.

"I thought your father's name was Robert?"

"Oh, my God, did I just say …"

A wave of confusion passed over Marista's face. The unspeakable reared its head—the lost millions of Camden, New York, and this one confused young woman who'd gone to great lengths to make her life into something. One of the three girls Marista had been had a father named Roger, another had a father named Robert. The third had a father named Greg. With a puzzled expression, Marista mouthed the name, *Greg*.

Uncertain what to do, Farya deliberately-accidentally knocked her globe of wine from the table. She and Marista jumped up to avoid the splatter, which caused Eamonn to get out of his seat two tables over, almost upending the table. Startled by the sudden burst of activity, Ronnie leaped from his chair, dropped into a crouch, and put his hand on the butt of the pistol in his jacket. Only a too-prepared waiter, rushing in with a stack of napkins, managed to keep a gunfight from erupting.

In the aftermath, Marista said she needed to go to the bathroom, and Farya offered to join her. But Marista declined the offer, dabbing at the corners of her eyes with her fingers. The men laughed over the narrowly averted firefight. Ronnie apologized and explained how the city had a way of setting him on edge. Bryan refilled his wine glass. Marista returned a few minutes later, her makeup redone. The waiter brought wooden planks inscribed with desserts.

"Finally, an indulgence I can indulge in," Marista said with a natural-seeming laugh.

They ordered cakes and puddings and ice creams and pastry. Farya and Marista together willed the conversation to children. Marista ran a daycare out of her parents' old house.

"It's scary because the vaccine doesn't always work," Marista said, "and the parents don't know that, and so they don't even check when the kids get a fever or cloudy eyes for a day or two. And these kids, some of them seem all right afterward, so the real extent of the damage is hard to tell."

"I know. It's terrifying. And the vaccines do work, but there are so many strains of Ripht-Schondles now. That's why my foundation is focused, first and foremost, on educating parents about the different kinds of vaccines and when children should get them," Farya said.

Normalcy reasserted itself—two old friends talking about things they both knew about. By the time the desserts arrived, their biggest issue was that one ran a daycare for a living, while the other married into enough money to have her own foundation. The foundation had been Lourdes's idea—especially the part about choosing a curable disease like Ripht-Schondles Disorder. It was just hard enough to keep Farya busy, fulfilled even.

The rest of the night stayed civil and sane for Farya and Marista. They may have parted without a clear sense of who they were to each other, or who they'd been, but they renewed a mutual commitment not to inquire too deeply.

✣

"Welcome, everyone. It's wonderful to see so many of you here tonight. And as you know, Ripht-Schondles Disorder is a neurological disease that affects more than three percent of all children between nine and twelve years of age in the United States. Symptoms start with small a fever, a cloudiness in the eyes," Farya said to the empty room, checking the screen behind her. "Hey, Claude, why are we still on the bar chart here? When I say *United States*, that's when we go to the eye slide, okay?"

Claude said *okay* from the soundboard in the rear corner of the cavernous dining room of a Midtown restaurant with waterfalls for walls anchored by a massive bar overlooking a glassed-in kitchen. Farya was nervous the afternoon before the gala, checking the venue, and doing a quick run-through. Giving away money—as Founder and Executive Director of the Navurian-Lomoigne Foundation—was Farya's main job. It was easy, Bryan explained, but there's also a way to be good at it if you want. He knew—he'd been dragged to these kinds of events since he was a boy.

Farya was good at it. She went on day-long site visits to the clinics, labs, and rehab facilities where the foundation contributed. She used Bryan's connections to get those facilities many of their supplies at cost, or for free. After a year, she had the kind of operation that could do more than just spend money and give Farya an answer for how she spent her time, and Bryan a subject of conversation besides business. In the first year and a half she ran the foundation, Farya developed a reputation and was invited to sit on the boards of two related organization. This was the foundation's first gala, a lavish affair where the nearly wealthy could be seen as wealthy, and where the wealthy could be seen in a flattering light.

"No, Claude, if it's *okay*, then why did you miss it?" Farya said. "You should have the whole speech in front of you, with the cues marked. Let's start from the top."

She had been planning the event for months, prepping the venue, hiring the band, selling tables, finding sponsors, and cadging items for the silent auction. Bryan helped. He had people who owed him favors, or who wanted him to owe them. So did Ethan, with his set of trust-fund layabouts and schemers. Ethan drew in people who wanted to find a way to get closer to his shadowy power-broker of a father-in-law. His wife Carolina was always suspicious of Farya and wanted to keep her close. She bought a table and contributed a week at the family's Montauk compound to the silent auction.

For Bryan, galas like these were regular occurrences. As a child, he'd learned how to endure them, how to hide if he had to. The country clubs, banquet halls, restaurants, and university clubs where they were held always seemed incredible warrens of intrigue and secrecy, like the unfolding of an unexplored sex. As he got older, he learned to watch the staff, to whom those august venues were as demystified as any place that you have to clean. Even grown up, Bryan still watched the waiters and busboys.

The event was tasteful, without anything so gauche as a red carpet. A simple *Private Event Tonight* sign in black and white outside of the restaurant separated the invitees from the public.

"… can be treated in nearly all cases when it's caught in time. But when it's not detected, or when caregivers don't identify the initial symptoms, Ripht-Schondles Disorder can ruin lives. And while some of the worst effects of it can be managed through medication and rehabilitation, the children afflicted experience a host of lifelong health problems, along with the disorder's signature lethargy and depression … Claude, I feel like the sound is more on the left side of the room than the right."

Claude responded that he was still setting levels. Farya checked the big screen and then her phone. The gala had taken more of her time than she ever expected. That week, she missed Edouard in a physical way, like an elastic made of guilt and grief tied to the center of her chest. She chastised herself—for all the overtime she was paying the nanny, she could have just hired an event planner. Maybe next year. For now, she was doing a good thing, and she was doing it all herself, more or less.

"… exactly because it's *not* deadly, and *is* treatable, that it doesn't get the attention it deserves. But I think the damage Ripht-Schondles Disorder does to its children and to families, is in some way just as tragic because, as one mother put it to me, you'll never know what that child might have been, what he might have learned, what she might have …"

After another half hour, they got through the five-minute speech and the slides to Farya's satisfaction. At home, she found Edouard in his room, smashing trucks into blocks. They played a little peek-a-boo. He looked like Bryan—the broad face, the sharp angle in his nose, but with her warm brown eyes.

After an hour, the babysitter arrived, and Farya left to get ready. She'd planned the whole day so she'd be too rushed to eat herself alive with pre-event nerves or last-minute dress changes. It took her almost four months to choose the right dress for the event, an open-back piece made of a fabric that flitted between gray, charcoal, and silver. It was light and moved with her. It covered enough, concealed enough in profile. While some might whisper about her being a dozen years younger than her husband, she wanted to keep them jealous without giving them any ammunition.

+

The first guests arrived, checking their coats. The Navurian-Lomoigne Foundation logos reflected off the waterfall-walls of the space, and the band—fronted by the recently exonerated Richie Reach—was playing on a stage by the restaurant's signature bar.

In the last year, Farya had been going to more and more galas, to be seen in the right rooms, and to learn. And she was glad she'd studied the bright doyennes who ran these events. For the best of them, these weren't parties, but a kind of dance, with their own moves—the clutch and release, the nod, the small bow, the walking wave and hello, the introduction of people whose names you don't remember, drinking and not drinking, handing conversation partners off to others, solemn nods, all while checking details like the passed hors d'oeuvres, who was drinking, and circulating in a fashion that made sense of the room itself, and making sure, informally, that the mood of the room was agreeable to everyone.

"Petra, hello. I've heard about you from Bryan. Thank you and the rest of Sevritas Capital so much for your generosity. I just saw him, let me …" Farya said to the precise but pretty woman in a tight orange dress with leather trim. "He's over by the oyster tower, with, uh, have you met Bill Van Harappan?"

"I have. And I think I'll stay here, for now, thank you."

For the most part, though, Farya danced well, and the people seemed to mingle, to drink and enjoy themselves. She even pushed and found a crack in her voice and a small but visible tear to introduce to the climactic finale of her speech. The applause seemed, to her, more than just polite. Of course, the night cured nothing. But between the tables, the corporate sponsors, and the silent auction, the Navurian-Lomoigne Foundation made enough to pay the bill for the party, and to fund its fight against Ripht-Schondles Disorder for another year. Sober and weary, Ethan was among the first to excuse himself.

"Even the oligarch managed to have a good time, which is no mean feat," Ethan said, gesturing to the coat check where the drunk, rail-thin old man was shoving a handful of green bills into a fishbowl while his daughter helped him get his coat on. He seemed sentimental, trying to get some point across to the girl behind the counter.

"I'm not surprised. You always made him out to be a big, brassy, Russian party animal," Farya said.

"Not lately. Carolina's mother has gotten worse. Just a few months left, the doctor says. Cancer."

"That's hard. I'm sorry."

"That's not even the *big* problem now. She's run off. No one knows where she is. She calls every week or so to say that she's okay and that she'll be back soon. But that's all we know."

"No kidding. Did she say why?"

"Says she needs to see *nothing but beauty* before she goes. She says she can't let herself be distracted."

"Distracted from what?"

"She says that when she dies, she's going to a world with no ugliness or pain. But she can't go there if she can't imagine it. She says she needs to focus, or she'll miss her chance," Ethan said, glancing over his shoulder to see his wife's progress with the scene at the coat check. "Anyway, I guess the old lady always ran the house, so they're just going along with it. The oligarch doesn't know what to do. It's a mess."

"It's death, I guess. How does anyone deal with it?"

"On that note, I have to go. But great job, lady. You sure can throw a shindig when you set your mind to it."

With dessert eaten, the auction completed, the band packing up, and Bryan's bow tie undone, Farya sat at the bar with a few lingering guests. The only person among them she'd known three years ago was Lourdes, who'd gotten a few real estate developers to buy tables. She congratulated Farya—on everything, as she put it.

"To everything," Farya said, raising a champagne flute.

"Everything indeed, and more of it!" Lourdes said, clinking with a squat cylinder of scotch.

The last of the hundred things that could've gone wrong that night now passed, Farya was giddy and exhausted. And there, at the pinnacle of a long year of hard work, she felt a dread, like reaching a summit and looking down—a space vast and terrifying, but the only place left to go.

She drank, smiled, and danced out the last few steps the evening asked.

✢

However much of a success the event was, it was over. And it quickly became less of a triumph than a standard that had to be met next year. After a warm fall, the weather turned on a knife's edge to a frigid, penetrating cold. Bryan's ex-wife had the older kids for Thanksgiving. And so, Christmas was the big holiday—their townhouse full with the kids from his first marriage, Elena and Charles, and Bryan's mother visiting. By Christmas Eve, it was full of people avoiding each other.

Elena was thirteen and sullen. She broke from her sighing, texting, and general impatience only long enough to try to get long-distance revenge on her mother by enlisting Farya as a kind of older friend she could talk to about boys, purloined beer, cigarettes, and sneaking out of the dorms at her boarding school. After one such story, full of exaggerations and inconsistencies, Farya threatened to tell Bryan. That was the end of Elena saying much of anything to anyone.

Bryan's still-glamorous septuagenarian mother, Alyx, still subjected Farya to a bland, patronizing civility reserved for someone she didn't expect to know for very long. Their conversation stayed within the realms of beauty tips to combat aging, how much the Village had changed since she was young, and the limited attention span and intelligence of males, including her son.

Charles, a lanky and oversized eleven-year-old, was too busy eating and reading graphic novels with lurid, blood-soaked covers, to have too much to say to anyone.

As for Bryan, Farya could feel the trouble building. She knew about the nightmares. And though he said he was thinking of making a change at work, he wouldn't say more. He checked his phone every few minutes throughout the holiday—not responding to demands so much as hoping some news had arrived. He kept checking to see if Eamonn and his men were nearby.

Even Edouard, a smart child who had gone from crawling to running that year, seemed depressed that Christmas. He was prone to terrible tantrums during which everything she offered to satisfy or distract him seemed to work for a moment before the toy or snack or bottle was discovered to be a lie and betrayal of the worst sort.

It was a week of being on her best behavior in her own home, of failing to find time to do her exercises, of ignoring slights, of trying to support her depressed husband, while hiding her own gloomy suspicion that this was going to be a very long winter. On Christmas night, with everyone sound asleep after a day of gifts, food, mutual aggravation, and malaise, Edouard broke the early a.m. silence with a shriek. Murmuring, Bryan rose from bed and staggered down the hall, past a guest-room-slash-home-office where Elena complained to whoever might hear about the impossibility of sleeping in *this stupid house.*

In the crying baby's room, Bryan shut the door and lifted the boy from his crib with a small grunt. Farya, awake now, padded out into the hall and listened at the door.

"Hey, buddy, what's wrong?" she heard Bryan say.

"I woke up. I was sad."

"Oh, no. Why were you sad?"

"I cried," the little boy said.

"You were sad because you cried?"

"Yeah."

"Oh. Why did you cry?"

"I cried," she heard the boy say, with a laugh in his voice. "The couch cried, the table cried, the cat cried, the music cried, the living room cried, Daddy's books cried, my books cried, the ball cried, the sofa cried, Daddy cried."

"I did?" Bryan asked with a small laugh of his own.

"Yeah."

✝

Finding the actual person behind LomoignAid1997, legally, had taken a considerable amount of time and money. Everick, the young man Bryan had hired for the job, said he could have done it faster the other way. But any lawsuit required that there be a clear and legally obtained chain of evidence connecting the screen name to the person who was illegally distributing copyrighted Union Skells and Jimny Lomoigne songs.

By the time they had the name and address of LomoignAid1997, the suits had long been prepared. Bryan's law firm had the young fellow served within the day. The suits were multiple, thick, and official looking, scary with charges and demands for enormous financial restitution. It didn't occur to Bryan, nor did the question of whom he was suing. He was desperate to believe that a successfully executed cease-and-desist on LomoignAid1997 might have a similar effect on his nightmares.

A week later, Ritchie Reach called. Bryan ignored the first call. He'd helped Ritchie a lot lately—overpaying for his share of the Union Skells' catalog, and paying a premium for the old man's private recordings and outtakes when he needed help mounting his criminal defense, and paid out of pocket for Ritchie to front the band at Farya's gala. He was ashamed for the old man—going back to the well so soon. But after an hour plotting out a fresh round of layoffs at Metacom, he decided that helping out the old rocker might put him in a better frame of mind.

"Why are you suing my son?" Ritchie demanded, his voice all Long Island rage, none of the Britishness he affected elsewhere. Bryan confessed his confusion, and Ritchie told him that his son had received a thick envelope of cease-and-desists, with demands for a few million dollars in damages. Ritchie said his son was in a panic.

"So, your son is LomoignAid1997?" Bryan said.

"What?"

"His screen name—LomoignAid1997—the name he uses online. Look at the suit."

"Yeah, I saw that. Screen name—like a stage name, but on a computer. That's funny. His name is Rick. Funny that he has a computer name. He always wants to be called Rick Toomey—even by me, around the house. He's a good kid, makes his own money. Plays in a band—bar band, but still. Lives the next town over. Quiet, but not a sponge or a fuckup. Named Ritchie after me, though he took his mom's last name."

"I guess it makes sense. What did he have to say about why I was suing him?"

"He said he was going to play some Skells for a friend and couldn't find it on YouTube. So, he put it up. And when it got taken down, he put it back up under a different account, and so on. It was like a game, like a *fuck you*. He's only twenty-four."

Bryan flinched at the age, though it didn't surprise him that Ritchie had such a young son. Among the children of rock musicians, the sense of a generation was often stretched to the point of ludicrousness. Bryan had his half-sister Leighton, who was his age but also had half-siblings by his father's later wives who were twenty years younger.

"Okay, well, you know I like to help out," Bryan said. "But you sold me that music, that intellectual property."

"Imagine that—calling the Union Skells intellectual property."

"Under the terms of the contract, under the law, that's what it is. It's property. Just like your house. If I sell you a house and you find me in there taking a shower a month later, guess what? That's against the law."

"Okay, no need to climb the lectern," Ritchie said, more British now. "How can my boy make this right? He can't afford a lawyer for all this."

Bryan could have mentioned that Ritchie lived in a multi-million-dollar home, as he could have in a few other instances.

But instead, they agreed to meet later that week in Bryan's office. Ritchie wore his Ritchie Reach uniform, the jeans, hair dye, gold chains, and a leather jacket. The young man, Rick Toomey, had Ritchie's features and his tendency to sneer. But where Ritchie was all gristle, stubble, and bony angles, the kid was like a squid, all soft and pale, like he could slither out of his polo shirt, sweater, and khakis if he wanted to. Bryan's attorney joined them in the Metacom conference room. The lights were at full brightness in a way that allowed for no shadows. It was unflattering and unnatural.

"So, Rick, it seems that you know by now that this is not a game," Bryan said.

"Yes, Mr. Lomoigne."

Rick Toomey didn't seem like the type to call people *mister* very often. Bryan wondered for a moment whether Ritchie had advised it to make Bryan feel respected or to feel guilty for becoming the square heavy. It seemed to have both effects on him.

"You've cost me a great deal of time and money," Bryan said, hearing the heavy dream-crushing tones of authority in his own voice. He couldn't help but like it a little. "And you nearly caused your father a fresh new set of financial difficulties."

"I'm sorry, Mr. Lomoigne. I was just trying to share some music—my dad's music. Your dad's too."

"I own that music. It's not yours to share."

"I understand that now. I won't do it again."

"Good," Bryan said, nodding to the lawyer, who produced a typed three-sheet contract and slipped it before the languid young man, who asked, "What's this?"

"This document states that you will not upload, download, copy, share, recommend, or mention online or elsewhere the music of the Union Skells or Jimny Lomoigne. In this document, you agree to severe penalties if you do."

"Oh."

"In it, we also agree to refrain from any further legal action, if you abide by the contract."

Rick looked to Ritchie. The old man nodded, the slow bend of his neck landing his chin on his sternum. His neck was a spider web of dry furrows, his cheeks sunken. He looked down at the conference room table, not wanting to be conscious for this. He seemed to have aged in his chair. The young man made a show of reading the first page of the contract, but gave up midway through the second one and signed. Father and son made the same face, like a genetic memory of a thousand inevitable rip-offs and defeats grudgingly acceded to.

In their resignation, Bryan saw his own father—not the short-tempered prima donna or the happy-go-lucky-at-all-costs rocker—but the one from his own dreams, trapped in a hell forged from his own songs.

"Son," Ritchie said after the young man had signed and dated the contract.

"Right. Mr. Lomoigne, I wanted to say that I'm sorry again for the trouble I've caused you, and to thank you for letting this matter go."

That was the one—the one too many *misters*. It made the power of the moment go sour in Bryan, made him eager to be done with this business. He rose and offered his hand. The young and old men shook it. The lawyer gathered his things.

"It amazes me, all of us here with a lawyer," Ritchie said. "I remember making those songs with your dad, some when we were younger than Rick Toomey. And now our two sons fighting with computers and lawyers and millions of dollars in damages … over music, over a bunch of sounds and best guesses about how to deal with time and with your heart, though it turns out, they're both unmanageable as hell. I guess sometimes music manages it, sometimes, but never for very long," the old man said, his thoughts gone off to a place preferred to the too-bright Midtown conference room, handing over the last of his patrimony to a middle-aged executive.

"Well, I'm just glad we could do it like this instead of going to court," Bryan said with the bland magnanimity of a conqueror.

Hand on leather-clad shoulder, Rick Toomey shepherded his father out of the room, to the elevator. Alone in the room, Bryan thought of father and son—the helplessness in captivity. He closed his eyes and tried to recall his own father's face from the latest spate of hellish dreams: deformed, surgically attached to jukeboxes. And focusing on that dim and slippery place, he could see that it wasn't his father in those hells. Looking at the chair where his lawyer had sat, Bryan thought of the lengthy and expensive quest to close his father's account with this world. This latest triumph sealed it. And Bryan was forced to realize that it had all been a waste.

After months of nightmares, and millions spent on music he could've listened to for free, it was all quite clear. Bryan had been trying to free the one person who didn't need freeing. At the same time, he'd spent every other waking moment of his life in an enterprise that kept millions in real thrall. Maybe he'd known this all along or just suspected it. But now, he was ready and willing to know. Bryan swallowed hard because knowing meant having to act.

✢

The thing about a truly and deeply private matter is that it's very easy to postpone.

While Farya's exercises were meaningful, and could even be enjoyable, every day offered some opportunity to say that her mood was off, or there wasn't enough time to do it right, or it would go better if she just waited until tomorrow. She had ways of dealing with this tendency, but the same tactic never worked for very long.

That winter, after the gala was over, Farya was uninspired. Edouard was a wonderful little boy with good sleep habits and an abiding affection for his mother. He was walking and talking, which was cute, and made her swell with pride. But as Ethan said the other day at a toddler-gymnasium date, "How much can you even say about a child? I mean, you're supposed to go on and on about them, but who cares?" Her love for her little son had a way of highlighting the areas of her life it left untouched. And it made her feel guilty about her own alternating restlessness, exhaustion, guilt, and depression. It was easier to focus on the battle the Navurian-Lomoigne Foundation was waging against Ripht-Schondles Disorder. She'd hired an assistant, Kathleen—a friend from Farya's very early days in the rarefied airs of the philanthropy circuit. Since they met, Kathleen's husband had been disgraced and effectively exiled to international waters, with the family's assets frozen for as long as the federal prosecutors needed to untangle just what had happened. As a result, Kathleen had found herself in need of a way to support herself and her two teenage daughters.

She and Kathleen met daily in the sunny home office at the back of Farya's townhouse, overlooking a cluster of minuscule Manhattan gardens. They held conference calls with experts, negotiated with pharmaceutical companies, and sketched the storyboards for a new informational video. Kathleen was grateful for the job, and for the sun-warm comfort and company of those afternoons. She distracted Farya and served as a reminder that she had no reason to feel as depressed as she did. Nonetheless, she did. Ripht-Schondles was boring. The cure was boring. The worst-case scenarios of its victims were boring. All this was why she'd chosen it. But raising awareness for it was like smearing boredom on a stick and poking someone in the eye with it.

Farya tried to give herself a break. She tried to get herself excited. She tried a lot of things. The net result, though, was that she let her exercises lapse a little more. She could feel the drift in herself and in the world, like a static of trivia. The suspicion of unknown things gone missing, followed by a few half-seen things suddenly vanished harmonized with the drowsy apathy of deep midwinter depression. And though she noticed the sensation and knew what it meant, it continued like a slow leak. It left Farya half-waiting for the sudden angry call from Lourdes, demanding she report to the room of masks, with warm instruction and hard admonition. But Lourdes didn't call. Nothing pierced the static until it was too late.

Farya was alone in her office when Kathleen called. She'd taken the day off for a pediatrician visit. On the phone, her breathing was louder than her words.

"We saw the doctor today," Kathleen said, "he said that Ellem tested positive for Ripht-Schondles."

Ellem was Kathleen's oldest, an athlete and honor student. Farya had met her.

"Well, no matter what stage it's in, there are plenty of treatment options," Farya said. "And we know some of the best doctors."

"I know. I know. We'll be brave. We'll make her as comfortable as we can for as long as we can. I just don't know if I can stand to think of her when they have to start cutting just so she can breathe," Kathleen said. Farya heard a door slam on the other end of the line, and then Kathleen broke down crying in earnest.

Farya knew Kathleen, and she knew Ripht-Schondles. Kathleen was a mature, composed woman who had seen her life overturned and shaken out the way a mugger handles a purse. And she had calmly picked up the pieces. And Ripht-Schondles, if treated at any stage, would leave its worst victims with periodic bouts of vertigo and a lingering sense of fatigue. Farya remained sure of that much as she listened on the phone. But at some point, on the cusp of offering fresh sympathies, Farya suddenly wasn't so sure.

The numb, buzzing depression, like a cashmere sweater separating her every thought from the ones before and after, intensified. Farya pressed the phone tighter to her ear. The sobs from her friend sounded farther and farther away, more like one another, in a squeaking, sucking pattern that simplified as it persisted. And Farya could see, as she'd never seen before, the threshold of her catastrophic seizure. And she could choose, as she'd never been able to before, whether to cross it.

This was the exercise that she should have been practicing. Farya closed her eyes and called on an image like a nail caught in the wooly coils of her brain: her father, purple-faced and alone asphyxiating on a piece of half-chewed steak in a grimy restaurant bathroom. With it, she pierced the static-membrane of depression and fought the pull toward the sweet deliverance that never-having-been will promise.

As she did, Kathleen's weeping became more irregular, more natural, and after a few attempts, she'd washed up again on the shores of dazed and ragged speech. Nauseous with a fellow mother's empathy, Farya wanted to say it would all be okay. But she wasn't sure it would. Past sobs, Kathleen recited the day, as if she could go back to the broken part and fix it. Farya could only listen. As she did, she turned on her laptop and visited her own foundation's site.

The site wasn't familiar at first glance. There was an image of a young woman on a hospital bed. Her contorted form, and the elaborate metal brace around it could be guessed well enough even from under the heavy blanket. Beside her was a family member, holding the young woman's contorted and clawlike hand. The young woman's face was asymmetrical, with half her teeth showing and one eye open as wide as seemed possible. Farya had seen pictures like this, but not from the United States, not from this century. It was the final state of Ripht-Schondles Disorder if left untreated, as no one had done since just before the first World War.

Kathleen talked about her day leading up to the diagnosis—shopping, the delays on the train to the pediatrician, why she'd kept the same pediatrician after they moved to Queens, the kindness of the receptionist, all the last normal moments she'd known. Farya read, in her own private horror, on her own foundation's website, that Ripht-Schondles was a fatal, degenerative disease with no known cure.

Farya swallowed a sob. She knew Ellem. And the violence of a memory newly minted by a reformulated universe struck Farya with the truth: Ripht-Schondles would ravage that girl. Ellem wouldn't just disappear. From diagnosis to pain-racked death, with the child's body and memory wrung beyond recognition, would take years. But Farya knew she had no right to weep. When Farya's cracking voice interrupted Kathleen, she comforted Farya. By the time Farya was coherent again, Kathleen was calm enough to say she had to go. There was so much to do, and she was so tired.

Alone in her office, Farya read the rest of her foundation's website. As she did, it became harder to ignore that she had, through her moody inattention alone, made a curable and treatable disease incurable and untreatable.

Farya had trusted herself. Lourdes had trusted her. And now it was clear that she could not be trusted at all, by anyone. Farya couldn't cry anymore—it seemed crass when she thought of Kathleen and Ellem. The years of shame and guilt surged, unbearable and unanswerable. Farya wanted to atone and returned to the thought of suicide. There had to be a way. She could ask Lourdes.

Farya heard Edouard wake in the next room. Without a second thought, she knew that her atonement would have to take another form. And no small thing would suffice.

"Oh, God," she said, feeling far past the reach of any prayer.

✝

Bryan and Bill Van Harappan, combined, made money off almost a third of the country's phone calls. But they never spoke on the phone. When they spoke honestly, they didn't even speak near phones. The warehouse where they met had a free-standing locker-slash-charger for cell phones outside its heavy door. As Bryan put his into a cubby and keyed in a combination to lock it, he noted Van Harappan's device—the thin plastic flip phone common to the powerful and secretive in those days.

"Newark, Delaware—you're full of surprises, Bill."

"The important places are never where people would have you think."

Nobody would have pegged this little corner of Delaware as important. Driving in, the area was as Anytown-USA as it got, and could have been in Maine, Georgia, or Wisconsin with its little main street of not-poor, not-rich shops and restaurants, its old protestant church in acceptable repair, and the interstate nearby. After a railroad crossing was an industrial district with oil tanks and hulking mill barns. But as they pulled into a nondescript industrial park, they met two armed checkpoints—one guarded by US Customs and Border Protection officers and the other by armed private security. The destination was a one-story cinder block so pristine that it glowed in the night.

The smell inside, Bryan recognized as the smell of college, like paste that floated on cool, dry air, almost sour, almost sexual. It was the smell of youthful whimsy and more than enough money.

Bryan followed Van Harappan to a door whose small digital sign bore the older man's name. Van Harappan looked up at one of the many cameras mounted throughout the facility, tapped his foot, and an audible mechanism within the heavy door began to whir and click. Van Harappan opened it, and the smell hit Bryan in all its fullness—the smell of a museum. The room was spare, the walls and floor white-washed concrete and lit like a museum, all the light sources muted, indirect, but bright. Paintings lined the walls.

"What is this place?"

"This is where things change hands," Van Harappan said. "Gold, gems, statues, paintings, companies. This one complex of warehouses is home to more—and better—art than the Metropolitan Museum. The main difference is that most of it is safely crated up. Consider it the greatest museum no one will ever see."

Bryan followed Van Harappan along the walls, past old oil paintings of battles, moments in the career of Christ, of horse-borne generals and pensive merchants. Hands in pockets, the pair walked and spoke.

"I've never heard of this place," Bryan said.

"It's a tax haven. I just acquired a collection here, and I wanted to appreciate a few pieces before I started to sell them off. This one, in particular," the older man said, stopping in front of a painting. In it, two young men with beards regarded the viewer with meek surprise. The greens, blues, and pinks of their clothes were rich and vivid, the patterns clear and intricate. Before them, across the mosaic floor, was an unnerving, long gray smear.

"What's this one called?" Bryan asked.

"The Ambassadors, by someone named Hans Holbein. And for now, it's mine."

"What are you going to do with it?"

"Sell it. It's well known and should get a good price. These major works are pretty liquid. So, what brings us together again after all these years?"

"I want to find a buyer for Metacom. The whole thing, as soon as possible."

"So, call a banker."

"You know how they gossip. And they're clever, a couple of them at least, when it suits them. It wouldn't take too long for them to find the big white elephant on our balance sheet. I have a lot of reasons not to want new people involved if I can help it."

"So, what happened to all that bandwidth you were going to buy on my network? You seemed very hot on the idea, but you never followed up."

"Something happened. I had to put that on hold."

"Something sudden and bad, I assume. I noticed your security."

"You have security. You know what's out there."

Van Harappan laughed at that, lowering his voice in the presence of the dead men in the painting. "I'm not surprised. The people you're in business with—you can't expect them to play by the rules. How did they come at you?"

"It wasn't them. It was kidnappers after a ransom. They must have drugged me. It was … I don't remember it well."

"Kidnappers, huh? They get their ransom?" Van Harappan said, turning to look straight at Bryan.

"No."

"Strange, given the timing—you trying to soothe your wounded conscience and kick your trusty old partners to the curb. You never considered the timing of it?"

"You don't think much of me as a businessman," Bryan said with some anger.

"Business is an amorphous thing. There's a lot of ways to do it, and a lot of ways to be good at it. And you're one variety of good businessman."

"Oh, yeah? Which one is that?"

"You're a good patsy."

Van Harappan opened his dry, thin-lipped mouth a half inch, and watched Bryan like an animal waiting to see what the young man would do.

But Bryan knew when he was being baited. He didn't so much as clench his jaw at the imperious old man. Instead, Bryan dropped to his haunches and looked up from the corner of the painting. Sure enough, from that extreme perspective, the long gray smear appeared as a photorealistic skull, while the rest of the picture became a jumble of shapes and reflected light on lacquer.

"Oh, I see it," Bryan said.

"I don't."

"The skull."

"Oh, that. Of course. It's famous. What I don't see is why I'd want to get involved with Metacom."

"Why would you get involved with this?" Bryan said, tapping the elongated skull on the canvas in front of him, knowing it would piss off Van Harappan. "Money. Money is why. I need to get this done quickly, and I'll give you a sizable finder's fee for your trouble.

You get paid and get to do someone a favor by landing them Metacom for cheap."

Van Harappan said a number that made Bryan wince. After a halfhearted negotiation, they shook hands, and looked at the painting some more.

"So, you sell this, and where does it go?" Bryan said, gesturing at the painting. "A museum? A college?"

"Based on the current market, it'll stay here, just move to a different locked room. Otherwise, the tax man comes knocking. It's funny—five hundred years, and the men like us rise and fall, come and go, succeed and fail. But these bastards get perennial air-conditioning, their lutes and globes and books and knickknacks forever. Pretty nice."

"Except for the skull."

"There is that," Van Harappan said, and cracked a smile. Based on the deal, the tall old man had reason for at least a grin.

At the phone locker, Bryan keyed his combination and saw that Farya had called, multiple times. He gave Van Harappan a distracted wave as the old man swept out with his three-person security team and two-person support staff. Bryan called his wife.

+

Farya was a little girl when she first heard the phrase *breakdown* as a thing that happened to a person. There had been times as a teenager when it seemed inevitable, but always not-quite-there. And those weeks in her mother and stepfather's house after Camden had vanished felt like a kind of sickness, a paralysis, and a brutal reckoning. She thought that maybe those weeks in bed rediscovering the cauterized world had been her breakdown. But it wasn't.

Alone in her townhouse with a toddler, this was her breakdown. The confusion was familiar: *Everything had changed forever, and no one else noticed.* But there was more pain and shame, the pitch and volume of which was unbearable and convinced Farya that she was the most dangerous thing she could be—not in control of herself.

It was a panic, and though her exercises came to mind, they fled just as fast. She grasped for some habit of mind, some safe object of contemplation. It was all on the other side of a surging wave of cold, numb turbulence, like trying to swim into the Atlantic in autumn. She tried to imagine someplace serene—a sleepy glade under clouds on parade.

She rose from her desk chair and wandered down the hallway to the front room. And looking out the second-story window of her townhouse, her blood lurched to a halt. The green and pleasant valley of her desperate imagining sat across the street, where other townhouses had stood just an hour before, and where a tranquil valley didn't belong. Farya flinched, shut the loose linen curtains, and turned away, gasping.

She sank to the floor. Farya did all she could to stop whatever came next—reciting what she could recall of one of the first exercises Lourdes had taught her: *Breathe, but don't let breathing talk you into anything. Take something other than a next breath.* Her own voice seemed to disappear in the sound of blood pounding in her ears. Eventually, she found an opening in that numb crashing sensation, enough to re-remember the buildings across the street into existence again.

And it worked. They reappeared. But the historic brownstones sprouted so suddenly that they deepened a horror that Farya had done her best to not to think about for most of her life: that all of reality was always entirely fluid, all of it up for grabs in her fallible hands. She could no longer ignore the possibility and couldn't help but test it.

So, Farya thought of a novelty she'd seen in a book—a four-story beachfront hotel in the form of an enormous yellow elephant. She didn't focus on the image too hard or for too long. But opening the blinds, there the pachyderm-hotel was, an elephant in profile, with a big blind window eye and red-saddle patio on its back. With it came the memory of a colorful anecdote the realtor had told her when she and Bryan bought the townhouse. There was more, too—memories of the walking tours blocking their stoop, while a ragged know-it-all regaled the rubes with the story of Elephant Estates and the eccentric who built it.

Looking at the elephant across the way, Farya did not feel a sense of whimsy or wonder, but nauseating grief. It was as if she'd been having an argument with someone for her entire life, and now that person—who was the whole world—had died by her hands. And now, whatever she said would be the final word, forever. And at the same time, what she said didn't and couldn't possibly matter because there was nobody for it to matter to.

She called Bryan again, and again, he didn't answer. In a panic, she checked her phone, and his name was still in it. She checked the bookshelf, and he was still in the framed pictures. So it wasn't that.

Looking around her well-appointed apartment, every item, every detail seemed to accuse her. A terrific dread informed her that home wasn't a smart place to be.

With careful hands unaffected by the unfolding nightmare, she scooped up her sleeping son and strapped him to her chest. The cold and the dark made the colors too vivid.

In Father Demo Square, Farya was relieved to see the people rushing past, the businesses, the old buildings, and the traffic—happy for everything that had nothing to do with her. Lourdes would know what to do, but Farya was hysterical and too ashamed to make that call. The cars and pedestrians came and went, in conversation with themselves and with each other. They reminded her of what Lourdes had said late one night after Farya asked what would happen when she died. "The sky will fill with eyes. And the eyes will open all at once. When they do, just hope the eyes aren't yours. If they aren't, you'll know you've done okay." In that way, the strangers restored her somewhat from the worst of her panic.

But it was cold outside. And there is, after all, no right place to have a breakdown. A breakdown seems to necessitate that you only find the most wrong places to be.

That's how Farya found herself crying her eyes out in the toothpaste aisle, beneath pale white lights in the wreathed plaster-molded dome ceiling of a pharmacy that had once been a movie palace. Farya regarded the aisles of powders and lotions she'd spent so much of her life learning and applying. "And they ask why women get depressed," she said to Edouard, who was looking at the colored labels of the items, deciding which one to grab.

A woman sobbing in a pharmacy with an infant on her chest may not have been normal, but it aroused little interest. The staff was underpaid, and she was dressed well enough. Finally, her phone rang. It was Bryan. He said he was in Delaware and would be home soon. She said to meet her at the massive, dreamy drugstore. He asked why, and she said just to meet her *at home, in the kitchen*, realizing too late how crazy that last part sounded.

✠

By the time Bryan got home, the crisis had cooled, congealed. The four-story elephant had become a four-story brick apartment rectangle whose contoured edges and accents merely implied the plump, fleshy outline of an elephant. The tour groups still paused by Bryan and Farya's stoop, the guide tracing the shape with his finger in the air, followed by the tourists making remarks and taking photos.

Edouard was eating macaroni and cheese from a small, red, plastic bowl. The house was warm with the appropriate lights turned on. Farya had poured herself a glass of wine. Farya met Bryan at the threshold of the kitchen and held him. He asked her what was wrong, and she squinted and shook her head, a jagged crease in her flower-petal eyelid expressing a strong pain as she said *not now* under her breath.

Bryan feared it was him and counted his sins: Leighton, or threatening legal action against a friend's son, or that she'd learned about Metacom's business practices. He could tell from her mood that it was serious. An hour and a half later, when Edouard was quiet in his crib, Farya offered Bryan a drink. He figured he'd better, and so poured himself two fingers of scotch, and thought his way through a few all-purpose apologies, the preamble to which he heard his wife say.

"I have to tell you this," she said. "I probably should have told you earlier. I think that I thought I could fix it, and I wouldn't have to tell you. But I can't live with this on my own."

The only way to tell the story was not to care if the audience thought you were crazy. And she cared. But honesty had come to matter more. So, she just started: "I was born in the Greater Majestic Anointed Commonwealth of Ohio. My family sailed there 1,500 years ago with the Osirian Coptic flotilla, fleeing the organized persecutions in Nantucket. My father was an astronaut and a duke. He anchored the first balloon-sphere city within the middle atmosphere of Jupiter …"

Bryan listened. Having been a lying fugitive to consensus-reality for his own reasons for so long and having heard tales at least as outlandish by his newest and most-relied-upon business partner, Bill Van Harappan, he was qualified not to balk at his wife's story. That said, he couldn't absorb the whole thing either. It had already been a long day before Farya's heartfelt confession of Ohioan astronauts, the elephant hotel across the street, the 50,000-year history of Ohio, and Thelonious Monk saving reality from a moody teenage girl.

Her tale made sense in flashes, the way a squirrel appears only to vanish into the foliage. The story struck him, as she spoke for a while, sparing no detail, both gripping their drinks with two hands, looking at each other, as if to break eye contact would be to break trust, with ruinous consequences. Farya knew she could not falter nor pause, soften the details nor apologize, nor ask for approval or agreement. She had to go straight and tie up the beginning with the end. Sense was the hardest thing to make of it. But she pressed on, telling of the obliteration of Camden, the foreshortening of Midtown, and the elimination of poor little Edouard's birth eye. It was hard, but the story had its own force once started.

She cried in places, talking about her father and his pathetic end, and about their son, to whom she'd introduced to such a precarious existence, and about Ripht-Schondles, Kathleen and her daughter Ellem, whom she'd consigned to a horrible fate through simple carelessness. But the words were more important than the sobs, and she kept willing them out.

It was painful to hear. But at the end of the story, Bryan knew one thing that he'd known before Farya began—that he loved this woman. And for reasons emanating in his nose, his chest, his crotch, and regions mysterious, she remained as close as he had to a credible source in his life of cosmic, dishonest scheming. She made Bryan, with his own unspeakable secret, want to follow, to tell all. She was the brave one. But looking at Farya, she was also overwrought and exhausted, wired and fragile.

"I believe you," he said. "What can I do?"

She cried and began to lift her arms. He got up from the kitchen table and embraced her again, kneeling on the kitchen's hard tile floor, not letting go. The kitchen seemed to spin with confusion, exhaustion, and the impossible transportation of love itself. Farya had no solution to offer, and neither did he. But they both felt that things would have to be all right.

Bryan's news about the sale of Metacom could wait. His young wife looked ravaged, and so Bryan offered Farya what little he could—one of his sleeping pills. Exhausted with her own mind, she nodded. Finally shutting off his phone, Bryan went to bed, where Farya was already asleep, the night-table lamp still on. Looking around, the sheets seemed to be a different color. Bryan didn't buy them or clean them, so he questioned his ability to notice with authority, so he had no way to be sure. He rose and went to the bathroom, thinking of her story and looking for things that seemed out of place, things that shouldn't be there and for things that should, but were missing.

By two in the morning, he cursed himself for not having taken a sleeping pill when Farya did. By four in the morning, he began to understand how a systematic suspicion of reality might unravel a man. There was no way for him to be ready for what would begin the next day, but more than two hours of sleep might have given him a fighting chance.

✦

The assault commenced the morning after Bryan's meeting with Van Harappan. It began in the corner of Bryan's eye, where a sleepless night had left a blur. That morning, he walked to work, hoping the cold would scrape some fuzz from him. Eamonn followed at a quarter-block remove, his partner in an SUV.

What came at Bryan wasn't anything his security could help with, though. It popped up on the digital ad screens at subway entrances, newsstands, and the big screens that had replaced payphones around the city and loomed over the sidewalks like elongated tombstones.

Occupied as Bryan was with selling his company and finding some way to understand what his wife had told him the night before, he missed the first few ads. As an ad, it was the same as most, showing a face, smirking, white, middle-aged, handsome with a firm, stubbled jaw and a cocky dimple before a background of bright sunset colors reflected off chrome. The show, the ad said, was on Weekdays at 7, on a network whose logo Bryan didn't immediately recognize.

But he recognized the face and the title of the show—*Jonathan Chearleederman*.

By the time Bryan realized what had been bobbing in his field of vision, he was a few feet past a subway entrance, where a digital screen flashed the ad. He froze there on the sidewalk, in front of a pharmacy where workers were installing a no-frills St. Patrick's Day window display.

He shuddered, looked behind him, and saw Eamonn pretending to browse the gated window of a souvenir shop. They exchanged a look. Bryan's first thought was of the month as a prisoner in that half-finished Maricopa County McMansion basement. His second thought was of Farya, and what it was to live bent around a secret you couldn't explain to anyone. He wondered: All this time, was it an untellable magnetic lodestone that they'd had in common?

As he continued down the early morning avenue, he saw more *Jonathan Chearleederman* ads on what seemed like every available street-facing screen, appearing as he approached and then shuffling out whenever he paused to examine them. Bryan started walking fast toward his office, which seemed a beacon of sense among these hopeless questions.

Seeing *Metacom* in brass letters bolted into the marble facing of the lobby wall always buttressed Bryan. That morning, he stopped to run his fingers over them. As he did, he feared for a moment that—after all he'd seen and learned in the last twenty-four hours—the lettering might recoil from his touch. After a moment, he put his head down, swiped his key card, and went through the glass doors with the same company name and logo frosted into their surface, and into his office.

Bryan thought he'd been careful. Since he'd made up his mind to sell the company, he'd made it a priority that no one could know about the sale until it was all but done. As Van Harappan had pointed out, Bryan's kidnapping had coincided too neatly with the last time he'd tried to get out of the soul-selling business. And now the appearance of the *Jonathan Chearleederman* ads. The best he could do was to put them into a *wait-and-see* pile in his mind, alongside his wife's sanity and his own utter moral failure.

His staff started to filter in. Bryan took a break to read the news, buy new pants. As he browsed, the same *Jonathan Chearleederman* ads followed him around the internet—in the same style as the ones he'd passed on his way to work. He clicked on one, and nothing happened. Bryan looked up the station that the ad said it was showing on—three letters and a number. Nothing like a television network came up. He restarted his computer and changed browsers, tried the private mode, but *Jonathan* kept on following him with that same smirk.

He reached for his desk phone to call in tech support. Maybe he'd come off as crazy to them. But he was paying for the privilege. Before he could dial, though, the phone in his jacket pocket rang.

"We have a problem," the voice said—a woman. It took Bryan a moment to place her.

"Leighton. This is a surprise."

"Is it? Didn't you get an envelope today?"

"Not that I know of. Why?"

"I don't want to say anything else on the phone. You're at your office, right?"

"Yes, why?"

"I'm nearby, at the Pierre. Can you come see me? We have a problem."

Bryan turned to the computer screen to open up his calendar and found *Jonathan Chearleederman* staring back.

"I'll leave right now," Bryan said.

✢

Nothing ever happens, except all at once, Bryan's father used to say. And though Bryan liked to remember the old man telling him these things, it was more likely from a magazine interview or a documentary. Jimny wasn't around much, and more of him wound up on tape and printed on glossy pages than with his first ex-wives and children.

Bryan rode up Fifth Avenue in the SUV with Eamonn and a second security man, dodging the smirk of *Jonathan Chearleederman* that peeked out from digital signs. The security at the Pierre was subtle but very tight. Leighton met him in the lobby, and Eamonn took a step to follow them into the elevator.

"No, not him," Leighton said, her fine and precise features wild like she'd missed a night of sleep or a meal.

"It's my security. He's been with me for years now. I trust him."

"I don't. In fact, I remember him. He waited in the car when you visited last. He can wait in the lobby now."

"Sir, I don't recommend this," Eamonn said.

"Don't worry. She's my sister. I've known her my whole life. I think we'll be fine. This is a secure hotel."

"You're the boss," Eamonn said, almost emotionally.

The inside of the elevator was gold and reflective, like a mirror made of scotch. Bryan and Leighton had it to themselves. They stood shoulder to shoulder, but Bryan snuck a look. Her makeup had been applied unevenly.

"He's quite pushy, your security ape," she said.

"He takes his job seriously."

"I'm sure he does. I wonder what he thinks his job is?"

The elevator opened, and they walked the silent hallway to her room. Though spacious and luxurious, the room had a squalor to it—clothes spilled across the made bed, half-opened wrappers and canisters of mini-bar snacks strewn about. Bryan excused himself to use the bathroom.

"Careful, there's glass on the floor," Leighton warned, clearing pantyhose and chips off the marble-topped table by the view of Central Park.

A strong smell of perfume filled the bathroom, and its floor was streaked with purple eyeshadow. There was indeed broken glass on the floor. When Bryan returned to the room, she was sitting on the edge of the night table, leaning forward, jumpy and enervated, with a glass of white wine gathering sunlight.

"So, what's going on?" he asked, sitting on the bed.

"These are what's going on," she said and pushed an envelope to him across the sheet. Inside, on glossy photo paper, he found about a dozen different photographs of the pair of them, from that night on her Maryland estate. In various stages of undress and in the act, at least one of their faces visible in each shot.

"When did you get these?" he asked, stacking and returning them to the envelope. He winced at the images, at memories from what seemed like another man's life.

"Yesterday. No demands, no nothing. Just the pictures in an envelope. But look at them, at the angle. We were on the second floor," she said, taking the pictures back out of the envelope, flipping through a few and finding a salacious full-body image. "See?"

"Yes, I see, Leighton."

"No," she said, poking her finger at the center of the picture. "Do you see the windowpane on the edge?"

"Yes, but what …" Bryan started to say, before remembering the sprawling property, like a country club. There were no buildings, no vantage points for miles.

"It had to be a drone taking the pictures," she said, finishing his thought, taking half a bite from a Toblerone. "But that's impossible."

"Is it?"

"The Secretary has the whole estate fenced with electromagnetic transmitters to keep things like drones from swooping in from outside. We shut the fence off for parties, so people can use their phones. But otherwise, it's always on. The only way a drone could fly there is if it was operated within the fence."

"But you don't think that I had anything to do with it?" Bryan said.

"I don't know. I do know that neither of us are feral teenagers anymore. You're in business. And my husband is an important man. The Secretary knows the kinds of things, does the kinds of things, and can say the kinds of things that move markets."

"What can I say? What can I do to show you that I had nothing to do with this?" Bryan said.

Looking Leighton in the face, he saw that the eye makeup on her left and right sides didn't match.

"I guess we'll see what they want. Incest, adultery—I don't know if the Secretary would survive the scandal. He and I, we each have our diversions, but nothing is ever said. There's a professionalism to marriage, at a certain point. And this is a bad breach of that."

"What are you trying to say?"

"I don't know, probably what I'm not supposed to—that I love my husband."

"I'm sorry."

"Sorry," she snickered, thin lips curling into a dirty smile that made him think of kissing her little mouth. "Not true and doesn't matter."

"Don't forget the problems this can cause me, too. I have a wife and a young son."

"So, what are you going to do?"

The question was like a slow-pinching vise that had finally caught hold of bone. The night before, Farya had touched wounds he'd thought healed and asked him to accept a dangerous reality. *Nothing ever happens, except all at once.* Out the window, the more ambitious trees of Central Park were putting on their tiny, pale green leaves.

"I'll start with Eamonn, see what he knows or what he'll say. Take it from there."

Leighton nodded into her wine glass and took an infinitesimal sip. Bryan rose to leave, and she met him on his feet, throwing her arms around him and releasing a half-anguished cry into his neck. The embrace lasted a few seconds before Bryan turned away and left.

He found Eamonn waiting in the lobby in a high-backed gold and brown armchair facing the elevators, talking on his phone. That was also out of character. Crossing the polished marble, Bryan's head swam with clever schemes and high-tech chicanery to prove or disprove Leighton's accusations. But he was tired. He was overwhelmed. He had no patience for the ruses that bubbled up.

"Can I see your phone?" he asked his hulking ruddy employee.

"It's just about out of juice."

"That's okay. Just unlock it for me."

"This isn't my business phone. It's my personal phone."

"Okay. Can I see it?"

"I was just talking to my wife. I didn't know how long you'd be up there."

"That's fine. I just want to see it."

"It's my personal property."

"So, are you refusing to show it to me?"

"I think I am."

"Then you're fired, Eamonn. Go get in your car. We're done."

"But you can't. I mean, I was just making a phone call."

"A personal call on time I'm paying you to do your job. I don't think I'm being unreasonable at all to ask to see the phone, given the circumstances."

"Fine," he said, tapping his password onto the glass and tapping open a screen and holding it up. "See. Look at the last two calls. They both say, *WIFE*. You're married. You know how it is."

Bryan held out his hand, and Eamonn handed the phone over. Scrolling through the recent calls, Bryan tapped the name WIFE, and it dialed. Eamonn made to reach for the device, but Bryan turned away, and the security professional remembered where he was before he took it any further.

"I thought you said he was getting out of the elevator—was the woman with him?" the voice said, clipped and rapid fire. "Well, tell me."

Bryan knew the voice, its cadences, and tone. He knew the voice intimately like he would any client.

"Hello, Petra," Bryan said.

"I'm sorry. I think you have the wrong number," Petra said, rattled. She didn't, however, hang up right away. Maybe she didn't know who was calling. Maybe she did and was waiting for some explanation. Bryan said nothing. They just sat and listened to the silence coming from each other's line for an excruciating minute.

When it was over, Bryan handed the phone back to Eamonn, whose broad face was crimson with embarrassment. Bryan could see some kind of excuse or explanation forming behind his hard blue eyes. He didn't need to say it, but Bryan told him he was fired anyway.

+

Farya looked out the window, where the four-story red-brick apartment house called Elephant Estates loomed over the street in the low late-afternoon sun, the subtle contours of masterfully laid brick lending the structure the supple appearance of animal flesh.

But one thing was gone from the street that had withstood the worst of her seizures since moving to the West Village townhouse—the black SUV. Farya had taken their professional security for granted enough to complain about it. Now, though, she felt its absence.

In her office, Farya tried to busy herself, but she still couldn't bear to look at the nauseating images of Ripht-Schondles sufferers that populated the foundation's materials. Downstairs, she played with Edouard and made small talk with the nanny, who was polite, though unhappy at the interruption of her routine. It occurred to Farya that she hadn't had the chance to say a proper goodbye to Eamonn, or Ted, or Jack, or D'Shawn, or any of the security staff who had watched her, held doors, and helped her carry in the shopping over the years she'd been married to Bryan. She watched the nanny, Cedella—from the islands. And Farya thought of how much better Cedella sometimes seemed to know her son than she did, how the housekeeper knew her home better than she did. And the day's surprises reminded Farya with evidence that she knew less about her husband than she thought. That sense of estrangement, of floating above the world but not quite touching it, haunted her all day. She sent the nanny home early.

When Bryan came home late that afternoon, Farya had questions. Despite the chill, Bryan was sweating when he got home. He gave Edouard a long hug, and seeing the look in Farya's eyes, promised to tell her everything after he changed his clothes and poured himself a drink. He came back down the stairs a few minutes later, in sweatpants and a T-shirt, as Farya had only seen him when he was sick. They sat on the couch, him with a few fingers of scotch, her with the paperback she'd been reading the same paragraph of all day, Edouard enacting a lengthy, revenge-laden traffic series of accidents with his toys on the carpet.

"You're not the only one with secrets," Bryan said. "And I want to tell you everything. I just don't know where to start."

"Okay, why don't you start with Eamonn. Why did you fire him?"

"Two reasons. First, I found out that he wasn't only working for us—he was working for one of Metacom's customers, as well, keeping tabs on me. And second, if the people I was worried about wanted to come after me, I don't think Eamonn could do much to stop them."

"What do you mean?"

"I mean, some of this is pretty scary. And most of it's my own fault. I guess I hoped I could get us out to the other end of it without having to explain the part of it that I do understand. But I don't think they'll let that happen."

"Well, now would be a good time to tell me. I mean, I showed you mine," she said, and placed her hand on his.

"It started in junior high with Nate Higgins. He was a rich-kid smartass, an heir to a mining family. His dad was in the Senate, and so was his uncle. Anyway, he was going through this loud, holier-than-thou atheism phase, and getting in everyone's face about it, and I said if you really don't believe, then sell me your soul. I think it was twenty bucks, which wasn't much at St. Philip's …" Bryan began.

He told Farya the story of his first profitable resale of a soul, to Senator Higgins, and of the dorm-run business he kept running through high school and college, which he did more for the satisfaction than the money. He told her about his third business out of college, a floundering mobile-phone business aimed at young people with no credit. It wasn't Petra who approached him, but a less-expensive version of her—an older woman with heavy poly-blend blazers that made him uncomfortable just to look at. She gave him the clause to drop into his phone contracts and started buying the rights to the souls of his subscribers. Bryan was already selling all the customer data the law would allow, and so he didn't think much of selling another slice of the animal. And the money she offered was more than good—it was enough to save his company.

Success, when it arrived, was intoxicating, Bryan explained. The world opened up; the price was right for everything he wanted;

every plan met with fulfillment, and the sky was the limit for years on end. His father died, his children grew up, and Metacom expanded. Everything was an idyll until the night he met Ritchie Reach in a banquet room in Southern California when the nightmares started—nightmares multiplied by nightmares.

"So, I tried to change my business," he said and finished his scotch. A scowl crossed his face, not from the liquor, but from what he would have to say next. He went to the kitchen and returned with his glass all but full. "I had it all figured out. I was going to celebrate when I fell down in the lobby of a hotel in Scottsdale."

He told her about the plan to eliminate the Non-Mortal-Element part of his business, and the immediate consequences, namely, the kidnapping. It was the first time since it happened that he referred to the event as a "consequence." He told her about the phony EMTs, the ambulance, the paralysis, the protein bars, tinned fish, *Jonathan Chearleederman*, and his struggle to stay sane in the half-finished basement of an abandoned dream house. He told her about when he got out, and the incredible disorientation, isolation, and shame he felt when he was told he hadn't been gone for a month at all—crying his eyes out in his hotel room—he told her everything.

Farya didn't flinch or doubt his story. She was surrounded by memories of things that no one else remembered. She squeezed his hand as he struggled through the telling.

"And there was the added security cost, the divorce, and the general exhaustion, so I just decided to put it off for a while," he said, looking down into his lap.

"I get it. I mean, what do you do with things that never happened? How do you act on information that's become less valid than a daydream?" she asked, a lump in her own throat.

"How do you protect anything?"

"What happened with Eamonn?"

Bryan told her about Leighton. That part wasn't easy for Farya to hear, and she glanced around the room to make sure Edouard wasn't listening. The little boy was racing a train against a robot on the carpet. Bryan told her about Leighton's suspicions, and about talking to Petra on Eamonn's phone. "That's why we don't have him around anymore."

"So, you're trying to sell your company, against the wishes of a soul-selling cabal with the ability to grab any of us whenever they want. And we have no protection."

"We never did."

"I guess that's true."

"But they need me. They need me to keep doing what I'm doing. And I have people I think I can trust. I think they can help us. Let's get some sleep tonight, though. We'll leave town tomorrow."

"Where to?"

"Someplace that's not connected with us. I think one of my mom's friends owns a house up in the Hudson Valley that they never use. I can reach out on a disposable phone. That's one idea."

"It would be good to get away for a little," Farya agreed.

Bryan nodded. She bent forward and kissed him on the mouth, hopped off the couch, and chirped at her son to get ready for bed.

Leading the boy up the stairs, she felt for the first time that the townhouse was indeed hers, that her husband was hers. Together, they had made that most elusive thing—a home. Her fear didn't vanish but became less important than it had been. Wrestling Edouard into pajamas, a certainty settled into Farya, that she was ready to fight any fight to protect her home.

✝

Fear you can face; dread is another story. Dread finds cracks between the curtains, the seams between dreams. Farya woke before anyone else, made some coffee, and plotted.

She did an inventory of her wealthy friends and their getaways. It was still cold and clammy in the Hamptons and muddy in the Berkshires. She had a story about emergency repairs, family staying at their own beach house, and a need to stay close to the city. There were a few friends, closer than most, who might have a house they weren't using. They could rent anywhere, but Bryan said they should try to keep things informal, off the record, if they could.

Bryan came downstairs, also early. He had a full day ahead. In addition to dialing for hideaways on a cash-bought phone, he was meeting with a kid who could set them up to be untraceable when they fled. He chugged a coffee, kissed her, and left.

Farya called Ethan. His in-laws had an ever-shifting collection of properties. Not long ago, there was no point calling Ethan before eleven. But a few years of sober parenting had transformed his habits. He agreed to meet for coffee at a little place by Union Square.

The coffee shop was crowded with people on laptops and sullen single parents escaping their apartments, infants and toddlers tied tight to their chests or kept near with steady entreaties, threats, and small screens of colored light. Ethan was the last of these. His boy was watching a troupe of wisecracking horses, robots, and talking airplanes as they worked through some kind of mystery. Ethan was happy to see her.

"You're a sight for sore eyes," he said. "Winter with this little beast, cabin fever, and the constant emotions while we wait to hear from Mrs. Oligarch. Even with *my* regimen of well-enough pills, it's been rough. But what's up? Why the emergency coffee meeting? Where are your goons?"

"There's more to it, but Bryan ran into some problems with his business associates. He had to fire his security detail, and we think it's smart to get out of town for a little while."

"I warned you about these captains of industry, didn't I?" he said, joking.

"Sage advice, given what you married into."

"I still say it beats working for a living. What do you need?"

"A place to stay for a few weeks—someplace we don't own or rent, that can't be traced to us, preferably not too far outside the city."

"Jesus. Do you want me to talk to my father-in-law? One thing he knows is security."

"Does he? How'd he lose track of his wife?"

"That's different—it's more of an arrangement, from what I can gather. And anyway, I guess she was the one wearing the pants all along. And when she told him she needed to go on a walkabout, he kind of had to agree to it. That's what I heard. Of course, I heard a lot of things."

"Oh, yeah. Like what?"

"He's spent big money to find her. And when he did—on some island in the middle of the Pacific—she politely told him to get lost. Death does funny things to people."

"How do you know she's still alive?"

"She calls, every so often."

"Oh, really? So, what? Did she meet a surf instructor?"

"Please. The woman's bones are balsa wood."

"You're bad. So, why did she call?"

"It was business. She called to warn the old man, so he could warn us. Apparently, I didn't marry into a few billion dollars, after all. Just a few dozen million. I know; it doesn't seem like a big *practical* difference. But you'd be surprised how deflating that was to hear."

"My condolences."

"Thank you. I've had to say farewell to some audacious plans. I was really going to enjoy myself—as soon as little Josef stopped screaming in my ear," he said, looking at his son, who was stupefied in the small rectangle of articulated light. "But, alas, I'll have to settle for my comfort pills, comfort meals, comfort pastimes, and general comfort."

"Speaking of comforts, do you have any comfortable properties you're not using?"

"You know what? I do. It's a compound out on the bluffs of Montauk. Actually, my mother-in-law bought it for the *beauty* she said she wanted before she decided the season was wrong."

"What does that mean?"

"If I had to guess, I think she meant it would still be cold and gloomy until after she croaked, which is really any day now if the doctors are right. But I've been over to this property a lot lately."

"Yeah. I never saw you as an off-season-beach guy."

"Anything to get a little break from this little hair-trigger air-raid siren," Ethan said, nodding down to the child absorbed in a five-inch-wide epic of small, tender animals solving the problems of giant robots. "I'm the useless, creative, or creative-ish one in Carolina's family, so they asked me to stage the house for sale. I went out and bought a lot of art prints, rugs, knickknacks, and overstuffed sofas—know your market. But you can have the place to yourself for a month at least. It's not priced for a level-headed, cold-weather investor, but for a rash Memorial-Day billionaire buyer."

"Really? I mean, I don't want to cost you money."

"Ha! My mother-in-law just spent billions, with a b, on some *literally* unimaginable thing that she spent her hard and prodigious life earning the right not to explain. We're all stunned. Even at a son-in-law's remove, I'm still numb from the shock."

"Numb how?"

"Numb like I don't think either of us knows what money even is, or what it's really for."

"What do you mean?"

"Just that—that we don't know. I mean, where does a dying woman spend more than a dozen billion dollars? What costs that? If it's ransom, I think I would have heard. Something else is going on. It has to be. And honestly, I only hope that I never find out what.

Mankind is a big herd, and I think I just want to stay in the middle. I don't want to know."

"That's a nice thing to hope for," Farya said, looking down at her cold coffee.

"I just texted you the code to the gate. I don't know what you're into, and you don't have to tell me. But good luck."

Meanwhile, Bryan was in his office with Ritchie Reach's son, Rick Toomey, who was showing him the features of a modified satellite phone.

"How did you even get this?" Bryan asked when the young, squid-like man in a long-sleeve T-shirt had finished explaining how the phones worked.

"Buddies in the army—counterintelligence," Rick Toomey said, dodging eye contact. "But your regular calls can be routed to it, and you can use it as a wi-fi hotspot, and anybody who tries to track you will wind up in Pakistan."

"Thanks," Bryan said, patting a canvas bag of cash. "I appreciate this."

"And if this works out for you …"

"*Then* we'll find a right way to keep the Union Skells out in the world. You know what I want, and I know what you want. There's a way to make it all happen."

Rick, pale and young and smart in that scary way, nodded.

The Lomoigne family was on the road late that afternoon, Bryan checking the rearview mirror the whole way. The traffic made it a four-hour drive, but he never spotted the same few cars behind him for very long on the Southern State. And on the dark Montauk Highway, there were no cars at all for long stretches.

In Montauk, Farya used a flashlight to read from a map to get him to the remote cliffside compound. The code at the gate worked, and there were no lights around or above the narrow, hedge-lined lane. At the end of the long curving drive, the house waited—a bulging blend of colonial artifice and modern sprawl. Bryan hurried in ahead, turned on the lights, found a bedroom, and set up the pack-n-play for their sleeping son.

Already in his pajamas, Edouard barely stirred as Farya moved him on tiptoes from car to crib. Bryan lugged the luggage and groceries, too many for a weekend but too few for a month, inside. When it was done, Farya stayed inside to unpack, while Bryan walked around the outside of the house. He didn't know what to expect but knew he wouldn't be able to sleep otherwise.

It was cold outside, and the early-spring waves crashed loudly below the soft cliffs. The whole place felt shamelessly unsheltered from the menace of water, wind, and cold. The dark was absolute in a way night in the city never was. But, looking through the bare shrubs at the end of the drive, there was no light, no other sound. And looking overhead, the only light besides the stars was a distant jet headed for Boston or Montreal. Bryan took a deep cold breath. They were clear, for now.

+

The next two weeks, they lived as they might have in another world. Their boy was cheerful. They had plenty of time for him and for one another. The food was simple but good, and the weather mild. The days were loose, anchored by occasional flourishes of activity centered around the two satellite phones. They waited, talked, ate, and played together. The three of them rediscovered their relationship there—that is to say, a way of being around one another. And they liked it.

On the patio above the fishing-boat-speckled plain of the Atlantic, while Edouard napped, Farya and Brian plotted. The first order was security of some kind. Ritchie's boy Rick Toomey was at their townhouse, redoing the electronic security of the place. And Bryan was talking to an old high-school buddy, Bernard Surulo.

Bernard came from a South American mining family that sent him to Saint Philip's. He was a small, sarcastic kid and shared Bryan's distrust of his upper-crusty classmates. In Bernard's senior year, the mines were nationalized, and the family fled to Curacao. Bryan and Bernard reconnected a few years out of college, after a chance encounter in the Cincinnati-Northern Kentucky International Airport. It was the kind of friendship that picked up without missing a beat, even after years. Bryan had just started Metacom. Bernard—never Bern, Bernie, Ben, or Benny—had just finished training to join the Dade County SWAT Team, of all things. He'd beefed up since high school and had a newfound quiet confidence that made his sarcasm funnier and more damning. Nonetheless, Bernard seemed to have that same surly dissatisfaction as in high school. Easing into middle age, it was refreshing.

And again, it was like old times again when Bryan called him from a satellite phone on the windy bluff. Bernard was working as an air marshal, a job he wasn't shy about hating. Bryan asked what it would take for Bernard to quit and come work for him for a few months.

"You in trouble?" Bernard said.

"Maybe. It's not clear. I'm selling my business, and I just want to be careful until it's sold. I'm in a spot where I don't know who I can trust right now."

"Say no more. I can get out there in a few days."

But there was more to say, and Bryan haggled the price up from what Bernard said he'd need for himself and a few trustworthy friends, along with a few long-term leases on SUVs.

Since arriving in Montauk, Farya had daily calls with Lourdes. On the encrypted line, Lourdes talked her through a new stage of exercises.

"Imagine you're everything, and you have everything ever within you—now what do you desire? What does desire do? What does it look like? What does it remind you of?" Lourdes asked, and the satellite-phone silence swelled and seemed to sparkle.

They always started with the exercises. After, Farya confessed what she'd done before they'd fled. Lourdes was impressed with Elephant Estates.

"This isn't perfect. But it's a new step. At first, you just destroyed indiscriminately. But you learned you could make places, things—even if it was sporadic, indiscriminate—you just made *more* reality. But this time you made a specific thing, that you *meant* to make," Lourdes said.

"So, you're saying I'm getting better at it."

"That's not the point. This is where things get dangerous. You're way out where you can say *yes* or *no* to whole broad categories and qualities of existence. What you need is to get better at staying silent, at least until you can be a lot more articulate. You need to keep doing your exercises."

"I think I can be silent. That should be enough, right? If I just stick with my exercises?"

"Maybe. I don't know. This isn't well-known territory. And you sound funny like there's more going on than what you told me. Do you want to keep it to yourself?"

"It's Bryan. He's selling his company, and he's worried about some of the people he's in business with. We're just staying off the radar until the sale is done."

"I wish I could say I was surprised. But you were never going to have a simple go of it. This is why being silent might not be enough. You've been able to live in a way where you have some control of yourself. But what if someone tries to hurt to you or your family? What will you do? What happens to them? What happens to the rest of us?" Lourdes asked. The question anchored the background static.

"I don't know. What am I supposed to do?"

"You're supposed to do what you're doing now—the exercises—but better and faster. You have to learn to daydream the right way, and to speak to reality in a very deliberate way."

Lourdes took her into a new exercise. Farya spent the rest of the week rearranging roots on the cliff face.

✝

Those weeks in Montauk, Farya did her exercises on the bluff overlooking the ocean. Sometimes, she managed to relocate a single shrub, roots to leaves, on the property—the goal Lourdes had given her. Other times, she broke up the vast distance of the Atlantic shrub-spotted outcroppings and returned the sea to its previous state. Other times, she overshot and eradicated the concept of a *shrub* from the world. The small things, she learned, were the hardest.

For as long as she could remember, the thing she did was like a seizure. Depression and boredom even, built up and triggered it like an avalanche. But it wasn't a switch she could reach down and flip. No matter how much of the world she annihilated or how much pain she caused, it wasn't an ability she would ever want to claim. But now, with her family in peril, that had changed. And willing to bear the responsibility, the way to ability became clearer with each exercise.

As she practiced, bundled up in an Adirondack chair, trying on new possibilities, it became harder to ignore a guilt like car sickness that kept surging. And the careen of that nausea buoyed her back again to Bryan's hurried, reluctant admission of how Metacom acquired and sold the rights to the souls of its customers. That scene in the kitchen of her husband, cornered, kept replaying on the darkness of her closed eyes. It illuminated the business behind a midnight-black absence that afflicted Marista, Jana, Ethan, and so on. Farya could feel in it more than a failure of imagination and enthusiasm. It was a lost future, a massive frontier palpably occluded. She could hear the echo of that unnatural absence where they broke off their sentences, feel it in the center of gravity to their jokes. It was a deep sense that they'd been outsmarted before they were born. What seemed like depression was, in fact, a truth that seeped backward from a greater doom, to inform the cynical glass rectangles of new luxury condos, the parking acres, and uncrossable state highways. It was the urge, written into the landscape, to get it all over with. It made the cities and highways and towns into a tolerable toilet-cathedral swirling around a Ponzi scheme.

Sitting in her wooden chair, under the bright sun in the bracing ocean air, Farya could feel the effect of all those souls sold off. She knew about eradication, but this was different. It wasn't a hasty rationalization of reality, nothing so blameless as a wildfire. It was a calculated and cold-blooded scheme of for-profit damnation and cosmic undoing. And she couldn't ignore her husband's role in it, or how she and her son had benefited.

Maybe she could find a way, after the sale, she hoped, when she was no longer complicit, to make amends. Farya shuddered at the thought of what she'd done with the Ripht-Schondles Foundation, and the phone calls she still had to return.

For now, she decided, there was nothing to do except for her exercises. And that's what she did.

+

In these idyllic days, Bryan waited for the call from Bill Van Harappan, who was searching for someone to buy Metacom. When they first arrived in Montauk, that call was all Bryan could think of. After a week, he was having such a nice time with Farya and Edouard that he could go hours at a time without thinking of it. The long afternoons of bright sun and cold breezes overtook his memory of what brought them there. He slept well. Each day was animated with an ease he'd forgotten was possible.

The call came in after they'd been in Montauk for almost three weeks. And hearing the old man's voice, a knot stuck in Bryan's throat—the idyll had ended. He answered the call in the house's dim little den decorated with antique fishing paraphernalia and watercolors.

"What do you have me on, a damn satellite phone?" the old man said when he heard Bryan's voice.

"Yep. I'm out of pocket."

"I don't blame you. Encrypted, I hope."

"You have a good ear."

"Just a little edge on the echo, but you get to know the sound of these things. I'd ask why so many precautions, but I think I already know."

"How'd we do?"

"Not too bad—a few bidders on individual pieces of the business. But we don't have time for that. I found some guys who want the whole thing, even the less-traditional assets."

Van Harappan told Bryan the buyer's name, a cable-TV provider based in Charlotte. Bryan knew them, and it made enough sense. Van Harappan said the price. Bryan factored in the finder's fee, the legal fees, and other costs. He'd still be a rich man, but not the way he'd been. He'd have his name in the gala program, the business-card-sized placard on the theater wall or park bench, but nobody's Man of the Year. Bryan, a little sad to hand over his life's work, but sadder to be returning to New York to sign the endless papers, said *okay*.

"Cheer up. You wanted out. This is out. And it could have gone much worse if you think about it. I'll let them know that you're on board."

"You're right. I'll get my lawyers started on an agreement, contact the FCC, put your finder's fee in escrow …"

"As always, a pleasure doing business with you, Mr. Lomoigne."

"I'm sure it is," Bryan said, surprised when he laughed.

"Good luck."

Bryan set the phone down on the den's lobster-trap coffee table and climbed the stairs to tell Farya the news.

☩

"What did we learn?" the voice on the satellite phone said, not even an hour after Bryan's talk with Van Harappan.

Bryan froze. It was the voice of the kidnapper—unmistakable after so many years, the cadence, the way a whisper infiltrated the nasal tone of it.

The kidnapper hung up. Bryan put the phone on the marble top of the kitchen island and pushed it away. Edouard was sleeping. Farya was in her usual Adirondack chair out in the yard. Bryan rubbed his fingers across his stubble, more to prove that he could control his limbs than anything else. He wondered if it was strength or weakness to keep the call to himself. But that's what he'd do—he had papers to sign and nightmares to live through.

With the car packed, Bryan looked at the clapboard sprawl of the estate and wondered if he'd ever feel such peace again, putting his chances at fifty-fifty. Bernard Surulo met them at a diner where the Southern State Parkway picked up the traffic from the Montauk Highway. Bernard drove a white SUV—the dealership was all out of black—following them on that grim drive to Manhattan and parked on the street outside their townhouse.

Bernard and his four like-minded former colleagues formed up a small team to shadow Bryan and Farya. She showed them around the townhouse and its security features. Expecting some kind of abduction at any moment, Bryan showed them around his office and routine. After a lifetime trying to escape life behind a desk, Bernard chafed at the long days at the desk outside Bryan's office—in Eamonn's old seat, with a view of Bryan's door and the approach from the elevator. The first day back, Bernard insisted on entering the office first. He checked the wardrobe, the desk, the bathroom, and the edges of the big windows. It was early, and no one else at Metacom had arrived yet.

For Bryan, the office promised normalcy, even if it wasn't going to be his office for much longer. Nostalgia mingled with dread as he looked out his window at the glittering spires and blunt ramrods of international commerce. With the end in sight, he pulled out his chair. But on his keyboard was a protein bar and a tin of mackerel, just like his kidnappers had fed him during his putative month in that Maricopa County basement. Bryan dropped to a knee as if to vomit into the recycling bucket under his desk.

He called in Bernard and explained the significance of the snacks. Bernard, no longer a friend who could ask if he was all right, instead asked if Bryan was certain that they were the same ones. Bernard said he'd get the security camera footage from the last few weeks and see what he could find. As they spoke, a quartet of lawyers showed up. Bryan mumbled to Bernard to find out what he could and nodded in the lawyers. They billed by the hour and Bryan wanted to get the deal over with.

With that, Bryan's life vanished in a blur of clauses, signatures, red-lined drafts, bleary negotiations, posturing, concessions, and X-ray bright halogen conference-room light. The week bled into and through the weekend. Alternately wired and exhausted when he returned home, Farya and Edouard were poignant and vivid presences. They sped by like the brief, shallow snatches of sleep.

The deal was massive, full of interlocking parts. Bryan struggled to keep it all in his mind, to track what mattered and what didn't, what parts would hold, and which ones wouldn't. He'd done dozens of these deals before, always as the buyer, and could spot most of the opportunities and traps. After ten straight days, his body rebelled with a back spasm. It locked up the space between his shoulder blades and forced him to thrust his head forward like a vulture. The spasm happened in front of Bryan's second-in-command, a former banker, whose eyes widened in anticipation, thinking it a heart attack.

Bryan caught his breath and dismissed the latest cohort of lawyers and bankers, and asked Bernard to help him into the car outside and to take him to his health club. "Better a healthy beggar than a sick king," Bryan recalled his grandmother saying as they walked gingerly together through the marble and flashing wall-sized screens of the lobby.

As Bernard helped him into the white SUV, the outdoors came as a mild shock. A light warm rain filled the avenue with a smell like soil and trees. In the backseat, he closed his eyes and tried to find a negotiating point that would unlock the wood-like flesh around the base of his neck. The ride to the club was a short one. The front desk clerk greeted him by name, and looking over Bernard, asked with professional circumspection whom his guest was. In pain and unwilling to stand still through the photograph-and-background-check required of all club guests, Bryan grunted that Bernard would wait in the lobby.

The clerk buzzed Bryan into the mahogany and brass locker room. It was empty except for a pair of old men powdering themselves, zipping up squash racquets, and joking about the Supreme Court. Bryan nodded hello, put on the swimsuit he kept there, and rode the elevator to the pool.

It was eight thirty at night, and the pool was empty. Given the average age of the club's members, Bryan knew it would be. A lifeguard sat in a chair at the far corner of the echoing room, with its bright lights and big picture windows overlooking the multi-colored phantasmagoria of foggy Manhattan. Bryan started down the lane with slow strokes and didn't stop until he was moving close to full speed. He kept at it for a while and climbed out of the pool, renewed. The elevator opened onto the locker room, which was dark. Bryan walked in and waved his arms to get the motion-sensor lights to come on, making a note to complain at the next members' meeting—they paid enough to keep the lights on. He waved and waved, and half the lights came on, barely illuminating the library-like room with its smell of liniment and aftershave.

Petra stepped from the shadows, dressed out of character in a tight silvery dress and stiletto heels. Heavy eye makeup mixed with the circles under her eyes to create a dramatic effect. Deeper in the shadows, Bryan made out a shape like a person.

"Bryan, we should talk," she said.

"Should we? Maybe you should call the office and schedule a meeting. This is the men's locker room," he said. "You shouldn't be here."

"I know. Rules are rules. But I'm pretty sure no one will bother us."

Bryan inched away from her, toward his locker, and retrieved a big, fluffy monogrammed towel, which he threw over his shoulders as nonchalantly as he could.

"What's this about?" he said. He considered changing his clothes in front of her as a power move. But he didn't feel that powerful.

"It's about the sale. I really wish you'd talked with us first."

"Petra, I don't have much to say to you about that. It's non-public information. And aside from your little protein-bar message on my desk, I doubt you have much to say that I want to hear."

"Fine. But I want to say that I never approved that. And before you try to sell, remember that this business of ours has its own culture. And it can take years to find partners that we can trust. That's worth a lot to us. And it's why, before you take a bad deal, we want the opportunity to make a counteroffer, a better offer."

"Whatever it is, I have your answer: no. Just no. And how did you even get in here? Who is that by the door?" Bryan said, looking past Petra to the indistinct shape. When he looked, his view seemed to just miss the figure, as if the sight of him was slippery. Petra turned, and when she looked, Bryan pulled on his pants over his bathing suit.

"Him? That's just the janitor. But I was saying, Bryan, before you say no, consider that we can offer more money, of course. But we can also offer more *than* money," she said, the lines rehearsed like she was reading from a PowerPoint.

Petra, for all her mystery and her direct line into the powers that be, lacked much charisma. And Bryan's attention remained locked in the shadows beyond her, on that flicker of a hint of a person that would neither vanish nor become clearer.

"There are things people say money can't buy. But we both know better. We know that we just can't talk about those things in front of people who can't afford them," Petra said, trying to look into Bryan's eyes. "The business we've done encompasses more than you give it credit for."

Petra suddenly looked different, her dress tighter, iridescent, her lips bright red and reflective.

"I have to go," Bryan said.

"Go where? To sell your life's work for a fraction of what it's worth?"

"It's enough."

"For what? Some cheap comforts on a long trek to death? I always thought you had more in you. I mean, your father certainly had more in *him*."

Bryan pulled on his undershirt and checked his pockets for the holy trinity of wallet-keys-phone.

"We're done, Petra."

"We'd always held that it's better if your side of the transaction was agnostic. That may have been a mistake. I'd love to see what you'd do if you were properly motivated." Some quality to the air changed and Petra's features took on a more severe quality—skeletal and mechanical, sexy and terrifying. She held Bryan's attention as if the room around them was vanishing. "I know now that money's not enough for people like us. And I think that could make you a better partner."

A hair or a limb emerged from the ambiguous character in the shadows beyond Petra. He looked up, his swimsuit soaking through his chalk-striped suit pants. Past the sight-slipping figure in the shadows, Bryan spotted the actual janitor, dressed in all white, professionally blind to the peccadillos of the members.

He began to dash toward the janitor, who was piling towels from little bins into a big, rolling laundry cart. The janitor seemed to be in his own pool of light in the dim locker room, which became farther and farther as Bryan ran toward it as if the room itself was telescoping out away from him. Bryan was sweating, breathless, and shoeless when he reached the circle of light and got the old man's attention. He said a calm, "Yes, sir," followed by a tranquil, "Can I help you, sir?" He watched Bryan with a dispassionate concern, gauging the bulge of his eyes, the sweat on his brow, and the disorientation on his face.

Looking at the old janitor, Bryan saw light behind him, light all around—all the lights in the locker room on at full brightness. He turned around to point out the woman in the men's locker room. But she was gone. There was only Bryan's towel, dress shirt, and tie on the floor next to his open locker. He asked the janitor to follow him to the locker and wait while he collected his things. The janitor, having worked at the club for more than thirty years, had seen far stranger in the locker room without even blinking. He followed Bryan out the door to the lobby, where Bernard waited.

"How's your back?" Bernard asked.

"What?"

"Your back. Is it better? You seem pale."

"Let's just go."

In the car, he asked Bernard if he had seen anyone come in through the lobby, a woman and a man, or just a woman. Bernard said no one. The pay for the job was high by security standards. But Bernard was still too much of a friend not to ask if he was all right. Bryan didn't have an answer.

✢

During those weeks, when Farya saw Bryan at all, it was late or early, with one of them either collapsing to sleep or rushing out the door. He was delirious, foaming with *soon*s. But *soon* could mean a week or six months.

The promised *soon* was a sale, a cashing-out, a final passing of the buck. After, as she understood it, they would be rich, safe, and less guilty. Those claims floated on deep shadows of doubt. But, looking around their modern, tastefully decorated townhouse, with its original art and top-of-the-line appliances, it seemed too late for questions.

Nonetheless, Farya's self-reproach kept her from New York in spring and its free-for-all of flirtation and good feeling, as the cool air of the subway mingled with the tentative warmth and the apparition of early flowers and buds against the damp concrete. She worried about her son inheriting his father's sins against his fellow man or inheriting his mother's ineffectual guilt. The only thing she could do was her exercises.

It was one such morning, right after the nanny arrived, that Farya took her usual seat in a leather bucket chair, her eyes half-lidded, unfocused on the window that looked out into the small backyard, where a few trees put forth their first leaves. The window was open a crack. Across the fence, a neighbor's housekeeper argued in Tagalog on her cell phone, repeating the same phrase in different cadences, her rage fading into sadness with each repetition.

Compared with other distractions Farya had exercised through, the housekeeper wasn't much. But Farya nonetheless fixated, trying to figure out what she was saying, and what was wrong. The housekeeper shouldn't matter to her exercises—just like her guilt shouldn't. But they took turns coming up until Farya could feel the outline of what at least the housekeeper was saying: Someone the housekeeper loved had done something foolish to get something they should know better than to want. What had led to the woman across the yard becoming so unhinged came down to a gleam—a reflected shimmer of spring sunlight. It could be the gold of an older man's watch, a young man's teeth, a man's new car, the clear skin on a young woman's cheek when she smiled, her dangly earrings when she flipped her hair a certain way, or the light on her shaved legs when she crossed them. That shimmer spoke loudly about what lay beneath all the dreary labor of being alive. It said sex was, if not the absolute truth, the closest thing to it, and if you could just hold it, you might not need to die.

The glimmer rang out through the housekeeper's voice as a bright regret and a hopeless warning. It was a small thing, a moment of delight in desire before it humanized into yearning. And doing her exercises, Farya isolated it, muted it, made it so the light that bounced into the eye of the beholder did so with less vindictiveness. The housekeeper's voice grew quiet, calm, a muted conversation with a teenage daughter who was in the yard with her.

Farya opened her eyes, and the yard seemed bigger, with more sunlight, because the buildings were lower, spaced farther apart. Looking up, past the peaked rooftops of the houses behind hers, there were no towers in the financial district, and, she sensed, no towers worth the name on the island of Manhattan. She heard the wind, with no car horns, car alarms, overblown car stereos, no helicopters, or jets roaring, no shouting in the street. The city was a smaller place, still a seaport, rowdy with sailors on its edges, but genteel toward its middle. Not panicking, Farya closed her eyes again and remembered the city she knew. She remembered with a singular focus to her exercises until the tumult and noise of the city returned, including the housekeeper whine-preaching into her cell phone.

Just a month ago, the misadventure would have frightened Farya out of her wits. But she'd learned some control. While it filled her with the dread of responsibility, it had also begun to calm her. For the first time, she thought, maybe she wasn't a wildfire, wasn't an earthquake. Maybe she could be the kind of person who could afford a conscience.

Farya opened her eyes, not sure how to feel.

✛

The next morning, she met Ethan at their usual place by Union Square. Her problems remained slightly beyond her. But she preferred sloppy sympathy to wisdom.

The cafe, at that hour, was a mix of parents with young children and actors trying to talk their way into jobs. Edouard kept busy trying to watch the cartoons on little Josef's tablet. Farya's new bodyguard took a seat at the counter, watching the door of the busy cafe. Ethan had been gaining weight since he got sober, but it had been gradual up until now. His face was flush and sweaty. His belly escaped the bottom of his button-down shirt, which paired with his expensive sweatpants gave the impression that he was wearing pajamas.

"It's good to see you. Ugh, what a week. Every day, we seem to find out we're poorer," he said, ordering a waffle platter without looking down at the menu or up at the waitress. "I mean, it's not like I'll have to go to work. But I'd hoped my boy wouldn't have to go to college, get a job, get married, any of that."

"I thought you were still pretty flush."

"I mean, we're rich. But we sat down with the money guy and started a budget. Right now, we burn through money like you wouldn't believe. Maybe *you* would. Anyway, the oligarch will have control over most of what's left once Feodora's gone. And he's an idiot—he'll get bled dry by some clever vixen in a year."

"What about your mother-in-law?"

"We never got a straight answer about what she spent it on. They always come up with something."

"Who's they?"

"The clever ones—the bankers and lawyers, the skimmers and scammers who write rules too complex and boring even to read. The ones who make it all impossible," Ethan said, pouring cream into his coffee.

"What about you? What about your pop-up store? What's going on with that?"

"With the little monster on me all day, who has time? Plus, the idea is played out by now. There's like three boutique-gallery-popups in Williamsburg already, I heard."

"Onto the next idea, I guess."

"Hmm. The store idea was fresh when I had it. But you don't get ideas by sitting around the house watching cartoons and arguing with the wife about where the sippy cup lids are. You get them from being out on the edge, up late, at secret bars, doing coke with artists, and talking. I don't think I'm going to come up with another idea like that. Anyway, look at me. I'm old and fat. I shot my wad, and this is my shitty pension."

"Sorry I asked. Maybe there's another way to live, another career. Maybe you don't need to take her family's money."

"Not take the money? That's like asking someone not to draw breath. You may run your dying-kids charity, but you still take the money. I mean, you do take the money, don't you?"

"Yeah. I guess I do. So, use the free time you have to, I don't know, create something."

"How about a children's book: *Daddy's Fat Because Life's a Joke.*"

Farya laughed and sipped her coffee. She knew Ethan's way of converting a pint of encouragement into a gallon of self-pity. A thin young man at the next table was asking the waitress to change or turn down the music—"the world would be a better place had she never been born," he said of the singer. The waitress apologized and said she would talk to the bartender.

"Thanks again for letting us use the place in Montauk," Farya said.

"Oh, yeah. No problem. We'll have to rent that place out this summer. Nothing is selling right now, not the real estate, not the art, none of it. That'll be a great summer, stuck in beach traffic, changing sheets in between renters," Ethan said, staring at his waffles. "Anyway, the whole summer is tied up by my mother-in-law—she could die tomorrow, or she could last until the fall. Constant visits to the hospital, or the hospice, if she comes back. Carolina is not handling it well; I'll tell you that. And people say I don't earn my money."

"Who says that?"

"I don't know. My in-laws, I guess. What was that—the trip to Montauk? Are you in trouble? God, listen to me bitching about weight gain and being relegated to the lower stratosphere of the global plutocracy, while you're on the lam from God knows who."

"It was just to be safe. Bryan is trying to sell his business. And he has some business partners or clients; he calls them different things depending on when I ask. Anyway, he decided we should get away for a while."

"Is that why the new security stud?"

"You noticed."

"Of course. It always seemed ironic that you had all this security when you should be able to, you know, if you were in real trouble, just make someone go, you know, poof."

"Yeah, you know it's never worked that way. Remember that bitch Beverly who made junior year hell for me? She's still alive and well, posting every five minutes on Facebook. And even when it happened a lot, it never happened when I was scared or angry. It was more when I was depressed. And I could wind up wiping away a whole type of person, or some entire city, or even an emotion or a color from the world. When it happens, it's more like throwing up than like deleting an email."

"And Lourdes, has she helped?"

"She's been giving me these exercises for a few years now. But I've barely gotten to where I can stop the worst things from happening. I mean, the exercises are better than Thelonious Monk. But it's only in the last few months that I can even control it a little."

"If you can, then you could, you know, *do something*," Ethan said, folding a thick triangle of waffle into his mouth. "Whatever this mysterious problem with those mysterious client partners is— you can do something about it. Something, anyway."

"The problem is that *something* is about as specific as it would be if I tried to do it. Anyway, let's hope it doesn't come to that. You have syrup."

"What?"

"Your chin—syrup."

✢

Farya walked home the long way with Edouard and her bodyguard, a massive, taciturn, tan young man. They walked through Washington Square Park, which was full of people. It was a warm day. Class was still in session at the colleges, and the jackets were off. The thin women seemed too much like children to be smoking cigarettes, and some of the coltish young men gave Farya the eye. People played guitars and sang songs, as they'd always heard was the thing to do.

But she felt very far from their excitement. Lunch with Ethan underscored the guilt and helplessness she felt.

Edouard, however, was immune to her mood and requested the playground. At its entrance, someone had set up a small fundraiser. It was a kind of high-concept marketing stunt—a spring-festival red carpet. Kids would pose in front of a step-and-repeat and play with the tiaras, boas, clip-on bow ties, and bowler hats. Farya noted it as an idea she could try for her own foundation if she could focus on it again. The event volunteers wore bright green T-shirts emblazoned with "Posing for a Cure" logos in big yellow letters. They carried brightly colored instant cameras, like the one Farya's parents had when she was a kid. They were taking pictures of the kids and giving them to parents, implicitly in exchange for a donation.

Set free in the playground, Edouard went for the trunk full of costumes. Farya followed to find the little boy talking about cowboys to a small, raw-boned volunteer in a bright green "Posing for a Cure" shirt. The ugly man angled up his clunky box of a camera and took a picture of himself with Edouard and handed it to Farya. She took the picture and handed the man a five-dollar bill for the canister on his belt and ushered her boy to the other end of the playground. She checked to see if the setup struck her security guy as odd, but it didn't. So little Edouard climbed and jumped for an hour before they met Kathleen and Ellem at a cavernous restaurant in Soho for a late lunch.

The restaurant, a few blocks from the park, was quiet. Ellem seemed okay, but Farya was afraid to look too closely, for fear of catching sight of an early-stage twitch, a stammer, or one of the disease's signature tics. Kathleen was brave as always. With no money, her husband last spotted in Eastern Europe, and a daughter in the early stages of a degenerative neurological disease, Kathleen seemed calm, positive—and like she knew what she had to do. Her daughter, facing an unimaginable fate, was also cheerful.

At one point, with their children engaged in their own conversation two tables over, Farya mentioned with some amazement how well Kathleen seemed.

"The thing is," Kathleen said, "I know that he's never coming back. I know my daughter's not going to get better. I know we'll never have what we once had. I know it's going to get worse, that it will be very hard, and very bad for a very long time. I know I have to do all I can so that Ellem has some kind of happiness in her life. And I know there's no way out for either of us."

"I can't imagine."

"It's shit. I know that. But in a way, it's freeing. I know what I'm up against. I know there's no higher court to appeal to. And I know what I have to do. Before, with all the money, and so many possibilities, choices, and so much time, I never had that. I'm okay now."

"Well, I'm impressed. And if there's anything I can do …"

"The job and your friendship are more than enough," Kathleen said. She had aged in the last few months, but in a way that made her seem harder, surer, as carved of oak and polished to a shine. "To be able to take on Ripht-Schondles the way we do is, well, the importance of that isn't lost on me."

"You inspire me."

"It's our job to do what we can, even when it's not much. You should meet some of the other parents I've met in the Ripht-Schondles support groups. They're inspiring. I'm going to an event tomorrow night if you're free."

"I should be," Farya said, eager to spend as much time as possible out of her house, out of her head. She could feel her conscience growing, pushing her to a conclusion she did not want.

"It's a memorial service for one of the older kids. Ellem knew him. I think you being there would mean a lot."

Stammering, Farya said she'd try to make it. She checked her phone, just to look away, and found a message from Lourdes: *Saw a steamboat in Newtown Creek for a minute the other day. Come by tomorrow afternoon. We're overdue.*

✢

The lunch with Kathleen left Farya chastened, but also less afraid. And when she and Edouard got home, she found, to her great surprise, roses waiting in the foyer. To her even greater surprise, Bryan was waiting there too, in the afternoon. Bryan. He picked up Edouard and tossed him, squealing with delight, in the air. Champagne and an array of delicacies waited on the kitchen counter.

"What is this? What's my husband doing home before ten at night?" Farya said, caught up in the excitement.

"We did it! We finished the sale! All the parties agreed and signed on the dotted lines."

"Really? It's done?" Farya asked.

"Pretty much. The FCC has to sign off. But that should be a formality."

He kissed her, and she remembered him—his voice and his body, his smell and how they'd fallen in love. It was like coming home after a long trip. Edouard was chatty as they sat at the dining room table, drinking apple juice and champagne, eating cheese, smoked fish, chilled King Crab legs with a zesty, piquant horseradish dipping sauce, or an organic heirloom prosciutto and a pickle charcuterie board and good French bread. Over the course of the meal, Edouard told his father about hats and cameras at the playground, and Farya explained the "Posing for a Cure" setup at the park.

"The man there said he knew you, Daddy," Edouard said.

"No, he didn't. Don't make up stories," Farya said.

"I'm not. He said Daddy fell down in the desert, and so he picked him up and gave him a place to stay, and fish and candy bars to eat."

"I don't know what he's talking about," Farya said. "We were only in that part of the playground for a minute. The guy was a volunteer—he wanted to take a picture, so we'd give some money."

Bryan wanted to write the story off to his son's imagination. But there was a sharp concern in his wife's voice.

"Here. I have the picture," Farya said, reaching into the oversized pocket of her fleece and finding the instant photo among the candy wrappers, toy parts, receipts, and hair ties. Seeing it, Bryan's hand started to shake. He tried to put down his champagne flute, but the horizon was blurry to him. The glass tipped over and spilled on the table, soaking the placemats.

In the picture, smiling straight into the camera, was Bryan's kidnapper only an inch from little Edouard. Bryan had never seen the man smile, but he knew the pug-nosed, gristly face. Edouard asked if Daddy was all right. Bryan shook his head yes and no at the same time and got up from the table. He ran to the front door and waved at Bernard and his partner, who were waiting in the white SUV across the street. He had other ways to alert them, small switches and buttons stationed around the house, but he couldn't seem to remember that or anything else.

They came running in. Bryan began to explain and to ask Bernard's partner just what he saw that afternoon in the playground. He reached into his pocket for the photo to show it to them but couldn't find it. Seeing his father in that state was jarring for Edouard, who started to cry. Farya took him upstairs while Bryan and the two security experts scoured every inch of the townhouse for an instant photo.

By the end of the night, the best choice for all three seemed to be that Bryan had misplaced the picture or his mind, and not to inquire which, but rather to forget about it for now. It was a familiar choice, a familiar shame. Bryan and Farya slipped in and out of shallow, under-nourishing sleep until the sun rose.

Farya was terrified. Bryan's mysterious partner-clients had threatened her son. All through the night, Washington Square Park—with its arch and all the countless songs, novels, and cultural ephemera it had inspired over the centuries—flickered, as Farya wrathfully elided it and its history from existence, and then remembered them back. By dawn, though, the park was there, a little misshapen, as an imperfectly recollected thing would be.

The night had moved Farya closer to a terrible choice.

"It'll all be over soon. It will all be okay," Bryan said as they dressed, both awake ahead of their son.

"I know," Farya said.

Feodora

By the time Feodora had visited the last of the best and brightest doctors with their enormous machines, and absurd healers with their enormous claims, the family jet seemed like another hospital hallway to her. But among the most optimistic and grandiose of the experts she met, her condition made even the liars err on the side of truth.

So, she stopped searching for a cure and started a final round of visits—to her grandchildren. She was in New York with her daughter's young son when she got a call from one of the oncologists—the one she could least bully, the one she liked the best. He said there was someone she should meet, but he wouldn't say more than that. He wasn't one to be coy or one to call for no reason, so Feodora did. The young man on the other end was named Troy. His voice was buoyant and polished—his smile was audible over the phone. She started to explain, but he said he knew who she was and who referred her, and why. He said he had something that would interest her but wouldn't say more. She said she didn't have time to waste. He said the meeting would be brief and promised it wouldn't be a waste of time.

Feodora suggested they meet at a restaurant near her apartment on Central Park South the next day, early, when her husband would be at physical therapy. The young man agreed, asking that they meet outside the restaurant, and apologizing for the strange request, given that it was winter. On the busy Midtown corner, the young man introduced an older, aloof gentleman, wearing what seemed like a back brace under his raincoat, as Arnold. While Troy was the quintessential salesman, all double-Windsor dimpled charm, well-calibrated eye contact, hairspray, and shoe polish, Arnold was another sort of creature entirely. His handshake was cold and soft as mist, and his body was discombobulated, as if composed of other bodies, poorly managed. He was hard to look at as if she'd been commanded not to look in his direction.

"Thank you for making the time, Ms. Andreyevich," Troy said, using a name no one had in decades. "I think you'll like what we have to show you."

"I agreed to meet with you, but I won't go anywhere with you. As I said …"

Arnold leaned in, saying, "Ma'am, it's not …" But during the last syllable he spoke, they were transported to another Fifty-Eighth Street. On it, the people were replaced with what seemed like ecstatic statues, exchanging shapes and sensations that coalesced into human forms, hieroglyphics eclipsing each other to speak a language that encompassed the entire avenue. Feodora couldn't take her eyes off the statues, each unique, still the person that they'd been, but also very much like the whole universe and like fountains, with luminous water bubbling from the tops of their heads. She knew instantly that this was no trick, no hypnosis or drug. The buildings on either side undulated with lazy pleasure. Even the old man at the pretzel cart on the corner and the hobo camped out on the exhaust grate of a high-rise gurgled with pure, elaborate enjoyment. The sun ran its fingers down a glass-and-steel curtain wall, and looking up, Feodora made eye contact with it—the sun was alive and deeply familiar with her. *Don't worry,* it said, *I've done those things too.*

A rat stopped to regard her, decided it had better things to do, and waved as it scurried off, promising they'd talk another time.

She wanted to ask what was happening, but she knew. The world, this world, like this—it was familiar. It was a place that had always been there, but it was a place for which she'd always carried a peculiar indifference.

"So, we've invited you here to make a very exciting offer," Troy said.

"Can you cure me?"

"No. We don't do that."

"So? What? Can I live here from now on?"

"I'm afraid not—no more than you ever did. But we can offer you something better. Would you like to be God?" Troy said, his smile clear as money.

Feodora, before asking more, asked the price. The answer shouldn't have surprised her: It cost what only someone who could have anything would pay.

That kind of price took some convincing. So, Arnold showed her wonders she had known or at least suspected all along. Troy explained what they meant, along with what was possible for her, with their help. It took what seemed to Feodora like an entire delightful week in that magical place. But she was home before her husband had returned from physical therapy.

She was convinced but called the oncologist to thank him and to ask a few questions. He confirmed that she had seven or eight months, adding that maybe she could get to a year with aggressive chemo, but it wouldn't be worth the agony. She asked how he knew Troy. He said *we all have to aspire to something, right?* It would be the last time she spoke to him. Feodora always controlled the family finances and began to liquidate or transfer the properties, shell corporations, and trusts that week. With payment arranged, the three of them went to work.

"You will make an entire world from your life," Troy explained during an early meeting in his office, just across town, on Park

Avenue. It was gray and freezing outside, and the sparse square tops of skyscrapers seemed to float in the concrete-colored air.

The thought excited and frightened Feodora. She knew her reasons for not being nice, and she was smart enough to know that wasn't an excuse. Her whole life, Feodora had been smart—never in a showy way, more like a squirrel on a branch who could tell when a rot had set into the roots, and when it would fall. She always made the right gambits at the right time, based on the baldness of the tires of a passing truck, the disparity between a neighbor's food and the plate it was served on, the fit of a clerk's shirt, the pace at which vodka was poured at a party, the pause before a man mentioned his wife. She never missed. She couldn't.

She had seen it all coming and jumped from branch to branch. And after she and her family were ensconced, wealthy, seemingly beyond want and from the whims of fortune—this betrayal, this ambush, this joke. After surviving so many people, so many huge doors crashing shut forever, Feodora was dying angry. That was bad material to build with.

"The creation will happen very quickly at first," Troy said. "Whatever you imagine and decide in those first minutes will be decided forever, for everyone and for everywhere."

Arnold wasn't at this meeting. The ones Arnold did attend seemed to take whole days. In them, she wouldn't get tired, and when they were done, just a few minutes would have passed. She was in a white leather chaise—firm but comfortable, like a stylish version of the examination table in a doctor's office. Most of the time, Troy sat beside her, facing her at an angle, in a hard, wooden chair. If someone opened the door, they might think they were interrupting a psychoanalysis session.

"So, you need to start to decide, or at least consider," he continued. "What will be in this world? Will it be like this one? Or should it be another kind of world entirely?"

"How can I decide everything? What's to keep the sky and the earth separated, or keep the land and sea apart, or make it so that it isn't too hot, or too bright, or too cold? I'm not a scientist or an engineer."

"Your knowledge of this world will be enough. You merely need to imagine it and will it. There are others who will bind the world together in an orderly, consistent way."

"Other gods?"

"No. You could think of them as builders. They take the raw material and interpret it in sensible ways. From your desire and your vision, the world will get its shape and its meaning. From them, it will get its consistency."

"Who are these builders?" Feodora asked.

"They're ordinary people, like the people you see every day, who cook and clean, who make your clothes and drive your cars. They've all agreed to do it, one way or another."

"Why would they do that?"

"The same reason they agree to dry-clean our clothes or cook our food."

"And what becomes of them?"

"Some of them will live on in the world you've created, and rule."

"Many?"

"Creating an entirely new, independent reality is a violent process. I won't lie. People are destroyed. But people are destroyed anyway," Troy said, solemn without letting the conversation sag. "The important thing is the whole world—what kind of place will it be? Do you want a place that's familiar or exotic?"

"Exotic how?"

"How many suns would you like it to have?"

"We can do that?"

"Absolutely—it's more a question of keeping it from happening. Many of the new worlds have multiple suns because even with the sun, people remember it differently. But just to change the number of suns is thinking small."

"Is it?"

"The sun could be an elephant, or a huge bird, or a bust of Ludwig Van Beethoven. What would you want the new world to be like for you? Some clients go picayune: think of Norman Rockwell planets around a Tropicana sun. On the other end of the spectrum, you have the ones who want undulating hive moons populated by snake-people, in cloverleaf orbits around black leather planets."

"Oh, really?"

"Sure. You could even have both and more. It is, after all, an entire universe. You don't have to decide now. But you should decide soon. We have to set the art department to work on the key concepts."

"Are they the builders?"

"No, they build simple models of the main things you want in the world. The moment of creation itself is very brief and very intense, and so we set images before you—dioramas and figurines of the things you most want to remember in that moment."

"So, this part is like shopping," she said, casting her eyes on Troy, with his tie knotted just so and golden speckles of late-day stubble on his pinkish face.

"Yes, it's shopping and wishing and dreaming all at once. This is my favorite part of the business."

Feodora, who saw small things, watched a small blue vein pulse on Troy's temple. He was an expert at showing no stress in how he comported himself. But she could tell that he was trying his hardest not to think about his least-favorite part of the business. She could tell that it had called up some subtle but very real damage that the business inflicted on him.

"I'll tell you what I always say to our clients," Troy continued. "You've spent most of your life anticipating and adapting to the world. You've done it better than most and carved out small spaces where you could have things as you believed they should be. Now's the time to tap into that. Now's the time when indulging that sense of *taste* isn't extravagant or selfish—it's the golden road."

Saying the practiced words restored the gleam to Troy's eye and restored Troy to the true glory to which he'd been born—an account executive to the gods of yet-unborn worlds.

Feodora never enjoyed shopping in the way some of the other wives did. And this work was harder than shopping. Consciousness is a legislature, and no one can decide if it's corrupt, incompetent, or both. Probing her own mind for her deepest wishes, she found it more like a frazzled chairman banging his gavel than a single narrator telling a story. And if a whole universe depends on it, then clear decisions are required, or else, who knows? These were Feodora's thoughts, walking one final spring afternoon down Fifty-Seventh Street, after another consultation with Troy. The salesman was, as she'd suspected, not as wise as he tried to appear.

"The only thing I would warn against is the Pegasus. You wind up with ponies who have short lifespans from carrying around huge, mostly useless wings," he'd advised. "I think someone made it work by having them glide off of cliffs. But you wind up with a lot of cliffs everywhere. Just another thing to consider."

The taxis tolerated the Central Park horse-drawn carriages and honked at one another. The buses sidled up and eased off. The point, as Feodora had taken it, was that she needed to take drastic action to feed her better angels better food.

Feodora had survived and risen to her quiet promontory in the affairs of men by being bold when others were terrified and terrified when others were warm and fuzzy. She had grandchildren in New York and grandchildren in St. Petersburg and a husband who didn't like to spend much time outside of his two homes in one or the other. She was an old, sick woman. Everything said to stay put, like a lamb before the hammer.

"You wouldn't understand, but you've trusted me this far," she told her husband in their pink marble dining room a thousand feet above Central Park.

Neither Feodora nor her husband had found a satisfactory way to speak about what would happen to her next, except in riddles and vagaries. So, they tried not to speak of it. Now she was asking him not to come barging into wherever she went for her last few months.

He was, after all, a very powerful man in every room around the world—besides the one he shared with her.

It wasn't easy. She invoked love, trust, loyalty, and the Almighty. Her plea was passionate, perverse for being a lie. And she wasn't sure that she'd succeeded when she left. From New York, she burned through a few weeks of misdirection, traveling legally to Helsinki and semi-legally to Khabarovsk. The landscape there pulled at her—the Cyrillic signs, the leftover Soviet murals, more faded than they'd been in her youth, the trucks and tractors gone to seed, hanging on like abandoned cathedrals. None of it could pull as hard as the husband she'd left confused and alone in New York, or her grandchildren, her son, and sometimes her daughter. Feodora, however, had always known that emotion was a constituency that could be ignored, for a while. Beyond that congress, beyond everything was the destination.

From Khabarovsk, she traveled illegally, with a weak fake passport and bribes, to Sydney. From there, it was a fishing boat, freighters, and a cruise ship—seamen always found a berth for an unthreatening old woman with cash on hand ... a frail woman with incriminating papers and a few vacuum-sealed bundles of five-hundred-euro notes stashed on her body. It was a risk, but eternity was on the line, and when you look weakest is when to make the strongest gambits. Everyplace was dingy, smelly, but far more vivid than the last safe decade had been.

She made it to the island she'd had in mind. It burst from the sea stony, sudden, and green like an impatient fantasy. The jungle relented here and there in dramatic clearings anchored by trees with trunks wider than the old American cars were long. Beautiful, the people were soft and patient as children. This was the place where she would feed her angels.

Feodora unwrapped her satellite-phone and called her husband, to tell him she was alive and well, and to ask that he not try to find her. She called Troy when it suited her, and they would discuss her happiest memories, about what she'd loved, what she had hoped to love or be loved by. She described those things and described the island.

For Feodora, even paradise was a calculation. She could seem to feel a pressure where she knew the tumors were. She tried to ignore the heaviness that seemed to be building in her inhalations, to pretend the coughing jags were from pollen. One day, looking from her porch over the gentle blue waters where dolphins played and peaceable turtles coasted through their long, long lives like dreams, it was clear: She would have to take the paltry beauty she'd found, and do what she could with it.

Troy had a helicopter pick her up from the island that night. A day later, she was at a posh seaside clinic in Long Island. It was early fall, but it felt as cold as the moon. Her children and husband visited her at the seaside clinic. That night, the ruse of the experimental procedure was the only way to get her husband to leave. Her children didn't need much convincing. Feodora rested.

Her husband was old when they'd married. Her children, greedily shielded from the harm they most needed, were spoiled, made wrong, she thought, imagining the world to come. They would all need money to live on, so Feodora had opted for a universe that was less than infinite—a galaxy, with a hundred billion stars and dozens of billions of years ahead of it.

After a nap, Troy introduced her to a friendly, well-dressed black woman named Charlize, who Troy said would answer any questions that she might have about what comes next. With big eyes and long fingers that drew out the things she explained in the air, Charlize had the sort of warmth that makes people comfortable, quickly, efficiently.

Feodora was weak. If it was a scam, it was too late to pull out now. If it was a scam, she'd be no wiser in a week. She gestured to Charlize and asked Troy, "She knows what she's doing, right?"

Troy said, "Yes, she's very good." Feodora nodded, now past concealing her weakness.

Doctors managed the pain and prepared her for the one last burst of energy that she'd need. Feodora didn't question doctors anymore. The sun set, and they injected a mix of vasodilators, steroids, amphetamines, and painkillers, all timed to reach their optimal mix not long after they reached the city in a blazing ambulance. Charlize, who was in the back of it with her, though busy with her phone for most of the ride, squeezed her hand and said everything was set up. It was late, and traffic was light. The night was clear, and the flashing city gleamed.

The building where they arrived, 432 Park Avenue, seemed impossible, bolting straight up in an unrelenting grid. It was just across town from where she'd lived with her husband. Feodora stopped, with the IV stand in her hand, and looked up, before Charlize suggested that they get inside, out of the cold.

The elevator took them up thirty-five floors in what seemed like a second. Feodora's ears popped. The drugs made her feel like she had when she was young—invincible. Though late, the office that the elevator opened into was bright and busy with people at screens everywhere. The doctor from Long Island checked her pulse and her breathing, injected a syringe into her IV, and said to Charlize, as though Feodora wasn't there, "We need to do this soon. I don't know how much longer she can keep this up."

This was a surprise to Feodora because she felt so good that she'd almost entirely forgotten the cancer. Her heart sank as she remembered, and they led her into a vast room. It was enormous, kind of like the stage of a theater-in-the-round, and kind of like the alleyway between two skyscrapers. A few men helped her onto a bed and told her to get comfortable. They gave her five seconds to get comfortable and began to pull bandages across her body. The bandages were soft but firm. While she could still move her head, she looked around the impossibly tall room—a cone with hundreds of widening circular tiers above her. And she was in that bottom part of the cone where all the melted ice cream would collect.

From a shadow, a large metal arm swung out over her. From it dangled a child's mobile, but enormous and detailed, with her mother's ornate tea set, the last thing they'd sold when she was a girl before she was taken from her parents. There were models of Palace Square and the Winter Palace from Leningrad, a model of the first home she'd had in Geneva. There was her newborn baby boy. There was a dolphin, a quilt, a small glass of vodka, and so on. She watched them play in the cold air until the straps pulled tight and she was immobilized on the bed.

It's time, Feodora, Charlize said over the intercom, her voice soft, but the words clipped. The attendants left the room. The way they hurried bothered her. The bother brought her back to the cancer. The cancer brought her to death. Death brought her to the hundreds of people she'd used, maybe as shields, maybe worse, while deep in the political blood sports of her young life. The thought of the people she failed to protect brought her back to the cancer—that rank betrayal in her tissues—which expanded and loomed ever larger in her thoughts.

The cancer, a terrible string of meat, coiling, spreading—Feodora tried not to think of it, tried to only think of what she was doing: creating a new world from a million impossible choices. But Feodora wasn't imagining so much as negotiating, pleading. *Maybe just a world without terrible beasts and impossible traps that force you to destroy one friend to save another.* She thought of Arnold, and what he'd said in one of their rare meetings, "With reality, the key is how much you want to talk versus how much you want to listen. It may seem like courtesy, but it's much deeper than that. You need to stop listening, and to speak clearly, or else someone else might."

But the radical unfed elements in the congress of her mind were howling and would not heed the gavel. It was too late to find a clear voice, a pure image to hold, Feodora thought, as the machine started. The tiers above her began to spin, the dim forms in the upper tracks catching the moonlight. The entire sixty-story chamber seemed to gyrate, the walls full of slithering.

Feodora knew what she'd done to get here, and that knowledge was like the cancer. It would follow her to the next world; it would infect the universe like the serpent in the garden. The new world would be full of pain and fear and injustice. She sensed this like she had anticipated everything in her life. The titanic slithering intensified. A vast and blinding light opened up on all sides of her, leaving just a spot of darkness in its center. Feodora began to move with a magisterial slowness into that spot.

The last of her physical pain became a concept, omnipresent, but mostly unnoticed, like the nose at the center of all you see. Alone in the rich and pregnant darkness, Feodora knew she could do whatever she wanted. She no longer had to listen. She was in control of everything, and all of existence could be whatever she wanted. But she also knew, with a vertiginous certainty, that she could not control what she wanted. She could not control who she was.

All of creation unfolded from her deepest wishes and desires. And Feodora, the only one true god of the universe, had a bad feeling. Darkness separated from light, time from space, matter from energy, the living from the dead at the dawn of eternity. And Feodora knew: her angels had not been fed; the serpent was the garden; this wouldn't go well.

Farya & Bryan

Farya was tired, but her exhaustion was nothing compared with that of the people she met the next day at the little boy's memorial at a funeral home on the Upper East Side. He was cute, and seemed happy, from the pictures. In his older pictures, closer to the end, his parents cropped the photos closer. But even still, the Ripht-Schondles contortions were impossible to miss in the last few.

She stayed close to Kathleen, shook hands with stricken strangers, and accepted thanks for the work of her foundation. She had never met the boy. But the tears came, nonetheless. Her tears were not the same as theirs, though. And Farya had to choke down her shame to look her victims in the eye. Each was a pointed reminder of the terrible seriousness of her actions.

From the funeral home, she went to see Lourdes. It had been a while, and her glass rectangle had been joined by a newer, cleaner, less-fortified sibling across the street. The two buildings still stood out against the previous generation's take on quick, opportunistic housing—the shingle- or vinyl-sided row houses that predominated in that part of the city. But change was afoot—the Dominican barbershop had turned into a coffee place, with salads.

Farya used her key and took the elevator downstairs. She passed the bike storage, the entrance to the garage, the boiler room. She went to Lourdes's special spherical basement room. Farya had always seen it as a kind of refuge and had used it as such when the only other places she could be were an open-plan office in Jersey City, and her room in a small apartment dominated by a raging vegan who never turned off the TV. And though Farya hadn't needed it in the same way in recent years, she still found nourishment and encouragement knowing that it existed. The windowless room with nothing but masks, busts and just faces, floor to ceiling, milling among themselves may have been a barometer to Lourdes. But for Farya, it was an anchor in a world to which she actually belonged.

Farya unfolded the TV table between the two armchairs and sat down. Lourdes met her down there, pizza box in hand, wearing sweatpants and a terry-cloth robe, and no makeup.

"Long night?" Farya asked.

"Very. Lot of comings and goings down here—poets, physicists, counterculture icons, folk singers, politicians gone, then back, then gone, then back again, some coming back the same, some different. I couldn't figure out a thread that connected all of them. Maybe you can help."

"Washington Square Park. I had an incident there. Someone threatened my son."

"And you tried to …"

"I don't know, really. I was upset. I couldn't sleep."

Lourdes started to speak, but stopped herself and just sat there, watching Farya. She tried on a few expressions—sympathy, disappointment, anger, and took a deep breath.

"The threat," Lourdes asked, "do you think it was random?"

"No. I didn't even know it was a threat when it happened. But it was a threat, and it was aimed at Bryan. It was some of the people he's in business with. It was more of a threat to him, really. But I can't let anyone, I mean anyone …"

"What kind of people are these?"

Farya looked around at the blind eyes of the busts and masks around them. The room had a sanctity. And if there was anyone in the world she could trust with a secret, it was Lourdes. So Farya told what she knew about Bryan's business, the souls he acquired, how he acquired them, and who he sold them to. She told Lourdes about Bryan's kidnapping and its many incongruities, his isolation and his deep fear. Lourdes listened, her broad face still, her eyes catching every nuance, everything not said.

"I was afraid of this," Lourdes said. "It's a serious moral problem. And it's probably why things have been going wrong—Ripht-Schondles and whatnot, you know?"

"No, I don't know. What does Bryan's business have to do with my morality or my exercises?"

"Think of your imagination like an ocean. It's vast, and in it, there are incredible creatures. Your imagination is a sea that leads to exotic lands and untold possibilities. And you're here, with me, on the beach, with a little boat. This boat is the exercises we do. But you can't get out to sea until you get past the waves on the shore. Now, those waves are the push-pull of all the harm you do to others. You want to argue with me about what's your fault. That's the push-pull of it. Those waves keep you on the shore, where you can only lash out at the water."

"That doesn't add up, though. I hardly even knew what Bryan did until after the whole Ripht-Schondles catastrophe."

"Maybe not completely. But you had some sense—even if you only knew not to ask. Bryan was your other half. And Bryan knew. How well did he hide it? Not well, I'm guessing. I mean, he was trying to sell the company. Whatever you knew was enough—to keep you off your exercises, to steer you in a vindictive direction."

"But it's his business. And now they're coming after us. What am I supposed to do?"

"That depends on you. After World War Two, the biggest problem with the nuclear bomb was that there was no real way to use it. They tried to make it as small as possible, so it could actually be used in a war. But it was still too much. The only thing they could use it for was the end of the world. So, how small can you get?"

"The new exercises are helping. But trying to *erase* someone is still ... I was at a child's funeral today. I saw the mother. I don't know what I'd do ... But I don't know what I'd do to protect to my son, either, if there was a threat in front of me."

"That may be the real risk. Maybe the best we can do now is limit the blast radius. Tell me again, slowly, everything you can about these people your husband's in business with ..."

✛

Bryan hadn't flown commercial in a decade and had been delegating his Washington meetings for almost as long. So, the DC shuttle from LaGuardia with its traffic, its halfhearted business-class amenities, and showing up at the airport an hour early for a forty-five-minute flight were all tinged with nostalgia for him. When he was younger, he'd have held onto these aggravations as anecdotes for a coming meeting. But now he wouldn't dare mention the trip for what it revealed: he flew commercial; he was worried; he had good reason to be worried. After six weeks waiting for the FCC to give its rubber stamp to the ostensibly straightforward sale of Metacom transaction, he was worried.

The deal was not going as Bill Van Harappan had said to expect. And now Bill was riding to the rescue, to set things straight at the FCC. Bill wasn't the FCC Commissioner, but he might be after the next election. And that afternoon, Bill had a hefty finder's fee on the line. He met Bryan just past the metal detector inside the Commission's headquarters, on the city's edge by the highway and the water.

The building was a standard federal office with too many antiquated touches forced into its bland gigantic frame. Just past security, a very thin, very young man showed them to a conference room with a view of the Washington Monument and sat down across from them. He introduced himself as Gary.

"Where's Cheryl?" Van Harappan asked.

"She had a conflict, and so she asked me to meet with you."

"Please, go get Cheryl," the older man insisted.

"Like I said, she has another meeting right now. *She* asked *me* to meet with *you*. So why don't you ask me what you wanted to ask Cheryl, and maybe I have an *answer* for you. If not, *then* you can try to schedule another meeting with her *later*," the small man said, enjoying the power he held over a giant like Van Harappan— baiting him into an outburst. Van Harappan didn't rise to it, but the ten-minute meeting unfolded fruitlessly from there, with no answers. Leaving down the wide, echoing corridor, Van Harappan mumbled a list of the people who would pay for this insult. Bryan was embarrassed for Bill and afraid for himself. The walk to the exit took forever.

Bryan alternated between looking at the floor and staring ahead at the endless and hostile hallway when he saw a familiar face—his old protégé, Cassie Ocampo. She was still pretty, but different. She looked calm and older than years alone would account for. A lanyard with an FCC staff ID bounced against her comfortable, understated clothes as she walked. Bill had taken to tapping his revenge list into his phone. He murmured a goodbye without looking up when Bryan excused himself and said hello to Cassie.

Her little frame stuttered to a halt, too stunned to smile. Bryan offered a smile and held out his hand. He had always felt bad about firing Cassie. And the sight of her reminded him of the wrong choices he'd made and the wrong people he'd trusted. If he'd stood by Cassie, things may have gone very differently.

"Hey—long time," was his first attempt to express all of that.

"Oh, Bryan—I heard you and Bill were coming in this week."

"Yeah, we just met with a Gary of some sort."

"Oh," she said, trying to look surprised.

"Can I talk to you?"

Cassie nodded, more resigned than pleased. Bill was gone down the hall, hissing now into his phone. Her office overlooked the wide highway of traffic-stalled cars and the Tidal Basin. The room was big enough for a desk, as well as a table with chairs, where they sat across from each other.

"It's been a long time," Bryan said again.

"Since you fired me. That's how long."

"I was always sad about how everything ended with us. I meant to reach out after."

"To be honest, it really hurt. I was doing my best, and I wasn't doing well, and you just dropped me—no warning, no nothing. When I heard you were coming in, I couldn't decide if I wanted to see you or not. I mean, you gave me my first big chance, and you taught me the business. I thought we were going to build something and work together for a long time."

"I did too. And I wish that could have happened. I wish we could have made Metacom into a different kind of company. And I'm sorry it had to end in such an unpleasant way."

"You had a lot to protect," she said. "You had—still have—your secrets. And they're the kind of secrets that make you do things you wouldn't otherwise do. I get it. Look what those secrets did to me. I used to be an athlete, up at five every morning, all of that. Next thing I know, I'm pulling on the shortest skirt I own to go see a doctor about another prescription. The secrets were more than I could carry. But I thought there was a way out the other side … forget what I thought …"

"How are you doing with all of that now—the pills?"

Cassie pursed her lips and brushed a strand of hair from her face. As she did, Bryan noticed the wooden prayer-bead bracelet on her wrist. That was new—as was the small golden crucifix around her neck.

"Do you know how long it takes to go through withdrawal for a real, serious Klonopin habit like I had? It takes two years. Two years of bad or no sleep most nights, of feeling like I was having a heart attack or cancer or was going blind. It was the hardest thing I ever did. But I did it."

"Good. I'm glad. And I'm glad to see you here. It seems like a good place for you."

"It's slow. It's boring. The pay is a joke. The people are mostly dull. But it's honest work, at least it is when I do it. It has to be. I can't live with side-deals and secrets. I can't quarantine parts of my life like I used to. I already tried to be clever and corrupt. At the time, it was a kick. It made my skin itch in a way I liked. Seeing you, I can start to feel that itch now. And I know I have to end this meeting."

"Cassie, I know what you mean. I'm doing what I'm doing not to have so many secrets," Bryan said.

"I know. I saw the transaction."

"And you know that it seems to have stalled—the clock stopped. I came down here to find out why, and for how long. But no one will give us a straight answer about anything. This was supposed to be a simple deal. Have you heard anything about the deal, the clock, any of it?"

"I heard it's indefinite."

"Heard?"

"I'm not on it, personally. That would be a conflict. But I'm close with some of the people who are."

"Could you talk to them, maybe see about nudging it forward?"

Cassie smiled to herself and shook her head. Bryan noticed that her face no longer flushed as it once had. It was tan, made sallow in the fluorescent office lights. It hadn't changed for their whole meeting.

"You don't get it, Bryan. I have talked to them."

"You have? So, what is this? Revenge? I thought you said that leaving Metacom was a good thing for you."

"I did. And it was. But what's good for me now is *not* letting things slide—moral things, ethical things."

"So, explain to me how using your official position to interfere with a legal transaction is a moral act," Bryan said, feeling the hair bristle on his scalp.

"You know how. You know why. You always said that our side of the transaction was agnostic, or atheist, I forget which. But this is Washington. People here go to church."

"Okay. But you're using insider information to hijack a legitimate acquisition. How isn't that just another kind of corruption?"

"I did not, and would never, violate the non-disclosure contract I signed when I left Metacom. I didn't tell anyone here exactly where to look. There are rules, and I respect them. But so long as there's any statutory precedent or institutional discretion, I will continue to do what I can to stop this sale. I will not let you pass this particular buck."

"So, for your morals, you'd leave me stuck in limbo with a dying company, at the mercy of God-knows-who, and no way out?"

"It's not my morals—it's my soul. And you've always had a way out, just not one that pays very well. You're in a toxic business. And even if I can't tell anyone—I still know. And I know what that obligates me to do."

Cassie's desk phone rang, and Bryan waited while she took the call. Eventually, he excused himself. All the way to the airport, through the chute and on the short, bumpy flight to New York, Bryan was pursued by the dry finality of Cassie's words. It was an uncompromising clarity that didn't often appear in Manhattan, nor among the CEOs he knew. But she was no fanatic. He realized that he'd exposed her to a situation that was toxic, fatal even. And she'd had to become uncompromising just to come back from that.

Bernard, at the wheel of the white SUV, cursed the traffic in Queens, cursed the rain, changed lanes, and changed again. Stoop-shouldered, Bryan all but fell through the front door of the empty townhouse that afternoon and sat at the kitchen table, unable to move. He tried to imagine what else he could sell, or retire from, that might alleviate the helplessness and exhaustion he felt. But nothing came to mind.

✦

Farya came home and found Bryan, still in his suit, dumbfounded at the kitchen table. She asked how the trip to Washington had gone, and he just shook his head, changed the subject, and said hello to Edouard.

The next few days, Bryan was evasive, responding to her questions about Metacom by saying *the sale's hit a snag*, or *we should have a resolution soon*. He'd go out in the morning for twelve or eighteen hours at a stretch. That he came home smelling of sour sweat rather than booze was no consolation. He tried to be genial and upbeat, but Farya knew better. She caught snippets here and there when he took calls from home—phrases like *asset stripping*, *deliberate loan defaults,* and so on. And every day, he seemed to return from his coven of bankers a little more defeated. When Bryan returned home after one too many late nights with a nostril-flared sneer of misery on his face, Farya demanded to know what was going on.

The FCC was blocking the sale indefinitely, he said. And without the ability to sell, he would have to keep running Metacom. It made so much money and carried so much debt that he'd be in court for the next decade if he tried to walk away. Impossibilities piled up wherever he and his klatch of consultants seemed to look.

"I don't know what to do unless you can just make Metacom disappear," he said and could tell immediately how the comment wounded her. "I'm sorry. That wasn't fair."

"I wish I could. But it's not like that. It's like shoveling a tide."

"I never understood how it works."

Farya nodded, took him by the hand, and walked him to the kitchen counter. She opened a drawer and pointed to the walnut flatware organizer tray inside.

"How many kinds of forks do we have?" she asked. "Look in the drawer and tell me."

"Three."

"What are they?" Farya asked. "This is serious. Tell me."

"Dinner, salad, and dessert. Three kinds of fork."

"Good. Close your eyes," Farya said, drawing a slow breath. It took a long minute, but Bryan was at too much of a loss to break the silence. "How many kinds?"

"Three."

"Look."

Bryan looked into the drawer. Comprehension lagged his sight, and then his fingers, as he touched the dark polished wood separators.

"Wait, I just said three?"

"And they were?"

"Dinner and dessert and …"

"So, the change is still fresh, and you might still remember the one that's gone. Look for it like you'd look for the details of a dream."

"A third fork? A sally's fork? A kelp fork? A salvage fork? A seasick fork? Wait … a salad fork?"

"Good. You can still remember it, a little. But it feels strange, right?"

"Yeah. It's awkward, like a sixth finger. It's like my other memories don't have room for it. If I try to remember the restaurants I've been to—the dinner parties— there was never any such fork."

"That's how it works," Farya said, half-lidding her eyes again.

"What are you doing?"

"Putting the forks back."

"Like that? You can do that?"

"Sometimes. For a few minutes, right afterward, when the memory is still fresh. After that, it's a lot harder. Memory gets distorted. Other dynamics come into play."

"So, if you made Metacom disappear? Made it so it never existed?"

"Is that what you want?"

"It's put us in danger. There's what happened in the park, with the camera. I don't think they're going to back off. So, yes, we have to consider it."

"But getting rid of Metacom could mean anything. It could mean that you don't exist, that you never existed," Farya said.

"The other dynamics, like what you said happened with Ripht-Schondles."

"It's never as simple as just forks. Even if you don't disappear, you could wind up a different guy. Maybe we don't meet. Maybe we don't like each other much. And what happens to Edouard? Metacom is only part of the problem here. These people you're involved with—what they did when they kidnapped you. We don't even really know *what* we're dealing with."

"It's insane, and I'm sorry. I'm out of my depth. And I think that, if there's a way to do this so that the risk is only to me—not you and not Edouard—then we should try, then I want you to—what's the right word for it?"

"I always liked the word *elide*. But I wouldn't know where to start. I couldn't do it if I wanted to. I just don't understand them. Salad forks are one thing—I have them right in front of me, and I understand what they do, how they work, and what the shape of the world might be if they'd never existed, and where reality might rush in to fill the gaps."

"Rush in?"

"Like I said, there's nothing exact about it. It's less like drawing a map and more like managing a pen of animals. I think I need to know more about Metacom, and about your partners."

"They're not partners. Sevritas is a customer. They're on the other side of the transaction."

"It doesn't matter. Explain how it all works to me again?"

Bryan took a deep breath. He was tired, but her questions seemed the last hopeful avenue. He started at St. Philip's. As he told the story, she pressed him for details, and to try harder with the parts he only guessed at or inferred. She asked for Petra's exact words, Van Harappan's exact intonation when he said this or that—

did he say the word God *with an uppercase or lowercase* G? It was a long, frustrating exchange. It ended when one of Bryan's nods went too far, and his sleepy head hit the burled olive wood surface of the kitchen table.

In bed, Farya pieced it together in her mind. Between her own life, Bryan's story, Lourdes's enigmatic fragments, she soon realized that she'd always had the pieces, but hadn't wanted to put the puzzle together. Once she did, however, the monstrous absurdity began to become, starting with the question of why it came together.

Once a universe begins to shrink, the scavengers take note, start stripping it for parts, Lourdes had said. *There's an essential somethingness of the world—a stubborn will to resist the appeal of being everything or nothing. That's why human souls make great fuel.*

Almost as unfathomable, as she climbed into bed, was how a few hundred strip-mall storefronts and a few million hours of idle, emoji-filled texting might ensnare and even destroy a person's immutable and private soul. She strained her imagination to understand what or who could connect the souls of the poor with the kind of buyers who would pay the prices that kept Metacom and supported the lavish lifestyle of Farya's family. And she found an answer in a comment from one of her long nights with Lourdes.

The sorts who guided human souls, Farya remembered Lourdes saying. *They look for work. Some find a partner in the world of the living—and show them how to make a buck out of the souls that they have access to.*

Piecing together the stories of Bryan and Lourdes—like with like—Farya traced the outline, the catastrophe, that had undone the very purpose of the universe. And that catastrophe, sensible to the smartest and the richest, had made them want to liquidate their holdings for a lifeboat. Bryan simply sold them the oars.

That made him and her just two more opportunists getting what they could from a decades-old catastrophe, a silent nightmare that had undone history and eradicated whole continents and peoples.

How many souls had lived in The Greater Anointed Imperial Ohioan Commonwealth, who now have no longer existed? How many in the Metro-Camden area?

Farya could no longer ignore: She was the catastrophe.

She shuddered and choked on her own saliva, coughed and went stiff in bed at the realization. Farya remained there, as still as she could be, and waited for Edouard's first cry of the morning. There would be no sleep that night.

+

For the next few days and late nights, Bryan and Farya tried to figure out what they were going to do. They considered every option they could think of, which ranged from asking the FCC to open an investigation into Petra and Sevritas Partners, to emptying their accounts and making a run for it with Edouard. After seeing that look on her face the other night, Bryan didn't ask her again what he'd asked. But Farya brought it up: Could she just make this problem *disappear*? She didn't think so—the cottage industry that Bryan was involved with was still too abstract, too mysterious for Farya to approach it with any confidence. The risks were too high.

At the office, one morning in between those discussions, Bryan got the call and learned the buyer had officially called off the deal for Metacom. He called Van Harappan, who didn't answer. Bryan stared out the window at the sun-drowned dreamscape of Midtown skyscrapers, which looked to him like an impassible and deadly mountain range. On cue with the last of his non-desperate hopes expiring, Petra called. The timing, Petra must have thought impeccable. Bryan did his best light-and-bright *hello* when she called. The weeks of slowly foreclosing options made his voice dull, like a drum gone slack.

"Thanks for taking my call, Bryan. I didn't know if you would."

"It seemed a better option than waiting for you to pop up in the men's locker room."

"I apologize for that. But we do need to talk. I heard that the sale fell through. That's too bad. Sevritas had done some business with your suitor. I'm in Charlotte right now for a meeting with them."

"So, you're just calling to chat?"

"We can chat if you'd like. But I believe that we still have business to do together. This is an inflection point, and there is still a way forward for you. But we do need to have a talk—in person. You know phones."

"Fine. I can try to open up some time the week after next."

"We've had enough meetings. We've talked enough. Come to Houston—a client is throwing a big party. It will be a good time, and I have things to show you—good things, important things, I promise. I've been working on a way for all of us to get what we want. And I think you'll be pleased."

When Petra clicked off the line, Bryan jumped up and started out of the office, waving for Bernard to follow him. It was still early in the afternoon when he got home, surprising Farya. Without another word, he gestured for her to follow him to his home office, which Bernard swept weekly for bugs.

"So, you said you needed to see them, to see the buy side. You needed to see Petra in her element, right?"

"You mean to do the ... Yeah, at the very least I need to see that, see who they are, how they act."

"Okay—great. I can get you a front-row seat with her, and we can talk through any part of the business you want. She just called and invited me to a party with one of their clients. She said she had something to show me. This could be our chance—maybe our only one—to really get free. What do you say?"

"It would be risky in every way, for us especially. Their money and their business ... it's been a big factor in your life, and in our lives. Even assuming I could get a clear idea of it at a party, it will be dangerous."

"This has been eating away at me, one way or another, for a long time. Even if I can sell the company ... it'll never feel right. Never mind who I want to be—I can't stand being this thing, this patsy CEO anymore. Maybe it will all be fine, but I can't stand the thought of that guy being Edouard's father anymore. You were right about that."

Farya nodded. They looked at each other, waiting for someone to blink, to laugh, to shrug and call it off in the name of safety or sanity or just a nice lunch. Everyone thinks that cosmology is someone else's job, but the two of them decided otherwise that afternoon.

"I could do it, I think," Farya said, to herself as much as to Bryan. "But this is so big and strange and complicated. I'd need to have it right in front of me."

"Okay. It should all be right there."

"But will it? For me, I mean. You're invited, but I know these people; they're careful. How would I get close enough? It's not like I usually come to these things. And if they can do what they say, who's to say they won't see me coming? After all, Lourdes did. How do you know they'll even let me go with you?"

Bryan looked over Farya's shoulder and thought. A smile cracked across his Irish features, which he tried to stifle, biting both lips in a look of boyish mischief.

"You may be right. But I think I have a way for you to be right there," Bryan said, nodding to himself.

"In person? How?"

"I don't think you'll like it. But there's a way."

An hour later, Farya called her mother and Marista in Camden, using the townhouse's scrambled landline. Bryan used the satellite phone to ask Ritchie's son to ask about a fake ID that would pass muster at an airport, followed by a call to his lawyer to finalize his estate.

✝

While it was still possible to call it all off, Farya did her exercises. These exercises were different, though—a private final exam. In the sunny front room, she stood straight, with her shoulders back, perfectly still, as she would have to be at the party. Ignoring the fatigue, she tried to manage her destructive boredom and restorative remorse to alter the world around her in the smallest, most specific ways possible. By a window overlooking the street, she dimmed her gaze and altered the patterns and initials inscribed on the manhole covers in the street, and beyond.

Parallel lines, crosshatch, grids, chains of diamond-rectangles, interlocking hexagons, radiating hexagons, radiating circles, interlocking circles, running bond, woven stripes, logos smoothed to an illegible, official status conferred by a million blind feet and a million blind wheels.

To change just the pattern on one manhole cover was delicate work. Farya was a forest fire, an earthquake, and this required a fine touch. It was harder than altering an aspect of human nature or rewriting the entire history of a major metropolis. At her first job in marketing, she'd heard a senior designer once say: *It is impossible to change just* one *thing*. That was true with the manhole covers—each change to the pattern demanded consequences, new names and acronyms of present and defunct utility companies and municipal agencies, rippling insidiously into the names for bands, restaurants, and street gangs, into the structures through which the ambitious had climbed or failed to climb, the start and end dates of wars, the people not born and the ones born in their place.

It was hard, but not hopeless. The difficulty of controlling each small detail—a zigzag replaced by a Greek key, a bull's-eye replaced by interlocking arcs—made Farya less afraid of what she might do next.

It was settled—they would go forward with their plan. Farya checked her watch and changed out of the ultra-high heels she was wearing. She had a full day ahead, at the bank and the tailor.

✛

July in Houston wasn't a destination of choice for the business traveler or vacationer. In the gloaming on the runway of the Post Oak Airport, it was 97 degrees, and the air seemed thick enough to hold a flipped coin midair. To Bryan, on the short walk from the private jet to the waiting sedan, it felt like the weather of prehistory. He'd come alone with one small bag. At the hotel, he showered and changed. He turned on the TV, turned it off, and on again, but low. With so much on the line and so little of it under his control, waiting was the worst thing.

The trip to Houston was harder for Farya, starting with a long drive upstate. One of the security men drove. And as they left New York City, Edouard fell asleep. Being so near to such peril, she felt permission to remember her father, her childhood as a daughter of one of the shining lights of The Greater Anointed Imperial Ohioan Commonwealth. She remembered him visiting the New York Straits as a diplomat when she was a girl. He told her about their family's history in that exotic land—fleeing through it more than 1,800 years before. That was the story told by relatives at holidays when Farya was young, and people still remembered such things. Her ancestors had been on the losing side of a religious war on the continent of Nantucket. To escape, they took the perilous sea-voyage along the edge of a horizon-spanning, telepathic beast whose blue-and-white-striped torso rose and fell with its breath, creating tides as it dreamed its dreams into passersby. After the Iroquois Catholics pursued them through the Paterson Archipelago and the Monongahela Gap, they crossed to the Lesser Cincinattan Sea to their new home, in Columbus.

Farya thought of the risk. So many memories would be gone from the world forever if she didn't return—memories now secret, memories she could still tell her three-year-old son as fairy tales.

Her fear and agony peaked the next morning when she left Edouard with her mother in Camden. Her little boy was mercifully oblivious, and Farya did her best to keep him that way as she said goodbye. He took her parting wishes as an interruption to the toys he wanted to play with. Her hug made him squirm. The thought of leaving and of the risk ahead made Farya weak, made her legs not want to walk out the door of her mother's house.

From there, Farya got a ride from an old, not-so-good high-school friend to a shopping center in Rome, New York, where she dyed her hair bright blonde, and who drove her to Griffiss International Airport, where she flew under a false name, with an ID she feared would smudge in her sweaty hand, to LaGuardia and on to Houston, Texas, where she skipped out on a connecting flight to Burbank. After the goodbye to Edouard, though, that was the easy part.

She saw Bryan in the hotel lobby and, without a word, followed him up in the elevator. The lobby, the elevator, and the hallway, would be the only times they might be seen together.

Putting on her latex dress was a minor ordeal. Farya's body had changed since her twenties, changed since the baby, and changed again with her trainer, a woman powerlifter who was into Tennyson and free weights. A fellow wealthy wife had introduced them. And after eighteen months, she had made Farya into a lean, efficient vision of womanhood, the lushness of her hips weaponized and sharpened, her breasts full yet tangent to the muscle underneath. Farya was beautiful, but not in the innocent way she had been. She knew as much.

That confidence was put to the test by the thin but opaque white latex dress, which would seem surgical, if not for its high gloss. After she bought it in New York, she'd practiced getting into it. It was only the astronomical stakes of the evening that allowed her to put it on and leave the room in under an hour.

The town car picked Bryan up, circled the block, and returned to pick up Farya, whose plain black raincoat concealed the skin-tight dress. Nonetheless, people in the lobby did notice her heels—the kind that take a childhood in ballet class to learn how to walk in. Together, they cruised along the tangled highways and low bridges of the city's flat sprawl. As the massive darkened stadium complex came into view, Farya pulled on the mask. It was the same material as the dress, with holes for her eyes and mouth, along with smaller openings for each nostril. She was careful, as she'd learned to be, to pull her ponytail out the top of it, and to be mindful of her heavy eye makeup as she pulled it on.

He started to make small talk. But she stopped him.

"Act like you're going to act when we're there. We have a plan. And we know the plan. I need to focus," Farya said, her face just latex, bright red lips, nose holes, mascara-ringed eyes, and a ponytail now.

The sedan stopped at an impromptu checkpoint on the service road leading to the stadium, where an old man asked if they were lost. No, Bryan said, we are *quite found*—the password Petra had given him. The old man nodded and waved to the others to clear the SUVs from the road. As the old man turned to wish them a good evening, Bryan saw a pistol under his reflective vest. They drove through a prairie of parking lot, to the main entrance of the gargantuan barn that was NRG Stadium. Farya finished applying her lipstick, slipping it into the pocket of her coat, which she left in the leg well of the town car.

Opening the car door, the nighttime air was a little cooler, but still thick.

"Hey," Farya said.

Bryan looked at his wife, half-hoping she'd call this off. But instead, she pressed the white rubber leash into his palm. Once he was out of the sedan, she hesitated, and wouldn't budge until he pulled her, firmly, out of the car.

+

The parking lot and the entire stadium complex was dark. Even the streetlights along the service roads had been turned off. And in that gloom, a low line of yellow lights led from the black-jacketed valet to the darker mass of the stadium. A small white man with expensive glasses greeted them, the larger bodies of yet more security in the shadows behind him. He asked Bryan's name and flicked at his tablet until he found it, sniffed about there not being any note of a plus one.

"What about pets?" Bryan asked, smiling.

His sophistication challenged, the small man nodded Bryan and Farya into a maze of vanishingly tall, thick velvet curtains, like the ones from the big movie theaters and concert halls of Bryan's youth. Then after a few bends, the sounds and sights of the party opened to them—a jazz orchestra playing swing along with a low rumble-and-cackle of conversation. The sight of it beyond the last bend of velvet was beyond what either of them—Bryan, the lifetime party guest and Farya, the planner of galas—had ever seen before.

The planners of this party had turned the football field and the first-level seating area of the seventy-two-seat venue into a full-sized phosphorescent forest. Some of the larger trees seemed to reach the two-hundred-foot ceiling. The branches and the vines along their trunks gave off a gentle, undulating light. Hedges and low artificial hills concealed bars and small buffets, along with little alcoves for conversation. Farya stopped in her tracks at the sight of how the barnlike space had been made gorgeous.

Bryan tugged at the leash and climbed a small hill to better see the band and the dance floor at what would have been the fifty-yard line. An air-conditioned breeze washed over them. The chill made Farya's shoes bite harder into her feet, made the edges of the rubber dress chafe her upper thighs and around her cleavage. Still, anxious perspiration gathered on Bryan's face. From the low hill, Farya and Bryan watched the dance floor, where married couples shared the floor with formal and informal courtesans, who stood out by being gorgeous, scantily clad, mildly famous, and in a few instances, all three. In her rubber dress, mask and leash, Farya helped Bryan blend in.

Bryan was tempted to nod some kind of acknowledgment to Farya when someone tapped him on his shoulder—Petra, in a short, bright red flapper dress with beaded fringes—her idea of fun and frivolous. His stomach plunged, but he forced a small, impatient smile. With Petra was a too-handsome, clean-shaven young man in a precise blue suit who was watching Bryan, waiting to pounce.

"I'm glad you could make it," Petra said and nodded at Bryan's rubber-wrapped guest. "And I see that I wasn't too far off about your tastes after all."

"Quite a get-together here."

"It's a send-off for a client, a big one, as you might imagine—I thought you'd appreciate it. Bryan, I want to introduce you to someone. This is Troy."

The handsome young man pounced, offering a practiced handshake and a smile as precise as his dark blue suit. "The *pleasure* is all mine, Mr. Lomoigne. I've heard a lot about you."

"Have you?"

"I work closely with Sevritas. And I'm proud to say that it's one of my clients whom we're celebrating tonight. Let's sit down and have a drink somewhere quiet."

They found a small bar in a secluded glade beside a hedge row and sat at its lone table. A winding branch from a nearby mock-elm enclosed and illuminated the cozy space where the two men and Petra sat. Farya remained standing, but she could hear everything. People walked past the small pocket but didn't stop. Farya recognized a few from television and a few from the charity circuit—men and women who'd achieved a meaningful and rare symbiosis with one major global corporation or another. They were tipsy from cocktails, and a little giddy with the scene.

"There are twenty two hundred ten publicly recognized billionaires in the world," Troy began, with unremitting eye contact and a smile that provoked and reassured in equal measure, "along with another six hundred or so that like their privacy. And, from what I hear, you're part of the reason that so many people would want that much money."

"That's right. You and Petra use the souls that I sell you to make a few of those billionaires believe they can be gods," Bryan said.

"That's a simplification, not the words I would use. But okay—broad strokes—it's a fair enough place to start."

"That's the thing," Bryan said. "I think it's the end. I don't want to be a part of it anymore."

"I can understand that. But is that true? Do you not want to be a part of it—or do you simply want to be a *different* part of it?"

"What do you mean?" Bryan asked and felt a shiver at how Troy smiled before he began to speak.

"I know successful men. My father was one. If I told you his name, you'd recognize it. I'm one too. You and I actually have a lot in common. And I know that in order to do what you do, to get up every morning and take on the next guy, to outbid, outplan, outwork him, you need a tight, consistent focus. You have to ignore the pull of a million emotions, opinions, well-reasoned arguments, deeply convincing persuasions, and so on. But at the same time, in order to do what you do well, you have to be aware of, and even sympathetic with, almost all of those enticements. I understand that. And I understand how it can make every successful man a kind of schizophrenic—like you're a collection of fractured pieces that can't be allowed to heal."

Bryan saw why Petra brought him.

"After reaching the top," Troy continued, "there may be another higher top, maybe one after that. But for men like us, there's no real end-goal, just a suicide-net of sensuous, never-completely adequate consolations."

Troy gave a knowing look up to Farya, docile and blank, but listening, watching the crowd, comprehending a little more with each passing second. Troy downed his drink, the diamonds in his cufflinks flashing in the low light.

"So," the salesman continued, "I can see where you might have started to get a little depressed. It's pretty much inevitable. But it's when you're depressed that some of those far-flung sympathies that have made you so effective and insightful can start to speak out of turn. That's why Petra asked me here. I can tell you with 100 percent honesty that it doesn't have to be that way. She asked me here to show you that you're wrong."

"Okay, I'll bite: Tell me what I'm wrong about—exactly," Bryan said, taking a drink and acting as though the salesman's opening salvo hadn't hit home.

"You're wrong to be depressed. You're wrong not to want more. I'm here to show you what I mean by *more*. We're going where no one else at this party—except the guest of honor—gets to go. We're going next door. But first, can you listen to what Petra has to say?"

Bryan nodded.

"Great," Troy said, his smile almost as bright as his cufflinks. "I'll get us another round. Does she drink?"

"No, it doesn't drink socially."

"I like your style," Troy said, laughing and gripping Bryan's shoulder, "I'll be right back."

Petra smiled, not warm, but less forced than in the locker room.

"I'm glad you made it," she said, a little coy. "I wasn't sure you'd come."

"You said that you could help move things forward. You said you had an offer for me."

"Brass tacks, huh. I always thought we might be friends," Petra said.

"You play too rough for me, Petra. I'm a businessman. If you have business, let's hear it."

"Well, as a *businessman*, you couldn't quite get a deal done, is what I heard. The FCC stopped the clock, and even Bill Van Harappan couldn't get it started again. But we can do things with the FCC that Bill can't, and we can get you a better price, a better buyer, and we can get it done in the next ninety days," Petra said.

"Okay. But you could have done that before and saved us both a lot of trouble."

"You didn't come to us. That's the thing. If you want cash, we can get you a buyer. But you have to stay on."

"So, why would I sell at all?"

"You get your name off the charter, a pile of cash, and a gigantic chunk of equity in a bigger outfit. You stay on for five-seven-eight more years and focus on growing the Non-Mortal-Element-contract business at the acquiring company. We can see to it that you'd build the team with your own people, help you ease the practice into the broader corporate culture, and make everyone rich."

"I see."

"No, you don't—not yet, anyway. You think it's just about money. And it's not. If you'll agree, now, at least in principle, then I have permission to show you this. And once you see it, I think you'll want to stay on board."

Troy returned to the table with cocktails as Bryan shrugged and offered a small *what-the hell* smile. Petra reached her veiny arm across the small table. He shook her hand.

"Is that the good news I think it is?" Troy asked. Petra nodded. Troy nodded, the rhythm infecting his speech. "That is *great*. Let's move on to the next part of our evening. This part—and Petra will tell you that I'm not exaggerating—is why I love my job."

"Where are we going?" Bryan asked.

"Just next door, to the Astrodome," Petra said, grabbing her shimmering red purse.

+

The Astrodome surprised Bryan. He thought it was far away or demolished long ago, like the shopping malls of his youth. It had been a kind of talisman of his youth—Neil Young on the living-room hi-fi singing *Maybe Marlon Brando would sit down by the fire, tell us all about Hollywood, and the good things there for hire, like the Astrodome and the first TV* ... His was never a sports household.

But there it stood, a giant dark blister against the sky as soon as they left the stadium through an unadorned service exit. It had a kind of geometric beauty that the formless complex behind them had been born never knowing. Flanked by Troy and Petra, with Farya trailing on her white rubber leash, they walked through the sticky night across the short distance between the buildings and continued inside. A strip of red carpet lent a fugitive charm to the derelict stadium, which was otherwise a mess of construction light fixtures, black tape, sprays and smears of dirt, and the outlines of hastily removed team logos on the gloss-painted walls.

After a series of narrow, low, and dirty concourses, the four of them emerged just above where the lower tier of seats would have been. The vast open space had been adorned like a cross between a factory and a mardi gras parade. At the center of the field, hung from the near center of the ceiling, was a mobile where different objects and images drifted—martini glasses, puffy pink nipples, blown-up photographs from distant Christmases, hamburgers and hot dogs, World War Two fighter planes, old muscle cars and animals, so many animals—cows, bulls, horses, sheep, pigs, chickens, turkeys, fish—helmets for football and baseball. It looked, more than anything, like the accumulated tchotchkes of a family-friendly bar and grill in suburban Illinois, or the junk cleared out from a teenage boy's bedroom, writ huge and strung up high.

The images were hung over a narrow hospital bed.

Bryan looked around. All over the stadium, men were checking, testing. There were hundreds of rails that went around the dome, across the seats, at all levels. On each rail, small boxes in long trains ran for a minute, then stopped. Bryan tried to estimate the circumference of the upper deck of the Astrodome and to count the rows down to the lowest rail, just above ground level. There had to be hundreds of thousands.

Petra and Troy let him look for a while.

"You want to guess?" Troy asked.

"Whew, better if you explain it to me," Bryan said, tugging on Farya's leash to remind himself why he had come to this place.

"One thing they said to me when I started is that *comprehension is a sucker's game*. But I'll try.

"In each box is the Non-Mortal-Element of one of your former customers."

"And how do they make it work?" Bryan asked.

"A lot of questions," Petra said.

"No, questions are a good thing," Troy picked up. "We like an inquisitive client. If you don't want to be agnostic, then at least you shouldn't be laboring under some medieval illusion of what we do. You're a smart guy, so I'll do my best. Do you have a science background?'

"AP in high school, and the *Physics for Business Majors* college classes to meet the requirements."

"Great. One uneasy fact of quantum physics, you may remember, is that the observer affects what they see. For the purposes of the machine, each box, essentially, contains an observer, who has been treated or refocused. The observers, yoked together into the client's single vision, make up a kind of reality engine, if you will. Together, they help set the dimensions of another reality, and keep its rules and regulations consistent, through a self-renewing mechanism of enforced attention."

"This enforced attention—just how is it enforced?" Bryan asked, looking around the vast space at the rows upon rows of boxes. As a single machine, it was huge.

"That's proprietary. And even if it wasn't, I'd hardly be the one to explain it. But among your former phone customers, I'm assured that no one is doing anything that they haven't, in some way, agreed to," Troy said, sounding a little disappointed in Bryan for his squeamishness.

"So, they agree to this?"

"Of course—they agree to it when they sign your terms of service. This is just one more element of that agreement. Just think of it like you think of their data. It's one more asset they exchange for your services."

Bryan wasn't supposed to be seeing this. Just in being there and asking so many questions, he was backing all of them into a corner where he would have to agree to their terms, or else they would have to do something still more drastic. So, he kept asking questions and prayed that Farya was getting what she needed.

"Okay," Bryan said. "So how does that asset come into play here?"

"Together, those Non-Mortal-Element *assets* help the client see a new world into being. And they help stabilize that fantasy into a concrete, lasting reality. The more of them we use, the more comprehensive, immersive, sizable, and lasting a reality they can build," Troy said. Farya could feel the sheer effort behind his pitch as he continued. "It's ingenious—their collective attention is aimed at a single tiny spot of darkness on the ceiling here. The machine spins them around the client. And when the boxes open, the force of that observation creates a new world, with the client in the driver's seat. That's why the pictures and knickknacks—it's to remind them of the kind of universe they want."

"So, this guy wants a fast-casual restaurant chain for a universe?"

"Good one. Petra said you were funny. It's not one-for-one like that. Anyway, tonight's lucky client made his fortune in livestock. That's why so many animals in this one. He'll be at the dinner tonight. I'll introduce you, and he can tell you what the experience is like for our clients."

"So, this thing you're selling—it's like an afterlife?" Bryan asked.

"Is it a loophole in mortality? Yes. But it's better, and more than that. Our clients literally become the creator and all-powerful master of an entire—an entirely real—universe. When the switch is flipped on this machine, the consciousness of these 144,000 souls will project a combined reality into the void. It's like a chain reaction. Reality will expand and refract almost infinitely. To get back for a second, to *Physics for Business Students*, it's like the 'white hole' on the other end of a black hole."

"And what happens to all of this when that happens?" Bryan asked.

"There's a couple fewer souls on a crowded planet. As for the place we're standing, any changes are subtle. Maybe people don't want to come to this part of town as much. Maybe they choose to drive home the long way, and not look at the building. Maybe politicians look for reasons to tear it down. But there's no radiation or anything."

"And what about the people in the boxes, the souls?"

"I think we should get to dinner soon," Petra said. But Troy just looked her off—she was clearly on his turf now.

"I understand what you're saying, and why you might be concerned," Troy said, going sincere before sneaking a smirk. "But are you? What about the caterers next door, or the welders and roustabouts working on the site here? What about the assets in your portfolio? How concerned are you about those assets, as long as they do what you want them to? No one knows how all this ends up."

"So, you don't know, or you won't say what happens to them?" Bryan said.

"I have some idea. But I can't honestly say if it's better or worse than what would have happened to them otherwise. I mean, here we are. And depending on who you ask, it's somewhere between eight thousand and fifteen billion years since the start of time—whatever that is. But what if you could be there at the beginning? Maybe you wouldn't be in charge. Maybe you wouldn't even be a person. Maybe you'd be the second law of thermodynamics, or the tendency of granite to melt at a certain temperature or the father of all squirrels. But you'd be embedded in that new reality from the start. And what if you *could* be one of those 144,000 souls at the beginning of creation? Doesn't that sound like an adventure?" Troy said, nearing the peak of his pitch.

Farya swayed in her heels, which had found a way to accentuate all the smoothed-down cruelty of Troy's words. Bryan pulled the leash taut to remind her that he was with her. She watched Troy, and Petra's studious quiet while he spoke. Farya could infer the immense misery in the boxes all around them—like eyes that could not blink or look away.

Bryan said nothing. He was giving Troy room to run, and Farya time to take it all in.

"I get it," Troy interjected. "Everybody wants to be a vegetarian, but everyone orders the steak. This is an old world, and every day it gets smaller. Make a billion dollars, and who are you? You're an old fool fawned over by liars and prey to anyone you might rely on. It's not getting any better. And why would you trust me?"

"That's a fine question, Troy," Bryan said.

"That's why our business isn't based on just me talking. You need to see the reality behind our technology to make the kind of commitment we're asking. That's why we brought along our managing director of presentation and fulfillment, Arnold."

+

Arnold appeared out of nowhere as soon as Troy had said his name. Arnold looked to be in his fifties, but like he'd been in his fifties for a long time. To Bryan, he seemed a creature of the office of another century—file cabinets, Rolodexes, and desktop ashtrays.

Arnold was very tall, but crooked like he had a spinal problem. His skin was yellowish, and his face had a canine aspect dignified by his age. The more Farya looked at the tall, older man, the stranger his posture appeared, as though his suit was full of buckets of different sizes. The man was wrong in too many subtle ways. The mix of emergency lights and work lights situated around them struck his oversized square spectacles, reflecting right at Bryan with an unnatural yellow harshness. It made Bryan think of being caught alone in the locker room that night, and his slow-motion dash toward the janitor. He shivered.

"Have we met before?" Bryan asked.

"No. We have not," Arnold responded with a stilted British accent.

With a startling quickness for a man otherwise half-combobulated, Arnold's snout-like face whipped around toward Farya. The corner of his upper lip jumped in a quick snarl, and he walked around Bryan to her, where she wavered on her heels. She recognized that he was someone, like Lourdes, who saw her for what she was, and who knew exactly what she had done.

"You don't need to meet *her*, Arnold," said Troy, an irritation in his voice. "My apologies. Arnold has certain gifts, but I wouldn't list social graces among them."

But Arnold drew still closer to Farya, his movements loose and coordinated like an animal.

"No. This woman. She shouldn't be here. She …"

"Can you please get *your managing director* off of my pet?" Bryan said to Troy, doubling up the white latex leash over his wrist and pulling her close.

"I apologize. Arnold—that's enough."

"No. This one—she …"

"Arnold, you can be *replaced*," Troy hissed. That last word was like someone threw acid on the strange man. He froze for a moment and stepped behind Petra.

"This is ridiculous," Bryan said. "Good luck with your train set, Petra. Please, don't call me."

"Please, accept my apology," Troy said. "Please. Trust me, Arnold has his talents, or else we wouldn't have him here. Just give me a few more minutes. Arnold, can you please show Mr. Lomoigne what he needs to see?"

"But he's not alone. You need to know that she …"

"Arnold!" Troy hiss-yelled.

Cowed, Arnold walked between Petra and Troy, and asked Bryan, "May I show you something?"

Bryan nodded impatiently, and Arnold walked a few steps past him. When Bryan turned to follow, Arnold gestured to the stadium, where a moment before, hundreds of tracks had been laid across the seats and the concrete tiers. But that was all gone now. He and Arnold were situated on a small island within circling rivers a dozen stories high, all the water roiling and volatile, yet contained within their banks. The workers who'd been tinkering across the stripped concrete field were themselves small fountains slopping bright water onto themselves.

"What is this?" Bryan asked.

"This is the world the living can't see. And these rivers, around us, are like an ocean waiting to be born. You've heard how someone like Troy says this works. Let me show you."

Around them, the rivers accelerated, as though a sluice had been opened, the water flowed fast and smooth, bubbling with what Bryan could tell were thousands of eyes. The water accelerated, boiled with a heat made of sight—hot enough to boil space itself. This was the opening of worlds into a patch of common darkness.

The force of the eyes within the wheels—seeing or mis-seeing that darkness—opened the darkness. Into it, teeming masses of common conceptions and unconscious suspicions, strange forms of familiar shores gathered together, compressed, conjoined under fatal pressure into emblems made of caricatures, of badges, and the winks of curbstones. And the emblems pressed against each other to create new, fatally familiar forms, molecules and continents, and snatches of nursery rhyme, then overlapped and piled to create another common, inadequate bandage on the unimaginable wound that the darkness had become.

Arnold showed him, within that darkness, the new world taking root, developing, articulate and mysterious, in a flash. But this universe, however vast, however eternal, would be at its core, a copy of a copy. And for the client who became its all-powerful God, this would be a comfort and an eternal frustration. Looking away from the cosmic scene to his companions, Troy was a fountain, as was Petra, each slopping a dim orange-brown light over themselves. Only Farya was solid, glowing tan through her white fetish dress. Above her head spun a halo or a bright tornado, wobbling. Bryan could tell that whatever it was above her head, it was deadly and barely controlled.

As Arnold turned away, Bryan had returned, or been returned, to the derelict stadium. The workmen were picking up their things and departing.

Farya didn't see the demonstration. She saw the tall, strange man turn away from them with Bryan and whisper a few words into his ear. Bryan froze for a moment before startling to attention, flush and agitated, his pupils wide and his breath uneven. Farya could feel the trick that Arnold had pulled: time within time, minutes bubbling from between seconds, centuries spent and collapsed into neverhood, evading suspicion in the space of a minute. Farya comprehended how someone might have abducted Bryan against his will, and contrary to the opinion of the larger world.

From Bryan's face, Farya could see that the important point had been made: this was no scam and no hallucination. Keeping her face impassive beneath the mask of heavy makeup and rubber was a struggle as Farya recognized in Arnold one of the corrupt guides of the dead that Lourdes had warned about.

The recognition was mutual. Arnold turned to Farya and started to whisper in her ear *can I show ...* But Bryan pulled her leash defensively, and Troy, now-red-faced with rage, demanded that Arnold leave or be escorted out. Arnold complied, mumbling in a language Farya couldn't place. Farya watched Petra, who was uncomfortable at having shown Bryan that much, and impatient with the whole demonstration.

"So, now that you've had the grand tour," Troy said, "how about if we go back to the party and talk particulars?"

Bryan nodded twice, three times, before retrieving the word *yes*—stunned like an agnostic summoned by what he did not want to know about. He fought the urge to look at Farya and tugged on her leash.

"Great," Petra said. "They should be serving dinner."

✢

They followed the winding red carpet out of the Astrodome and into NRG Stadium. The forest inside was brighter now, so the army of uniformed waiters and waitresses could bring plates to the dining valley that had been opened up off the end of the dance floor. Petra showed them to their table, which they shared with two old men whose tuxedos were festooned with unrecognizable medals, and the young Asian women with implausible figures who accompanied them. The men nodded, and the women tipped champagne flutes to their table mates.

"Is Arnold joining us?" Bryan asked.

"No," Petra said, "he still has work to do. And he's not, by and large, client-facing."

"I'm sure that's not a complete surprise. Anyway, he doesn't eat," Troy said, "just kidding."

Farya watched as Petra shot Troy a look of exasperation.

"Really, just kidding. So, I know you have your reservations, Bryan. And I can only answer so much. But now that you've seen it, what do you think, Bryan?"

"It's really something. It's a real, uh, machine, a real process you have here."

"That's the word I like to use—it's *real*. I talk to people who want to leave their fortunes to the arts—painting, architecture, music. They want to fund symphonies or keep a cathedral standing for another hundred years. They say they want to support *real* art. But I say that if you want to talk about scams, the first place to look is the Parthenon, or Mozart, or the Sistine Chapel. All of them were just fantastic advertorials commissioned by brutal, savvy aristocrats and church officials to dress up *their* rules and regulations as gorgeous angels and sympathetic devils," Troy said as a handsome uniformed woman set a charred rib eye before him.

"Maybe that's why people paid for the paintings and the symphonies. But they didn't own them completely. They can't control the feelings that they evoked," Bryan said, just to slow the young man down.

"That's my point; they *evoked*. And evoked isn't the same as delivering."

"Delivering?"

"Delivering reality. It's the same with history—I mean, you put up a war memorial to sell the *next* war. Name the college after a tycoon to trick the next stupid genius into being a tycoon. That's the scam—trading people's lives and their real power for a nice story. But until now, no one had been able to deliver on that last exchange."

"Deliver what, exactly?"

"Deliver a real payoff for the whole pyramid of human society. Maybe back in the day they had beauty, endless catechisms, and baffling prose to seal off the ceiling. But we have *that*," Troy said, gesturing across the football field of diners and servers toward the Astrodome. "And *that* proves all of this— this world—isn't just a scam that lost its bearings. At least it's proof to us precious few," Troy said.

"I couldn't put it better myself," said Petra, raising her glass, flush, inspired. Troy turned his attention to the table.

"Is that okay? I had you down for a steak. But there's also lobster and crab."

"No. This is fine," Bryan said.

"Great. Oh, hey," Troy said. "Bryan, you need to meet Graham. Tonight is Graham's big night. In a few hours, he'll be making the trip next door."

Graham was a suntanned older gentleman with deep dimples and a military-straight posture. He wore a blue blazer with gold buttons and a white shirt open at the collar. He smiled as he shook Bryan's hand.

"Graham, this is Bryan. He's in telecom, and he's looking forward to a send-off like this one day himself."

"Well, I'm here as proof that it can be done. Work hard, be smart, and who knows?"

"Congratulations," Bryan said. "If I may ask, how did you get here?"

"Graham practically invented the veterinary vaccine market," Petra said, offering her hand, which the gentleman bent to kiss.

"I had no idea," Bryan said.

"Believe it. How do you think our food can live cheek to jowl like they do? It was the fish, though, that made me. You probably never asked how we can raise so much Tilapia in stagnant pools of their own waste. But it's the way we do it with our customers—vaccines," he said to the group, winked, and was off to other, more important tables.

"In just a few hours, that man will be the single all-powerful god of a universe as massive and varied as our own," Troy said once he was out of earshot. "Think about that."

"In five or so years, you could have a similar outcome—be a similar, *singular* success," Petra said to Bryan, smiling. "Maybe not on Graham's scale—but imagine your own midsized spiral galaxy for maybe ten billion years."

"What about my family?"

"They'll be fine. Our business is growing. If my projections about the opportunity to scale up your Non-Mortal-Element business line is correct, you can have that galaxy, and plenty to leave them. Imagine being the father of a new family, a family of billions," Petra said.

"I mean, Bryan, you have to see it," Troy jumped in, "there are no other universes to explore here—not with liquid-fuel rockets and vacuum-suited company men waking in ten centuries to plant the flag of a then-forgotten nation on some half-hospitable rock. That's just so *not it*. But to create, well, that's the thing. Am I right?"

Bryan wanted to say *no*, just to slow the young man down and buy Farya more time. The night felt like it was getting away from them. But when he thought about those early years building Metacom, storefront by storefront and region by region, he caught himself nodding—it *was* about creating. In his reverie, he saw Troy nodding in time, smiling between bloody bites.

"So, brass-tacks time. Do you agree that what we're offering is real?" Troy asked.

"I do."

"And is this idea of selling your company going anywhere?"

"It's not."

"And do you believe what Petra said about her team at Sevritas putting you in a position to do very, very well?"

"I do," Bryan said, feeling the pull as if a leash was on his own neck. It was the old *if-then* magic spell that could make a subject into an object, and a living person—silently and faultlessly—into an asset.

"And have we proven that enough wealth can deliver immortality and the real fulfillment of your every desire?"

"Yes."

"So, do we have a deal?" said Petra. It was, after all, her deal to close.

+

Physical agony vied with overpowering anxiety. Farya's shoes were impossible, and the conversations long. She forced herself to listen as Troy and Petra began to close the deal with her husband. Toe by toe, Farya lost sensation in her feet until it was like standing on burning pegs. Sweat filled the spaces inside of her rubber mask and dress and made a paste of the makeup underneath. She could taste the stray drips of sweat that found their way down her philtrum and over her heavy red lipstick.

But Farya knew more. She knew no one had accounted for her. Even Arnold had been surprised and dumbfounded. She spotted his face on the edge of the woods just outside the dining area, obscured by table-hopping guests and racing waiters, watching her.

She could smell her own pungent mix of sweat, fear, and rubber. Her ears chafed against the zippered openings in the tight rubber hood like little clam shells. The stink and the pain pushed her to where listening and seeing were her only escape. She heard the words and knew the faces, the smiling eagerness, the telegraphed reasonableness, Troy's pushing and anticipation, Petra's thinly veiled disdain. And she recognized, from behind, an affable fear and assent on her husband's face. His forehead high, his ears back, smiling too much, tiny ripples in the patch of scalp where he was balding. She leaned out a little to pull the leash taut and remind him she was there.

Her eyes disguised in thick waterproof mascara, within a mask like a mockery of a face, Farya saw that Troy and Petra were trying too hard. That was Farya's way in—after all, they'd kidnapped Bryan, distracted and intimidated him, spied on him, and blackmailed him. They'd threatened the people closest to him. That same pressure showed in the cadence of the clenching and unclenching of their features, even as they ostensibly won Bryan over. Tonight, she could see, was their last resort. They didn't want him to see the machine because it was very wrong, and they knew it.

Farya could see just how it was wrong. She could see the billion-dollar scheme aimed at the imperfect understanding that might exalt someone to such huge and peculiar success. They wouldn't see the cost at all—eternal isolation in an echo chamber operated by immortal slaves. And they wouldn't give a second thought to the cost to the world they departed. Petra and Arnold might call it a fire sale. But it was one that only worked if you kept the fire stoked. After so much cleverness on the part of the lawyers, salespeople, engineers, guiding spirits of the next life, and party planners, it was nothing more than a money-making scheme for another crude survival gambit.

Farya's sweat ran cold. The business, the fly-by-night machine next door, and the pure chicanery of it made her afraid and depressed. And there she found the weakness in the scheme. The weakness flashed like the creases in a plastic milk jug as you crush it for recycling—the whole business was an evasion, a cheap trick. She could see it stretch out into the future as one more perversity the next generation would take for granted, while the gloss on reality faded, the food no longer fed as it had, the water no longer quenched as it had, and friendship no longer comforted as it once did.

Looking past the table where Petra and Troy worked out a deal with her husband, past the two hundred or so diners in the staged fairyland of the stadium, Farya comprehended the vicious pressure on the guests—even in this moment of vicarious triumph among good food, wine, and conversation. The phosphorescent sylvan scene strung from the beams and constructed on the acres of sod they'd rolled in was there as a disguise over a desperation born of a terrible bareness. Farya comprehended a little more.

The pressure and the bareness pressed on the wealthy at the top of the known world; even Arnold must be under some kind of pressure, too. It was the pressure of a shrinking world.

The vista was unfolding faster now, like a chain reaction. Farya could feel, on the vibrating strings of an invisible guitar, just who Arnold was, what he did, and what he had access to. And it was no celestial hierarchy—the heavenly command lost track of their habits long ago. But that wasn't how Arnold had been betrayed. His gripe and the gripe of those like him was underemployment in a badly shrunken world. The scheme to build the machine next door was no tantrum or revenge. Arnold and his like had always been practical creatures, navigating the endlessly second-guessed and renovated mixed-metaphor kingdoms of the afterlife.

And being practical, Arnold and his colleagues located their loophole.

Their plan to yoke the ambitions of man was a stopgap, a ploy that had fallen from repute in the weary shadows of another age's abandoned urban plans. In the long term, on a large scale, the scheme that Arnold, Petra, Troy, and God-knows-who-else had cooked up wasn't good for anyone. But it gave them a purpose. It kept their jobs in place, even if it would eventually bankrupt their employers.

Farya could feel the seizure approaching. She could even see the exact loophole that Arnold had exploited, written in a language as legible as the side of a cliff. But she could feel it—an awkward knot where the dictate and design of reality couldn't entirely accommodate one another. It was a small gap in nature. And nature in its wisdom had been stupid enough to assume that no one wise enough to locate and understand the gap would ever be dumb enough to exploit it.

Feeling that gap, that loophole, and feeling who had felt it before, Farya could understand, and lidded her eyes. She couldn't close that gap, but she could manipulate it—make it into a costly opportunity, one that had always been and would always be too unprofitable to exploit. It was all in view—the fabric of reality, the gap, the crisis she'd begun as a little girl, the terms of service, the financing, the sales pitch, the clients, the machine, the sensation of a shrinking universe. Farya could think the thoughts and sympathize with the cabal of underemployed angels and greedy Ivy Leaguers who'd convened, assessed the redacting galaxy, and marshaled their considerable forces to make a grubby buck selling knock-off universes.

The entirety of it flashed at once, clear—no longer varnished over by a million foggy layers of sighs and shrugs—and Farya declared it boring, and a little sad.

What came next wasn't a seizure, though she wished it was. She'd won too much control and too much culpability.

+

And, so, it began. Farya elided the remunerative edge of the cosmic loophole and the cottage industry that had grown out of manipulating the world's spiritual infrastructure. It would seem subtle—the annihilation of careers, hopes, institutions, and pretensions—but its effect was profound in the stadium that night.

The result, despite the justice of it, despite the greater-goodness of it, was excruciating to Farya. No understanding comes without pity. And pity was the squeal of the cart that carried that whole party to the true oblivion of never having been. Farya couldn't see it through without pity.

Pity for Petra, the world-beating overachiever, working impossible hours and terrified that all her ambition and work had overmatched the prizes to be won.

Pity for Arnold, who was just trying to look out for his demoralized and half-mad angelic peers by punching their tickets to a tepid, but busy, exile.

Pity for Troy, the child salesman who never heard *no*, who was just looking for the biggest thing to sell.

Pity for even Graham the fish-vaccine mogul, who'd listened to the voice all successful men hear, that there is no limit to what he might do, and no real cost to doing it.

And lastly, pity for Bryan, the square son of a cool idol, the rich kid just trying to prove he belonged somewhere.

They, and more, all had to go, it seemed.

The world around Farya collapsed into one intolerable form after another and returned—violently, physically, painfully—again and again. Across the floor of the stadium, across the crunching and expanding flesh and architecture, the screams emerged and were swallowed up into small vortices of shadow. As Farya vacillated mid-seizure, trying to find a tolerable form for the world in which her husband might remain, one thing persisted.

It was Arnold. He was moving toward her.

But the stadium kept collapsing wrong, with the broader world becoming a place with no room for the warm core of happiness in her life. It began with her attraction to Bryan, the sustained pressure of it, the rapport, which came from a secret, living with it. Secrets had warped Farya and Bryan similarly so that their customary evasions were never betrayals, but an extension of the suspense. And that suspense held wonder.

Holding the scene in her mind as Arnold came closer, Farya located the only possible seam along which the world could be tolerably folded. It came to her like a lightning strike—she sensed it and did it so fast that she couldn't identify its beginning from end. But she knew it would keep her from the hundred worse outcomes she was close to committing. Arnold, Petra, and Troy folded into themselves, vanished into puckering specks of air. It stopped the leaks in the tired world. It saved most of what was left and even some of what wasn't supposed to be there.

Once begun, Farya's terrible dismissal had a force that she could not check. She redacted the world around Bryan, then Bryan, as well. The moan of pity ripped the roof off NRG stadium, as the man she'd loved vanished and took so much of her away with him. She'd feared this, maybe even there was no way to save reality without eliding Bryan as well. Saving her child was all she could have ever hoped for, perhaps. With the pieces in motion, it was no choice at all.

At the party, the faces of the guests folded over faces like plastic masks on a pharmacy rack. Diamond rings doubled, trebled onto other rings, watches onto watches, phones onto phones, sternums onto sternums, hips onto hips, all reducing and reducing, losing track of itself and vanishing to patterns on the bulging surface of an eroded hillside.

All the people, their fortunes, the décor, and the stadium itself folded in on that unseen crease. It was logical, symmetrical. There were no survivors. However distinguished those people and their accomplishments may have been, the waters of reality closed over them without a hiccup or ripple of memory.

At that moment, in elsewheres beyond elsewheres, a couple hundred secondhand universes drifted. And the memories of the nouveau divine and their slaves ceased to drain the world of its somethingness. Though gods, the former clients of Arnold and Troy would never thereafter recall who they'd been before. As of that moment, they had sprung from nowhere, fully formed as themselves. And though they'd create pine trees and pimply teenagers and New York cities, they wouldn't quite know why and would attribute it to their own unique and mysterious prodigiousness.

They were gods, after all, and who would dare imagine otherwise?

As everyone inside and around the Astrodome and NRG Stadium vanished, millions of souls, living and dead, were freed from their contractual obligations. And the world became a little less depressed, a little larger.

✢

When it was built in the 1960s, the Astrodrome was supposed to look like a hill, at least from behind—with bright green grass atop a clean landfill on a steel-and-concrete hill-shaped frame. But long ago, the fill had shifted, and the sod died or slipped away to reveal the lattice of rebar and broken sprinkler pipes underneath.

Wild-eyed radio raconteur and real estate magnate Ray Halfheinz had designed and built the Astrodrome. He loved ancient Greece and wanted Houston to be home to the biggest Orpheon in the world. So, he built the open-air theater with a massive proscenium and forty-thousand seats carved into the side of the artificial hill. Critics argued whether Halfheinz was in love with the past or simply feared the future. At the ribbon-cutting, Halfheinz said mankind was the story of missed opportunities, and that the Astrodrome was a chance to have another crack at one of the biggest of them. The powers that be in Harris County weren't about to tell a man what he could do with his own land. And it was a lot of land. Halfheinz placed the Astrodrome at its center, imagining a new Athens would grow around it. The theater opened with Euripides' *Madness of Hercules*, which shocked the thousands who came that afternoon, many with their children, to see the grand new stage. Worse than scandal, though, was low attendance.

Houston was too hot for outdoor shows most of the year, and the Greek drama Halfheinz insisted on was too boring or too upsetting, and often both. The artificial hill leaked and slumped. The new Athens never materialized. The Astrodrome became a cruising ground, a shadowy free-fire zone for prostitutes, drugs, drag racers, and the abandonment of whatever needed abandoning.

The city fenced it off. The balding concrete supports of the slump-shouldered Astrodrome are still visible behind cyclone fencing.

Farya held onto the fence with her painted fingers, bent and vomited the bile and remnants of the airport food she had in her stomach. The rubber hood, with its ponytail-hole at the top, held her hair clear of her face as she retched.

She was all alone in the hot night.

✛

The dark hump of the fenced-in Astrodrome was ringed with the aura of the city beyond it. At least Farya hoped the city was still there.

She looked up at the sky. Stars twinkled. Where she was and how she got there would come to her—it always did. Reality, however raw and new, had its way of becoming plausible sooner or later. As it did, she looked around at the empty, dark landscape—the construction site of someplace more than a year from being built. There was heavy equipment and foundations sunk. In the distance, she could see low houses and streetlights.

The questions she had were immense and of dire importance. But before anything, she had to take those damn shoes off. She sat down on a cracked sidewalk between a freshly paved service road and the cyclone fence and undid the buckles with trembling fingers. The relief of taking off those shoes was a pleasure that would shame any decent person. In the afterglow, Farya wrestled the white latex mask off her face and over her bright blonde ponytail. She wiped her sweaty, makeup-smeared face with it as best she could and threw the mask into the deeper, damper shadow by the fence.

Sick from what she did and afraid of what lay ahead, Farya remained on the cracked sidewalk. Wherever the wet rubber dress could dig into her, it dug. When she got up, she saw a sign under a single orange streetlight maybe a hundred yards down the cyclone fence that the sidewalk traced.

Astrodrome Commons - An Innovative Mixed-Use Community, was coming, the sign warned—a promise had been made a long time ago. The architect's rendering plastered onto the plywood had already faded. Its edges flapped. Farya could see that it was a long walk to anywhere. Without a mirror, she made an educated guess as to how she looked—latex dress, clownish makeup smeared, shoes in hand.

She felt the glossy rubber beneath her armpit. As she'd practiced getting into her rubber dress, she'd found a secret pocket—glued not stitched, just big enough for some dollar bills, a credit card, and ID. Located on the one flat surface least likely to attract erotic attention, and even padded to make it almost invisible to someone with an armpit fetish, it was a small mercy.

Farya dug into the sweat and talcum powder between her skin and the rubber and pulled out the driver's license, credit card, and twenty-dollar bills she'd stashed there. In the orange penumbra of streetlight, she could deduce that she was still Farya Lomoigne, that there was still a New York City, a United States, and that Andrew Jackson had once been its president.

Looking at the empty road, she jammed the money and cards back into the secret pocket. The sidewalk was cracked and unswept. The road whose shoulder she relied on after the sidewalk ended had seen more than one car wreck. But barefoot, careful, and slow, remained a better option than the outrageous heels. On her way, she picked up a dry tree branch. Maybe it wasn't worth much for self-defense, but it did make her look crazy. So, she kept it.

She was slow, and Houston was huge in the warm, clammy distance. It was still an hour or so before dawn when she reached a gas station. From a payphone, Farya dialed a number she'd known for what felt like her whole life. Her mother picked up.

"Hello," her mother said, awake and alert, despite the hour.

"Mom, it's me."

"Farya. That's so strange. I had this terrible dream. I don't remember what, but I woke up worried about you. Are you all right?"

"Yeah. I should be. I should be fine."

But Farya called for another reason—Edouard—if he was okay, and more importantly, if he was. But she couldn't find the words or the will for it. So, she waited, stammering while a stray trucker stared her down.

"You probably want to talk to Eddy," her mother said.

"Eddy?"

"We call him that sometimes. You know, your father, when I met him, went by Eddy with his friends. When he got into the astronautical academy, it became Edouard again. But Eddy's still a nice name for a little boy."

"When did they call Dad, Eddy?"

"Before Ohio State. That was a big deal. Not everyone went to college back then."

"How is he? Little Edouard?"

"He's good. I've been up for hours now. But he slept well."

"I'm sorry," Farya said, wanting to laugh with delight that her boy was safe and healthy. "About your nightmare."

"It was only a dream. And nights like these, when I'm by myself reading a book in the kitchen, it's so cozy having a little one asleep upstairs."

"Thanks, Mom. Listen, Mom, I love you, and I'm heading home now."

"How did it go?"

"How did what go?"

"Your trip—you said you had a big meeting."

Farya remembered the person she had left herself being. She was a single working mother, but otherwise not unlike herself. She was in Houston visiting a Ripht-Schondles treatment center, on behalf of the foundation she worked at.

"The meeting was good. It went well. I should see you in a few hours."

Farya hung up and used the otherwise untouched yellow pages on the windowsill to call a cab. For almost an hour, she haunted the gas station while she waited. She focused on the details of the convenience store, the metal racks, the packaged donuts, the two glowing walls of alcoholic and soft beverages. And her life came into focus, but she wasn't ready to accept it or to mourn the old one. She had to get home first.

The wait was vivid—the side-eye that the early-morning patrons gave a strung-out woman in a rubber dress, the hum of the overhead lights, the purchases to keep her in good stead with the Indian clerk. The cab was an old Buick that smelled like hamburgers and was driven by an old, unwashed man who said nothing after she said *airport*.

They neared the city and ever-more-frequent streetlights reflected off the white sheen of her latex lap. Farya knew airports. She would have to endure strange looks. But there would be little shops selling sweatpants, tacky T-shirts that repelled the eye, and ugly, foam-rubber shoes that felt like eager, forgiving confidantes to her feet. There would be fatty food prepared anonymously. Maybe even a neck-pillow to embrace her on the plane.

Sitting up as the flight-control tower of the airport came into view, her rubber-clad bottom squeaked against the vinyl seats. She wanted to see the sun, finally rising over the flat landscape. As it did, the Classic Rock station in the cab seemed to get a little louder.

The song that came from the speakers was the Union Skells, playing "Now Just Stars." Farya knew it well enough to murmur along with every third word.

Belly to the double yellow line
It ain't right, but that's just fine
Ain't been home in a year or two
I've been better, but what's it to you?
From the heave and swell of the bars
A jailbreak empire with heaven in play
A hide and seek in moving cars
All of them gone now, gone wide and far
Gone away, now just stars

Farya's face buckled, and she wept. The exact reason why was something she had to keep from herself. She had to breathe and see her son, and she had to forget. She knew she had to forget, though she couldn't let herself know what, or why. She wept. She forgot. And the sun rose.

The End

About the Author

Colin Dodds is a writer with several novels and books of poetry to his name. He grew up in Massachusetts and lived in California briefly, before finishing his education in New York City. Since then, he's made his living as a journalist, editor, copywriter and video producer. Over the last seven years, his writing has appeared in more than three hundred publications including Gothamist, Painted Bride Quarterly, and The Washington Post. His poetry collection *Spokes of an Uneven Wheel* was published by Main Street Rag Publishing Company in 2018. And his novel, *Vice Nimrod, Communications*, was longlisted for the 2019 Beverly Prize. Colin also writes screenplays, has directed a short film, and built a twelve-foot-high pyramid out of PVC pipe, plywood and zip ties. One time, he rode his bicycle a hundred miles in a day. He lives in New York City, with his wife and daughter. You can find more of his work at thecolindodds.com.

Made in the
USA
Middletown, DE